Wild Innocence

By

Moody Holiday

Pretty Paper Press
East Orange, NJ USA

Wild Innocence
By Moody Holiday

Copyright © 2009 Moody Holiday

First Printing - May 2009

ISBN: 978-097463156-1

MHoliday®

The MHoliday design is a registered trademark of the author.

Printed In The USA.

The Encounter - 1980

St. James Prep, 1980. A cold crisp smell in the air was a sign to New Jersey natives of the imminent snowstorm. It's funny. I didn't care how much snow fell that night. Nothing could keep me from seeing Derrick. Besides, I lived a stone's throw from St. James and I was going to lie to my parents no matter how late I stayed out.

My mounting love and affection for Derrick didn't need Cupid's arrow. He's the type of brother that any woman would drop her panties for upon sight. His ancestral legacy commanded hair as fine as silk passed down from the Blackfoot Indian Tribe. If Derrick stood up in church and proclaimed that he had Indian in his family, I would have jumped up and shouted, "Amen!"

His cocoa brown skin glistened with life unfettered by stress or acne. He stood long and lean at six feet tall and weighed two hundred and fifteen pounds. His upper thighs were chiseled to perfection. His muscular calves ruggedly supported his six pack stomach and sculpted chest. When Derrick smiles, I instantly hold my breath to contain his masculine energy. His scent fulfills me like the air at the dawn of a new day. My heart is pumping right now just thinking about him, but that's how he makes me feel when I'm around him, girly, giddy and sexy.

The game plan was to play it cool and sophisticated. My hormones were raging and I was ripe for some flirtatious titillation. One last check in the circular compact mirror heightened my need for Derrick. The "do," was done, slicked back in a pony tail, not a follicle out of place. I used a small eyebrow brush to sculpt my baby hair into four little swirls. Maybelline mascara whipped my eye lashes out long and thick like a brand new baby doll. Gloria Vanderbilt Jeans and a burgundy v-neck sweater with matching boots from the Village adorned my frame. No turning back, I walked straight into the gym and down the sidelines against the blaring noise of the electrified crowd. I passed the wanna-bees, the nerds and the curious boys burning a hole through my sweater as I strolled by their wandering eyes. I reached the middle section of the court and climbed each bleacher with cool confidence. I kept to myself and avoided the cat and scratch crew. Those horny bitches threw down in an instant if they thought you were after their imaginary boyfriends. Half of them looked like a pencil sketch from a witch's picture book with spiked hair, pointed shoes and ten pounds of make up. Without my girls to back me up, I had to stay away from a possible catfight.

I took final position and began to search for Derrick. The anticipation for his touch and not knowing how we would ever become an item drove me into flights of erotic fantasy. They were fueled by four chance meetings that sealed our fate.

Our first encounter occurred at the South Orange Library. I was perplexed over algebraic equations until Derrick came to my rescue. He strolled up to the table. A simple hello was his calling card. Derrick sat down and offered to help. I stared at him feverishly as the words he spoke began to form life inside of me. My fingers and toes began to tingle. I had no idea what he was talking about regarding algebra, but it sounded beautiful. I registered every inch of his handsome face in my brain. He had soft hair that swept and curled in different directions. Some strands spiked straight up like he couldn't tame it, perhaps a little pomade would do the trick, but he looked too rugged for beeswax. His eyebrows were smooth and thick. They also complimented his almond-shaped eyes. The first time he smiled was magical. Because of him, I began to smile more, but only when there were thoughts of him in my head. After giving it careful consideration, I damn near smiled all the time, but never at home. As Derrick spoke, I watched his lips ease and relax. His skin seemed so soft that I wanted to stroke his face and ask him if he used Noxzema. I remembered thinking, *"Damn, he's so fine,"* but he wasn't a pretty boy.

Derrick slid my notebook and pencil back to me. I took a deep breath and relaxed my hands. He told me he wasn't in a rush, so we went to the periodical lounge and talked. It was a simple conversation about common acquaintances and teachers. He was smooth in his approach and I was on fire from the feel of his body brushing against mine. Time was running away from us as the light faded through the library windows. Derrick had to go to basketball practice so he offered to carry my book bag to the bus stop. He was kind enough to wait until it came and watched me as I boarded. Derrick waved goodbye as I continued to stare at him. I strained my neck to see which direction he walked and whispered his name under my breath. Surely a guy as fine as Derrick had to have a girlfriend, but I never asked and I didn't give a damn. I wanted to see him again, but he never asked me for my number. I thought to myself, *"Good thing,"* because our phone was cut off for months. He only knew the name of my school and that I also played basketball. Derrick mentioned coming to one of my games, but I didn't take him seriously. I felt so stupid for not asking him for his number, but I didn't want to appear aggressive. It was also the first time I felt an overwhelming need to tongue kiss a guy.

The next encounter happened at the Livingston Mall. Thank God I was by myself and wearing a new outfit from Persuasions. I let Derrick notice me first, a risk that was daring for me, because I would have cried forty nights if he didn't see me. He was leaving the mall with his mother, an activity that most of us avoid on any given day, but he seemed to enjoy her company. He called my name. I glanced up pretending to be so surprised.

"Hey, Derrick right?" I asked, smoothing away a wrinkle in my top. He seemed pleased that I remembered his name. Derrick signaled me to come over with a curled finger.

"What's up Shanelle? Meet my mom, Ms. Johnson."

She grinned and waited for me to speak.

"It's nice to meet you Ms. Johnson. Taking in some shopping with your handsome son?"

Derrick chimed in to avoid embarrassment. "Don't answer that."

They were a content mother and son team, unlike the world unraveling around me.

"Are people really this happy?"

Derrick asked his mother to browse at a nearby store while we talked. His broad chest brushed my shoulder before he spoke.

"You've been on my mind since I saw you at the library Shanelle."

His lips pressed against my ear.

3

"This time I'm not going to let you get away without a phone number."

I wanted to beam with lust, but my heart fell to the ground and splat into mini pieces.

"How could I tell him it was disconnected?"

Quickly plotting an escape, I blurted, "I have a game at five-thirty," biting my lower lip. "It's tomorrow. Can you come?"

He rubbed his chin, delaying his answer, watching me rock back and forth.

"Sure, I'll be there."

I started to get anxious about my phone dilemma and flitted away with a side-eye to his mother. My right hand flashed a timid Miss America wave.

"It was nice to meet you Ms. Johnson. See you tomorrow Derrick."

I headed out of the mall and caught the bus back to North Orange. The long ride home was enough time to go over every detail. I leaned my head against the metal bars with relaxed eyes as Chaka Khan's *Sweet Thang,* played from the driver's small radio.

"Did I say the right thing? Did I smile? Was I polite to his mother? Was I cute enough?"

Despite my self-critique, I desperately hoped that Derrick would come to my game. Lucky for me, he did and he was by himself. I didn't have a great offensive game, but who cares. I was thrilled at the thought of it and couldn't wait for the game to be over. He waited for me in the parking lot and I immediately got excited the moment I spotted his car. I scrambled through the exit doors still damp from my shower. My perfume was the first thing he mentioned. Derrick leaned forward tilting his head against my neck.

"You smell good. What are you wearing?"

I teased him.

"Oh, a little bit of this and that."

His top teeth sunk into his lower lip. He stared at me so hard that silence overcame us. The friction of my goose down jacket was the only noise between us. We gazed at each other simultaneously and busted out laughing. I felt so silly not knowing what to say. I couldn't believe he couldn't come up with a good line or two. I asked him if he was nervous. He strummed my lower lip and leaned into me as if we were going to kiss.

"Yeah, you make me nervous, Shanelle."

Wide eyed and curious, I locked in on his thick, smooth lips. "Why?"

Derrick's head tilted to the side.

"I think about you all the time Shanelle."

"Me too," I added as I watched his hand settle on my thigh.

Derrick offered to take me home. Our short time together was quickly ruined by the distraction of police sirens and their cherry bomb lights. Derrick didn't ask any questions as he pulled up in front of my house. There were rumors about my crazy ass brother. Everyone knew him and I wondered if people thought differently of me because of his reputation. Silence filled Derrick's heated car as he searched the street for signs him.

"Shanelle," he swallowed, "Can I get your number? I wanna' talk to you by phone sometimes you know?"

I decided to give him an honest answer.

"Look, thanks for the ride, but I don't have a phone."

The news went right over his head as he leaned forward and retrieved a slip of paper from his glove compartment. His warm skin and rich cologne excited me as my nipples turned into rocks.

"Not a problem lady."

Derrick scribbled his number down and pressed it into my palm.

"It's up to you. Call me, or come to my game." His mouth met mine with a soft kiss. He licked my lower lip before pulling away.

"I can't wait to see you again Shanelle."

I clutched my tattered winning lottery ticket with teeth clenching relief. The cool expression on his face assured my place with him as Kitty swelled into a soft pulsating ball of pleasure.

Rumors swirled about the jock and the wild child. Word eventually got back to him that his girl Portia wanted to get to know me better. I didn't care. Little did she know that I was a scrapper. I called Derrick from my girlfriend's house to talk about it, but he never entertained the question. Each conversation lasted until the early morning. We seemed to have a destiny that no one could understand. We loved children and strong families, even though mine was crumbling around me like a sand castle on the shore. The more we talked, the more I wanted him in every way. To make things right, we made a pact that tonight would be our fourth encounter. By showing up at his game, win or lose, we were going to make it happen.

The lady in me took the stage to perfect our liaison. Cheering for Derrick in a quiet frenzy, I watched him leap, shoot and rebound the basketball. Pity though, it seemed like the excitement was too much for them. St. James lost, double overtime and by two points. Despite the loss and fat chunks of snow falling outside, I was determined to be with him just like we planned. I gaped at my watch thinking, *"Damn, its nine-thirty, thirty minutes shy of my curfew. Fuck it. I'll tell them I was at the library."* I had to take my chances.

Derrick threw the ball to the referee barely missing the point guard from St. Thomas High School. For one quick moment, he perused the top of the rafters and spotted me. The hairs on the back of my neck rose. I gave him that, *"I'm so sorry you lost,"* pout and with that he turned around and headed straight for the locker room. *Great!* At least we made eye contact and he knows I'm here for him in every lust filled way. I could only imagine how nuzzling in his neck through his varsity jacket would turn my pink panties into sweet cream.

By the time Derrick made it to the lobby with his boys, the only remnants of tonight's defeat were sticky gum wrappers, wilted pom-pom strings and Gus the maintenance man. I quickly turned around and leaned against the windowpane. Even though no one knew about our rendezvous, I had to make it look good. Dumb ass Mookie called me out first.

"Yo, yo, ain't that Shanelle right there?"

In sheer disgust I thought, *"Damn, I don't want Mookie to look at me, let alone ask me for a ride home, but he's going to ask me with his goofy ass."*

Don't get me wrong, Mookie's a nice guy, but he's also a weed smoking illiterate who spent his entire education being socially promoted. No one gave a damn. Everyone spoke openly about how dumb he was, but bragged about the skills he possessed on the basketball court. Mookie filled the gym to capacity crowds that spilled out the campus doors and onto the sidewalk. Even though he was just a freshman, he was well on his way to a coveted college scholarship with a division one school. For now, if you got in his car, he would light up a spliff, smoke it with the windows rolled up tight and then stop at the Number One Chinese Spot for three quarts of beef fried rice. He needed ten duck sauce packets to kill the craving. I wasn't interested in Mookie, his car or the Burger King wrappers on his front seat. I needed to be with my man in the worst way. Derrick seemed to know it too, because he swerved past Mookie and right behind me. The wool on his varsity jacket brushed the back of my hand. Derrick whispered, "Let's go Shanelle. It's all about us now."

Boisterous heckling followed as one of the Brat Packers belted out, "Yo man, you know you can only get booty from Nicky when we lose like this."

Derrick put his arm around me and led me down the snow trampled steps. Half of his scarf blew sideways into the fierce and steady wind. The fringes brushed my nose and landed on my breasts. The scent of Paco Roban overcame my nostrils along with the cold air. He spoke to me like we were the last two people on earth.

"Don't pay any attention to them, they're all crazy from the loss tonight and each one of them wishes they were me right now."

Surprised by his comment, I looked up and asked, "Why?"

He licked his big beautiful lips and grabbed my hand to strengthen the intensity in his answer.

"Because Shanelle, you're a lady, a beautiful lady and any guy would be crazy to let you out of his sight."

My chest was heaving under my coat. I bit the lower corner of my lip and put my head down. He immediately lifted my chin with his finger.

"Did you hear what I said Shanelle?"

I quickly remarked, "Yes, I heard you Derrick."

Against the frigid evening air, Derrick responded to my nervousness with a soft kiss. He pulled away slightly and stuck his tongue in my mouth for the first time. Derrick tasted absolutely delicious as he made love to my mouth with mint and orange citrus candy. Maybe a Starburst occupied his time in the locker room after he brushed his teeth. No matter the flavor, the wet thickness of his tongue slicked a layer of silky juice onto my panties. My eyes began to well up with tears while my face eased and softened. I moved in closer and slid my hand down his tight ass and up the center of his back. He felt wonderful against me, like a leather glove on a delicate hand. A ferocious beast fired up in his pants and spoke to Kitty.

"I want you young lioness."

Kitty purred back, "Raaaaaaarrrrrr!"

A thunderous roar erupted from the lobby. Nothing seemed to matter because I was simply swept up in his kiss and the soft powdery flakes of snow melting on my face and neck. To avoid the onslaught of laughter, Derrick turned around and grabbed my hand as we darted off into the wintery storm.

Cutting into the cold wind, we ran past his car, dodged the mini salt trucks and headed for lot number two. To get there, you have to scale a three-foot embankment and slide down the other side. I was breathing so hard I could barely clear the wall. We reached the top, fell backwards into the snow and rolled down the hill. Hysterical laughter shot into the air as the snowdrift draped our frames. Like flour in a wind storm, snow clogged my eyes, nostrils and belly button. It was cold, yet so exciting. Derrick propped himself on his elbows watching me brush away wet pellets.

"Come here," he ordered, reaching for me.

"Where?" I chuckled, biting my lip in girly delight.

"Girl, don't make me have to come after you."

"Come get me," I gushed, sprinting away. I was a fast runner. Kicking my feet into gear like the 440 relays, the tap of his fingertips hit me in the center of my back. I fell face first into the snow behind a white pick-up truck. He was barely breathing as he pounced on top of me. The beast in his pants seemed longer and harder this time as he pressed his weight down. Distant voices drifted away, chained tires scraping the ice-slicked ground, echoed into the distance. Rusting engines from salt trucks driving by suddenly disappeared.

Another kiss ensued and I was completely and physically his. Heavy petting filled my freshman existence as we kissed behind that pick-up truck for what seemed like hours. The nape of his neck contained the sweat I was craving. I kissed him, caressed him, stroked his hair and called his name. He grinded me and molded me into a sculpted piece of art. I pretended there were no coats, hats and pants between us. My brain was gone, as rhyme and reason swayed back and forth. I was confused, but everything felt so good.

Floating above my steam of lust rested, "Ms. Nemesis." She was my daily guide and anti-sex coach.

"Virgin girl, oh virgin girl, where are you, virgin girl?"

Oh yes, every good girl has one.

"Will Derrick pop the cherry or are you sending him home with blue balls?"

He used his right knee to spread my left leg. My eyes started rolling around in the back of my head.

"Damn, could it get any better than this?"

Derrick enhanced the feeling by whispering, "Shanelle, I need to be with you now. I need to be inside of you."

"I know," I breathed, trying to control my chattering teeth. "I don't want this night to end…, you feel so good, but please, not like this."

Hot air rushed into my ear. He stood up and helped me off the ground. Derrick took off his varsity jacket and put it around my shoulders for warmth as the reality of the late evening jarred my nerves.

"Dammit, what time is it?"

Derrick checked his watch. "Just after eleven. Why?"

"Shit! My mom is going to kill me, that's why."

Derrick rubbed my arms up and down. "Well there's no sense in rushing. You're late anyway, let me get you dry and then I'll take you home."

Even if Derrick had my back, my ass was grass. For the time being, I didn't care. On the way home, I leaned against him with a smile. The feeling was light and euphoric. The homes nestled on South Center Street became a story book of ginger bread houses dipped in white frosting. Tree branches bearing the weight of the season crackled under the icy sheeting. Crippling silence pierced the night. Drivers crept along the road just to admire the scenery. I nestled closer to Derrick as we enjoyed the snail pace home. With the heat on full blast, enhanced by a vanilla freshener, his free hand settled between my thick thighs. Derrick turned the corner and pulled up in front of my house. We kissed goodnight one last time as my heart began to beat rapidly. Fear and anxiety seeped into my blood stream. Out of sheer nervousness, my eyes shifted to the front window. Since our phone was back in service, I wrote the number down on a small piece of paper. Out of frustration for the unknown, I slid closer to him and buried my face in his neck.

"Is it that bad in there?" Derrick asked, peering over my head. I wanted to lie like Penny from Good Times. She wasn't the only one with fucked up secrets.

"Yeah."

It was past my curfew and too late to describe my version of the trilogy of terror on the third floor, so I kept quiet. Derrick conjured up a plan. "Why don't you just come home with me? My mom works nights and doesn't get home until eight o'clock in the morning." He wiped my tears away with his basketball towel which left his scent all over me again. It gave me the strength to slide out the door.

"I can't, but I'll call you if I need you."

Derrick put the car in drive and pitched, "Baby, I hope you don't need me, but I'll be here if you do."

I headed up the walkway, twenty paces short of a whipping. My mother Mrs. Viv was ready for me because the vertical blind swayed back and forth revealing a glimpse of her yellow house coat. I waved goodbye to Derrick and used the storm door to clear a path to the main door. A mental pause froze my hand.

What will happen to me tonight? Should I run now or face the consequences? Will evil be waiting for me?

I knew I was in trouble and couldn't wish it away. At a minimum, I could expect a suburban curse fest with a few jabs to the head.

Ding, ding, ding, in this corner, weighing in at one hundred and thirty-five pounds and five foot five inches tall, Shanelle Brown. In this corner, weighing in at two hundred and eighty pounds, Mrs. Viv Brown.

The fight began the minute the door opened.

"What the hell is wrong with you?"

Crack!

A back handed blow to the head. I was barely through the second door quickly lunging forward to protect myself from the metal key rack. I took two steps forward to avoid another backhand when Mrs. Viv yelled, "Don't you walk away from me."

Slap!

"Get your ass over here."

Dear daddy had a front row seat in his crushed velvet chair. The enforcer held his cigarette between his pointer and middle finger taking in the fight. Brightly lit embers rose slowly up the cancer stick to compliment the interrogation.

"Didn't I tell you to bring your ass straight home from school?"

Whack!

A firm right hand to the collarbone knocked me into the bubbled unfinished wall. I began to float away.

Fade away Shanelle. Think about how wonderful Derrick felt up against you in the snow. Take in the hits and just laugh. It'll be over before you know it. Let her win. She loves to be right. She loves to be in control.

I turned quickly pleading my case with a trembling lip.

"I'm sorry mom; I was with Der…,"

Pop!

I couldn't finish my sentence without another smack in the face.

"I forgot to tell you about the game."

Whap!

"Don't you lie to me girl. We're not playing. Take your ass to bed before I slap the shit out of you for lying."

There she goes again, slapping the shit out of me. To think, there's no toilet tissue downstairs to clean up the shit when it flies out of my mouth.

Hiking up the old creaky staircase, my face felt raw and achy. The smell of snow, sweat, cologne and cigarettes in my damp hair began to clog my nasal passage. The first stair squeaked in the voice of a crumpled old witch.

Who knew if my evil brother had gone to bed?

I didn't feel like being bothered. He was surely listening to the boxing match and loved the negative attention I received from Mrs. Viv.

I think I got smacked and cursed at so much because my drug-crazed brother held my house mentally and physically hostage. Dear mother and father were so frustrated with him that they took their frustrations out on my minor infractions. He was in and out of the hospital for drug treatment more times than I can recall. He ate, slept, dined and passed his bowels with the richest druggies in Essex County's drug rehabilitation center. Movie stars and singers graced his neighboring hospital room. He bragged about it every time he escaped. At least six police officers had to be called to the house to escort him back to the hospital. Each time, Detective Jackson took the time to console dear mother as she watched Steven's rage rock the disappearing ambulance.

"It's for the best Mrs. Brown, you've done the best you can do with him. He'll only end up killing you and Shanelle if he stays."

Kill? Oh that's an understatement. That mother fucker would slice your throat in a minute if you didn't lock yourself in your room with a skeleton key during a full moon. Weed mixed with angel dust was too much for him after a football injury in 1978. His poor brain must have short circuited when he took that hit from the opposing linebacker. His helmet flew east and blood rippled from the crack in his skull at the base of his cerebellum. A team of doctors told Mrs. Viv that dear brother would be fine as long as he took his prescribed medicines and avoid the use of marijuana. The strain of sitting on the sidelines and watching his friends soak up the glory during that championship year sent him into a binge of drugging and drinking. The chemical substances seemed to affect his brain in the worst way. He turned into a classic schizoid case and on any given day chased me and Mrs. Viv up and down the creaky stairs. He shut the power off in the house, blasted Richard Pryor albums, and smeared his own feces on the attic walls. Steven adorned his room with pictures he stole from my photo album. All of my good friends were plastered into the dried shit like a fecal photo gallery. There was Candy, in her black two-piece bikini at Coney Island. Sexy Bonnie wearing her grape flavored lip-gloss in the 4x6 head shot I took of her in front of Upsala College. None of us could control his unusual behavior, nor dare enter his room. He wore Chuck Taylors and blue jeans with two scullys fitted together like a two-tone hat. That crazy fuck walked everywhere too and stayed in the best shape ever.

When Steven's rages climaxed and Mrs. Viv needed a break, she would change the locks and throw him out for a week or two to fend for himself. While she was at work, dear brother would knock on the kitchen window like a Gino's drive through for two mayo sandwiches before dad got home. After twenty-three years of marriage, the only acceptable bad habit that could legitimately take up residence in our house was dad's cigarettes. He told Mrs. Viv on a cold day in January that it was either their son or him. The vows they took prevailed and Mrs. Viv kicked dear brother out in the blistering cold escorted by the North Orange Police. But before he left, the demon that ravaged his brain burned emotional scars into my mind for a lifetime.

I took another step up and Steven started to laugh. Each step became increasingly sadistic. It was the sound of tapping metal to wood. The small taps became increasingly consistent and obsessive. It was part of his calling card and you had to accept it as his personal accessory. As I reached the top landing and faced my bedroom door, dear brother was waiting for me.

"Hey fat bitch, got any money?"

He was sitting on the third hallway step leading to the attic carving a butcher knife into the step. This wasn't your ordinary sibling spat. This was psychological warfare with twisted, sour lemons. I faced him agitated and weary. My hands settled at my sides.

"Not tonight. Leave me alone and go to bed."

My retort had little effect. Steven was a tactical athlete and a drug head. The two combined enticed his terror strategy. He held his knife up and pointed it towards my bedroom. I turned around. My door was slightly ajar. Steven quickly mimicked me in a high pitched voice, "'Not tonight, not tonight.' Yeah well, you left your door open bitch. You better buy a new coat with that weak ass pocket change you get babysitting pee-pee boy across the street."

Yeah, he was cruel, even when it came to innocent and mildly disabled children. But for the moment, I was consumed with the thought of possibly leaving my door unlocked. Maybe he was lying this time and I was spared from his get high thievery. I started to get warm inside, rushing to the closet to find my coat. My throat began to clog with saliva. I could hear Steven jabbing the knife into the steps as he read my mind. The last push revealed an empty coat hanger.

"Go ahead and cry you fat fucking baby, I got some good money for that shit." A Jimmy Hendrix tune hummed from his vocal cords as he ascended into the demon filled attic with his untouchable stolen treasures and erotic filth. Defeated, I cursed myself for being so stupid. I washed off my mascara, jumped into the shower and released my tears into the hot stream. The screeching sound in the shower pipes muffled my wailing. That old pipe and showerhead muted my cries for years. I always bathed slowly to wash away the sins I committed and the ones hatched by my brother. I toweled off and donned a gray sweat suit. As I pulled the top over my head, I thought to myself, *"I need Derrick."*

I put some Visine in my eyes and dialed his number with one hand. The sound of his voice released a bellowing ache from my womb.

"Yeah, what's up?"

He was disoriented, but woke right up when he detected my voice.

"Shanelle, what's wrong?"

"I need you."

"Sure baby, hold on," he jumped as his feet crashed to the floor. "I'll be right there. Meet me downstairs in fifteen minutes."

I quietly hung up the phone and threw some clothes in my favorite duffel bag. All of my toiletries stayed in my room because dear brother loved to masturbate with scented soaps or wipe his ass with my toothbrush. I slipped past my parents' room and headed downstairs. Steven was directly behind me in a calm and calculated tow.

"Hey you fat ass whore. Are you on night patrol?" He pressed for an immediate answer with blood filled fingers wrapped around his knife.

"What time is pretty boy picking you up?" he smirked under his breath. "I bet he's light skinned too, you love those Shalimar looking mother fuckers."

I laughed shaking my head out of fear and frustration.

"No you crazy fuck, Derrick's not light skinned, but let's focus on you. You're always on night patrol, slithering past our rooms and skipping the creaky stairs to get to the first floor."

Think it, yes, but if I expressed his psychotic behavior, the cool steel blade would have pressed against my neck with smooth precision. Steven skipped the stairs so much he wore out the side floor moldings three times. The banister came off the hinge and the opposite wall supporting his downward flight exposed his sneaky compulsion. Mrs. Viv worked out her maternal codependency by wiping down the walls with Mr. Clean humming Sunday gospel tunes. The Clark Sister's rocked her in the bosom of Abraham and lulled her into a quiet existence. As she cleaned the walls, Mrs. Viv rhythmically clapped in rejoice of sweet redemption, *"I'm climbing up, on the rough side of the mountain; I'm doing my best to make it in."*

Satire ruled me as I listened to her singing, *"No momma, dear brother is going to get you up the mountain and push you over the cliff if you don't get him out of this house."*

But since I had to put up with him until Derrick came, I picked up my duffel bag and stood in the vestibule. Steven invaded my space and jabbed me in the back of my head with his pointer finger.

"Run along now whore. Goodnight bitch."

The strain from his constant pursuit and mental aggression was all I could take for one night. I opened the front door and stood outside in the blistering cold. Once there was a barrier between us, dear brother was fine. I embraced the frigid air in order to escape his menacing ways. But at the same time, I cursed winter's serenity. It was forced upon me in the night without recourse or justification. Steven locked the peeling white door behind me. I turned around to face him one last time. His eyebrows grimaced in the window as he smiled. His mind was working up more terror as his breath forced hot steam clouds on the small windowpane. He slid his nose up and down and made piggy faces at me. Sometimes there was comedy in his routine when the threat diminished. I thought to myself, *"Oh God, it's 1:00 am in the morning and I'm dealing with this crazy shit."*

Suddenly, white lights turned the corner in the distance. When Derrick pulled up, the insidious disease of my life whispered away in the unforgiving wind.

Portia

As for Portia, she had Derrick below the waist for the past three years and that was the "shit" that had to be straightened out. It wouldn't be long before Mookie started blabbing about the tongue kiss he saw after the game. He dropped a dime on us to one of his groupies at St. Clark's Academy. In less than twenty-four hours, Portia put the word out that she was looking for my ass.

Everyone was interested in her because she was a stuck up fly girl from Maplewood. Back then, only six percent of the town was African American. Upwardly mobile blacks trickled into Maplewood enticed by the commuter friendly neighborhood and top rated school system. Portia's father was a pediatrician and her mother was a stay at home functional alcoholic. Her mother entertained Portia's every whim, including swimming lessons, art lessons, tap, ballet and Suzuki method piano. Every material need was met, every emotional need denied. Her family lacked affection in the worst way and it manifested in Portia's adolescent and adult behavior. She looked for love in all the wrong places, showering herself with tennis bracelets and gaudy bamboo earrings. Everyone knew her. She drove a black Camaro which was rare for brown beauties in 1980. That car stayed clean and blazed out everywhere she went. Every Papi Chulo, B-boy, homeboy and fly guy turned to see that crimson brown face and detailed car. She took her Kitty to Livingston, Nutley, East Orange, West Orange, Belleville and back to Maplewood searching for her claim to fame. She loved to hook up with pimped out boys whose parents owned box seat Mets tickets, floor seats at the Garden and NCAA Final Four tickets. In her down time, Derrick was her steady because he was the local boy, who, along with Mookie, received plenty of press coverage. Portia knew that she was going to break it off with Derrick in early July. Since Derrick was committed to four years of college and then medical school, she was determined to divorce herself from any more medical drama. In order to keep myself sane, I mapped out the life of Portia on my own terms. That way I could write that bitch off instead of kicking her ass. Here's Portia's story:

By August, Portia would be on her way to Spelman College. She would immediately join an elite sorority based on skin color and her father's social status. Like a wild fiend, Portia would screw every Kappa male in her path. A train here or there came in handy when she was real horny. During March madness, Portia would go to a step show at Morehouse and be blown away by dark and sexy Rashan slammin' down his mighty feet. Rashan had sexy dreads that fell and swooped in different directions as he tapped his cane to and fro in a warrior's chant.

Rashan's style was popularized by his father's love of Bob Marley and Peter Tosh. He was one of the first non-Jamaicans to sport his style on campus and Portia the man-eater was riveted by his physical appeal.

Visually locked onto her target, Portia sized up his manly existence, black oak skin and persistent sweat. She envisioned herself yanking the belt from the pants that hid his long hard dick. Rashan spotted Portia coming in the door. He was skilled at visual multitasking; *onion booty at three o'clock, my boy Diggs in the third row; honey in the black jeans I hit last night.* But after seeing Portia, it stopped. The step show moved into the quad and by eleven o'clock that night, Portia and Rashan were hitting a spliff and discussing black conservatism. Rashan was just what Portia needed in her shallow ass life. A five-year EOF student from Prince Street in Newark who didn't give a fuck about anything except getting high and opening a barbershop back in his neighborhood. His thugged out body blazed through his black fraternity slacks. He peeled off Portia's clothes just when the munchies set in and ate her Kitty to kingdom come. He didn't care about her long ass hair either. He put so many knots in it fucking her he had to cut four inches off with his professional scissors. She loved the new look and found new energy in fucking Rashan. Every other weekend, Rashan and Portia weeded up and headed back to Jersey pumpin' Luther and Teena Marie on I-95. Portia's father flipped out at the mere site of Rashan and Portia's short hair. Her mother giggled under her drunken breath. She was happy for her daughter's new style and fifteen pound weight gain. Rashan didn't give a shit what either one of them thought because Portia was all his. The Jersey weekends included banging the headboard on three day old sheets and going to the Irvington Beauty Supply Shop. Rashan kept a steady supply of blades and cheap black doo rags for his special clients at Morehouse. They jetted to Cuts Above the Rest on Springfield and Clinton Avenue to earn enough money for tolls and a lunch break at the Maryland House. Rashan's best friend from Quitman Street Elementary School was holdin' the shop down until Rashan finished school. Portia sat in the shop, read Essence Magazine, picked up $5.00 dinners and swept the hairs off the floor for her man. In two years, Portia and Rashan would be married with two kids, Hasan and Nicole. Portia's ass was so sexed out; her fat ass size sixteen jeans pleased her every time she pranced in front of a full length mirror. The memories of her father, Derrick and binging were long gone.

•

Wayne Valley High

Wayne Valley High in North Orange, New Jersey was the shit back in the day. Walking into the hallway was like visualizing "The freaks come out at night," but in the daytime. The door shut behind me as I flitted up the stairs. Raheem, aka, "Ralphie" was waiting at the top. Nobody knew whether he was Italian or Puerto Rican, but it didn't matter because Ralphie just knew his ass was Black. Chunky gold chains and a brown Kango adorned the upper half of his skinny frame. He got his ass kicked every day for trying to front, but you had to admire Ralphie because he kept coming back for more.

"Yo, yo, what's up Sha-Nelli-Nell?" as he grabbed his crotch.

I scowled back, "What's up with you Ralphie boy?"

Ralphie sucked his teeth in frustration. "Yo, I keep telling you my name's Raheem, Ralphie's my slave name."

He was so funny in an annoying way, but the ladies loved Ralphie. He took my duffle bag and escorted me to my locker.

"Yo, I saw the way you shoved your tongue down prep boy's throat in the car. I hope you're saving the real stuff for me though."

He was starting to get on my nerves.

"Yeah, just for you." I replied. "Have you seen Candy?"

"Yeah, your crew is downstairs eatin' breakfast but yo, you better tell Candy to lay off the sweets yo, her titties are big as hell."

The bell rang for first period but I was in no rush to go to class. I reorganized my duffle bag, dappled my pink lips, took out my algebra books and headed for the cafeteria to meet up with my girls.

The cafeteria was filled to maximum capacity. The jocks were ordering their hungry man breakfast and turning around to see where Candy was sitting. My girl had that effect on the entire football, basketball and baseball teams. No matter the season, Candy's slim hips, big tits and full lips had the jocks talking about her on the regular. Candy was a wild child and we clicked the first day we met. She liked my genie pants and I liked her bob haircut. We loved club music, plum lipstick, Teena Marie, double cheeseburgers and hot boys who could make us laugh from the bottom up. We had different taste in boys and men. Our rule of engagement was simple, "If he were ever my man, he can never be yours."

Candy liked them tall, pecan tan, chiseled face with a big dick. No matter the shade, I liked them stocky, broad shoulders, deadly smile and a cut jaw line. I wasn't too interested in the piece. I was keeping it tight for Derrick and having him lay on top of me in the snow mound locked Kitty down for him.

Candy was poised at the table sliding petite pieces of a brownie down her throat, carefully avoiding a lipstick smudge. At 9:00 am, she could eat whatever the hell she wanted. Barely a size six and a strut to match, her persona fell from the pages of a fashion magazine. Hanging out with her was good for me because at five feet five inches at one hundred and thirty-five pounds, I was always conscious of what I ate. Candy gave me my props all the time. She made me buy cut off tops, sweaters and sweatshirts. Or she would take my shit and cut it herself.

"Show your stomach off girl, guys love that shit!"

It felt good to have a friend like her in my corner. Trust me, I knew I was cute, but it took a lot of work to maintain that frame. Speaking of frames, my other girlfriend Bonnie had a face and body like a work of art. She was sitting next to Candy at the table surveying the eclectic crowd. Bonnie was a feisty half Spanish, half Black girl. Her Puerto Rican father blessed her with the thickest black hair imaginable. It didn't matter whether it was natural or chemically treated; she had waves for days and the flair to fling it around. She had fiery eyes and thick eyebrows. The braces she wore in grammar school paid off in a major way and that smile drew guys into her web like a black widow spider. Bonnie's mind was always at work, like Portia's future husband Rashan. She always eyed you up and in a flash she could read the lips of two new pieces of school gossip.

"Check out Joey over there with his big ass head, I hope he can convince the dentist he brushed his teeth because I can smell his funky ass breath from here."

Bonnie was funny as hell.

"Damn, what's up with Jameel? That boy got the munchies like hell and it's only nine o'clock in the morning."

She saw a familiar face dodging by and said, "Mieda Papi-Chulo, call me tomorrow, I got that stuff for you."

Eric, a sophomore point guard for the varsity team, gave a nod of approval and kept it moving. Bonnie could kick that Spanish lingo back and forth and kept some secrets for herself. That was cool with me because we all had a few good secrets that were important enough to hide. Bonnie knew we were trying to figure out whether she and Eric kicked it last week. Guys were attracted to her exotic flavor, so they had to work real hard to get her attention.

I took the empty seat next to Candy and jumped into the conversation. Only the popular girls sat with us at our lunch table. We were a bunch of make up wearing chicks that had eye and lip application down pack. It didn't matter whether you were Black, White, Greek, Portuguese, Cuban, or Italian. If your ass was fly, you deserved to sit there. That table blew up with scents of Knowing, Escape, Safari and Fendi. Hair spray was a must for the Portuguese and Italian set. If someone lit a match, the whole school would have blown up from the chemicals we emitted.

When the bell rang, Fendi bags and key chains jingled and swayed as the clicks bid each other farewell. As usual, Bonnie, Candy and I said goodbye with the peace sign and a wink. We didn't leave because we needed to catch up on gossip.

"Shanelle," Bonnie leaned forward, "Don't even ask me if I'm coming to the game because my mother is pissed off about that shit with Andre."

"Damn," Candy gawked. "She's not over that shit yet, that was like three months ago."

Bonnie's mom wouldn't let her to do anything after school except come straight home and fire up the pots and pans to cook rice and beans. Bonnie had to do her dirt from 8:30 am until 2:30 pm and then turn into the good Catholic school girl.

"No, she's not over it yet and Papi took my gold chains. I can't even go to Great Adventures."

"Dang Bonnie!" Candy shouted, "you need to run away from them. Fuck them gold chains. You know Andre will buy you some more."

Andre was Bonnie's man since the eight-grade. A mighty mouth entrepreneur, he sold gold, silver and egg rolls if you wanted one bad enough. He was on his way to the top, once he figured out what he really wanted to do with his life. In the meantime, he had Bonnie's back day and night.

"I'm cool Candy; just make sure you bring me back a cute shirt."

"Ok, just make sure you give me ten dollars so I can buy that shit." Candy had a smart-ass mouth, but she always got her point across with no regrets.

"What's up with you Shanelle? I called you last night and your mother hung up on me. You need to tell me when you want me to cover for you. She thinks I lie with a straight face and she couldn't even see me."

I shrugged my shoulders in disgust.

"Same old bullshit, Steven started smoking again, knife and all."

"What?" Candy replied.

"Yeah, I booked up and went to Derrick's house."

"Did you give him any pussy yet?" Candy asked.

I sucked my teeth to prove a point. "Come on now, he's not ready for this yet."

Candy fired back with wide eyes. "Girl, you've got that boy so strung out, he's gonna come in two seconds the minute you let him in."

"Shut up Candy," Bonnie laughed. "You know Shanelle is into that corny ass endless love shit!"

They both broke out into simultaneous laughter. Candy started to serenade Bonnie like Lionel Richie to Diana Ross. She grabbed Bonnie's face for added drama.

"Two hearts, two hearts that beat as one." Bonnie ended it with a joke singing, *"I think I'm gonna come."*

They cackled harder and gave each other a high five as I picked up my book bag and tray.

"Real funny assholes, you know I'm sensitive about that shit. Let me get my ass to class, I can't fuck up this quarter because the coach is gonna bench me."

They were still caught up in their comedic moment, so I left thinking about Derrick and wondering what he was doing. Sometimes they teamed up on me about my good girl nature, but I didn't care. I was willing to stand alone in the virginity department as long as necessary.

Night Vision

The game against St. Bridgette's was a bust. The senior point guard from St. Bitches, as we coined them, was on fire, knocking down twenty-two points, six assists and four rebounds. Derrick came to the game, but I couldn't enjoy his presence with such a heavy loss. The coach was on my back to stick and box her out, but her game was just too tight for me. I was distracted and tired from playing the house bounce. During half time, I kept thinking that this would be a good night to get some sleep in my own bed. Little did I know that when the 2:30 pm bell rang, the demon was back at 122 Crescent reeking havoc. Everything intimate and personal was sliced, cut, shredded and smeared. Years worth of jewelry, perfume, clothing and shoes were frantically shoved into a black garbage bag to sell to the highest bidder. The intense desire to get high ravaged his taste buds and demonic hands. Steven wanted me to know that he was there and violated every inch of my room. He tracked mud with his old boots. He brought our overweight German Shepard named Kiko into my room to romp on top of my bed with his favorite bone and tennis ball. It took five days to vacuum and air out the dander. Steven enticed Mrs. Viv by calling her at the Pride House Community Center.

"Get home Leo the Lion before I burn your fucking house down."

Mrs. Viv knew this was one of his big rages because she could hear Kiko thrashing and barking in the background. He took every phone out of the wall and put it in his loot bag. Mrs. Viv had the sense to quietly call Detective Jackson from the office before she left. It was a twenty-minute drive up Central Avenue to Crescent. By the time Mrs. Viv got there in the Chrysler, three police officers were in position with their guns drawn. Two knives were placed on top of each other in the sign of the cross as a warning. Steven was long gone. He cut through North Orange Park like the black grinch, slipping and sliding through the thawed snow as he headed towards Oakwood Avenue. Arriving at the Garvey Street projects, our possessions were sold in fifteen minutes under the darkness of the broken courtyard lights. People peered from their apartment windows as new items transcended from the garbage bag. Some wished they were downstairs braving the cold to get a phone, a leather jacket or my gold watch. Dope man waited in the hallway of quad #1 waiting for Steven to make a purchase. He brought more than five ounces with some dust to mix it with. The high blazed his lungs and crystallized his brains for hours. The demon zoned out after five hours, but he had enough conscience about him to plot new vengeance and domestic havoc. Time would only tell.

My vision was clear during the bus ride home. I wanted to take a long hot shower and get some rest. I thought to myself, *"There will be peace tonight,"* until I reached South Center Street and Crescent Avenue. Cherry Bomb lights lit up the block. There were three squad cars with two-armed officers accompanying each car. The neighbors had seen so much drama over the years, only two showed up this time. Mrs. Viv was out front pacing and surveying the block. She slouched up to me trying to remain calm. Her quivering voice was a dead giveaway.

"Your father is packing a bag for you. Steven had another episode and the police are checking the area for him."

"Ma, I need to go up..."

"No!" She shouted, "wait for your bag and…"

"I don't want any bags, I've got too many bags, and I'm tired of going here, there and everywhere. He's not here, so what!" I gasped for air to fight back the tears. "This is crazy, I didn't do anything wrong and everybody's dancing around for him. Commit his ass and forget about him!"

Mrs. Viv bore a hole right through me as her eyes searched for his arrival. My thoughts were cloaked in sarcasm.

"Always creeping, dodging, peeking and peering, this shit is ridiculous."

I ran past Mrs. Viv and bolted up the stairs. The landing was full of soot and wood shrapnel. Dear brother took a saw from the basement and ravaged each bedroom door just to get high. The magnitude was unbearable. Poor daddy, he didn't know what to say.

"Don't worry baby, I'll buy you another necklace."

Humility fell at my feet.

I don't need a necklace. I need my bed. Grab your bag girl, the damage is too deep. Combat boots, leather belt, crop tee shirt, maxi pads and Pamprin.

Dad handed me a twenty-dollar bill. I grabbed the money and said, "I'll be back Saturday night. No, I'll call first, so make sure mommy buys a phone tomorrow."

I picked up my bags and descended the creaky stairs one by one. Each step had a voice, *pain, sorrow, bitch, liar, thief, denial, anger, kill, run away*. The last step was reality. My parents were so wrapped up in the crime scene; they didn't offer me a ride. I headed back to the Forty-Four Bus and transferred to the Ninety Grove at Central Avenue. I didn't pay when I boarded. Mr. Jenkins, a solid NJ Transit employee, drove me to Penn Station on many a night.

"Hey young lady, what mischief are you up to this evening?"

The bus jerked forward as I grabbed the metal bar to brace myself.

"No mischief tonight Mr. Jenkins."

I walked to Candy's house in five minutes, shifting my bag for comfort. My confidant was sitting on the porch filing her nails.

"No questions asked Shanelle. Go take a shower and crash in the blue room. Oh yeah, Derrick called. He said he would pick you up tonight."

My voice cracked and returned to normal. "When?"

Excitement filled my lungs with hot air.

"A minute ago. Don't forget to lather up Kitty. She may come in handy."

Candy stepped on the porch and grabbed a pen, scripting my future married name.

"How does this sound? Shanelle Monet Johnson."

She raised her arm and showcased a scene from Romeo and Juliet.

"Yes Derrick. I'll marry you my love joy."

"Quit it, Candy," I saddened, sweeping the floor with my duffle bag.

"Ok, ok, girl, I'll leave you alone."

The Test

Derrick arrived promptly at eight. I bolted down the stairs and barely said goodbye to my home slice. I jumped in the front seat and plastered his cheeks with three quick pecks.

"Hmmm, happy to see me huh?" he smirked.

"Not really," my lips parted, "Well, maybe a little."

I decided right then and there that I was going to start letting my guard down with Derrick. After weeks of supporting each other's basketball games and constant dry humping, it was time to get down to business. Derrick put the car in drive and headed for home. He glanced at me and joked, "Are you hungry?"

"No, I'm cool. I need to watch my weight."

"Why? You look fine Shanelle. Don't start with that I'm too fat..."

I quickly covered his mouth as he playfully bit my fingers.

"Stop Derrick," I pouted, "I am kind of hungry. I'll watch my weight when you're not around. Can you take me to Burger King?"

"Sure," Derrick replied. He drove to Central Ave and turned into the parking lot. Scrutinizing the meals on the menu screen made my stomach growl. I leaned over him and planted my resting hand in his crotch. Derrick leaned into me and nibbled on my neck as I giggled through my order.

"Yeah, let me get a Whopper with cheese off the broiler, a lil' lettuce, a little bit of ketchup, no mayo, no onions and cut in half!"

The scratchy voice came back over the intercom.

"Wow, is that all?"

I belted out, "No, gimme a large onion ring, a small fry and a small vanilla shake. I also need extra ketchup packets, at least five!"

Derrick reeled back with laughter. "Damn girl, I need to rob a bank to pay for that order."

I whipped out the twenty dollars my dad gave me. He pushed my hand away.

"Save it, you're going to need it when you take me out to

dinner."

The last thing I wanted to do was to be *"out,"* I needed to be in a house and Derrick needed to be *"in,"* me. He paid for the order at the window as I snuggled against him.

"Derrick, I really don't want to go out tonight. I just want to be with you."

My puppy dog expression won him over. He tucked strands of my hair into place and said, "Ok baby, have it your way."

Giggling, I puckered my lips. "Just like my Whopper?"

He chuckled, "Yeah, hot off the broiler, but don't try to cut my ass in half."

"Oh you got jokes now huh?"

"I got something," Derrick echoed.

The irony of good jokes and food didn't last long. We cruised back to his house with the radio turned down low. The drive would surely take us past my block if he went down South Center Street. I held the warm package on my lap dreading his sense of direction. The aroma of French Fries distracted me for a little while and released another stomach wrenching gurgle. I fed Derrick three hot fries at Tremont Avenue. As the light turned green, my throat started welling up. Derrick cruised past Crescent Avenue. Whether he slowed down in sheer curiosity, or to give me a glance at the house was anyone's guess. We witnessed a patrol car parked in front of the house. He noticed the physical change in my demeanor and patted my lap. We barely said two words to each other until we reached his house. When we plowed inside, a sweet baked smell aroused my senses. Ms. Johnson left a pound cake on the table with a note sticking out from the bottom of the plate. The cake was golden brown mixed with crimson edges. We took off our coats while Derrick took my bags upstairs. Before he got to the second step he stopped, turned around and professed, "I hope you're staying for the weekend. My mom went to a fellowship convention in Philly and won't be back until Sunday night."

There was no need for him to mention his dad. A new job split the family when he was three causing Derrick's father to relocate to Southern California. I was starving and confused.

"Why only one squad car instead of the usual three?"

My response was quick.

"Yes, I'm staying. Can I wash my hands in the sink?"

He ascended the stairs adding, "Sure, get comfortable."

Once Derrick was temporarily out of sight, I washed my hands with lightening speed, dried them with the Burger King wrapper and tore into my Whopper, damn near devouring it whole. I had to remind myself to slow down because with three large bites down, Derrick would think I was a hog. I slowed down to savor the taste. He came back downstairs and picked up a banana. He stared at me wide-eyed and teased, "Are ya hungry?"

"Stop playing!" I choked, cupping my mouth to preserve my face.

"Ok, enjoy your food. I'll let you eat in peace."

He washed his hands and cut me a piece of cake. I think I was caught up in an anxious eating frenzy. I ate the cake with my shake and it was heavenly..., for a little while at least. After the last swallow, the squad car came into focus and the food seemed to sit in my throat. I started to panic and needed an escape.

"Derrick," I quivered, holding my hand to my mouth, "I made a pig of myself, can I use your shower?"

"Go ahead, you don't have to ask. I put some towels and a washcloth on my bed for you, the last room on the left."

On any other day, his answer would have sent me into the passion pit, but I knew that riding past my house awakened the anguish in my stomach. I started up the stairs feeling the food slowly sour in my belly. There were no creaky noises, but the voices were in my head.

"Die bitch die, die fat bitch. You slut, whore, bitch."

Like maggots feasting in warm bile, the sour food crept back up my throat. I spotted the bathroom and plunged my face into the toilet bowl. There was never a need to put my finger down my throat. Anguish and stress sat in the pit of my stomach like a power lifter, forcing food up in times of stress. The vile hurled out of my mouth for an eternity. My stomach heaved and jerked until my eyes felt like they were going to pop. Relief finally came. The cold rim of the toilet bowl cooled my sweat tremors. My fingertips relaxed as I searched for tissue. I wiped my mouth, stood up and stared into the beveled mirror. My eyes were dark and blood shot. I was ugly. Focusing on the floor, I settled the voices in my head.

"Stay cool Shanelle. He can't hurt you here, you're safe."

I turned the shower knob for hot water. The two temperatures merged and relaxed my aching muscles. I began to take slow deep breaths. Air swelled my brain as I began to sob, deep and steady. There were no creaky pipes to muffle the sound. The bellowing went straight to Derrick's ears and in seconds he was banging on the bathroom door. Panic ruled him.

"Shanelle!"

Bang! Bang! Bang!

"What's wrong?"

Bang! Bang! Bang!

"Shanelle, please don't cry baby, let me help you!"

His plea of help weakened me straight to the floor. He heard the thump of my palms hitting the basin tile, so he kicked in the door. Derrick took his shoes off and stepped inside with all of his clothes on, picking my rag doll frame off the shower floor. Forcing his hands under my armpits, he spoke to me with his cheek against mine. The water confused my need for him, as my eyes fluttered open.

"Whatever it is, let me help you. Don't do this to yourself. Hold me and don't let go. I love you, but you need to let me help you."

With that declaration, I was free. I relaxed my arms and wrapped them around his neck. I was afraid we were going to slip, but with one arm he held on to the peach tile wall and secured our exit. He carried me to his bed soaking wet, toweling off every inch of my body. Derrick applied lotion to my arms and shoulders like a professional masseuse. There was no sexual awakening in me, just peace and tranquility.

The clock struck two a.m. when I stretched. Bunkering down into his arms, relishing his fingers against my scalp, I yawned, "How long have I been sleeping?"

"Three hours. You fell asleep during Eyewitness News." Guilt set in.

"Derrick, I'm so sorry."

A soft kiss tapped my forehead.

"You deserve to be happy Shanelle. Let's get you some tea."

Once downstairs, we played footsie under the table and

thumb wrestled until *"she,"* popped up. Quickly letting go, I strummed the table and asked, "So, what's up with Portia?"

His eyes shot to the floor. Derrick stood up, keeping a well maintained distance.

"You need to know that this basketball thing is short lived. The only people that do know are Coach Mahoney and my mom."

I quickly interrupted, "Well, I'm listening, but I didn't hear anything about her."

"Let me finish Shanelle."

"Ok, ok, I'm sorry, go ahead." The suspense was killing me.

"I was accepted to Duke University in the early admission's program. Even though it's a sure thing, I took the state Regent's Exam for an early exit out of St. James Prep. In order to get a jump on things, I have to take some advanced biology courses at St. James University. Duke is going to accept those credits as long as I keep an A average."

Derrick had a solid academic background and this news would be of no surprise to anyone that knew him, even Portia. I had to wonder how she fit into this picture. Derrick continued, "Once basketball season is over, I'll be at the university buried in books Shanelle."

I silenced him with fingers against his lips.

"Is this what you want Derrick?"

He stared at me with a reassuring smile and boasted, "It's what I've dreamed about."

"Well, then Dr. Johnson, I'm happy for you."

Derrick chimed in.

"Not so fast, Sherlock, I haven't answered the million dollar question."

"True, true," I surmised with restless hands.

"Well, didn't you notice that she wasn't at the game?" he asked.

"Do you think I come to your games to check on her, or you Derrick?" I thought to myself, *"C'mon now, you're pissing me off."*

Derrick chimed in, invading my space with a stern face. "School comes first and besides, Portia's just a fling. She wants the fast lane with a ball player strapped to her hip. Besides, she's been messing around with a football player name Malik from Shabazz."

Staring, refusing to let go, Derrick lifted me up in one swoop. I felt light and incredibly sexy as he charged up the stairs with athletic prowess. I tightened my grip around his neck so hard that the garnet ring my father gave me brushed against my cheek. I thought to myself, *"Not now daddy, this is too good to be true."*

We entered his room. It was the first time I really got a view. The décor was fashioned in hunter green and navy. Trophies, hooded sweatshirts and scattered pictures accented his humble surroundings. Derrick laid me down as his weary mattress melted against my body. He stood between my legs and licked his lips, longing for his freshly served appetizer. His pointer finger shot up as he searched the room.

"It's just us Shanelle," he backed away. Derrick thumped across the bed yanking a tattered lamp string. The room faded to black as the Whispers came on. *Why did it have to be Chocolate Girl?* I was through. Kneeling down, his slight razor stubble brushed my skin as he kissed my inner thighs, quickly hardening my nipples. Tears began to well in my eyes from his warm hands. He put his lips to my ear and begged, "I want you. Do you want me?"

"Yes," I softened.

Derrick began to kiss each sensual point on my body. My hips, stomach and belly button were all at his command. I tried to connect with him, but he put my hands back on the headboard.

"Be still, or I'm going to tie you up."

I thought to myself, *"Oh, I really think I'm going to enjoy that."* I laughed out loud. It was raunchy and mature. My cackles were usually high pitched and petite. It didn't sound right. I perused the room, taking in my physical reality. I wondered if Portia had the same experience. I squeezed my eyes to bury thoughts of Nemesis. Just in time, Derrick kissed me below the belly button as I melted. He quietly breathed, "Shanelle, you smell so good baby."

"Smell good?"

I wasn't wearing any perfume, Steven stole it and I didn't have the money to buy a new bottle. Nemesis quickly warped into my conscious.

"Giving up the Kitty tonight my pretty?" She prattled.

"Shut up," I fired back, *"You'll stop at nothing to see me miserable!"*

"Miserable?" Nemesis preached. *"Your father's miserable right now.*

Hill Street Blues just went off and that kid smoking pot on the commercial said to your father, 'It's 10:00 pm, do you know your daughter's at Derrick's house trying to fuck?'"

I mistakenly growled out loud, "Ughhhh, leave me alone!"

Derrick jumped up, gaped faced and startled.

"Shanelle, what's wrong with you?"

I felt so stupid and betrayed.

"No, it's not you," I blabbed, grabbing his face. "You're wonderful. It's just that, it feels so good, but…,"

"What is it? You don't want me to make love to you?"

Before I could answer, Nemesis fired another shot, *"Surely ding-a-ling, this is lust, not love."*

I squeezed my eyes to shut her down, but she was in control.

"No ding…, I mean… dick, no Derrick, I'm sorry, I just get so caught up." My rationale failed as he interrupted me.

"Here, put these on," he rushed with a frown. Derrick turned on the lights and cracked his neck on each side as he headed for the shower. I picked up his sweats but I didn't put them on. It was bitter cold outside, but his room was roasting warm and I felt comfortable naked. I got under his covers and rubbed my nipples to dull the sensation of Derrick's rapture. From a distance he shouted, "Shanelle bring me a towel."

"Well at least he's still speaking to me."

I obliged and strolled into the bathroom. In all of his naked God given glory he was dripping wet with beads of water perspiring down his abs and legs. He started laughing and exclaimed, "Don't mess with me; I gave you that sweat suit for a reason."

I put the towel on the sink and got in the shower with him.

"Can I join you, oops, I already did. Tee hee."

"Oh, now you want to be a bad girl. Don't start something you can't finish Shanelle."

"I'm a good girl." I replied. "Let me wash your back. Turn around."

His body was beautiful and lean underneath the swell of the steam. I couldn't resist kissing his smooth skin.

"If you don't wash my back you're gonna be mine on the shower floor."

A loud snort escaped my mouth. "At least I can remember

our shower."

I lathered up the washcloth and washed his beautiful back. With all the strength left in me, I massaged the soap into his skin and rinsed him down. Derrick turned around and kissed me with an open mouth. The warm water caressed the two of us as his lengthy manhood pressed up against me, but I wasn't ready. He took one of my breasts in his mouth and the other in his hands.

"I want you so bad girl, but I'm cool."

I searched his eyes and whispered, "Yeah, I'm cool too."

Derrick leaned out the shower and handed me a towel. He spanked my ass with one pop and replied, "I need you to get out so I can take care of big man. Put something on Shanelle if you want to stay with me tonight."

Focused and still, he meant business. Derrick tamed his urges by watching me dry off as his release swished down the drain. I pretended to hand him the towel but instead I smacked him with it to shock him out of his dazed response.

"Owww! Now you've done it!" He jumped out of the shower and ran after me, wet hair, bodies and all. He chased me to the bed and dove on top of me laughing like we did during the snowstorm. I felt so comforted by him and my need to feel safe, even though we were completely naked. He tickled me so hard my stomach began to hurt. I couldn't get away, so I begged for mercy.

"Please stop, I'll do anything!"

My laughter reached a high pitch as Derrick continued to trap me in his grip. "Anything?"

I screamed again, unable to get away. "No, just about anything. Let me go, my stomach hurts!"

He released me and I let out a loud sigh. I stretched out across his bed reaching for my pocketbook. It was a great time to wind down so I decided to read a poem I wrote for him.

"What's that?" Derrick asked.

"Oh, just a little something I wrote to keep me sane. Do you want to hear it?"

"Sure, and it better be good."

"Ok," I said. "This piece is titled, 'This or That' by Shanelle Brown."

Derrick crossed his arms as I cleared my throat in jest.

"At the age of thirteen daddy gave me to hold, three carats garnet, wrapped in white gold. He slid it on my ring finger to have and to hold. 'Lead with your mind, it's stronger and bold. Your heart will mislead you, this I fear, and I'll take that boy out like a hunter to a deer.'"

I held up my left hand and proudly displayed my shield of virtue and protection.

"So if it's this that you want, you can't have it, it's mine, we'll meet in ten years for a meeting of the minds."

I stood up and took my bow as he clapped for me.

"You don't think I'm a boy Shanelle?" he asked.

"No, but my daddy does," I boasted, sliding my panties up with a snap.

"Hey, my poem is corny, but it's a general thing, don't take it personal."

Derrick rubbed the side of my leg and said, "I'm not. Anyway, I've got something for you."

My eyes lit up with excitement.

"For lil' ole' me?"

Derrick got up and went to the closet. I sat up with curiosity as he pulled out a brown hatbox. He put his hands on top and said, "Shanelle, I hope you don't think I'm as crazy as you are, but I've been meaning to give you these things. While I'm gone, I want you to get through this. It's one of the reasons that I stopped when you asked me to because I didn't want us to make love knowing that I couldn't fully commit to you."

My eyes welled up. I wanted to tell him everything, but it wasn't his problem. Derrick continued, "I wish I didn't have to leave you behind, but I am. I won't be able to pick you up or keep you safe when you need me. So I put some things in this box for you to keep you close to me."

The open box exposed a green felt leg. With little girl glee I replied, "Kermit the Frog!"

I gave him a big hug as Derrick's chin settled into my neck. With Christmas morning anticipation, I exclaimed, "What else have you got for me?" Derrick grinned and said, "Close your eyes pretty lady."

"Ready when you are." I felt something familiar rest on my

shoulders. I opened my eyes and confirmed that it was his varsity jacket, a coveted trophy for any girl in my town. I jumped up on the bed and began to cheer for him, "Derrick, Derrick, he's my man, if he can't do it no one can!"

He couldn't resist a comeback and joked, "So you're going to let me do it?"

I chimed in on top of his sentence, "No, silly, but I'll be willing to wait for you."

His face instantly soured.

"What is it?" I asked as my eyebrows knocked together.

Derrick grabbed my hand, gingerly rubbing my palms.

"Shanelle, a lot is going to happen to the two of us over the next year and I hope things will get better. But if I know you the way I think I do, it won't be long before you find a perfect guy. I'm just in the wrong place right now, but I would love to be that guy."

His words seemed so silly. I couldn't conceive liking anyone as much as Derrick.

"Don't get crazy on me Derrick, you're all I need."

Hushed by my whimsical feelings, he paused, searching the room for answers.

"Ok Shanelle, I won't think about it anymore, but I would love it if you were still here waiting for me when I come home."

I gave him a heart-felt hug, breathing his energy into my soul.

"Baby, we've just begun, I'll be here."

Little did I know my fate was about to change.

Eyewitness News blared across the TV screen. Unseasonably warm weather from the Midwest changed the weather pattern to sixty-five degrees. Derrick sat up and announced, "Wow, that's crazy for December, we need to take advantage of that."

"What do you want to do?"

"Drive to the beach."

"Derrick, its freezing." The idea sounded absurd to me. I had very little exposure to the New Jersey shore up until now, but I was open to the idea.

"Well we're not going swimming silly, but the ocean view will get your mind off of things."

I snuggled into his neck and sighed, "Well I can't wait, as long as I am with you, I'm cool."

"Yeah, we're cool, huh?" he asked, pulling me against his warm body.

I laughed and closed my eyes with the security of Derrick holding me. It was picture perfect. He in his sweat pants and sweatshirt and me in my varsity jacket, no bra and pink satin panties.

Vision of Him

By morning we were heading down Parkway South to exit 98, Belmar, New Jersey. With just four hours of sleep, I was alert, chatty and craving a hot chocolate. I memorized the railroad, the WaWa and the turn onto Sixteenth Avenue. By 9 a.m., there were people out and about strolling and jogging on the boardwalk. We plowed onto the beach with our shoes on. I was wearing a navy Nike track suit with sneakers to match. The pants were a new cotton spandex blend that absorbed sweat and gave my legs incredible form. Derrick stood out in his trademark sweats with a black turtleneck underneath. He led me to a spot on the sand about fifty feet from the shore line. Derrick opened his sand chair which was big enough for the two of us, although I chose to sit in between his legs. Off in the distance, a group of guys caught my attention as Derrick wrapped his arms around me. The sun was very bright so I used my hand as a visor to see them. They were playing touch football, appearing as silhouettes in the distance. One of them seemed to stand out among the rest. Derrick nuzzled his face in my neck and snuggled into me for warmth. The position on the sand gave me a better angle of the game. As I watched them play, Derrick sang love songs to me and nibbled on my ear. It complemented the moment, but as he continued, the game grew closer to us. I took a deep breath as the mighty one in front took a stance. His face turned in my direction as he positioned his pass like the poster boy for the Heisman trophy. Like a match connected to a Fourth of July sparkler, I sat up to embrace his physiology and chocolate vision. He was cinnamon brown, with glistening skin under the sunlight. He was slightly over six feet tall with a firm husky neck and broad shoulders. I found myself floating away from Derrick's love song to behold this mighty warrior. The game drew nearer, at least three feet and I began to feel loose particles of sand as they ran by. He turned to receive a pass. His burgundy sweatshirt said a little bit about him. I thought to myself, *"Hmmm, Lakewood Athletics."*

One thing was true; he was a man and not a boy. His body

was absolutely beautiful. He had a cut waist and powerful thighs. Derrick began to stroke my hair. I smiled as the warrior watched Derrick's innocent affection. Marching closer, his muscular thighs and big feet parted the sand. He motioned for Derrick with the football. In a deep burley voice he gruffed, "Yo man, you want in? We need another player."

The base in Derrick's voice tripled. "Nah, I'm cool."

To my surprise, the brazen Dark Gable towering over us peered down. "How about you little lady?"

My mouth dropped open but nothing came out. Derrick sat up, pulling me closer. He answered before my lips parted again to speak.

"Nah man, she's cool too."

The guys in the game laughed in jest, waving their hands. "Leave 'em alone Q-Dog and get back in the game."

Derrick squeezed me tight, kissing my neck.

"Damn. I can't take you anywhere. Even the college fellas want you, but you're all mine."

I wondered how Derrick knew they were in college, but I didn't ask. I was curious about Mr. Q-Dog and what his deal was. He was arrogant, self assured and down right brazen for patrolling up on us, but I was incredibly excited to get his attention. More importantly, I wanted to know his name. Kitty nestled around and snuggled in for a nap, but I wanted the warrior to push Derrick down and carry me off into the sunset. The thought of what he would do to me with his powerful hands made me suck my thumb for a second.

Derrick needed to go to the bathroom. I in turn wanted a hot chocolate to soothe me while I watched the rest of the game. He asked if I needed anything and I told him I was going to go across the street for something hot. He gave me twenty dollars and asked for bottled water. Derrick headed down the boardwalk. I crossed the street at Sixteenth Avenue in pursuit of Dunkin 'Donuts. My mouth started to water as I mentally resisted the thought of thirty mini Munchkins. Just then, I felt a presence brush against my back. I continued to move up in the line, but every time I inched forward, the person behind kept invading my space. A male voice spoke to me.

"So, is the prep star your boyfriend?"

I turned to face my aggressor. To my surprise, it was the mighty one. I reacted abruptly, facing him with a frown.

"No, he's just a friend, why do you ask?" I paused and said, "Oh would you excuse me please." A dollar bill graced the counter.

"A large hot chocolate," I paused, fumbling for currency, "sweet please." One hand planted against my hip.

"Why do you ask?"

His smile stretched and retreated into a frown.

"Well, he's not your type that's for sure."

"No he didn't just say that!"

He advanced the tease by mimicking my expression with a cocky ass grin on his face. I fired back.

"Oh, you know my type?"

He cocked his head and belted out, "He can't handle you. You're a wild child and I know you wanted to get up and play some contact football. Maybe even one on one."

He smirked with a wink, "Anyway, you're young and I don't want to mess up your puppy love. But here's a tip, if you want to get rid of those dark circles under your eyes, give up hot chocolate, get more rest and drink water."

My pitiful lip fell to the ground supported by an iron skillet.

"Excuse me, I didn't need all of that and besides you're in this Dunkin' Donuts with me." I grabbed my hot chocolate and put the change in the tip jar while the warrior cleared his throat.

"Yeah, but I'm just buying the news paper. If I knew you better, I would offer to take you to church with me to get some of that worry out of your head. You're too serious little girl."

I wanted to smack him. He was breaking me down layer by layer and he sounded like a religious fanatic to boot. He crushed the air around me and asked, "You're not from around here are you?"

I clutched my dark eye inducing drink and gripped it firmly, silenced by the sight of Derrick crossing the street. The warrior followed my eyes and scoffed, "Go have a talk with God, get organized and you'll make a way on your own terms without that dude. When you're finished kicking it with pretty boy in a couple of years, take the Parkway back to exit 98 and bring those big pretty legs with you."

As he edged out, Derrick swaggered inside shaking his head.

The cashier shouted, "See you next week Alex."

Through the glass pane Alex waved a peace sign and winked at me behind Derrick's back. I couldn't believe I forgot to purchase his water. He put his arm around my shoulder and said, "I can't leave you alone for a minute."

Flushed from the inside out, I was ready to leave. Everything "Alex" said to me was the truth. My only reference was my drink. I took a sip and threw it in the garbage. Derrick dropped his guard.

"Hey, I thought you wanted that?"

I searched for the warrior, watching him climb into a Mazda RX 7.

"No, it wasn't that good. I want to go home…, I'm getting cold."

Derrick didn't ask what was wrong. He met my every need, no matter what I said. We went back to our spot and folded the chairs and blankets. I glanced at Derrick and wondered what would happen to the two of us once we got back home.

"Derrick can you promise me one thing?"

"What is it?" he answered, brushing sand from his calves.

"If I run into you and you're with your boys, will you promise not to act shady?"

"What makes you think I would do something like that?" He seemed puzzled by the question.

"You know how you guys are, pretending to be something different around your friends and when it's just us, you act yourself."

Derrick folded the blanket and rested it on his chest. "Shanelle, the only thing I did different around you was keeping it inside. That's not me. Besides, there's a lot to be said about me taking a cold shower for you. You'll see I am not the average guy."

He picked me up as my legs wrapped around his waist for a reassuring hug. I nestled my chin into his shoulders taking in the panoramic view of the ocean. I held on to his hug as Derrick rubbed my back. The pounding waves crashing onto shore enhanced the mystery and excitement of my unknown life ahead. I was comforted by Derrick's caress, but the invitation Alex extended piqued my immediate interests. Sighing once, I slid down as Derrick packed up the car while I searched for answers.

On the way home I revisited the scene as he held my free

hand. Derrick the rescuer and provider, always there for me, but along comes a mysterious stranger who blows my mind with a few simple sentences.

Sure, I know how to pack a duffel bag, but what about my life? Where was I going and why was I in constant flight?

He was right and he barely knew me. I needed to do those things and I definitely wanted to see him again. I took my journal out and wrote a poem to remember him. I held the front cover of my journal up so Derrick couldn't peek. I didn't want to disappoint him. I fixed a gaze into my compact and smiled. The circles around my eyes were dark, but sleep and water could cure those issues. Crossing the bridge on that unseasonably warm day in December, I should have thanked Derrick a million times or more. Our journey was my prelude to someone new. Little did I know it wouldn't be long before we would meet again. About him, I wrote:

Drawn to him,
his skin
so cinnamon.
Will you let me in,
to your mind,
unwind,
my thoughts of you
like the suckle of sweet honeydew.
I need to get to know you.
I need to know your name,
sitting with this current boy,
visions of you
driving me insane.
Oh that's your name
your boy just exclaimed,
"Yo Alex, I got next."
But wait a minute,
I want a turn.
Your cinnamon vision,
fires and burns

a critical synapse
in my brain
look at me
make me sane
but take your time,
I'm just a girl.
You are certainly a man.
This sunny day I understand,
That contained in your vision,
A master plan
unearth my girlish gem to woman from man.
I need to be me,
this precious star, drawn to you
wherever you are…, Cinnamon.

I smiled when I closed my journal shut. It was a clever piece and poetry seemed to calm me in my crazy reality. I began to focus on Derrick again as we talked about his future plans. I was genuinely happy for him, but I knew his absence would overwhelm me just the same.

We ended up in North Orange Park and talked before he took me home. I wanted it to last forever, but it was overshadowed by a familiar face lurching up to us. Steven had a way of making you pay attention. He walked right up to Derrick's window and made his presence known by knocking on the driver's side.

"Yo, what up Shalimar?"

Derrick barely flinched as he rolled down the window.

"Do I know you man?"

Steven started laughing, "Yo, I don't give a fuck if you know me or not, but you know my sister now don't ya?"

I gave Derrick the look.

"Yeah, that's crazy ass, can't you tell?"

He got out of the car and I immediately jumped out and ran around to their side. He was taller than Steven and he weighed more, but I was sure Derrick never carried a weapon. A police cruiser just so happened to drive by on South Center Street. Thank goodness it passed by slowly because it broke dear brother's concentration. Steven slouched away laughing, "You better be glad they're out here or I would bust a cap in your ass."

We jumped in the car and sped past him. Even though dear brother was fucked up, we still went through sibling rivalry with Mrs. Viv and I wasn't taking any chances convincing her that I wasn't at Candy's house.

"I'll call you later Derrick," I ended with a quick peck, "don't worry, I'll be fine."

My luck ran out as soon as Steven turned the corner and greeted us with an evil grimace. He gave Derrick the middle finger and sidestepped to the front door. I grabbed my bags and ran to the door feeling desperate and five minutes short of a whipping.

Breathing heavily, I begged for mercy.

"Steven, please don't tell mommy, okay Steven, please?" I rummaged through my pocketbook hoping to find ten dollars to pay his ass off until I got paid. He surveyed every inch of my bag, sizing up his loot and ordered, "This one's gonna cost you, I want whatever you have now, plus fifty when you get paid next week."

I pleaded, nodding my head in approval. "Ok, ok, but please don't tell." Mrs. Viv opened the door and started raging, "Get your ass in here Shanelle and clean that damn refrigerator out like I told you. Next week you better have your ass in church instead of hanging in the streets."

My lips puckered together with a quick peck to her cheek.

"Ok momma, do you want me to clean the mirrors too?"

Her weighted fists jammed into her full hips.

"Do you need to ask Shanelle? Don't get cute with me. I want this place clean, do you hear me?"

I quickly replied, "Ok, no problem."

Steven scowled, clenching his jaw. I was sure he wanted to kill me in front of Mrs. Viv, but he needed fifty bucks on Friday and that would certainly stall his sibling homicide plot. He retreated to the attic without a word. Mrs. Viv had no work assignments for Steven. She yelled upstairs parting her mouth wide, "Steven, I'll call you when dinner's ready."

He slammed the attic door. With that little episode working well in my favor, I cleaned the refrigerator and wiped down the glass mirrors. I was in a great mood and the smells emitting from the kitchen enhanced my good feeling. I was humming so loud, Mrs. Viv couldn't resist a motherly inquiry.

"You're in a good mood missy, what's new with you?"

A waterless fishbowl of marbles rattled inside my shaking head.

"Nothing!"

She leaned back and raised one suspicious eyebrow.

"I was just asking a simple question Shanelle."

"Oh, I'm sorry; I've been preoccupied with the season and all the games coming up."

Temporarily satisfied, she leaned against the wall for strength.

"I've been meaning to talk to you about that Shanelle."

"What about it?"

"Well, your father and I have been struggling with all these medical bills and we're going to need you to get a job when your birthday comes around to cover your personal expenses."

"What!" My tone was high pitched and hostile. Mrs. Viv stood up and mashed my face with an open palm.

"Lower your voice. You heard me girl. Your father and I are barely making ends meet."

I was irate and frustrated. I leered at her and screamed, "Why can't Steven get a job? He sits around here all day listening to Richard Pryor, getting high and stealing from us all the time. It's not fair!"

I bolted upstairs. The drama was too much for dear daddy as he marched to my bedroom door. I made sure to lock the door with the skeleton key so they couldn't get in and gang up on me.

"Shanelle, open this door now!" Nobody's going to lock doors in my house."

Tears trickled down my face. I needed a way out. Maybe I could just run away. Candy's parents could adopt me. They didn't have that kind of drama going on. She didn't even have a brother. I yelled into the pillow, "God I hate this shit, if I can just find a way out of here I swear I'll never come back!"

"Get out of there Shanelle."

Alex was right. I wanted to see him again and ask him how he knew so much. For now, my only resolve was to figure it out myself.

Devil's Dormancy

The next day the temperature dropped twenty degrees. Derrick dropped me off to a tranquil house. He made his announcement, I flunked my Spanish exam and I didn't want to talk to Derrick about not seeing him for two weeks because of his hectic academic schedule. To make matters worse, my period was due to arrive and as each day crept up on me, all I could do was sleep. Five minutes into my nap, I was quickly interrupted as Steven started his reign of terror. He pounded on my door shouting, "Get up bitch and take a shower before I cut the fucking water off!"

My hands smacked into the bed as I sat up like a woman possessed.

"Go take your fucking medicine and leave me the hell alone!"

He used one finger to bang on the door this time. Steven was furious and hell bent on proving it to me. "I only need cold water bitch, you better hurry too, the pipes are frozen."

I shook my head in disbelief, discouraged that we were going to have another obsessed winter. "Steven, daddy never shuts the water off, don't get crazy on me again with that pipe shit."

His voice dipped deeper.

"Well I'm turning them off, so leave bitch and take your fucking bags with you."

His fist drummed the aging wooden frame.

"I'll be sure to lock the door behind you and while you're at it, bang on the window for a fucking mayonnaise sandwich so you can see how that shit feels." Silence followed for a second until his creepy footsteps hollowed into the attic. A symphony of terror played in his chosen music. Super Freak, Voices, and Super Nature blasted through the ceiling over and over again. He stomped his feet to deepen the effect and shouted, "Three more inches and I'm fucking shit up. I'm starting with you first Shanelle and I'm going to gut you like a fish."

I immediately grabbed my bag, threw on some sweats and

opened the door. His victory was apparent.

"This is my house bitch, so get the fuck out."

Stomping with conviction, I headed into the winter snowstorm. For my own safety, I turned an eye cautiously watching the haunted house. He was standing in Mrs. Viv's window mimicking his pointer finger across his throat like a knife. The conquering snow sliced my face and stung my eyes. Plowing, I trudged through the deep, powdery trenches without consideration of nature's fury. There was one back at the house that made up for every weather pattern. If my parents sent the police after me, I was going to cry child abuse. A good foster home was a better shot than living with Steven. Searching, I looked up, although the heavens offered no answer.

"Do You hear me God? I'm talking to You, did I just leave the devil behind because I can't take it anymore."

The faster I trekked, the heavier my cramps became. Tears streamed down my face at the corner payphone. Faithfully, Bonnie answered, stalling with a quick breath.

"Stay at the Exxon station, me and Papi will be there in a few minutes, don't cry."

A house filled with warm smells and Tito Puente serenading in the background. At last I finally got some rest. I think I slept for twelve hours. I was awakened by Mrs. Viv, fidgeting with regret. I was so disoriented it took me a while to figure out that I was still in Bonnie's room. Mrs. Viv rubbed my arm again. Her eyes were blood shot red. She uttered with bitterness welling in her throat. "Steven's in a psychiatric institution, he can't hurt you anymore."

I sat up in disbelief.

"Where?"

Mrs. Viv took her time as she spoke. "The police took him to East Orange General Hospital for a twenty-four hour evaluation. He was in bad shape Shanelle. It was enough to commit him to Marlboro down in South Jersey. He won't be coming home anytime soon."

She skimmed Bonnie's surroundings and smiled. "She has such a cute room, we should get your room painted and fixed up just like Bonnie's."

That went right over my head. Every deal came with a heavy

price. Bonnie greeted me at the hallway landing.

"Shanelle, hopefully you'll feel safe now."

The ride home was deafening. Dad drove hunched over with paralyzing remorse. I guess he meant what he said and the choice came at a hard price. We were a family of three. Hopefully, dear brother's revolt would seem like a shallow memory even though the wounds were deep. Even if Mrs. Viv wanted to forgive her son, the police and the prosecutor's office wouldn't let his acts go unnoticed. With enough probable cause, they entered the attic and removed three duffel bags of domestic weaponry, including a bat with nails sticking out of the head. I shutter to think what would have happened to me if I stayed that night.

I couldn't help but think, *"Is his mind that crazy? Am I crazy too?"* Lord knows the voices in my head made up for a twenty-piece marching band. Thinking about it became too much to bear. It was easier to close my eyes and let my dreams carry me away.

Something Old Something New

Our high school graduation sailed through with the excitement of summer nipping at our high heels. Mrs. Viv, suffering from bouts of limbo loss, mourned and celebrated dear brother at a whim. She was happy one moment, and sadistically sad the next. The house was never clean enough for her and she was constantly making an extra plate of food for him. Me and dad refused to question her habits, not knowing whether it would deepen her into further silence. We probably all needed counseling, but I'm sure mom and dad couldn't afford the treatment. Financial strains deepened in the house as more and more medical bills came funneling into our lives. I didn't play basketball or try to see Derrick. The hurt and embarrassment kept me away. The whole town knew what happened and we were too emotionally drained to care. Derrick's mother was a nurse at East Orange Hospital and I'm sure word got back to her about my house. I was convinced she told Derrick to stay away for his own safety. I buried thoughts of everyone, Derrick, my brother and my parents. I needed to do that one thing that Alex talked about, getting organized. For starters, every Saturday I ran to North Orange Park and practiced foul shots for one hour. I meandered the long way home and headed up Crescent Avenue. By the time I got to the intersection, my hair was drenched and my arms were exhausted from dribbling the ball. A car from behind me beeped as I crossed the intersection, but I refused to glance back or give the harasser my time or attention. A familiar voice quickly caused my heart to flutter.

"Hey, number thirty-two, can I get your autograph?"

The driver side opened and my handsome black prince stood up towering over his vehicle. I screamed his name, instantly rejecting my prior thoughts of him.

"Derrick!"

He dashed to the front of his car and stretched his arms out smiling ear to ear. I dropped my basketball and jumped into his arms squeezing him tight. Derrick squeezed me back. I was glad he was used to sweat because he didn't react to my damp, clammy skin. He picked me up off the ground and squeezed the life out of me. "Ahhhh, damn girl, are you happy to see me or what?" I buried my face in his neck.

"I am happy to see you Derrick. I missed you sooooo much. Look at you, you're taller and smarter. Meanwhile my life sucks!" Derrick started laughing.

"Girl, c'mon and get in the car," he beamed, "I need to take you out and catch up with your life," he laughed, throwing the ball into the backseat. Like the gentleman he was, Derrick opened the passenger door and waited before it slammed shut. My disheveled appearance caught his attention as he slid in the driver's side.

"Shanelle, you're all over the place."

"It's a long story," I replied, shrugging my shoulder in one heap. "I don't want to waste your precious medical time. Let's stop by my house so I can take a quick shower."

Derrick gave me a familiar wink from the past. "Are you sure you want to do that?"

I nudged him, chuckling with a wrinkled nose. "I'm positive. Besides, you wouldn't want to mess around in my house."

Derrick made himself comfortable on our old living room couch. I skipped the stairs by twos to get ready. A hot shower rinsed the sweat out of my hair as I brushed it wet into a tight ponytail. Blue Magic grease layered the surface for extra sheen. I dabbed on Maybelline mascara and a pat of lip gloss. Turning left to right in the mirror, an old friend came to visit.

"So, off on another rendezvous with 'hit it while you can' Derrick?"

I tapped my lips to dull the sheen and ignored the jealous one.

"Oh so you think you're grown now huh? Got your life all figured out, like you and Derrick are going to play house somewhere. Get real; you're just a kid to him, a play thing."

I shut my eyes tight to think her away. I ran downstairs and showed off my new outfit. He didn't seem excited at all by the sight of me. He was examining the family pictures on the mantle.

"Is this your brother?"

He pointed to his early high school days at North Orange High while Nemesis came back.

Yeah, he's studying that psychology and disorder shit, maybe he thinks you're crazy too."

I grabbed his arm and pulled him away from the use to be memories.

"Yeah that's him. Let's go, he's not here anymore anyway."

"Where is he?"

I gripped his wrist and pulled him out the door.

"It's a long story and who cares where he is as long as he's gone."

I slammed the door and jiggled the battered lock, securing the fragile trappings inside. Constant fear of dear brother finding an escape route plagued me. Derrick opened the passenger door and calmly asked, "So, where do you want to go?"

It was already two o'clock in the afternoon and I wasn't sure.

"I don't care, as long as I'm with you baby."

Snapping his fingers once, he replied, "There's a West Indian festival in Brooklyn off of Atlantic Avenue. Let's get out of New Jersey and hang with some of my people."

My rendition of the Caribbean dialect made him laugh.

"Ahh, dem your people 'eh?"

"Girl we all 'dem people," he joked, pinching my cheek.

He put the key in the ignition as fast as he completed his sentence. Derrick usually gave me a little wink, but it didn't happen. Memories of watching the final scene in Cooley High swelled my heart as I faced the passenger window.

Driving to Brooklyn was a great getaway. The pedestrian hustle and bustle from the view of his car was exciting. Derrick talked about molecular biology, human psychology and physics. I looked out the passenger window and spotted a woman tying a balloon on her daughter's wrist. The little girl looked at me as I made a funny face. She smiled just as Derrick pulled off towards the entrance of the Brooklyn Bridge. I turned back to witness her success, but from the little girl's pathetic teary eyed face and wide mouth, the balloon dashed into the sky. Witnessing the sadness resting in my wrinkled forehead, he said, "Shanelle, you know I can't pull over and hug you, but everybody goes through life feeling the same way you're feeling right now, even me. I'm out of my league studying all this advanced material, but it just feels right. As for you being in my life, I never said that you had to stop your life for me, but I know that I love you and wish that you were the one girl who could share this with me when I'm finished school. Maybe that's not what you want to hear, but it's the truth and that's all I've got to give you right now."

Tears welled in my eyes like the water below the bridge. It looked so clear and tranquil as the sun took temporary rest. Derrick poised himself upright and said, "I still love you and I always will no matter who we end up with in the future."

I don't know if it was me or Derrick going through some life cycle, but with all the color and splendor of the Caribbean festival, we both knew that we were not the same anymore. We strolled through the scenery holding hands and admired feathery junkanoo costumes. A simmering five-dollar curry chicken dinner invited our taste buds as we licked each other's fingers under a bountiful shaded oak tree. There were lapses of silence as we kissed and caressed each other like old times. Derrick stepped on my unblemished white sneakers and turned them into a tracked shade of brown. I sat behind him for a while and whispered fake molecular equations as he laughed and caressed my ankles. He left for a minute to buy some sweet Goombay punch someone had on sale direct from Nassau. We ate cotton candy under the tree and shared the sugary substance with long French kisses. An old Trinidadian gent broke our romantic stride and sat down with us for a game of dominoes. We played three hands as the wise one beat us mercifully. I kept looking at Derrick, the skilled competitor, thinking how mature he looked in such a short time. He didn't need to say we were coming to an end, I could feel it in my bones.

The ride home from Brooklyn was long and quiet. By the time we reached the Holland Tunnel, Derrick settled into a decent mood.

"So what are your plans for the rest of the summer?" he asked.

"Getting ready for college," I snapped back, leaving the air testy and tight.

Derrick clenched his jaw. "I'm leaving on August 10th for North Carolina."

"Good for you Derrick, have fun," I sniffed, before gazing out the window to hide my grief.

"Damn Shanelle, I'm sorry your life isn't gravy, but there's nothing I can do. It's not like I can take you with me, your father would have me arrested."

Derrick sped up as I released my pain with tears. "I don't want you to leave me, I want you to stay. You're the only thing safe and warm in my life. The world isn't so crazy with you around and people don't bother me."

I sat up to relieve the pressure in my head watching him pass our highway exit. "Where are we going?" I asked, wiping my trickling nose.

He grabbed my hand.

"I can't take you home like this."

We parked at the Eagle Rock Reservation in West Orange. Derrick put his arm around me as we ambled to the end of the pathway.

"Can I still call you Shanelle?"

"Sure, as long as my phone is connected."

He laughed, planting his chin on the top of my head as my ear connected with the beat of his heart.

"If I write, will you write me back?"

"Sure, as long as you send me a stamp."

His last question was our final romantic interlude of days gone by. He placed his lips within a breath's reach.

"Can I have a kiss Shanelle?"

Like that sweet winter evening so long ago, he slid his tongue in my mouth and made love to my senses, rubbing my back with his heavy hands. Whether the feelings I had for him were misplaced or misdirected, at least I could be proud that I was still a virgin. A soft breeze rippled goose bumps up my arms. I took the first step towards the car.

"Can you take me home?"

Leaving on happier terms, he pinched my chin.

"Sure Shanelle. Just remember, I'm coming back for you."

Time Flies

The summer after graduation came with incredible excitement in the air. Out of all my friends, I was the first one to get my driver's license. Bonnie and Candy were counting on me because we knew it wouldn't be long before it got hot enough for beach season. I passed my road test with flying colors. Candy called first, wide eyed with relief.

"Ok Shanelle, you know we have to get new bathing suits and lay off the Ring Dings and double cheese burgers."

I laughed at her calculated plan. "Girl, you are the bug out! I'm trying to find a way to get the car now, bump the beach. Well maybe not, I've got to get to Alex if he's still there."

Candy laughed, nodding with pressed lips against a mirror. "Shanelle, that was so long ago, do you think he'll be there this summer?"

"Oh hell yeah, it seemed like Belmar was his second home. Anyway, I think I'm going to run errands for Mrs. Viv so she can start giving me the car. By the end of June we should be straight."

By all accounts, I was right. I gave Mrs. Viv a break from grocery shopping, trips to the mall and I even took her to visit dear brother in the hospital. He was relocated to a secure facility with little opportunity for escape. We all had a tiny place in our hearts for Steven, but for Mrs. Viv, the grief was like a slow pendulum of hope then disappointment. I dropped Mrs. Viv off for her dental appointment and took a quick trip to the mall. Candy was there with one of her soon to be ex-boyfriends. Poor sucker didn't know it, but we did. Candy was planning to go to airline school to become a flight attendant anyway. She walked up to me just as I was about to buy my favorite chocolate chip mint ice cream on a sugar cone with chocolate sprinkles.

"Sure you want to do that Shanelle?"

The familiar voice sent my shoulders in a quick hunch, laughing as I licked the savory mint cream.

"Positive."

She took my cone and licked the other side. I snatched it back. "Damn, I would have bought you one; I don't know where your mouth has been." Candy shifted her eyes towards Macy's. "I'm here with big head and I can't wait to leave, he's getting on my nerves. Oh, listen, I'm going to my cousin's wedding this weekend in Asbury Park, if you want to go."

My face slouched with disinterest, but it wouldn't be long before Candy headed off to school. Two weeks was just around the corner.

"Sure, I'll be your date. What are you going to wear?"

"I think I'm going to sport my black pant suit, but let me know Shanelle. We're not going dressed the same."

We were together so much we had to discuss outfits to avoid looking like twins. Our fashion sense was the same and we had to be careful about our adult image.

"I think I'm going to show some legs this weekend, just to celebrate the summer. Probably my fuscia jacket and matching mini skirt."

Candy gave me that, *"excuse me,"* look.

"Ok cool, but don't forget how bad your feet are going to hurt when the party's over."

"I'll take my chances, Asbury sounds corny as hell and I'm sure there won't be any cuties there."

I checked my watch and instantly thought about Mrs. Viv.

"Oh snap, let me get my mother, I'll talk to you later."

Dummy finally lumbered up to Candy and put his arm around her. The sound in her voice was sheer aggravation.

"Bye, call me."

"Ok girl!" I didn't look back and headed for the car to pick up Mrs. Viv.

Playing Lil' Miss Driver worked in my favor. She let me take the car and I headed to Candy's house. I pulled into her driveway and beeped the horn. Candy's father Leonard came out to greet me with a smile.

"Where you headed today kid?"

"Nowhere special, just hanging."

Leonard was a caring man and always tried to let you know he was something back in his day.

"Drive carefully and don't get sassy with that car. Times are not the way they used to be."

Another lecture, but I didn't care, with the engine running and new club music, it was worth it. Candy and I went downtown to Persuasions and bought two more outfits. We bought Jordache jeans, size six for Candy and my usual size ten. I looked in the dressing room and surveyed my changing body. My waist seemed slightly narrow and my ass filled out the back of my jeans. I thought I could squeeze into an eight, but Candy assured me that Jordache wasn't cut for girls like us. It didn't seem to matter that much because I liked the fit. We left Persuasions and hit the Academy Fish Market and split a shrimp and whiting dinner. We loved that spot, especially when they changed the oil. The fish and shrimp were always fresh and it was enough for us to eat without feeling full. On the way home, we pumped some club music. Candy bopped her head planning our next move.

"Hey, let's go to the Village. Leave the car at your house and let's take a cab. We can come back around nine and you can drop me off home."

We laughed the whole way to Penn Station, plotting our lives out for the summer and what Candy would do once she got to Pittsburg. I knew I was headed straight to Bloomberg College because it was the only college that accepted my pitiful application and transcript. They had a dormitory and a cafeteria and that's all I cared about for the time being. Freedom wasn't too far away and I couldn't wait for September to move on campus. Sometimes the laughter stopped between us because we knew our lives were rapidly moving forward. When the cab arrived at Penn Station, we jumped out arm in arm like two silly schoolgirls. She was definitely the sister I never had in my crazy world.

Saturday came and it was time to get ready for the wedding. I felt good as I got dressed. I sat at the mirror and applied pink eye shadow and lipstick. I took my time styling my hair in a simple French roll. I decided to wear pearls to look more mature. It was just the right accessory with my hair style. Feeling complete, I grabbed my purse and went downstairs. The full length mirror was the last check and everything looked cool, especially my legs. The phone rang, but I chose not to answer it because Mrs. Viv was in the kitchen. She picked it up and greeted the caller. "Yes, how are you Dr. Levitz?" I dismissed the thought knowing I would hear about it later.

The ride to Asbury was long, but the Parkway traffic was light despite the beach revelers. Candy's mother was infamous for not showing up at the church so we went straight to the reception. I was happy because the long drive grappled with my hunger. We went to the bathroom to tinkle and glam up our face and hair. Candy's mother left us as her eyes orbited with pressed lips.

"You two live in the mirror." We brushed her comments off and went inside. There were three older women inside but one girl appeared to be my age. We looked each other up and down. The oldest lady glanced at Candy.

"You must be on the bride's side of the family. You look like Sabrina."

Candy reciprocated with a wrinkled nose.

"She's my first cousin on my mother's side."

The woman's eyes lit up. "Oh, you have such a nice family. I'm best friends with Sabrina's mother, Florence."

"Oh," Candy sweetened with sass, "Florence is my aunt and my mom's sister."

A full eyebrow arched with dumb suspicion.

"Right."

The nice woman turned towards me. "Are you related to the family?"

"No, ma'am, Candy and I are best friends."

She gave me the once over, nodding with approval. "Well I think I'm going to play match maker tonight, because my son is in the wedding and I would love for you to meet him."

She stepped into my space and started the first round. "Where do you live?"

I feared the worst.

He must look like the Creature from the Black Lagoon.

I didn't want to be rude. "North Orange."

She looked disappointed. "That's far, but my son loves to drive."

Candy jumped in with the ultimate question. "Is he cute?"

Before she answered, we were ushered out by the hostess who announced that the DJ was about to introduce the wedding party. We scurried inside and searched for Candy's mother. She flagged us down and pointed to two empty seats. Candy sat head to head with me so we could critique each person. The flower girl was simply gorgeous as she paraded out with a pea head ring bearer who graciously picked his nose. Candy dipped to a whisper. "That's my cousin, Shirelle; she just got a print ad with a big clothing store. I can't remember the name of it though."

We clapped and smiled at the half way cute couple. Candy grimaced and pointed at the little boy, "I don't know who pea head is, he must be on the groom's side."

We laughed in an unlady like manner as Candy's mother cut a glare in our direction. We didn't care because our loud raucous behavior blended into the applause. As the bride's and groom's parents were introduced, I surveyed the room for cute guys. There were none to be seen except two who were under heavy lock and key by their insecure nymph looking girlfriends. They looked so skinny I looked around for food. There was fresh bread in the basket but the uproarious laughter from the crowd broke my concentration to see the humorous commotion. People were pointing in the direction of the next groomsman as the announcer held the microphone to his mouth.

"Next we have Bridesmaid, Tammy Foster, accompanied by her brother and Groomsman, Alex Foster."

The crowd clapped louder this time for the brother and sister duo. I extended my neck to see the pair, especially the groomsman. He was engaged in a comedic act as he escorted his cute, but chubby sister. I couldn't get a visual, so I stood for a brief moment to witness the commotion. Blinking twice, my lips parted. My neck extended as all my breath escaped through a thin wind tunnel. Candy jabbed me in the leg. "Sit down, I can't see girl."

Stuck in an asphyxiated trance, I continued to gaze at him. *"No, it can't be? Could it?"*

His sister took her place on the receiving line next to the other bridesmaids. I sat down in shock.

"What's wrong with you Shanelle? You look like you've just seen a ghost."

A tiny smile nestled in the corner of my lip as I slowly began to clap. Years passed between us and there was an innate need for me to become a lady in that very chair. From head to toe he was covered in a black Armani double breasted tailored tuxedo. He was as fine as the day I saw him at Belmar. The tuxedo was definitely Armani, fitting him to perfection like a GQ magazine spread. As the crowd quieted for the entrance of the bride and groom, Alex began to survey the crowd with sun blinding eyes. Within an instant, the fuscia in my jacket and skirt caught his attention. I nudged Candy as air began to clog my throat. He looked at my legs and slowly carried his eyes up to my face. As I watched him survey my appearance, Candy leaned her ear towards me as I gasped for breath. His eyes finally met mine. I breathlessly whispered to her, "It's him."

Alex looked perplexed.

"No way, is that?"

Candy nudged me and searched my eyes for answers. "Who?"

I continued to clap as the possible realization ignited him. There it was again, that slow slide grin, bursting into a full, devilish smile as he continued to stare. Candy pressed for more information.

"Tell me girl, who is it?"

He read my lips from a fifty yard stance and dropped his calling card with a wink. Sinking my teeth into my lower lip, I blushed with sheer enthusiasm, "Its Alex."

Alex

The groom began to dance with his mother as the bridal party took their seats. When they concluded, the DJ mellowed the crowd with some light R&B and jazz. Candy and I collapsed into a frenzied whisper.

"Are you sure it's him?" Candy gripped my wrist for an answer. I shook my head in confident affirmation, "Yes, it's him and he's fine."

I sipped some water to control my nervousness, "Oh, it's him alright; I can't believe he's here at your cousin's wedding."

As I put the water back on the table, my glass hit the plate which signaled the first "cling" to get the bride and groom to kiss. Candy took her knife and began to hit her glass to drown out her excitement for me.

"Girl, don't you fuck this one up, he is definitely the one for you."

She started laughing as she whispered in my ear. "His eyes are all over you, look at him!"

I smiled at Candy and surveyed the room in his direction. I was interrupted by the woman from the bathroom. She came over to the table and chatted with Candy's mother about meeting us in the powder room. The regal lady edged up to me and said, "Well, I only have one son and he carried on so bad up there, I'm sure you saw him."

Candy rescued me from my bumbling behavior.

"Alex is your son?"

She looked at Candy with reassurance and turned to me. "Yes, that's my son and I would love for you to meet him young lady."

My heart beat tripled its pace as Alex raised his beverage in our direction. His mother leaned forward with a smile. "Looks like he approves an introduction, but I'll wait until later." She put her hand on my shoulder as I delicately assembled my lap napkin with refined table manners.

"I'm sorry; I didn't get your name sweetheart?" she asked.

I cleared my throat. "Shanelle, Shanelle Brown."

Sweeping her hands against her silk sleeves, she relaxed with a sigh.

"Well it's nice to meet you Shanelle. Don't run away from here without meeting my son okay?"

"Yes ma'am," I gushed, "it would be my pleasure to meet your son."

Luckily I didn't have to wait that long. Candy made me push the food around my plate and limited me to vegetables and a breath mint.

"Girrrrrrrl," She ordered, "You betta' pick at your food, your prince charming has arrived and I don't need you farting or burping around him. Go to the bathroom and touch up right now."

She slipped me her lip gloss as I quickly departed. When I opened the door to exit the ladies room, his voice filled the space between us and vibrated against my breasts.

"So, we meet again."

He extended his hand to shake mine. I looked up into his eyes with a coy smile.

"Looks that way, huh?"

"Uggghhhh," I thought to myself, *"Did you have to say 'huh'?"*

Nemesis even popped in for a minute.

"Listen, he's not looking for an air head so snap out of it, you're acting like a jack ass."

I gathered my thoughts and gazed at our hands interlocked in a soft, yet firm grip.

"Belmar right?" I asked.

He smiled like the Joker.

"Time sure flies when you think you're having fun?"

"Think?" I asked, "What do you mean?" A cute grin etched my face. He let go of me and motioned an outbound pass like he was holding a football.

"You still owe me a football game on the beach."

"Touch or tackle?" I shot back with wide eyes that quickly batted and fell to the floor.

Alex exposed his deep, warm dimples. His eyes locked with mine.

"Your choice."

Nemesis returned.

"Quite the officer and a gentleman. Ask him what he's been up to over the years. Lord knows you need a handsome black prince right about now." I blinked her away. "I don't want to be rude, but shouldn't we go back inside?"

Alex stepped into my space, leaving a thin silk ribbon between us.

"After years of hoping to see you again, we don't owe the bride and groom anything but a white envelope."

He offered his massive, weighted arm.

"There's a gazebo outside, let's talk. I won't take no for an answer."

"Sure, let's talk," I whispered.

We walked on to a crimson brick patio. Lights and assorted impatiens graced the walkway. Begonias were nestled in big potted plants that sweetened the scenery. Alex escorted me to a white wooden bench and waited for me before he obliged. He sat close at first before shifting his weight away. I was tickled pink from the inside out. It piqued his curiosity.

"What? Did I do something wrong?"

Abrupt, but poised, I tapped his hand. "No, no, you're such a gentleman now." He laughed and looked the other way to see who else was outside with us on that summery night.

"Thanks. I have to add that you turned into quite the lady."

His finger rested against his temple.

"Before I forget, let me reintroduce myself, my name is Alex Foster."

I gingerly shook his hand. "I'm Shanelle Brown."

He temporarily searched the sky as his eyes danced with excitement.

"All this time your name was Shanelle?"

"What do you mean all of this time?" I blushed.

"When I met you that day I wanted to talk to you and find out more. You looked hurt and abandoned, even though you were wrapped up in whatever his name was. When I asked you if you wanted to play, I knew you wanted to leave him and jump into a new challenge. I'll admit I was wrong for the things I said, but part of me thought, 'give it a try, she may want to meet you after all.'"

I threw my shoulders back and smiled.

"Yes, you did say horrible things to me, but you also said things that made sense. I wondered if I knew you from a past life or something."

As Alex sat on the bench, he shifted his weight and folded his hands at his crotch. I noticed his massive size and thought about what it must have taken to assemble his wardrobe.

"When I spotted you sitting at the table, I said to myself, 'this time, she's not going to get away.'"

I laughed at his apparent nerve. "Oh really, you think?"

His broad chest rose and relaxed as I glanced at his handsome side profile. His thumb and pointer finger softly pinched my chin. "No, I'm serious; you're not going to get away this time."

The entrance doors to the gazebo burst open with search warrant surprise.

"Alex, you're being rude. I don't care what ma said. There's no one to dance with, so come on right now!"

He rolled his eyes, tight lipped and caught up. "My kid sister is a royal pain in the ass."

It was enough to break up our interlude. Alex stood up and held his arm out again.

"Duty calls, but promise you won't dance with anyone but me." He laughed swaggering down the hall. "Chill sis, chill, I'm going to dance with you."

He turned around and winked as I went into the bathroom to check my makeup. Candy was hiding in stall number two waiting for the scoop. She jumped out and scared the living shit out of me.

"Ah Haaa!" my zombie-like friend shouted, lifting her arms reminiscent of Night of the Living Dead.

"Stop playing, girl, you know I hate that scary shit."

Candy didn't care, she wanted all the details. "Well, what happened? What did he say? Did you get his phone number?"

"No," I calmly replied.

"What do you mean no?" her shoulders collapsed, "don't play with me Shanelle."

"I'm not playing, we were talking and he didn't get to ask me because his sister interrupted us."

Candy put her hand on my shoulder for support.

"Yeah, I saw chubba-liscious. After she wolfed down her food she was looking around for a pitiful soul to dance with her. I guess Alex comes in handy."

I nodded in agreement.

"Yeah, now she's guarding him like Joe Dumars on Michael Jordan."

Candy laughed, sharing a common secret.

"Well Miss Thang, one thing's for sure, little sis can't give him what you got."

Our giggles switched to silence with the arrival of Alex's mother into the bathroom. She brushed off Candy and sauntered next to me.

"So, you met my handsome son."

"Yes we've met."

She squeezed my upper arms.

"My daughters are very protective of their only brother, but don't mind them, they're harmless."

"How many daughters do you have?" I asked.

Boasting proudly with direct eye contact she deliberated, "I have five daughters and one son."

Candy's manners flushed down the occupied toilet.

"Damn, you got six kids?"

"Excuse me, I have six beautiful adult children and I'm proud of all of them, especially my son, who also happens to be a police officer."

She looked at me with motherly joy.

"Well, let me get Tammy off of his back so the two of you can enjoy yourselves. Are you having a nice time? I talked to Candy's mother and she said you were going through some rough times."

My face flushed with embarrassment.

"I feel like Cinderella tonight."

Her wrinkled nose and relaxed hands turned to the door. "My son is a gentleman. Enjoy his company, you deserve the best."

I sauntered into the reception hall and took my seat. The last entree emitted flavorful steam, but fidgeting fingers preventing me from touching a fork. I wanted to search for him, but I was trapped in a puppeteer's controlling head lock. Candy swayed her hips towards the dance floor while I leaned into my plate and inhaled, quickly sitting back to continue my surveillance. A vibrating microphone jolted the audience as the DJ concluded, lowering his voice to a deep whisper.

"Ladies and gentleman, no wedding would be complete without this special request from the groom to the bride."

Suddenly, a firm hand brushed my shoulder. The puppeteer released me as my head turned sideways towards a rich scent of cologne.

"Alex," I paused, finding his hand slipping onto my waist.

"Let's dance," my cinnamon vision replied, leading me to the shiny hardwood floor musically enhanced by the Whispers. I could have melted right there before the words to Chocolate Girl wooed us into one being. Alex placed his hand on the small of my back and put his mouth to my ear. Crooning over the song, he romanced me with those beautiful words every brown girl loves to hear.

"If there was, such a thing, as a wish come true..."

I began to melt in his caress as he changed the words to the song and spoke to me.

"Let's take that day back at the beach and make it ours this time. My heart and soul is telling me that tonight is our chance."

Our breathing paired with excitement.

"Let's go," I mouthed with a whisper.

Alex beamed. He held me close until the conclusion of the song. Without saying a word, we separated on the dance floor and made our way back to our assigned seats. I sat next to Candy and hatched our plot in her ear. She was more than happy to hear it as she grinned from ear to ear.

Candy switched to detective mode. "He's a cop so you know you can trust him. Is he going to take you home?"

"I'm staying at your house. Remember the back-up plan for Mrs. Viv?"

"Oh yeah," she winked, before concluding. "Girl, be safe and don't do anything I wouldn't do, which is just about everything."

I hugged her tight and quickly pulled back. "I'll see you tonight."

Alex met me near the exit. He held out his hand like we were runaway love slaves.

"You look beautiful, if I haven't told you already."

I grabbed his hand and headed out the door. I wanted to pique his interest so I inquired, "Do you still have that Mazda RX 7?"

"How did you know that?"

"I watched you drive away that day."

He leaned on the passenger door and looked at me like I had some surprises in my back pocket.

"Are you in law enforcement too?"

Laughing, I surveyed his immaculate vehicle and smelled the aroma of a vanilla flavored car tree.

"You keep your car in excellent shape."

He looked at my legs.

"You've kept yourself in pretty good shape too, but I'm going to be a gentleman tonight."

I playfully punched him and pulled my skirt down.

"I'll make sure you do Alex."

The clock in his car was off by ten minutes, but it was eight thirty by the time we reached Belmar Beach. My feet took a heavy toll in his cramped car. I grabbed his wrist, confessing my shortcomings.

"Alex, my feet are killing me."

He looked down and asked, "What's your favorite color?"

"Pink." I gushed.

"Ok, I'll be right back."

I took off my sheer stockings and let my feet dangle in the cool evening breeze. In an instant he was back with a cute pair of pink flip flops. He took them out of the bag and held them up for my approval.

"How about these?"

I didn't care if they were camouflage. He was so handsome and engaging in his Armani tux. Anything he did would have been irresistible. Alex went to the trunk and took out a blanket.

"I always keep one handy in the car. Let's go sit down."

We marched down the boardwalk stairs leading to the sand. Alex hoisted the blanket watching it parachute down. Just as we got comfortable, the tide rushed up and crashed between my legs. I jumped up as Alex rescued me.

"Hey, it's just water, let's move further back."

I dodged away from the spot to avoid another rush. I could feel him watching me with baited breath as I headed for dry land.

"I wish I had some shorts or sweat pants to give you," he offered with a steady hand as I sat down, "the store was closing when I got there."

Pleased at his apparent fuss, I could also sense his nervousness. Facing him, I wrapped myself in his scented tuxedo jacket.

"I'm fine really; you're so sweet fussing over me. Let's just sit over here and talk. I want to meet you all over again."

The rumble and crash of the ocean broke my silence. Cool mist moistened my face and the space between us.

"I wrote about you when I left the beach that day."

His warm demeanor flushed in disbelief.

"Stop playing, you were so wrapped up in that dude."

I invaded his space, fixing his collar.

"I wrote something like, 'your cinnamon vision fires and burns a critical synapse in my brain, make me sane, I want to know your name,' or something like that. I have it at home if you want a copy."

Shock fixed his face. "Wow you were feeling all of that?"

His self glorification tickled me.

"Yes, the entire situation was so mysterious. You told me to bring my big pretty legs back to you."

Alex placed his hand on my knee.

"And here you are. I have to confess, I didn't write a poem about you, I just played Al Green all night. I'm going to have to play some new songs now."

"I love music too, what song would you play?"

"Definitely, Luther, *Never Too Much*."

I nodded in approval. "Yeah, that's a good song."

Alex entered my space by grabbing my hand.

"Is there any song you can think of Shanelle?"

Wondering, my lower lip edged out. I didn't have any song in my head. I was praying it wouldn't be *Casanova Brown* by Teena Marie. For once in my life, I wanted to wish for the best.

"I'm a poet, but I'll let you know if one comes to mind."

I tried to make small talk before my body chemistry took over. I was definitely feeling him and I didn't want to ruin it with my sexually charged virgin ways. I was also surprised that Nemesis didn't visit me during this exchange. Caressing his hand with my thumb suited me for the moment.

"So, you're a police officer."

He licked his thick beautiful lips, peering down at my coy gesture.

"Yeah. It pays the bills and keeps me honest."

My tone softened against the evening breeze.

"I like honesty, it's a good quality."

"Well be honest with me and tell me why you looked like a girl on the run."

Searching the swell of the ocean, the crashing tide became my reflection.

"You were right Alex, I was on the run. But I'm starting college this fall and staying in the dorm. Maybe the taste of freedom will set me free."

He put his arm around my shoulders and replied, "Is your mind free or are you physically trapped?"

I looked at the gleaming light blanketing the calm sea, trying to search for a rational answer.

"I think I need to be mentally free, I'll never be physically trapped from anything as long as I live."

Alex turned my face towards him and said, "Believe you me Shanelle, we've all been there, no matter how hard we try, it takes fortitude in the individual to break those mental chains, whatever they are."

I wondered where his philosophy came from and asked, "Are you free Alex?"

"Shanelle," he softened in a deep voice, "I've always been free. Maybe I'm just different, but there's only one hurdle that will follow me until the day I die. I'm sitting here with you, content with my life and even happier that I'm looking at you again. What more can I ask for except the unknown. When it comes, whatever it is, I'll be ready for the challenge."

Alex let go of my hand and pulled me into him for warmth. "When you finally feel free Shanelle, I hope I'm the one that can share it with you."

I relaxed my shoulders and gingerly placed my head on his chest. The feelings I had for Derrick were not the same feelings that were beginning with Alex. I felt like I could relax, instead of being a wild child. I pulled him towards me and softly kissed his lips.

"It's nice to meet you," I paused, "my name is Shanelle."

He brought his lips to mine and whipped his tongue into my mouth. Alex tasted minty fresh with a hint of chocolate mint the bride and groom offered as favors. Our kiss seemed to last forever in his arms. We sat on the beach until sunrise. Alex didn't have to work, but he wanted to make a respectable woman out of me and gassed up the car to drive me home.

We stopped at a diner on Highway 35 for breakfast. Patrons smiled as we staggered in like two tussled love birds. We played footsie under the table and exchanged phone numbers. He asked about my college and the directions so he could visit me. We talked about his time in the police academy and his experience as the second black police officer in Lakewood. Our conversation flowed rhythmically as the sun took the day hostage. We went to Bloomberg College for a driving tour and then headed to Candy's house. We planned a date for the following weekend and promised to talk every night at his expense. Alex grabbed my chin.

"I had a wonderful time Shanelle; I can't wait to see you again."

He pulled my face into his and kissed me with his beautiful lips and tongue. Watching him from the stairs, he got into his car and drove into the early morning sun. Slamming the door, Candy came barreling outside. She damn near jumped on my back in complete happiness.

"Tell me every wicked detail or I'll kill you." Stepping back, worried this time, she pressed her lips together.

"Oh, by the way, Mrs. Viv called; she really wants to kill you if you don't call home."

I bolted up the stairs for a shower. Our post adolescent screaming was driving her father nuts so he banged on the door as a warning. Candy sat on the bathroom floor as I told her every detail of our time. She screamed at all the juicy parts, especially our first kiss.

"Work it, work it."

We gave each other high fives as Candy smacked the bathroom floor during the footsie scene at the diner.

"Hand me a towel and my bag so I can get dressed."

She gave me two minutes of privacy. We crawled into bed for a daytime slumber party. I held the sheet up to my chin and finished the story. The ringing telephone jolted us as we began to giggle like sugar filled preschoolers. Candy picked it up.

"Hi..., oh, hello Alex."

She kicked me with her foot. "She's right here hold on." A game of hot potato ensued. I put my sexy voice on as Candy shared the phone's ear piece.

"Hello."

"Hi Shanelle, it's me Alex."

Candy pinched my arm.

"Hi, are you home yet?" The phone hollowed out with background static.

"No, I'm at a rest stop, but I wanted to let you know that I was thinking about you and I'll give you a call tomorrow."

I was dying to say, *"Call me in five minutes, then again and again and again!"*

Candy gave me the thumbs up.

"Ok Alex, I had a great time, I'll talk to you tomorrow."

Candy laughed into the crumpled sheet.

"Not bad skeezer!"

A loud bang on the door jolted us out of our teen frenzy.

"Y'all quit all that raucous in there, I have a headache!"

Candy pressed her fingers into my lips as we shared a silent laugh. I didn't want to go anywhere because I wanted to wait for his phone call. When it rang again, Candy shoved the receiver in my hand.

"It's Mrs. Viv."

I cleared my throat as my eyebrows shot up and settled with a sigh. "Hey mom." I was short and to the point without offering any excuses. My nonchalant greeting bounced off her last nerve and returned with sheer annoyance.

"Shanelle!"

"What?"

"Don't you what me girl, what is this all about?" she angrily pitched.

"What do you mean what is this all about?" I teased, in a happy cheerleader tone. Candy's face was riddled with confusion as Mrs. Viv began her tirade.

"Do you think our house is a hotel or something? Maybe you think you can just check in and check out at your leisure?"

"I never said that," I calmly replied.

Losing ownership and control, she roared with the intensity of a losing basketball coach during the semifinals.

"Well that's how you're acting and your father and I are not going to tolerate your behavior. You've been gone for two days and not once did you call home and let me know what you're doing."

I flipped over and smoothed out the sheet on top of me.

"I've been with Candy the whole weekend. This is routine to me and I don't understand why you're yelling Viv."

Candy burst out with laughter.

"Ooooh girl!" she cheered clapping her hands.

Mrs. Viv slammed the phone down ending the call with a bucket filled spilling over with obscenities.

Candy clasped her hands and stared at my parched lips.

"Girl its okay, you'll figure everything out."

The sheets peeled away as my feet hit the floor. My bag floated above the carpeting and settled at my side. Candy's arms stretched towards me as we shared a comforting hug.

"Are you sure you don't want a ride home?" Candy sighed, leaning her face to the side. "Who needs the headache right?"

Turning towards the window, my shriveled lips retreated to a solemn grin. "No, the walk will do me some good, thanks anyway."

Exit Wounds

Even though I had enough money to get home by cab or by bus, I decided to walk home. The three mile hike back to North Orange was filled with so many visual memories of days gone by and days I didn't want to remember anymore. Even Portia drove past in her new Celica GTX, but it didn't faze me. There were a few cars parked in front of the house. I edged inside to a host of family and friends gathered around the prodigal son. Once again, he had returned home in true familial style and grace.

A pathway cleared as they stared at his clear skin and tight fade hair cut. He was welcomed with open arms from everyone except me. I hurried away and went upstairs while Mrs. Viv made excuses for my rude behavior. I entered my room and started to pack a new bag. A few things were necessary to accompany my exit, a driver's license, social security card and acceptance letter. Taking a final trip down the stairs, no noises or whispers followed me. The squeaks in the stairs were the regular sounds an old house resonates after years of growth and passage. I closed the door behind me as curious family members peeked out the window to follow my path. Without question I was going to take the bus back to Candy's house until classes started at Bloomberg College. There was a quiet bed in the blue room and a sense of calm from the roof to the basement. I was going to rest and get organized until school started. It made sense to live there instead of running with the dead. New life came to me that day and adolescence seemed to wash away in my mind. There were new things to think about, including *Alex*.

Hope

Candy's parents supported my decision to stay, especially since I was going to college in the fall. Thoughts of Alex drowned me. Deep down inside I was longing for his phone call. It was one full day since I saw him and I needed to feel the magic of last night again. I helped Candy carry a small dresser from the attic to the blue room for my personal belongs. As we were cleaning up, the phone rang. Candy's mother began to smile as she talked to the mysterious caller.

"Yes, she's here, hold on please."

"Hi Alex."

He sighed with relief.

"Shanelle, is everything ok? I called your house, but I think I had the wrong phone number."

"Why, what happened? Who did you speak to?"

"A guy picked up the phone and said, 'Shanelle's dead asshole.' After that he hung up on me. He thought it was funny, but I didn't, who was that?"

"That sounded like my brother. It's a long story."

"Shanelle, you don't have to apologize, but that was messed up. I would never do that to my sisters."

"Rightly so," I thought, but Alex was no Steven, nor was anyone else in the world. I leaned back and inhaled. Alex's deep voice swelled my breasts, yet thoughts of Steven caused bile to settle in my throat. The shame of hiding secrets began to get the best of me. Pressure filled my neck and shoulders as forced air expanded my lungs and throat. I sat down and rubbed my stomach.

"Alex," I quickly pitched, "Can you hold on?"

"Sure."

A fast shuffle led me to the bathroom. I turned on the faucet as cool water ran down my fingertips and into my cupped palms. I wiped the watery residue away and searched for resolution in the mirror.

"Breathe Shanelle," I whispered aloud, "just breathe."

Calm returned as I reached the phone. Changing the subject put his worries at ease.

"So," I replied with calm enthusiasm, "I'm alive and I've been thinking about you."

I didn't sound pretentious or anxious, I was glad he called and I wanted him to keep calling me, so I had to make him think my life wasn't as flawed as I appeared some three years ago. The pause between us forced him to finally speak.

"Well, I'm more than happy to hear you're living and breathing and I would love to see you again if that's ok with you."

"Sure, I would love to see you again, but you'd have to do so much driving Alex."

He paused as a slight chuckle escaped.

"What?" I asked.

Alex cleared his throat.

"Shanelle, you've been on my mind since I left and I didn't want to leave. I don't have to go back to work until Tuesday so help me think good thoughts before I go back to rounding up the bad guys."

"But you live so far," I sympathized with a long sigh.

Protecting his masculine pride, he quickly ordered our time.

"Shanelle, leave the driving up to me. I'm used to long distances and I'm in Essex at least twice a week for narcotics training. Don't get the wrong impression; I'll bring you home both days."

I began to melt, releasing the cord from my asphyxiated finger. I crossed my legs like a lady in bloom.

"Three o'clock?" he offered.

"Sounds great," I replied. "But what do you want to do?"

There was a brief pause.

"Dinner and a movie?"

"Fine."

I stood in the doorway and leaned against the frame.

"See you then."

With less than two hours to get ready, I screamed, "Girl, Alex wants to see me in two hours!"

Candy immediately abandoned her plans for the evening and transformed into a fashion designer and consultant.

"Ok," she said, "Let's think, I know, you need to wear all white, something crisp and clean."

I didn't have any new clothes to wear, but there was some left over wardrobe in her closet. Candy pulled me into the blue room and closed the door. She fell to the floor scrambling for bags shoved in the back of the closet.

"Here, I bought these for you last week but you need them now. Wear my scoop neck tee with your white strappy sandals and sailor cap."

We rushed to the full length mirror. My shoulders began to sag as Candy pushed my frame in an upright position. She comforted me by saying, "Shanelle, you don't look fat so don't even say it, you look nice."

"You're right," I replied, as I remembered that December day with Alex.

"Do you remember what Alex told me?"

Candy popped me in the back of the head and said, "You've said it a million times, take the Parkway South to exit 98 and bring those big pretty legs with you. Damn Shanelle, you are so conceited, I swear."

She smacked the fatty part of my thigh.

"Just remember I brought you and those big legs right to Alex, so when you two get married, don't make me wear an ugly dress with goofy ruffles or I'll kick your ass."

We laughed so hard, I didn't realize how much time escaped. I looked at the wall clock and said, "I have an hour and a half to go, let's hurry."

In signature class and style, I jumped in the shower, washed my hair with Cream of Nature Shampoo and Conditioner. Candy passed me her St. Eves facial scrub and cut up cucumbers for my weary eyes. I rested for five minutes while she applied facial moisture to my face and neck. I sat in front of the full length mirror as Candy oiled my damp scalp and brushed my hair back. She put some Nunile along my hairline and donned a scarf on my head to keep my wavy edges down. We sat on the bed and chatted as Candy gave me a quick manicure and then dried my nails with a blow dryer on a cool setting. We stared at each other once or twice and giggled as Alex's arrival stirred to a boiling point. Candy checked to see if his car was outside.

"Mazda right?"

"Yes that's him."

Candy pushed the shade back smiling with pure elation.

"Girl, he's got a single white rose and a big ole' brown teddy bear."

A warm sisterly hug fortified my new adventure.

"Listen Brown, don't screw this one up. Act like a lady, even though we know you're a brute."

As my heels tapped against the living room floor, Alex focused his eyes away from Candy's father and stared directly at me. My dark brown cinnamon vision was well suited in a crisp white shirt with small navy pinstripes and navy linen slacks. Pleasingly cool and absolutely charming, Alex nervously handed me a rose.

"One single rose for a beautiful single lady."

Candy sensed my nervousness and took the rose from my hand. "She rolled her eyes at me and said, "Let me get a vase for that flower."

He picked up the stuffed animal and said, "If you ever need a hug, you can hold on to him until I get here."

Candy's family scurried off the porch. Candy mumbled under her breath, "I guess Kermit the Frog is going right in the garbage when she gets back."

Even Leonard chimed in, wittingly adding, "Yeah, I like that cat."

I quickly closed the front door to avoid embarrassment. Alex grabbed my hand. "You are so beautiful."

I wanted everything to be perfect, but it was hard to find the words to say.

"I can't stop staring at you Alex, but I don't think I can help myself."

Alex put my sailor cap on my head.

"Shanelle, you can look at me forever."

I wanted to say more, but I kept my feelings inside. I was nervous and my palms were getting sweaty. Alex opened the door as I slid into the front seat, crossing my legs at my ankles. He darted around to the driver's side and adjusted his frame. Alex politely excused himself, reaching for the glove compartment to retrieve his sunglasses. He put his specs on and inquired, "Where to lovely lady?"

"South Street Seaport."

The drive into the city was pleasant and cheerful. I was so enamored by Alex's charm and conversation that I didn't look at the beautiful scenery around me. He paid the toll at the Lincoln Tunnel. A pretty brown sister in the booth collected his money. Like any real woman who is confident in her own spot, she gave me that look like, *"Girl, he is fine, work it, work it!"*

The world around us at the port lit up with energy as we strolled into shops. Confidant and self assured, I watched him purchase a few shirts and eye up a white linen dress for me.

"Is this your size?" He asked, placing the dress along side of me.

My lips pressed together with the sweetness of strawberries resting there. I looked at the cashier and confirmed with a wink. "Yes."

We found a quaint restaurant by the docks. A female hostess escorted us to an intimate table in the corner. When our meal arrived, Alex and I dined on lobster tails dipped in warm butter. He grabbed my left hand and stroked each finger. Chatting away about my precious friendship with Candy, Alex fixated on my garnet ring. Pausing mid sentence, I watched his face relax as he stared at me.

"What?" I asked.

He stroked the stone as his voice dipped to detective mode.

"A gift? An old friend?"

Even if Alex was trying to stir up my past, my ring offered no clues. Feeling free, my lips parted as an escaping tear crashed into my napkin.

"My father gave it to me. It's a symbol of my virtue."

His jaw clenched. One eyebrow rose and resumed position.

"Did it work?"

"Yes," I blushed.

Alex's broad chest heaved and settled. A devilish smile took up residence across his chiseled face.

"I knew you were different Shanelle."

By the time Alex and I finished our conversation, it was ten o'clock. We stood up, stretched and held hands as we walked back to the car. I made myself comfortable as Alex paid for the ticket. He got into the car and offered me a mint before putting one into his mouth. Alex played Sade for the ride home as her sultry voice wooed us back to New Jersey. There was a sobriety check inspection after we exited the Holland Tunnel into New Jersey. Who knows why they did it, but traffic was backed up for miles. The slow crawl stopped to a standstill as the music ended. Alex put the car in park and made our moment special. He turned my garnet ring around exposing just the band of gold.

"My parents are still together after all these years, I think I know why my mother's simple gold ring means so much to her."

Silence filled his car amidst the evening traffic and blaring lights. His heavy hand landed warmly against my bare thigh as a girlish flutter spiraled through me. Alex's lips brushed against my ear as a whisper spilled into my ear.

"Tell me you believe in fate Shanelle."

Like a line out of a famous holiday classic, I rattled on like a princess, "I believe, I believe."

The car behind us beeped to edge us forward. Alex put the car in neutral and rolled fifty feet. He glanced back to see who the impatient traveler was and scoffed, "Some people...,"

It was the perfect opportunity for me to talk about my virginity because I didn't want to him to rush me. If it didn't go my way, the pain of him leaving me wouldn't be so tragic.

"Alex, I need to ask you a question."

"Anything," he replied, turning the radio down.

I twisted my garnet gem back to its original position. My eyes drifted into the lanes of traffic as his massive hand covered mine. Instant goose bumps spoiled my timing. Alex instantly read my mind.

"As long as you're my lady, you can wear your ring with pride. When you're ready, I'm sure you'll let me know. I mean, let's face it Shanelle, I'm no angel, but I am willing to wait. I think I told you already, you're different. I need commitment and someone to be there with me when the chips are down. That kind of love takes time to mature and I want to spend that time with you."

The tips of my fingers stroked his cheeks as he kissed me. My stomach fluttered twice before a knock beckoned our attention. Alex rolled down his window and flashed his badge. The officer stepped back and let Alex ride the shoulder as he signaled a clearance sign.

"Must be nice," I teased, licking my lips to savor the taste.

Alex replied, "Right now, you're nice."

The next morning came with lightening speed. Before I knew it I was in Alex's world, engaging in fellowship at his church. Everyone, including Alex's family, was warm and inviting. Mrs. Foster gave me a generous hug as she rubbed my back in small circles.

"You look radiant and I'm so glad you met my son Shanelle. His sisters have been teasing him non-stop, but I think it's wonderful that the two of you found each other again."

Alex's chubby sister Tammy was slightly reserved but to my surprise, after engaging in some idle chit chat, we discovered that she played high school basketball. Tammy was going to attend Pitt and had not heard of Bloomberg College. I didn't feel insecure because our common bond squashed her jealousy.

There were stolen moments between Alex and I in the kitchen and living room. His sisters shared secrets about Alex's boyhood pranks and opened up the family album for a trip down memory lane. Mr. Foster, the proud father spent most of his time grilling steaks and tossing a baseball between six grandchildren of various ages. Alex and I took his twin nephews outside to play tackle football so I finally got a chance to playfully chase him and catch the ball. His sisters admired my tomboy attitude, but Candy would have smacked me for getting sweaty in my linen dress. Alex's police partner Jack called to talk about work. He pulled me into the kitchen. They exchanged a few secret messages.

"Yeah, she's right here, do you want to say hello?"

I had no idea what they were talking about but I endured.

"Hi Jack, this is Shanelle."

He smirked. "No kidding, he's been talking about you day and night. I can't wait to meet you."

Alex's mother came from outside with steaming steaks, burgers and shrimp. Mrs. Foster proclaimed with pride, "Girl, I hope you can cook. My son can put away some food."

After lunch, Alex announced an early exit from the gathering as they hugged me goodbye.

"They love you Shanelle," he said with a kiss, "especially my father. Once you've got his attention, you're in."

I laughed, parading back to his car.

"Are you surprised?"

He grabbed my waist, pausing to gaze at me. "No, but it means a lot to me that you came today," he ended with a yawn.

"Alex, I'm worried about you not getting enough rest, aren't you tired?"

"Shanelle, I'm beat, but I really don't have a choice if you need to get home. I'll be more than happy to sleep on the couch, but only if you're comfortable. You'll have to find a way to occupy yourself while I'm at work."

I wanted to say yes right away but I knew I needed clothing. He seemed to read my mind as he looked at my soiled dress tucked in a used grocery bag.

"If you need clothes, it's not a problem."

We drove to JC Penney. I bought some cute panties, a short set and a long pajama top. We went back to his apartment in Lakewood. I was amazed at his simple sense of style. He had a cherry wood wall unit with a matching leather sectional. His kitchen was black and white. The entire apartment was clean, even the bathroom. Alex threw his keys in a basket.

"I'm usually a slob, but I have a cleaning lady come in twice a week, just to keep me sane."

I was afraid to put my bags down so I stood in the middle of his living room clutching my meager possessions. He was in the kitchen taking water and fruit out of the refrigerator.

"Put your bags in the linen closet. Wash clothes and towels are also in there to the left."

Alex washed his hands and wiped them dry as I opened the door to his closet. He cantered up behind me and said, "Shanelle, make yourself at home."

I told him I was going to take a shower and closed the door to the bathroom. The water felt wonderful and soothed away all the knots and stress that riddled me throughout the day. I toweled off and put on my pajama shirt and panties. I quietly left the bathroom and pulled my clean hair back into a ponytail. I went into Alex's room and closed the door for privacy. There was lotion on his nightstand so I took my time and rubbed it into my skin. I was so tired I didn't realize that my need to take a five-minute snooze across his bed, turned into twelve hours of wonderful sleep. When I woke up I was under Alex's comforter wrapped up in a fetal position. I felt lightheaded and incredibly aroused. I looked around the room to focus on the world around me. There were hangers on the doorknob and a spare gun holster near the nightstand. A hand written note with my name on the top read, "Good morning sleepy head, I was more than happy to see you sleep so soundly. If you need me, page me at 732-5555. Help yourself to anything you need and I'll be home for lunch around 12:15 pm."

What struck my heart in the deepest way was his farewell, *"Falling for Shanelle, Alex."*

I gently held the letter to my face and smelled him. I rolled around in his bed with the morning sun basking against my skin. I sat up and looked around his room. Every inch of it was decorated in testosterone. I didn't get out of bed because I wanted to read the note one hundred times before I got up.

By 12:00 pm I donned one of his sweatshirts. I prepared a light salad with turkey strips, feta cheese, tomatoes and balsamic dressing. Alex's body was perfect just by looking at the contents in his refrigerator. Protein and vegetables were his primary foods, fruits and nuts were secondary. He did have some sherbet in the freezer so I crushed up some strawberries in a cup with light cream and let it chill in the refrigerator until his arrival.

I called Candy and luckily she was home. She was screaming with delight about all the things I told her. I gave Candy Alex's beeper number in case she needed me. Smiling ear to ear she asked, "I leave in four days, when are you coming home?"

I knew the romance wouldn't last forever.

"Probably today."

"Ok, cool. I'll be waiting for you while I pack, don't forget one detail," Candy ordered.

A sisterly tone followed, "I love you girl."

Candy was quick to respond with sultry flair, "Forget about lovin' me, you better start lovin' that man."

We hung up the phone and within five minutes a key was turning in the door. When he stepped inside, I had to catch my breath at the sight of him in his uniform.

"What happens when you pull women over?"

"Why?" he quipped, removing his hat.

"Because I would faint if you stopped me."

Alex's weighted arms wrapped my back while he surveyed the room.

"I'm starving. You made lunch for me?"

"Just for you," I blushed.

I pulled him towards the table, but he resisted.

"Come over here Shanelle, I need to talk to you baby."

There was longing in his eyes like he wanted me and I didn't know what to do. He sat down, pulling me between his legs as his head pressed against my titties. He breathed in all of my energy and released it like a bull. Alex palmed my ass like a basketball in his manly hands.

"Shanelle, I'm glad you're here, but it's only been four days and I can't get you out of my head. The temptation is too much for me. I wanted to wake you up and make love to you."

He cleared his throat. "I couldn't concentrate at work and I need to stay focused."

I stroked the back of his head and neck as he continued, "Did you know I slept beside you last night?"

My heart skipped in twos.

"No."

"The need to be near you and to feel you is incredibly overwhelming, even now. But I'm not going to jeopardize how you feel."

I kissed his forehead in three places. Alex fondled my breasts as our breathing paired in unison. I straddled his lap and tongue kissed him long and hard. A moan bellowed in his chest as his thick Adam's apple slid down and rose with the swell of his member. His face strained as he sucked my tongue with thirst and frustration. I could feel the power in his pants swelling against Kitty with ample strength and size. Alex was so strong he could have easily taken me and fulfilled his needs, but I wasn't ready and we both knew it, no matter how hard we had to resist. With his mighty hands, he hoisted me off his lap and laid me down. My breasts swelled before his eyes as my nipples craved his open mouth. He wedged himself along side of me and picked up my left leg with a whisper, "Did you like the massage I gave you last night?"

My eyes danced with delight. "So that's why I slept so late?"

"Yeah, and that's why you can't stay overnight anymore."

Alex sighed and sat up on the couch. He pulled me into his arms, strumming my neck with his massive hand. His thumb swept my lower lip before he kissed me again. A gentle hand caressed the inside of my thigh as I leaned into him, yearning for more. Alex pressed his forehead against mine, peeking at his erection.

"I need to take a quick shower just to cool off before I go back to work."

Alex quickly finished and entertained me during lunch. He smiled at me every time I held the fork to my mouth. I couldn't understand why, so the next time he did it I paused and asked, "What is it?"

"You need to eat, you're too thin Shanelle."

"Too thin," I droned. "That's an understatement, I already weigh one hundred and thirty-five pounds and that's embarrassing."

Alex leaned across the table. "Trust me; I'm going to get your weight up to one hundred and fifty pounds of lean muscle."

I held up my fork like a weapon and replied, "You're going to have one big fight ahead of you because I don't want to be fat Alex."

He stood up and wiped his mouth in astonishment.

"Oh, tough girl huh?"

My pouting lips did little to persuade him. I hugged him across the table for sympathy.

"I don't want to be any bigger than what I am now, so don't pick on me please."

Alex picked me up off the floor. "I'm sorry, my little cocoon, I thought you were turning into a butterfly, but I'll wait." He put me down and headed for the door. "I've gotta' get back, be ready by 4:30 pm and get some more rest, it becomes you."

The ride home was all too quick. As soon as we got to the Union Toll, I asked him to take me to Bloomberg College. He parked and escorted me inside. I was an incoming freshman with a hefty tab to pay. Alex looked at my bill and the names of the classes I was taking.

"You have a political bug?"

I took the paperwork and examined the financial damages. "For now. All I can think about is this bill."

"How much time do you have?" Alex asked.

"I can pay it in three parts. I have half of the first payment and that's not including books." Alex sighed and ushered me out the front door.

"Here, take the keys. I need to use the men's room before I go back to Lakewood. Wait for me in the car."

I obliged, looking up to admire the brick inspired dorm building. Alex was taking his time, but I didn't care because I didn't want him to leave. As he exited the Bursar's Office, I noticed Alex shoving papers in his back pocket. A long sigh accompanied his question.

"Are you smart Shanelle?"

"Yes, when I enjoy the subject."

"Good because it's a shame to waste money on an expensive education."

We stopped at the grocery store for weekly essentials at Candy's house. Alex made me carry the bags while he put the cart back. When I got in the car, I noticed a piece of paper with the Bloomberg College insignia on top. Glued to the financial details of my life, Alex slipped inside the confined space and snapped his seatbelt, quickly leaning towards me with his lips at my ear.

"No turning back my little cocoon, it's a done deal."

"Paid in full," I gushed with surprised, "Alex, why did you do that?"

He tugged my earlobe and quietly enjoyed a soft spot on my neck.

"Remember Shanelle, if you're not running, then I'm here for you. That only helps us in the future."

Overwhelmed with relief, my arms spread wide for a tear filled hug.

"Thanks Alex. Thank you for everything."

He searched my eyes, thumbing my cheeks until his hands rested at the base of my neck.

"That was nothing Shanelle. I want the best for you."

Butterfly

By fall of 1984, I was nestled in the comfort of Alex and his loving ways. Little communication came from home because my brother was still there. Mom and Dad were absorbed in silence and sent subliminal messages in cards and phone calls. By that time, I had experienced so much of Alex's uncomplicated world; it was easy to ignore my emptiness. I made the honor roll and filled out an application to St. James University for my sophomore year. Alex paid my bills and dorm fees. The happiness I felt inside increased my weight to one hundred and fifty pounds without missing a beat. Since I was sleeping at his apartment again, he picked me up every Saturday and brought me home after the Sunday beach traffic died down. In between visits to his family, the Fosters whispered behind our backs about how much we were in love and wondered when we would get married.

By March, I received an acceptance letter from St. James University. I was elated because they had a great English Department and I wanted desperately to become a writer. Alex begged me to write poetry and purchased a camera to take pictures of me while I scripted pen to paper. Each time we went to his apartment, simple treasures of our love were everywhere. Alex had so many photographs of me that a psychologist would have termed it a "Narcissist's delight and a stalker's dream gallery."

Candy was nestled in Pittsburg having the time of her life and begging for money every week. I usually called her from Alex's house on Saturdays, but Miss Party Girl was having so much fun, I abandoned the phone calls for letters. Candy knew the momentum was building between us. She told me that the "first time" would hurt. She also said that when the pain subsided, making love to Alex would feel like pure pleasure.

Alex and I were in the "I love you" stages. He wanted me to transfer to Ocean County and take classes in the fall, but I didn't have the time. There were signs of an unofficial engagement everywhere we went including the goofy smiles everyone gave us.

By June of 1985, our love blossomed into a full courtship and the intensity of us making love grew deeper and stronger. I wanted him inside of me in the worst way. The monthly calendar placed me at the peak of fertility by the Fourth of July weekend. The weekend before was intense for the both of us. I took a shower with Alex and jerked him off with my hands. I knew I was in trouble by his size and wondered if I could truly make him happy. He washed my hair and kissed me long and hard. His fingers explored my swollen clit and gooey vulva.

"Shanelle," he whispered, "It's going to hurt, but I love you and I want you to feel all of me." I wept in his arms at the thought of going through the experience with him while he caressed me. He carried me to the bed and rubbed me down with Jasmine oil. Alex spread my legs with his hand and towered over me with a kiss.

"This is just the beginning of our lives and I want you to feel love from me in a pleasurable way before I make love to you."

Alex kissed my breasts and danced his tongue around my belly button. He reached my clit and used his fingers to spread my lips apart. Softly, gingerly, he smacked his lips against Kitty as my body shuddered inside and out. His kisses were fast and then slow before his tongue lapped her up like warm milk. I felt light headed and crazy as he made love to Kitty. A sensation stirred from my head to my toes. My back arched off the bed.

"Alex," I cooed, "what is this?" as my vaginal walls trembled and burst into an abyss of coital pleasure. I called his name as he slowed down for me to take in the entire sensation. I was so overwhelmed; my thighs tightened until the sensation swirled away and left the soles of my feet. Alex held me close, kissing me as his finger danced around the pool of creamy silk between my legs. I turned on my side facing him, begging him to make love to me as my hips pressed against him.

"Not now Shanelle," he laughed between breaths, sliding his hand down my back. "You're too tight. I'll hurt you if I do it now."

Curling into a fetal position, Alex rested behind me, snaking his arm to the front as his hand probed Kitty now thick and creamy in his hands. He used his middle finger to show me how tight I was as he slid it in and out of my tunnel, listening to me moan and coo as I wrapped my hand around his bicep.

"You're ready, but I wanted you to feel that before we make love. You need to understand how your body works."

Alex took my hand and slid it down between Kitty.

"Don't be afraid to pleasure yourself in front of me or by yourself baby. You'll be a better lover for the both of us."

July 4th came and the stage was set for my liberation. A new swimsuit fashioned in black and white fit like a leather glove as we lay on the beach. Feeling free, the warm sun beating against my skin, I kissed his cheek and declared, "I love you Alex and all that you do for me."

Searching deep into my eyes, he whispered, "I'm taking you into custody for three days."

I rubbed my thumb across his mouth and giggled, "Three days?"

Alex jumped up, thumping his heavy feet into the sand. His towel rolled into a tight ball. He pulled me up and wiped away residue from my legs. Trudging through the sand with a tight grip, Alex led me to the car door. He got in on his side and sighed, "Shanelle, I've been very patient with you, so yes, three days."

Despite the beautiful morning, gray storm clouds crept in like a pregnant cat eyeing us from above. Stretching with a wide yawn, I noticed my garnet ring, so delicate in appearance. The prisms were mysterious and hard to gage as I twisted my hand from side to side. Suddenly, an old friend came to visit in a soft sultry voice.

"Hello Shanelle."

I closed my eyes. *"Greetings Nemesis."*

"Greetings indeed. I've been quiet for a few months, but I come to you with love and concern as you appear to be like the lioness in full estrus. Check well young maiden that you are protected from his seeds of life, perhaps a Trojan or two will do the trick."

"I know, we're responsible."

"I don't doubt your intentions, young love child, but the love you feel will surely cloud your judgments as he enters your being with pain and pleasure."

"Is everything ok baby?" Alex asked of my sudden lapse into silence.

He handed me a bouquet of flowers that went unnoticed in my exchange with Nemesis.

"These are beautiful Alex, thank you."

The close proximity to the scented flowers overwhelmed me to tears.

Alex's faces contorted. "Shanelle why are you crying?"

I buried my face into his neck.

"I love you so much and I need to know that everything is going to be okay. I mean, I know it is but,"

Alex quieted me with pampered circles against my lower back.

"Just say the word Shanelle and we'll wait, I told you before, I love you and I wouldn't do anything that you're not ready to handle."

The tight squeeze around his neck revealed the red garnet, so beautiful and delicate. Alex was calm and steady as he wiped my tears with his thumb. I grabbed his hand as he continued to stroke my face.

"Let's go," I reassured him with half a smile, "It looks like a thunderstorm is coming."

Alex started the car as Sade escorted us home. Once inside, I put the flowers in a vase. His apartment, now mixed with hints of estrogen complimented the kitchen, living room and bedroom. I placed the flowers on my nightstand and searched the room. Shades of darkness rolled into the window as Alex sauntered in to close them. He came from behind me and said, "I love the rain."

I turned around with confidence. "I love you."

Alex's lips brushed my neck. "Well maybe after I make love to you, you'll love the rain as much as I do."

Alex snapped his fingers, leading me into the living room. By the looks of things, Alex took care of business. Condoms were sitting on the table as I sighed with relief. Darkness fell with a heavy blanket of urgency against the blinds. Alex took the phone off the hook. I smiled like an innocent college freshman glancing at the clock. It was 1:00 pm as serenity rested in the room. He turned the air conditioner down while I fired up the teakettle.

"Do you want some tea? My hands nervously shook.

"No," he groaned as he hastened up behind me and softly nibbled my neck. My feet quickly left the ground.

"Alex!" twisting my neck at the potential fire hazard on the lit stove.

"Shhhh," he hushed, planting his weighted finger on my lips. His heavy feet carried me into the bathroom. I gazed into his intense eyes. There was a sensual flutter in my stomach as Alex lifted my beach cover. I closed my eyes and bit my lips as my bikini bottoms peeled away from my damp skin. Seaweed and sand stuck to my ass as Alex carried me to the shower. Water beads cascaded down and swished away the weary remnants of the sea. He dried me off, locking eyes with me the entire time.

"You okay?" he whispered.

Nodding once, my body froze. My fingers stiffened at my side.

"I think so," I softened glancing at his massive erect penis.

Alex licked his lips and applied soap to my body. His hands swooshed away suds with delicate care. Soaking wet, Alex picked me up again and sat me on top of the bathroom countertop. A burst of thunder and lightening rang outside jolting my body.

"Don't be nervous baby," his mouth smacked as it traveled to my nipple, gingerly sucking away, leading my hand to his firm erection. Moaning once, he left my breast as his hand reached my lower back. He pressed against me and whispered in my ear.

"It's your dick baby, all yours. "

Stroking him up and down, I watched his free hand leave my lower back and reach the liquid soap. It filled his palm and spilled on my ring instantly slipping away. The glass cabinet became its new resting place. Tears trickled down my face as he kissed each one away.

"You're safe with me Shanelle. I'm yours for life. That ring is a thing of the past. You're my precious gem."

His thick lips pressed up against mine.

"I promise to treat you like a delicate butterfly. If it hurts, just tell me. We'll take it slow."

My breathing began to calm. We talked about this day for so long, I knew Alex was going to respect each and every moment. He pinched my nose and kissed my forehead.

"You're so beautiful Shanelle."

He carried me to the room and placed me directly in the middle of the mattress. The smooth cotton sheets felt cool as I searched for the sound of the falling rain. Alex went to the kitchen and came back with a bowl of strawberries. The first bite was sweet as Alex used his thumb to force the juices back into my mouth. He crushed a strawberry in his manly hands and carried it to Kitty's den as she purred and cooed in sensual delight. He kissed my belly button and stroked my thighs as I begged for his thick dick.

"Alex, I want you inside of me."

He got up and put another strawberry in his mouth. Alex shifted it to the corner and bit into the sweet fruit. Walking strong and proud, he went into the bathroom and started singing Magic Man to lighten the mood. Rain pellets increased with intensity as an unwritten ceremony romanced our time. Alex entered the room with a white towel wrapped around his waist. He took a condom off the nightstand and slid next to me. Pulling me on top of him, I straddled his waist, unsure of what he wanted me to do. I removed his towel as he followed my eyes and hands. His face was strained as he reached out and stroked my neck. I watched Alex protect us from his seeds of life. He sat up and gently laid my shoulders back on the bed, watching my breathing accelerate. He placed his hand on my stomach to calm me.

"Breathe through your nose and relax baby."

I placed my hands by my sides. Alex placed his body on top of mine and whispered words of affection through his calm breath. A brief preamble caused goose bumps to ripple up my arms.

"Hold onto me and don't let go. Bite me if you have to."

His weight bore down on me. I could feel the massive head of his dick toying at my tunnel, wet and slippery from my urgings. Wiggling under him, Alex positioned himself.

"Easy baby. I'll be gentle."

The heat between us became unbearable as my insides popped like the snap of a juicy hot dot. My skin began to burn as his dick traveled inside of me, filling me up with intense pain. Crying out, gritting my teeth, Alex kissed me softly, sliding in and out. Each time the pain grew worse.

"It's going to take time before it feels good, but I love you. What you feel is natural."

Alex took my arms and relaxed my grip around his neck. I dug my nails into him cringing from the cruel intrusion that entered me accented by his loving words of calm happiness. Alex took his time, patiently waiting as small depths of pleasure came in quick spurts and disappeared. My teeth sunk into his skin, my eyes bore down into crinkled slits, waiting for the intense fire to burn out. Without flinching, he moaned, "It's okay Shanelle, bite me harder if you have to, I can take it."

Wiggling beneath him, feeling me ease and settle Alex bore all of his weight on top of me grinding this time.

"Damn its so hot and tight baby. Keep it like that for me. I love you Shanelle. Don't ever leave me. I'll die if you leave me."

Alex began to pump his dick harder as small bits of pleasure began to rise up with the comfort of his voice and the oneness of our skin. I stroked his back listening to him moan and grunt with heated interest, this time moving faster as my nails gripped his back. He slowed down a bit, pressing his lips against mine as his pace and excitement intensified. I couldn't make sense of the time, pain and his sheer strength, but I could feel his gentle hands smoothing away sweat from my hair line.

"It's so big baby," I cried, a haze of excitement charging my womanhood.

"I know Shanelle, it'll get better, you'll see."

He hushed me into silence as his pace sped up again, riding me, seemingly never ending. His stamina maintained as my tunnel continued to burn. I could feel him growing, trembling. His back rippled with goose bumps as he groaned into my ears.

"I'm coming baby, ah shit baby, I'm coming. Damn it feels so good."

He called my name as his body collapsed and crushed my frame. He buried his sweaty head in my neck, listless and exhausted.

Alex kissed my neck and stomach while holding my hand. Damp beneath us, remnants of our love soiled the fabric.

"Are you okay?" he asked, looking up, watching me settle as I wiped his brow. Alex used the sheet to towel my face, smiling at the newness of our relationship. Gently, he lifted me up and carried me to a cucumber bath. After a lingering soak, I felt at ease to stand up and dry off. I looked in the mirror and smiled while Alex held me from behind. Our faces merged together like a beautiful picture book of love. We climbed back in bed as Alex massaged my scalp with his large hands. He pulled my body into his so I could rest against his massive chest. He also caressed my empty ring finger.

"Where once a garnet wrapped to protect, a pear shaped diamond lays to rest."

I smiled at the romantic play on words, but I was too tired to find meaning in his verbiage. Alex rocked me in his arms for twenty minutes, pushing the covers back to admire my healthy ass. The visual excitement stirred him up again as he prodded my legs open. Cooling Kitty with his thick tongue, he ate her until a glorious rush burst inside. Sexually drained, I slept for three hours under the pitter patter of falling rain. I felt Alex slide next to me clothed with cotton underwear. Four hours passed as I woke to the sound of fireworks. The thunderous noise pierced red and blue flashes through the blinds. Alex snuggled closer as I pulled his arms around me. I stroked his beautiful cinnamon skin and smiled with the embrace of our love. Facing him I whispered, "Are you awake?"

Alex shook his head. "No, I'm in love Mrs. Foster."

"Mrs. Foster?"

Alex laughed. "You're right, you're right, I stand corrected, soon to be Mrs. Foster."

I pushed back in order to comfortably wrap my arms around him as we nestled under the sheets. I held my head up and to my surprise a pear shaped diamond decorated my ring finger. I gasped as Alex held my hand.

"Say yes, Shanelle."

Beaming, biting into my lower lip I squeaked, "Yes!"

We hugged under the explosion of fireworks resounding with a grand finale. Alex kissed me all over as our twelve months of courtship brought the two of us into one being. The pain was beginning to subside as he held me tight. The time spent making love this time came without a shield of protection. Tiny seeds of life were mercifully pumped inside of me. We ended our evening with a hot soaking bath and quiet conversation. It was complimented with buttery pancakes in bed. I ate heartily as Alex spread syrup across my lips and licked his fingers. Alex called his mother and announced that we had something special to tell her at tomorrow's family gathering. I massaged my swollen stomach with my right hand and held my pear shaped diamond in the air. Alex took a call from the station and rested on the side of the bed. He kissed my forehead and said he would be back in one hour. I nodded with fatigue. Whatever he said was barely audible as I lay wrapped under the covers.

I drifted off to sleep settling into a quiet meadow. The grass beneath my toes felt warm and inviting. Delicious smells filled the air. I felt someone caress my face. I opened my eyes temporarily. Alex was back and had filled the room with white gardenias. Gazing into his loving eyes, he kissed my cheeks.

"I love you. Welcome home butterfly."

Welcome to Sweet Redemption: Part II

Alex Julian Foster, the man of my dreams, lover and fiancé. What more could a girl like me ask for and did I deserve such a good man? From his soft kisses to his powerful hands, I didn't want to leave his embrace for fear he would never return.

The holiday weekend of making love for the very first time left us as the Tuesday morning sun arose. Alex returned to his regular routine as a police officer for the town of Lakewood. As a result, I woke up alone, nestled under a thin yellow sheet surrounded by empty silence.

The warmth of sunlight began to pierce through the blinds. I rolled over to look at the clock on the nightstand. A small note on Alex's pillow caught my attention. In anticipation for reading his heart felt words; I sat up and carried my feet to the floor. The note read, *"Sleep becomes you Shanelle. Get pretty for me so we can tell my family the good news. After we leave my parents' house tonight, we're going to North Orange to tell your parents."*

In an instant, my mind went completely blank as the clock stopped ticking and the world's orbit ceased. The delicate note was set free from the nerve endings in my hand. Fear and anxiety slowly seeped into my blood stream. I opened my mouth and mimicked the written words in slow motion. *"Tell your parents the good news."*

I watched the note fall to the hardwood floor like a mature leaf on an autumn day. Although it possessed no beauty or color, it rippled to the ground with such declaration that I could not fathom an outcome except sadness and shame. My face contorted into a state of confusion. *"How could such a tiny piece of paper contain such a powerful message?"*

Destructive contemplation set in as the ball of my foot began to push the note towards the darkness beneath the bed. A soft creak in the floor quickly changed my course of action as I listened for Alex. My foot stopped moving as he trudged towards me. I bit my lip wondering how I could hide the tiny message. The floor below me quickly changed into black shiny shoes. Alex lifted my chin and announced himself, unaware that his message was resting on the floor.

"Hey, you finally decided to wake up sleepy head?"

The smile on Alex's cinnamon face was confident. The love we made over the weekend sent me into endless dream sleep and he knew I was finally his with a sealed engagement ring on my finger. My body relaxed just by the sound of his voice. It had just the right base and on any given day, all I could do was melt. A response flowed from my mouth as if I swallowed a succulent truth serum.

"Good morning," I replied, as my chin continued to rest in his mighty hands. Alex stroked my face with a caring smile. I contemplated pulling him on top of me, but his written words diminished my need to make love to him. I didn't want to lose focus with my plan to destroy it, but I was fading fast. My heart started to beat slowly as his eyes shifted to the floor. Alex bent down and retrieved it from under my foot as a tiny voice buried deep inside of me crept to the surface, *"You're busted Shanelle, he's a cop remember? You can't get shit past him girl."*

I quickly accepted ownership by concentrating on the things that pleased him. "If sleep becomes me, I'll sleep for you all day."

Alex toyed with my untamed hair, quickly pinching my earlobe. "You can't sleep all day Shanelle; we've got too much to do." His car keys quickly whipped around his pointer finger. There was no sense in distracting him because he was completely focused on two things, going to work and spreading our good news.

"What about the note?" He asked, placing it in the palm of my hand. A formulated answer never came. Thank goodness Alex exercised patience on a daily basis. He was rarely at a loss for words, but his actions commanded an answer. Alex cleared his throat and sat next to me. The weight of his body gave way and pressed our shoulders together. His large hands crisscrossed to retie his shoes ending with a tight snap. Our eyes locked for a momentary pause until his lips parted.

"Look Shanelle, you owe it to your parents. Let's get this over with and make peace."

I stared at our photograph filled bedroom. There were enough pictures to occupy myself and avoid his answer. To make good use of his time, Alex stood up and adjusted his bulletproof vest. He continued to stare at me and methodically adjusted his belt. Even if he was waiting for a response, I could not speak. Alex began to massage my shoulders and said, "Ok Shanelle, we'll talk about it at lunch."

Alex's love for me led him straight to the floor on his knees. He spread my legs and tucked his massive frame against me. A warm embrace eased my worry. Alex nestled his head against my breasts and pacified himself before he left. He also whispered reassuring words.

"Baby girl, you're gonna be fine. I'm here for you, and I'm not going anywhere." No matter the comfort, it did little to diminish my anguish.

"Derrick used to call me baby girl too."

I wondered if Alex thought I was a child in his eyes. More troubling to me was the voices that began to carry me away. The Big One spoke first.

"I hope Mrs. Viv takes a shot at the back of her big ass head, that's always a good laugh."

The Little Meek One replied, *"No, no way, she's going to make her clean out the fridge."*

The Big One chuckled and retorted, *"Better yet, wait till dear daddy sees her new ring."*

I shut my eyes tight and wished them all away. I needed to soothe my own sense of worry so I began to rub Alex's back in large circles.

"Why are they so chatty today?"

Even though Alex could barely feel me through his weighted armor, the sensation always relaxed him before work. I was glad he had to wear his vest because I could not imagine life without him on any given day. My love for Alex was so great that I was in no position to let him go to my parents' house like a sitting duck. Steven's rampages and small dark closets festered in my head. The note only brought the images back to the surface and I was determined to suppress them.

"He doesn't know Shanelle...he doesn't have to know about the voices or the closets."

Realizing that duty called, Alex snapped out of his trance and stood up. "Baby, I'll call you during my break." He grabbed my hand with care and added, "Oh yeah, I'm definitely coming home for lunch."

One last hug satisfied us as Alex headed for the door. I tip-toed behind him like a little school girl as his handcuffs and keys jingled in tune. As we stood at the door, Alex swept my lips with his thumb.

"I love you girl."

"I love you too Alex."

I locked the door behind him as Alex's whistling disappeared through the secondary entrance. The tips of my fingers adjusted the blinds for the right shade of sunlight through the window. My other hand stroked the places that Alex aroused. As he pulled out of the complex, I stared at our apartment. The sensation of Alex's unforgiving hands left my body as soft murmurs began. Among the quiet walls and hollow doors, my world felt occupied by demons and voices, some strange, others as witty as Richard Pryor. I did not want to know them, but they escaped and found a way to find me in my new world with Alex. Time could only contemplate their intentions.

Voices

I needed to get ready for Alex's lunch break so I closed the blinds and turned off the TV to prevent any distractions. Mental interruptions plagued my mind in various forms. Questions, doubts and rhetoric fused together like a spider's intricate web. I scuttled into the bathroom and took off my clothes from the previous night. My arms began to itch as goose bumps permeated my skin with thoughts of returning home.

"I don't want to go back there, please leave me alone, I'm fine just where I am. Everything is clean now mama. Leave me alone Steven. Help me daddy. Who are you Shanelle?"

The audible words began to settle into a small whisper, but wouldn't go away. As each murmur continued, I hastily closed the door to hear the intruders. I stared into Alex's bathroom mirror and pressed my nose gently against the glass. The need to focus forced me to look down and meticulously spread toothpaste on the brush. My hands began to shake as I tried to talk my way through the process.

"Stay cool Shanelle. You're okay, take deep breaths."

The calm of my voice brought me closer to the creamy texture. It was blue mint with stripes of white and red gel. The substance was too alluring to waste on brushing, so I held my head back and began to squeeze the creamy substance into my mouth. It was cool and creamy going down my throat like the frozen yogurt machines at the mall. I looked up at the swirling texture and forced it down my throat with hard concentrated swallows. It happened so quickly that I didn't realize I swallowed the entire tube. I forced the remaining toothpaste out of the tube by curling it down. The creamy droplets that followed were escorted to the back of my throat with my pointer finger. I plowed into the kitchen without clothes. The world stopped moving for me as I reached for the peanut butter in the kitchen cabinet. In a gothic trance, I returned to the bathroom and closed the door to my sanctuary. I washed my hands without toweling them off and dipped my fingers into the plastic jar. I shoved the substance down my throat bringing immediate relief to my tortured existence. It was hard to swallow, but I was able to eat half of the twelve-ounce jar without feeling nauseous. The sensation of feeling full settled the whispers.

Remnants of my demise were stuck to the tile walls as I stood up. The immediate head rush sent me back to the floor to avoid a dizzy spell. A shower was my next release. I sat on the floor of the tub as the water pulsated into my open mouth. The feeling increased my need to relax as I looked at my swollen stomach.

"You look so fat you fucking bitch, you need to go on a diet, look at you."

I shut my eyes to block out Steven's voice, but it was controlling and persistent.

"He's going to find out how fat you are and leave you bitch."

The internal messages continued with more voices from my past. I covered my ears with my hands, but it served little purpose as they continued.

"Shanelle, you're a disgrace, the bottom of the barrel and you won't amount to anything."

My courageous plea for help did little to stop them as rapid breathing took over. I placed my head into the shower stream and began to moan.

"That's it Shanelle, good girl, no more crying, we prefer soft moaning. That way, no one can hear us. That's it, take your time, we love you when you're weak."

I slammed my fists on the bathroom tile.

"Stop the bullshit, I've had enough!"

I began to lather my washcloth with soap, rethinking what went wrong. The peanut butter vice used to work all the time, but had little to no effect today. I clenched my teeth as I began to curse Alex's decision.

"This is not going to work Alex. I hate you for doing this to me!"

My breath quickly escaped as I began to choke and babble.

"Mama is going to be furious, daddy is going to call me a sugar shack whore and Steven is going to put an end to my misery."

Drool escaped my mouth and slipped into the shower stream.

"I don't care what you think of me Steven and if I never see you again, it'll be good for me!"

Pleasing Alex meant going home. Losing him was unacceptable. With little or no choice, it had to be done. The shampoo sat in eyesight as I poured it into my hair shaft. The massage made me more alert, even defensive about what could happen tonight. I was so deep in thought I could barely hear the phone ringing. I answered it dripping wet as the soapy residue trickled down the side of my face. The tone in my voice was riddled with frustration.

"Hello."

Alex paused. "Hey baby girl, what took you so long?"

"I'm sorry," I said, as I paused to catch my breath. "I was in the shower and I couldn't hear it with the door closed."

"Oh," Alex replied, "Are you okay?"

Before I could think of an answer, a radio dispatch blared in the background.

"All units respond to a 302 at the corner of Chestnut and Amsterdam."

Alex didn't hesitate to end our conversation. "Got to go babe, I love you."

The dial tone blared into the earpiece as I stood dripping wet. Loving him the way I did forced me to speak even though he was out of earshot. "I love you too Alex, be safe."

My worry for him was so great that it was just the right trick to settle the voices. I pictured his face in his patrol car talking to his partner Jack. It comforted me to know that I could conjure up images of him until he got home. After my shower, I went to the bedroom and turned on the TV to keep me company until he came home. I toweled dried my hair and turned to Eyewitness News.

There was a special news report on the arrest of a reputed drug kingpin in New York who was responsible for a high distribution of crack cocaine throughout the metropolitan area. For a while, New York looked like an ugly city. I worried about Alex's safety and hoped that it didn't come to New Jersey. We talked about the news all the time, but drugs and weapons were the only things he avoided in conversation. I knew there was talk at the precinct that several officers were going to special narcotics and weapons training, but he made it his business to keep me out of the loop.

I stared at the TV and watched the kingpin trudge to a white Chevy Caprice as two officers carefully lowered his head into the vehicle. A pretty Latina reporter wrapped up the news coverage as I held the remote in my hand.

"More news at 12:00 noon, this is Carmen Rivera, live from the Brooklyn Criminal Court house, back to you Bill."

I looked at the clock and turned the TV down as I jumped off the bed. With less than an hour to go, I needed to get ready for Alex. I ran around the apartment picking up various pieces of clothing and the newspaper. As I scurried past the bathroom, I suddenly remembered the remnants of peanut butter stuck to the wall. I grabbed a paper towel and feverishly wiped it away.

By noon Alex was home putting the key into the lock. A few dishes were left over, but I abandoned them as soon as he appeared. He was deep in thought which was unusual for him. I grabbed his wrists to get his undivided attention as he looked at me like visual eye candy.

"Hey babe, what's wrong, tough day?"

He gave me another once over from my pink toes to the top of my head and escorted me towards the bathroom.

"Yeah, it's crazy out there and the heat isn't helping."

I stopped at the bathroom door entrance and watched Alex methodically wash his hands. Placing one hand on my hip, I began to stroke my collarbone as I admired his thick frame. My eyes spoke to him as he smiled at me.

"What? Tell me," he grinned.

"You're so damn sexy Alex, that's what."

"Yeah, well we need to do something about that. All I want is you right now Shanelle."

My eyes began to widen as he grabbed the tube of tooth-paste. His face contorted with surprise. "What happened? We just brought this."

Quickly rising to the occasion, I answered, "Oh, I got carried away and cleaned all of my jewelry, sorry."

The officer in Alex didn't seem to care. A tiny visitor spoke to me in my left ear.

"You're so stupid Shanelle, Steven stole your jewelry."

He brushed his teeth and spit into the sink without flinching. I began to worry if my lie had any impact.

"Take a shower with me Shanelle, I missed you."

I freed myself from his grip and kissed him while I stood on the tips of my toes.

"Get in the shower with me now," he whispered.

At his command, I flashed him a dreamy smile and stepped in with my clothes on. There was no sense in complaining about wet hair or taking a second shower because Alex didn't give a shit. I searched his eyes for suspicion or interrogation, but there was nothing but love in his eyes. He handed me his washcloth as I scrubbed him from head to toe. Alex ran his fingers up and around my wet tee shirt. He was so focused on teasing me that I started laughing.

"Alex stop! That tickles."

He licked his lips and forcefully popped the right seam of my panties.

"Keep playing, you love to waste money."

Alex grabbed the other side and threw it to the floor. He swept Kitty's curly wet hair exclaiming, "You can buy as many as you want, I'll rip those too if necessary."

He turned the water off and grabbed two towels. The floor resonated with a loud thud, with me falling on top of him. He slipped his dick inside of me as I screamed in pain. We rolled over, as he quieted me with a whisper. My back cooled against the tile floor as Alex made love to my mind. He swept words into my ears that drove me crazy as he continued to fuck me.

"Being inside of you makes me whole. I love you so much."

I bit his ear and whispered, "It's all yours baby, make me whole."

Alex covered my mouth with his hand to silence me as his body tightened and settled.

"Don't talk, don't talk, that drives me crazy."

He lifted my leg up and kissed my calf. He used his other hand to force Kitty into an orgasmic rush as my back arched off the floor. I called his name as he rested his thick hand on my throat. Alex looked at me and calmed me with a quiet kiss. Time quickly escaped us as he succumbed to our rhythms and released his seeds of life inside of me.

The bathroom floor was the perfect place to be on that muggy day. I knew what he was thinking, but I didn't say a word about protection. The comfort and safety of Alex's arms was all I wanted for the moment. I placed my hand on top of his as we rubbed my stomach together. Alex whispered in my ear, "I want a son Shanelle."

"I know Alex; I'll give you a son one day, just wait and see."

He looked so happy when I said those words, but deep down inside, I knew his need was more immediate than my spoken promise. For the moment, the rush to his head was the first thing he had to deal with. I jumped up and poured him a glass of orange juice. Alex gulped it down like a mighty giant, placing it down before he entered a hot shower. As he lathered, I wrapped myself up in a towel and kept him company.

"Shanelle," he pitched over the rising steam, "there was a big meeting today with some heavy hitters from the Federal Narcotic and Tactical Weapons Task Force. Captain Fisco assigned me and Jack to the Tactical Weapons Squad. Apparently a major sting is under works on your side of town. If the operation goes well, we might be assigned permanently. For now we're going to be on loan to the feds."

I sat up and looked at him through the shower door not knowing whether that was good news or bad news. Alex extended his hand.

"C'mon angel, get in and wash off."

He greeted me with a soapy fingertip. Alex decorated my nose with bubbles as I giggled and stepped aside. He made his exit and quickly dressed himself.

After five minutes of whistling in the bedroom, Alex came into the bathroom with more information.

"Captain Fisco said I can take my vacation time to take care of personal business, but when I get back, I'm going to be gone for a month in Philly for special weapons training."

My heart started to race. I peeked through the shower door anxious with wide eyes. "I won't be able to see you for a month?"

Alex grabbed my hand and wrapped me in a towel. In that short period of time, he was fully dressed in a fresh uniform except for his shoes, bullet-proof vest and shirt. I sat down next to him but he wasn't satisfied with the seating arrangements. He patted his lap and said, "Sit here."

I stood up and straddled his waist as the towel fell to my waist side. Alex smiled, kissing my cheeks and neck. He pulled me closer to him as our noses began to twiddle.

"You know I love you Shanelle, right?"

My smile was met with worry.

"Yes, I know."

"Good. I need you to be strong for me until I get back. Don't get me wrong, I know you're strong, but it can get a little lonely sometimes."

My stomach quickly became his focus. His large hand rubbed my back in small circles.

"Baby," he whispered, "I want you to be safe and happy. You can stay here or at my mother's house in my old room until I get back."

My head rattled at the thought.

"Alex, everything is changing so fast, I don't even know what I'm going to do for the rest of the summer."

Laughing this time, I watched his teeth bite into his lower lip. A smile suspended his response. Alex boastfully breathed out loud and sighed, "Hopefully, morning sickness will set in as soon as we get back from our vacation."

I squeezed my legs tighter and grabbed his face. Stuck on happiness, I blurted with delight, "Vacation! I've never been on vacation, where?"

Alex placed his hands under my armpits and placed me on the floor.

"The Bahamas."

An immediate parade followed Alex to the door as my hands shot up to clap.

"Be ready by five o'clock and don't cook anything, my mother's got that covered."

"Okay babe!" ended our interlude as I locked the door.

"Lucky me," I thought, thumbing my chin with an arched eyebrow. "Wait till Candy hears this."

I breathed a sigh of relief when she picked up the phone. For once she was in the dorm room and studying for a change. Flight attendant school rewarded her with a love interest. The lucky pilot swept Candy to two exotic destinations in one week. She gushed over her Dominican tan and couldn't wait to hear my news with the exception of sex.

"What do you mean he doesn't use a condom?"

A long pause filled the phone. I shrugged my shoulders and sat on the bed.

"He doesn't want to and he made himself pretty clear about that."

"Well I guess you're going to be pretty pregnant if you keep that up. Are you ready for all of that Shanelle?" Candy continued honing in on my maturity. "Damn, that's a bit much don't you think? You're nineteen."

"You're right Candy, but…,"

She quickly short-changed my unfocused life.

"I know I'm right. You haven't finished partying and trying to figure out who you are. Damn, we all like Alex, but the two of you need to get to know each other first and see how that shit really feels."

Her sentiment filled my eardrums and escaped into the day-time air. The world around me including Alex was seemingly perfect. Candy continued.

"Shanelle, you know you're my girl, but I think you forgot about all the hopes and dreams you had about going to college and graduate school. You and Derrick talked about that shit all the time. Now that you're with Alex, is your life going to be school books with a baby strapped to your hip?" She changed her tone after my high pitched sigh. "Damn Shanelle, at this point, we have to do what makes us happy. So if you're happy, then I'm happy for you."

Gripping the phone to relay the vacation news, I fell back on the bed. "We're going to the Bahamas to get married. I don't know the dates yet, but it would be so nice if you could join us."

Candy laughed.

"Girl, you've got big dreams."

As long as those dreams were with Alex, I didn't give a damn.

Just like clockwork, Alex picked me up at five o'clock. His entire family greeted us at the door as his sisters pulled me into their huddle and grabbed my ring finger.

"Oh girl, it's beautiful," Mary said. She was the oldest sister who always had kind words to share. I turned towards Mrs. Foster. She was proud as a peacock in her jeans and sweatshirt staring adoringly into her son's eyes. I knew they shared secrets, but I didn't care. I knew in my heart that Alex would be good to me just by the way he treated her. Alex cut the conversation short and announced our plans.

"Listen up family, no bridesmaids and drama for this family. I'm taking three weeks vacation to spend time with Shanelle. We're going to have a quiet ceremony in the Bahamas. You can do whatever you want when we get back, but my job is sending me to Philly for a month and I need you to look out for my lady."

My chin rose to the occasion facing his family.

"I'll be fine. Thanks everyone for caring about me so much."

Tammy, the youngest sister slid her big hips next to mine with a few plans of her own.

"We can hang out before I start school. Don't worry sis' I'm going to miss big head too."

Mr. Foster stood up and extended his hand to Alex, pulling him off the couch.

"I'm proud of you son. If you remember everything I schooled you on, you and Shanelle will be fine."

Mr. Foster focused on me and pitched, "Girl, I know you're a strong woman and maybe you're being too kind by not showing it. We take pride in our family by doing things our way." His voice rose to the ceiling. "Don't let these women smother you while Alex is gone. But if you want to come by and get something to eat or just talk, one of us will be right here anytime."

Alex broke his father's momentum with part two of his plan. "Let's get you home Shanelle, I know you miss your family."

I didn't care what the plans were; I would have married Alex over a chipped plate of black-eyed peas and rice. He was a gem given the life I left behind. More importantly, short of the trip home, there was nothing that could stop our happiness.

Alex's sisters made such a fuss over me that I never had a chance to help Mrs. Foster with the dishes. I entered the kitchen with a weighted head and shy smile. Two plates balanced in my hands. Mrs. Foster laughed, closing the dining room door.

"Shanelle, you and my son have your whole lives ahead of you to make up for soiled dishes. I've never seen him so happy."

She grabbed my wrist and patted my hand. "Alex can't wait to have children so you've got your work cut out. Lawdy," she drifted to the ceiling with her eyes, "If you give him a son, he'll be the happiest man on earth."

Losing rhyme and reason with Mrs. Foster's happiness, I let my guard down. "I can't even tell you how many times he's rubbed my stomach like there's already something in there."

Mrs. Foster bellowed, exposing a full mouth. "Girl, ever since Alex was a little boy, it's been his way or the highway. He loves his family, but he's ready for his own little brood. With all these women around him, I know he is tired of periods, weddings and proms. In fact, his nephews are the only ones that keep him sane."

Our heads nodded in unison as she continued. "Alex told me this morning that he can't wait until you're pregnant."

There was so much happiness in the house that even if my smile turned into a frown, no one would have noticed. I looked at my stomach and grimaced at the thought.

"When you get pregnant? I don't want a baby. I'm fat enough as it is."

Alex dashed in and declared our departure. The combined statements sent me into temporary shock as I kissed and hugged the well-wishers goodbye.

Alex draped his weighted arm around me as we ambled to the car. The stiffness in my limbs riddled him with curiosity. He stopped. His lower lip poked out with doubt.

"What's wrong? You feel like a robot."

"Nothing." I was curt and to the point.

"C'mon Shanelle, I think I know you better than that."

He opened the door as I got into the car. The seatbelt wouldn't give way for me to lock it into place. Frustration settled into my hands as I pulled on the strap in a long jerking motion.

"See how fat you're getting, you can't even get the damn seatbelt on in a two seater."

Alex quickly reached over me and loosened the strap.

"Shanelle, what's wrong?"

I pushed his hands away as tears began to fall. The tips of my fingers flicked away the drops.

"Everything is wrong. I'm just frustrated."

Alex fired up the engine and leaned forward as if a rattled mouse crossed the street. Focused on getting us out of eyesight, he pulled over. The car jerked into park. Alex wearily rubbed his face in two swift circles. His upper body turned to confront me.

"Shanelle, just say what's on your mind, start anywhere, I don't care."

I buried my head in his chest. A muffled tone burst into his thick sweater. "I'm fat and I hate myself!"

Alex's hands stroked my hair.

"Girl, girl, girl, there's not an ounce of fat on your beautiful body. Why are you doing this to yourself, you're beautiful baby."

"I feel fat," I pleaded, "and I'm not even pregnant."

Alex grabbed my face and gazed into my blotched, tear streaked eyes.

"Well I don't think you're fat. Don't get me wrong, you're thick, but that's what I liked about you from the very first day I saw you." He kissed my neck and whispered into my ear, "I'm not leaving you fat, thick or skinny."

My breathing reached a snails pace as the voices gathered in a huddle and attacked me.

"Quit that fucking crying Shanelle!"

"Dang, she ain't nothin' but a bitch ass baby."

"Girl, you better get to the real problem before he finds out."

I squeezed my eyes to shut them out. Alex kissed my forehead.

"It's getting late, let's get on the Parkway and take care of business."

One million highway divider lines passed until I spoke.

"I don't know what to expect when I get home, but my brother is not well."

Alex slowed down to pay the Union toll. He hesitated before he pulled off to look at me.

"Shanelle, I figured that out when he told me you were dead."

I knew Alex was an astute police officer, but I wasn't sure how much he could figure out on his own. I shrugged my shoulders and replied, "Well, I think my brother wants that to happen and that's why I left home last summer. Hopefully he won't be there when we get to the house. He's been in and out of the hospital and even though it's been a year, I can't imagine that Steven got any better."

Alex sighed, shaking his head with little concern.

"Shanelle, I've seen so much out here in my short time as a cop, nothing seems to surprise me anymore."

"I know Alex," I lamented, rubbing my legs down, "I just didn't want to keep secrets."

"Baby, you're not the only one with secrets in your family. We all have secrets, good, bad and indifferent."

He pinched my earlobe, confident of the outcome.

"We're going to be okay, trust me."

We turned the corner of Crescent Avenue. To my surprise, the block looked the same, but my childhood home grew weary. The aged grass needed clipping. A few shingles slipped from their positions before falling into a mangled, rustic planter. Alex put his arm around me as he stared at the exterior.

We reached the door. There was complete darkness inside with the exception of a flickering hallway light. I peeked through the small windowpane to see if there was anyone standing there, but it was too dark. I could hear music in the distance, but could not discern the location. I placed the key in the lock. Alex cleared his throat and stood up straight. To my surprise, I still had access. Searching, peering, extending my neck, it was clear that Steven prevailed. The lingering stench was the sign of his demise. The house smelled like an old mop and expired moth balls. All the windows were sealed shut. Alex held my hand as he wiped the back of his neck and closed the door behind him. I walked up to the flickering light switch. Alex squinted and tightened the tiny bulb. He pulled a tissue out of his pocket and wiped away the dusty residue from his fingertips. I stared, embarrassed by the condition of the house. As soon as the light brightened the room, I gasped for air at the sudden transformation. The mirrors that I cleaned so many times were glazed over with smudge. Signs from the attic made their way down stairs in the form of old photographs, newspaper clippings and Richard Pryor albums. Our apparent stir reached the third floor as I looked up. I stepped back into Alex's space as scraping footsteps descended. Whispering, I squeezed Alex's hand.

"It's Steven, he's coming."

Alex barely flinched. The attic door opened from a distance and emitted the sound of an Earth, Wind and Fire tune. My body began to tense up in terror as dear brother began to take his flight down the creaky stairs. His head was hung low, but he was alert as the day he terrorized me during the winter snowstorm. As soon as his face was visible, I knew that little had changed. His hair was matted and disheveled. A small beard twisted into a curl spurt from his cowardly chin. His face was riddled with acne. His once muscular frame evaporated into an aging human string bean. Hunched in the shoulders, his boney frame mimicked the late stages of scoliosis. Laughter was his introduction to our creepy reunion.

"Well, well, well, look what the cat done dragged in," he snickered. "Looking fat as usual Shanelle, but it's always good to see my chubby ass little sister."

Steven took position on the fourth step from the landing. It was a safe stance as his hands remained rooted in his tattered pant pockets.

With Alex at my side I muttered, "Where's mom and dad?"

His voice, deep and lethargic lodged in his throat and droned out, "Probably at church praying for you fatty. But let's face it Shanelle, do you really give a fuck, you've been gone so long." He sucked his teeth and peered down at the last step before his menacing eyes rolled up.

"Besides, you don't live here anymore remember?" he asked as his fingers toyed with his crunchy bearded curl.

Alex came to my rescue. He bypassed me and extended his hand for a formal introduction.

"What's up man? I'm Alex, Shanelle's fiancé."

Steven's legs shot up to a full stance. His empty hands swung to his back as he set his sight on the new and improved light bulb.

"Smells like fuckin' pig in here. I don't give a shit who you are Negro, but I'll tell you one thing, you need to get the fuck out of my house, unless you actin' on a warrant."

Alex stomped up the first two steps and extended his neck just enough to look Steven dead in the eye.

"No warrants, no bullshit man, just a friendly hello. As you can see, your sister is very much alive, but if you keep smokin' that shit, I'm gonna' be saying the opposite of you."

I was so frightened, I thought that Alex was going to pull out his glock and shoot him while my back was turned. Instead, Alex escorted me to safety. I squeezed his hand tight to secure our exit. He took one last look at Steven and said, "The life you're living is a time bomb man, take care Negro."

I could hear Steven descending the stairs as we stomped down the cemented steps.

"Farewell you punk-ass motha-fuckers." Steven laughed, as I hunched down expecting a rock to hit me in my head. I was almost free and clear from dear brother, but we were moving too slow and his mind was racing with strategy. As Steven closed the creaky door, he shouted, "I see the toothpaste and peanut butter are working just fine fast ass."

I stopped dead in my tracks, turning to face him. Steven nodded, twirling the knots in his hair.

"Yeah, you heard me right bitch."

Alex's pointer finger shot up like the barrel of a gun.

"Yo kid, we'll meet again and trust me, the word 'bitch,' will be the last word you'll be able to say."

Steven's response was his usual psychotic routine. He stuck his middle finger up and pressed his nose against the small window-pane. A contorted glare etched his face. I bowed my head in defeat as I thought about Steven's verbal assault.

"Oh God, not one, but two vices exposed? How could you Steven?"

Alex jumped in the front seat, slammed his door and started up the car. I was frozen in time wondering what would happen next. As soon as Alex sped down the street, he started his own tirade.

"I think it's a little more than being fat don't you think Shanelle?" Placing pity in a trash can, I looked at my feet and found small bits of courage to answer.

"What do you mean?" I asked swallowing a mouthful of spit.

Alex shifted the gears back to first at the red light.

"Shanelle, your brother was high as a hell back there, not to mention that he's not operating with a full deck. He attacked you the entire time."

"I know, I told you he was sick."

Alex cocked a quick glance at me and faced the traffic light. "No shit Sherlock."

My hands slammed into my lap.

Alex quickly apologized, smoothing my thigh. "I'm sorry baby, I'm just pissed off."

I lashed out at him with a roaring mouth.

"Don't you ever curse at me again! I didn't do anything to deserve this. I didn't want to go and I warned you about him!"

The voices rallied behind me with bats and Billy clubs as I quickly looked outside the window. Whatever they were saying did little to squash my frustration. Alex sucked his teeth and laughed. I wondered if he saw too much of my mini time bomb. He pulled into the parking lot of North Orange Park.

"Why can't we just go home?" I asked, scratching my arm.

Alex unbuttoned his shirt collar and turned the car off. He was sweating profusely as an enlarged vein surfaced on the side of his neck. I immediately looked around. Even though the park was well lit at night, I had no interest in being there. I wanted to go home and close the blinds. My palms were itchy and my face felt extremely hot. Alex got out of the car and ambled to a park bench, wiping his face clean. He turned, scowled in the face.

"I need to think," he angrily replied.

I watched him put his hands in his pocket and search the sky. I didn't know if he was going to call it quits or start hitting an innocent tree. Tears began to well up in my eyes as I began to contemplate Alex's plot to get rid of me like rotten garbage. For once, instead of crying, my defenses festered up old habits. I searched my pocketbook for spare change. I looked in the direction of the bus stop to see if the Forty-four bus was approaching. I could start all over again and make a clean break without judgment. New Jersey Transit was the easiest way out before I let Alex dump me.

I was so distracted planning my escape route that the sound of Alex opening the passenger door caught me off guard. My pocket book dropped to the ground as all of its contents spilled out. I immediately stepped out and started picking up the silver pieces. I made sure to count the fare in my head as Alex stood over me.

"Baby girl, forget about the change, you can't even see."

"I need to get out of here," I trembled, "the bus will be here soon."

Alex grabbed my wrists. He searched my eyes for rationale, leaning his head to the side with empathy.

"Shanelle, stop talking crazy, you're not going anywhere."

Alex dragged me like a rag doll to the park bench as I looked back for more coins. He gently sat me down and put his foot on the bench.

"Shanelle, you don't have to run. You're safe with me. I'm not going to hurt you or leave you." He took his foot down and knelt down in front of me. "I can't imagine life without you, despite what you've gone through. You had enough courage to leave, so give yourself credit for that." Alex grabbed my chin and stared at me. "Your brother's got a bad habit and beat your head up in the process. Things seem to make sense to me now, but I need you to open up so I can help you." He stood up and pulled me into his arms as my body slumped against him.

"Girl, every family has secrets. I'm going to help you get all of that garbage out of your head if it kills me." Alex's baby soft stubble brushed my cheek.

"C'mon Shanelle, don't do this to me, I love you, just squeeze me back and let me know you're with me."

Holding him brought a small sense of comfort, but I wasn't ready for anything else. I looked in the direction of the bus stop and abandoned the thought of catching an old habit. Alex stroked the back of my head.

"I won't ask you to do that again. I'm sorry your parents weren't home, but I am worried about them too. I'll make a few calls tomorrow and see if I can contact your father. That way, you'll know they're safe. Our news can wait."

I couldn't find the words to speak. I was curious about Alex's need to talk to my dad, but I was too tired to care. As we walked back to the car Alex said, "The only thing that prevented me from killing your brother was my love for you Shanelle and I'm not going to lose you over his addiction."

My eyes opened wide despite the emotional weights resting on my lids. A chill in the air forced me to slide my hands around his waist. He hugged me back and breathed a sigh of relief in my neck.

"Ahh, that's better. Now, I know you're not going to run for that bus once I let you go, right?"

A small giggle escaped. Alex kissed my forehead. "You know I'm a skilled running back and I'll catch you anyway right?"

I nodded yes as he pecked my pouting lips.

"Ok then, let's go home and get those fragile wings fixed."

Alex went to the trunk and took out a blanket. He draped it over my legs as I slowly put the seat belt on in silence. A storm cloud took up permanent residence over my head. Steven always had a way of messing things up for me. Alex had a sharp mind and keen strategies of his own. Mentally drained and wounded, I drifted off to sleep. Kindness came to me in my thoughts.

"Rest now Shanelle, you're safe for now."

Unsettled Sheets

By the time we got home, exhaustion absorbed my weary body. The only thing left to do was to take a shower and go to bed. As I pulled lingerie from the dresser drawer, his hand landed on top of mine.

"Put them back."

Looking up once, I snatched them out the drawer and quickly headed for the bathroom. The steam left over from Alex's shower melted my senses as I turned on the water. From a distance, I could hear him talking on the phone, but I didn't care who or what the conversation was about. Alex returned, leaning on the edge of the sink. The look in his eyes offered no direction or purpose. He began to towel me off, spreading my legs open as he licked my titties. Soft kisses ensued on my neck in three different places. He picked me up and carried me straight to the bed. Alex slid beside me and stroked my damp nipples. He made his way to Kitty and swept me unconscious with his tongue. Alex got up and went into the bathroom as I lay there wonderfully wounded by his love. As he gargled, I squeezed my legs tight to maintain the last ripples of pleasure. He climbed back into bed throwing the covers to the hardwood floor and asked, "Are you sleepy Shanelle?"

"Yes," I whispered, turning into his cinnamon frame. The vibration of the sheet beneath me felt soft and poetic as Alex moaned, "Let's make love right now beautiful."

I grabbed his face and pulled his soft lips towards my mouth. Alex lay on top of me as Portuguese Love by Teena Marie serenaded his entry. I gripped my nails into his back to bear the pain of my swollen region. My entire body melted as he delved inside. Alex buried his head in my neck and scooped his hands under my ass for maximum penetration.

"Tell me it's all mine baby," he grunted.

"It's yours, all of it."

I squeezed him tight and wrapped my legs around his waist in pure ecstasy. Beads of sweat formed on his neck and back as he rocked me in his arms. I whispered his name over and over again until he finally came. He pulled me on top of him and stared at me with a loving smile. His thick chest rose up and down. Focused on his needs, I bit his chest, looking up once with puppy dog eyes.

"Don't ever leave me Alex."

Alex's fingers found a resting place in my tousled hair. A gentle massage settled me as my cheek lay delicate against his firm chest.

"I told you, I let you go once and I'm never leaving you again."

The last thing I remembered was Alex wrapping us up in our crumpled yellow sheet and falling fast asleep in his arms.

Deadly Arrangements

When I woke up, Alex was in the kitchen huddled into the earpiece of the phone. He was officially on vacation and making flight arrangements with a travel agent. He called me from the kitchen and asked, "Shanelle, do you have a passport?"

I yelled back, "No, I don't!"

When I reached the kitchen, he covered the mouthpiece and said, "its okay, get dressed, you don't need a passport, only a driver's license and your birth certificate." Breathing a sigh of relief I went into the bathroom. Guilt flushed through me when I spotted the toothpaste, but I was resourceful. I cut the tube open and wiped the residue from the corners, making sure to leave some for Alex. By the time I got of the shower, Alex was dressed and shuffling around the apartment looking for papers and receipts. From the looks of things, he was pulling out financial statements, life insurance policies and his pension plan.

"We're leaving two weeks from Sunday, so make a list of the things you need for the trip. We also need to take care of some business at the bank and the clerk's office."

I stood over Alex surveying his financial records and statements. At a quick glance, he must have come into some money because there was no way a rookie's salary afforded him that much income. Alex sat me on his lap. He lost focus for a moment and started yawning. I thought the drive home and our interlude wore him out, but to my surprise, he was still worrying about me.

"How are you feeling today?"

There was slight hesitation in my smile.

"I'm better now that we're home."

Alex rubbed the side of my leg. "Yeah, I like the sound of that too."

His eyes appeared blank and sullen. I grabbed his chin.

"Hey, what's wrong?" I asked, watching him slide away.

I sat down on the couch and extended my hand. Alex joined me and laid his head in my lap. Distant, yet relaxed, he rubbed my legs up and down. He turned over and trailed my face with wide eyes.

"What is it Alex?"

No words followed. I stroked his forehead and held his other hand as he began to speak.

"Sometimes people make you take on responsibilities you just can't handle Shanelle."

I continued to support him by stroking his hairline. For a minute, I thought he was going to talk about last night, but the tone in his voice was deep and reflective.

"Remember that night on the beach?" Alex asked.

"Yes baby, I remember."

"Well," Alex replied, "I told you that I only had one hurdle that would follow me until the day I die. Remember that too?"

Soft spoken, I nodded, "Yes, I do."

Alex's chest rose and fell. "I love you enough to know that the two of us can get through anything as long as we stick together. After last night, I said to myself there's nothing that can stop us except secrets and lies."

"Alex, I don't understand."

He quieted me with his finger.

"When I was thirteen, my father took us to a family reunion in Pulaski, Virginia." Somber and anguish etched his face. "My sisters were so excited to get down there and play with all of our cousins. Most of them were girls so I was definitely outnumbered. We were supposed to spend four days together as a family, but like the old cliché goes, 'things fall apart.'"

Alex shifted his weight and turned his head into my stomach as I stroked the outline of his ear. Our breathing continued in unison as he recalled his story.

"During the drive down, my father promised to take me fishing on the lake as soon as we settled in." He smirked at the thought and continued. "I was happy about it. I remembered asking him at the Maryland House where the bait and tackle store was in Pulaski so we could buy some for my rod."

Alex opened his eyes. I stroked his skin and replied, "Go ahead, I'm listening Alex."

I was intrigued by his tale and wondered how the story was going to end. Alex sat up. "Humph, when we got there, it seemed like he made the whole story up just to keep me busy. As a matter of fact, there was one thing he said that I'll never forget."

Our eyes locked. A subtle blink broke our concentration.

"What's that?" I asked.

Alex looked down at the ground. "He told me to look after my sisters. After that, he jumped in the front seat of my uncle's pick up truck and headed down the road."

There was no unusual meaning in what he said or what his father did, but the words that followed had rippling effects.

"Instead of looking after them, I should have kept my eyes on my mother."

Alex got up and wobbled into the bathroom. His head was hung low and lifeless. I wanted to help him get through his story, but I wasn't sure how I could. Luckily he found the strength.

"I remembered the look on my mother's face when he pulled off. She was so disgusted that she barely said hello to my grandmother. My so called relatives weren't helping the situation either. My Aunt Carol came to the car and started talking junk the minute she saw her."

Alex looked around the room searching for a prop. He picked up the newspaper and rolled it up while he acted out the scene. Alex said of his Aunt, "Girl you should have known my no account brother was going to run off with Ray. You probably ain't gonna see him for a few days either. So y'all come on in this house and fetch yo'self somethin' cool to drink."

Alex locked into the moment like it was yesterday.

"I can't stand my aunt Shanelle. You'd think she could have been cordial to my mom knowing that she felt like an outsider. That was only the second time we went to my father's side of the family."

Alex's face flexed with anger.

"I headed in the house with most of the bags and looked up the road for my father, but he was long gone. I damn near wanted to cry, but Willie James added his two cents before I got used to the idea." Alex's face scowled as he described their encounter.

"Boy, don't you come on this porch with that face all twisted up like that. Your daddy done all that driving and he's tired, so you best leave him alone."

"Alex," I pleaded, watching his mood swing to and fro. "Let's sit down and talk. I'll make some tea."

He back up and planted his hand against the wall.

"This is hard for me Shanelle."

"Talking about it?" I asked, rubbing his forearms.

"Yeah." Alex grimaced with regret.

"Whatever it is, I'm here, you can tell me anything."

Alex ran his fingers up the middle of my back. Taking comfort in our physical reconnection, he finally sat down. The kitchen was close enough not to be out of ear shot, so I walked to the cabinets and pulled out his favorite mug.

"So is Willie James, your cousin?" I asked, carefully avoiding clanging dishes. Alex dropped his head in his hands. "Everybody called him Willie James, a second cousin from two towns over. They said he loved to drift back and forth just to eat and do odd jobs for Grandma Mae. The only talent he had was his good looks. I knew I didn't like him because he acted like he was trying to take charge in my grandmother's house."

I put the teakettle on and sat next to Alex.

"Shanelle," Alex gruffed, "He was as sick as they come, eyeing up my sisters and flirting with my mother. That bastard even had the nerve to steal my sweat socks and undershirts." Alex cocked his head back just thinking about the so-called thief.

"I remembered looking for some clean socks and not being able to find any. Grandma Mae warned me, 'Boy, you better put your good stuff up because Willie James got sticky fingers and he'll deny everything with somebody else's clothes on his back.'"

Alex's southern dialect made me laugh. His drawl was highly undesirable, but he brought brevity to his anguished tale. He put his head in my lap again enjoying the feel of my fingertips against his scalp.

"Shanelle, I was pissed off at the world. My family never felt so divided and my mom was so alone. There was nothing I could do to please her and it seemed to me that the only thing that could get her attention was that damn Willie James."

The teakettle imploded to a deafening pitch. Alex jumped up and turned it off. The noise seemed to pierce his brain as it resounded to a mild hiss. Alex poured the piping hot water into the mugs.

"I thought my father was coming back that night, but by the time we caught up with him the damage was already done." Alex stared at the rising steam and slammed his mug down.

"Shit," he said. "I don't want any damn tea."

I quickly ushered the cups to the countertop and led him away.

"Come sit down Alex."

He spread his legs and pulled me between his thighs.

"I love you so much Shanelle, I couldn't stand the sight of you with someone else."

I immediately kissed his lips.

"I wouldn't do anything to hurt you Alex. I promise."

Settling next to him, he continued.

"The next day was too much excitement for me to handle. Grandma Mae was the only person to keep a promise. We didn't have planning committees and dates for our family reunion. They just went by whatever Grandma Mae said the night before. She planned a big cat fish fry down by the river and everybody had to bring a dish. My sisters cut up sweet potatoes at Aunt Clara's house. They were happy being over there because it was a house full of women and good gossip. My mother stayed to herself and sulked the entire morning. Grandma Mae asked me to go cheer her up and see if she was coming to the fish fry."

I interrupted him. "Well did you ask her if she wanted to go?"

Alex looked disappointed. "Yeah, I did, but she got pissed off."

Alex forced back his tears.

"Take your Alex, I'm here."

"My mother told me to get the hell out of the room."

"What!" I exclaimed. "It wasn't your fault."

Alex nodded. "I know Shanelle. Now that I think back on it, I guess she was mad at my father, but took it out on me. I knew she wanted to say those things to him but she couldn't. I even sat on the edge of the bed to console her, but she pushed me off. Grandma Mae's bed was real high, so I had to hang on to one of the posts to catch my fall."

Alex scratched his head with worry. "That bed was old and damn near ready for the junk yard, but Grandma Mae couldn't part with it. When I leaned on the post it toppled right over and landed on the floor. It was the loudest noise I ever heard Shanelle."

"Did you fix it?" I asked.

"It was a temporary, but it came in real handy that night."

This time I lay in Alex's lap hoping he could remain calm as he finished his story.

"Everybody went to the fish fry except my mother. She stayed behind with a bottle of wine and the daily newspaper. I felt sad that she didn't want to go, but I needed to watch out for my sisters, especially with Willie James around. It was so hot that day even with the lake around us. Everyone was laughing and having a good time singing songs and tellin' jokes. I tried to get into it Shanelle, but I couldn't. Every part of me felt like my mom did. I just wanted to go home."

Alex began to stroke my hairline with his hands.

"Grandma Mae asked me to run up to the house to pick up some more sugar for the lemonade and you know me, I was looking for something to do and I wanted to check on my mom. I felt bad and I was hoping she changed her mind. I hopped on my cousin's bike and headed up the hill back to the house. The dust from the road kept clogging my throat. I spit a few times to clear it, but that didn't work. By the time I got back, a strange silence seemed to kick in around me. Call it childhood police work, but I was curious about the surroundings of the house since everyone was down by the river. I dropped the bike by the front door and walked around the back."

Alex squeezed his eyes shut.

"When I looked up ahead, I thought I walked up on a dead animal being devoured by a bigger animal."

Alex gripped my head as he stared at the wall. I had to grab his hands to slow down his massage.

"My mother was leaned up against Grandma Mae's house tongue kissing Willie James."

My mouth gaped open in disbelief, but the look on his face negated my doubt.

"The next step I took was on a small twig. I threw up on the ground and damn near passed out. I don't know if it was the heat, the juice I drank, or my mother kissing Willie James. At least they stopped when they saw me."

"Are you ok Alex, you look sick."

Alex immediately shook his head to quiet my worry.

"Yeah, yeah, I'm fine baby; it just feels like it happened yesterday. I started to run towards the woods just to get away from them. Willie James was laughing out loud while my mother ran after me. He said, 'Oooooooohh weeee, look at that little piglet run. That's one fast youngin' you got there girl.'"

"Alex," I grieved, "I'm so sorry you had to see that, what were you thinking?"

Alex held his head in his hands again as he yelled out. "I wanted to kill that bastard!" His lips began to tremble. "Damn Shanelle, why did my mother do that? She followed me into the woods and Willie James came behind her with his stupid country ass saying, 'Boy don't you go worrying about grown folks business, your mama was just having a little fun.'"

With a gentle nudge to my shoulders, Alex stood up and slouched to the cabinet. He turned around and braced himself against the counter.

"I remembered facing Willie James and punching him dead in the jaw, but he didn't even flinch."

The tone in his voice changed. Alex looked out the kitchen window.

"I was surprised my mother could run so fast. She caught up to me and grabbed me like she never wanted to let go. Instead of hugging her, I pushed her to the ground. Willie James caught up to us and started laughing like a hyena. He looked at me and said, 'You little sissy, you ain't got no business pushin' yo mama like 'dat boy.'"

Alex closed the blinds and turned to face me as I sat up. "I ran up to him and clocked him right in the jaw again, but he acted like it didn't faze him."

I crossed my legs on the couch and folded my arms.

"What did he do next?"

"He picked one of his big ass bucked teeth off the ground and spit." Alex's shoulders bunched up with laughter. "My mother jumped up and said, 'Don't you talk to my son like that Willie, he was only trying to stop me from doing something stupid.'"

Alex's face instantly soured. His lips parted slightly with a quick breath. "Willie James walked off in a huff. We went back to Grandma Mae's house. I felt bad because my mother sprained her ankle from the fall. All she could do was apologize. Part of me wanted to forgive her and another part of me wanted to run."

Alex sucked his teeth and headed for the bathroom. "Take a shower with me angel," he ordered, "I need you right now."

Alex's command was my unconscious will. I left the unfinished story on the couch and took off my clothes. Alex's hands traveled up and down my back and legs. I lulled him into a quiet calm by turning up the water. He pulled me into his body and locked me down with a kiss. Whatever stress he had began to leave his body as he whispered my name.

"Shanelle, I need you so much."

I put my hands through his arms and held him tight. Pellets of water bounced off his shoulders as I looked up at him. Alex wrapped his arms around me and said, "I killed him Shanelle."

My body became numb.

"Killed who?"

Alex grabbed my hands and said, "Willie James, I killed Willie James." He began to tremble as I held his face and pleaded with him to tell me what happened. He finished showering off in silence as I stepped back to give him some space. I felt lost, scared and helpless. Alex wrapped himself in his towel and put a hand cloth over his head. He closed the toilet seat and sat down in perpetual shame.

"The fish fry lasted until the early morning. Most of the adults were so drunk; people were saying and doing things that didn't make sense. Grandma Mae fell asleep rockin' on the porch well into the morning and I stayed in the front room just to give my mother some space."

I began to dry off and spread lotion on my legs and arms as Alex shambled into the bedroom. He handed me one of his tee shirts and struggled through his vivid memories.

"I remembered falling asleep, but not long enough to fall into a deep sleep. There was movement in the house and a draft coming from one of the windows." Alex folded his hands.

"You know how you think you hear something when you're sleeping but you can't figure out if you're awake or dreaming?"

Yeah, that happens to me all the time."

Alex replied, "I stayed in bed for a while and decided to get up to see if my father came back. I thought it was him at first because I heard a commotion coming from Grandma Mae's room. I walked up to the door and noticed a man, but it wasn't my father. It was Willie James."

My lips parted in suspense. "What happened?"

"He was on top of my mother with his hands covering her mouth. That son of a bitch tried to rape her."

Alex shut his eyes tight and clenched his teeth.

"I ran into the room," he struggled, "I grabbed the post off of Grandma Mae's bed and busted his head wide open."

Fear draped my face as he stared at the floor.

"Alex, I'm so sorry."

He wrestled his fingers together and said, "There was blood everywhere. My mother was screaming so loud I thought she was going to wake up the whole town."

"What did you do?" I asked.

"We didn't do anything. My mother kept screaming until Grandma Mae came in the room with a broomstick ready to beat somebody. She looked around and said, 'What in the hell happened here?' It didn't take long for Grandma to gather her senses. She said, 'I aint' gonna make no judgments on you girl, but whatever happened, blood is on my grandbaby's hands.'"

Alex fixed his sight on the wall.

"She was right Shanelle; blood was all over me like splattered red paint."

I covered my mouth to bury my own screams. Alex quickly squeezed me tight, rubbing my arms. He rested his lips against my mine and said, "Shh, Shh, girl, I told you I had some hurdles, you do too, but we're gonna be okay, don't worry."

The whole thing sounded crazy as I paced the floor hurdling questions at him.

"What happened? Did you go to jail? What about your mother?"

Alex matched my footsteps and turned me around. His thick hand covered my mouth as he delicately whispered, "Nobody knows but us."

My eyes shifted back and forth like a confused lab rat.

"What do you mean just us?"

Alex replied, "It didn't take Grandma Mae more than a minute to declare herself the judge and jury for Pulaski. She made us wrap him up in three of her heaviest quilted blankets and two extension cords. Before we covered his face she did the craziest thing."

"What?" I asked.

"She spit in his mouth and pulled a lock of her hair out."

Alex paused briefly to collect his thoughts. "She told us that we had to bury our secret in the dark. The sun was coming up in an hour so she made us carry his body to the pick up truck. We drove a few acres onto her property and buried him in Grandma's animal grave."

My mouth sprung open. "No one ever asked for him Alex?"

"Shanelle," he nodded, "nobody cared. My grandmother said he was a raggedy ass no account man. He brought so much shame on the family; I think Grandma Mae was glad to see him go. It didn't matter to me though. As numb as I felt, all I could think about was the spectacular sunrise at dawn from the back of the pick up truck."

My stomach began to churn. I didn't know what he meant, but I was too exhausted to ask any more questions. Alex lay back on the bed and pulled me onto his chest.

"We went back to the house and cleaned Grandma's room from top to bottom. It wasn't until I dumped the last pail of bloody water down the drain that my father came through the door with a stupid grin on his drunken face. He looked at all of us and said, 'Well what the hell happened to y'all, did you slaughter a pig this morning?'"

Alex's hand trembled against his face as he described his mother's pain. "My mother ran up to him and started slapping and scratching him any place she could find bare skin. I wanted to jump in too, but all I could see was dried dirt and blood buried under my fingernails."

I mustered up the energy to ask one more question. "What about the body?"

Alex held his head with his eyes stiff and wide. "Its right there were we left it, in the animal cemetery. No one knows but my father, mother, Grandma Mae, me and now you."

My body stiffened as if I had been inducted into a deadly cult of sin and abysmal secrets. I laid next to Alex in silence, stroking the soft hairs on his chest. I couldn't get up if I wanted to. He used the tips of his fingers to fondle my neck ringing a commitment in my ear. "Shanelle, promise me you'll never leave me."

"I love you Alex and I'll never leave you no matter what."

Oddly enough, he laughed, confidently stroking his chin.

"I know you won't baby, that's why I'm gonna make you my wife and the mother of my children. I felt like God gave me a second chance when I saw you at the wedding. I was trying to atone for my sins until God gave me a sign that it was going to be alright. That sign was you Shanelle."

I snuggled into him as his words melted my soul. Nothing mattered with Alex, even things that were beyond his control. Alex squeezed my hand.

"Girl, having you in my life is like sweet redemption." Alex shifted his head as we lay in the warmth of the afternoon sun and asked, "Is there anything about us that you want to change Shanelle?"

"I don't know what you mean Alex."

Alex cleared his throat, "I had to tell you about my life so you could really understand how much you mean to me. You deserve your own downtime if you need it Shanelle."

My focus shifted to my stomach. Everyone seemed to have a claim on its shape and the progress going on inside. I wanted to answer him immediately and say, *"Please, spare me with the baby stuff,"* but that was too risky. His words made me feel queasy.

"Shanelle, so far I've lead this entire relationship, but I want you to let me know if it's too much."

Blinking twice a wishing well appeared. The sheet crushed beneath me as I faced him.

"I want to be everything you need me to be Alex, but I'm not ready to give you a son."

Alex began to stroke the back of my head.

"That's a rough one Shanelle, but I understand after what happened yesterday. I promise not to put too many demands on you."

I wondered what forced him to change his mind so quickly but there were other emotional barriers to work on. Alex sat up and said, "I didn't forget what your brother said about the peanut butter."

Dumbfounded, I began to scoot to the edge of the bed. Alex grabbed my arm.

"C'mon now Shanelle, I'm not here to judge you, but don't lie to me. Toothpaste? Peanut butter? I have sisters too," he gruffed, crossing his arms. "I'll tell you one thing; you need to work that out before you get pregnant."

My once comforting wishing well dried up to dust. My common tears fell leaving no room to hide. Alex sat next to me and handed me a Kleenex from the box on the nightstand. I realized the one thing that could get by him was the voices in my head, but for how long was anyone's guess. Alex covered us with a sheet as the warmth of the afternoon rested my weary eyes. My deep settling sleep was enhanced with the notion of putting motherhood on hold. Little did I know my body was engineering a different plan. The reality of making love to Alex on that warm 4th of July day without a condom began to take flight. As we lay in each other's arms, deep inside the core of my womb, an embryo was fashioned from a fertilized egg. My innate need to sleep fostered the early signs of life that Alex so desperately craved.

Splendor in Paradise

Just as Alex planned, on the third week of our vacation, we boarded a non-stop Continental Airlines flight to Nassau, Bahamas. There was very little conversation because I was overcome with dumfounded sleep. Alex shook my shoulders to witness the view of the crystal clear water as we landed at the Bahamas International Airport. The only thing that consumed my thoughts was a good meal and my tight pants. Alex glanced at my apparent preoccupation using his pointer finger as a reference.

"Yeah, you filled out a little," he pitched, "but I like the new you."

I tried to fix my clothes but abandoned the idea as the sound of steel drums greeted us at customs. There were a few slinky girl wonders behind us giggling and chatting about their soon to be exploits on the island. One of them accidentally bumped into Alex, bending her wrist as she tip toed back with apologies. Alex barely flinched as he planted his arm around my waist.

"This way babe, we're almost done."

His hand left my side and locked into mine. Alex looked down with a reassuring grin.

"I love you Shanelle."

It was all the strength I needed. Alex hailed a taxi and quickly ushered me inside. My future husband acted like a native Bahamian as he chatted with the driver. Our transportation came to a halt at a local fruit stand. Straining my eyes against the blaring heat of the sun, I watched Alex stock up before we got to the villas. As he paid his tab, the driver leaned his head back.

"Chile, you in the Bahamas, there's no time for sleepin' less you got baby."

I sat up wiping away sweat from my brow.

"No sir, not me, we're getting married."

His head jerked forward.

"If you say so."

Alex didn't' entertain our conversation as he bit into his fruit. He pressed his head against mine and asked, "Do you want a bite?" I shook my head no as the driver wittingly replied, "That's how Adam got in trouble man."

A warm chuckled suspended our time as Alex tipped the driver at the villa's regal entrance. One bag hoisted on his shoulder. He smiled throwing his shoulders back at attention. Slight annoyance riddled his face.

"Are you planning on sleeping the whole trip Shanelle?"

Before I could answer, a familiar face and flailing arms barreled out of villa number two.

"Shanelle!"

"Candy!" I gleefully yelled.

Our mad dash led us straight to the sandy ground. Alex brushed residue from his pants.

"Damn, I don't get that kind of a reception."

Candy jumped up happily grabbing my face.

"You lied," I chuckled. "I thought you weren't coming!"

"And miss your big day? I don't think so."

Bearing a wide grin and confident gait, Candy turned for a formal introduction.

"This is Clinton everyone, that's Shanelle of course and her fiancé, Alex."

The two of them gave each other dap like they knew each other from back in the day. I quickly caught Candy looking at my midsection and smacked her arm. She noticed the look on my face and pinched my cheek.

"Hey," Candy said, "Let's go inside where it's cooler." I grabbed her hand to follow, but Alex had other plans.

"Yeah, but let me get settled with Shanelle and we'll hook up in three hours for dinner."

Clinton nodded his head in approval as he started pulling Candy back to her villa. I waved goodbye to my girl like old times. She was the perfect surprise for our wedding.

Alex and I checked in at the registration desk amidst a small crowd of young couples in the lobby. There was nothing I needed to do except wait for him to take care of everything. I looked at some brochures and surveyed some of the tourist attractions. The flight and cab ride began to overwhelm me. My feet and hands felt tight and heavy. Alex handed me the paperwork and room keys as the bellhop loaded our luggage onto the cart. By the time we got back to the room, I was ready to pass out. Alex took one look at me and said, "Shanelle, you need to eat something, you slept the entire flight remember?"

"I know, I know. Can I order from room service?"

"Sure, you don't have to ask Shanelle, get whatever you want."

I surveyed the menu and ordered a garden salad but Alex wasn't satisfied. "Shanelle, order some food, a salad isn't going to fill you up."

I grabbed some fruit and said, "I'll be fine, I'll make up for it at dinner, I promise." I traipsed into the bathroom to wash my face and hands before I took a shower. Alex didn't get in with me like he usually did. Instead, he chose to lean against the sink and watch. He left for five minutes and came back with a towel and handed it to me.

"Your food is here. I added some chicken breast to your meal Slim Jim."

Funny, I didn't feel slim, but I knew I had to go along with the program. Alex sat on the bed and turned on the TV while I ate at the table.

"Feeling better?" he asked, removing my towel and tossing it to the floor. "I want you Shanelle."

"I want you too," I gushed, looking around. "Did you bring any condoms?"

"No," he quickly laughed. "Did you get your period yet?"

Puzzled, my hands gripped my waist. "I don't think this is about whether or not I'm getting my period, I thought we agreed."

"We did," Alex lightly chuckled, "but from the looks of things, you may not get your period."

"Stop playing Alex, that's not funny."

He pulled me closer, dropping his tone to a whisper. His head nestled against my neck.

"I know what we said mommy, but it may be too late."

I got off the bed and went into the bathroom, slamming the door behind me. The mirror presented no clues or revelations. I looked the same, except for the swelling. My skin looked clear and my eyes didn't look so dark.

"He can't be right. I'll talk to Candy about it later."

Alex knocked on the bathroom door in rapid successions.

"Are you okay mommy?"

"Stop calling me that," I snapped.

"Ok, babe, but I still want you."

"Okay, I'm coming," I yawned as I scurried out of the bathroom. Alex continued to stare.

"What?"

His shoulders jerked up and down. He pinched my chin and recited, "Absolutely nothing, I love you and you're all mine."

Alex took a shower while I stretched across the bed. Before I knew it he was peeling away at my tee shirt and panties with his teeth and hands. I pushed his head away sliding sideways off the bed.

"I need to use the bathroom." He picked his head up and said, "Make it quick, we're going to dinner at six."

I ran to sanctuary and shut the door. This time the mirror told a different story. I didn't realize how much weight I put on in the last two weeks. We never bothered to work out with all the planning to get to the island. My breasts and stomach looked extremely swollen.

"Maybe it's the food."

The voices had a different version.

"Don't even think about it. I think you've just made Alex a happy man."

Defeated, I dragged my body to the foot of the bed, locking hands with him. A hollow ache filled my heart.

"Pregnant?"

Alex thrust himself inside of me. He whispered my name and rocked me in his own pleasing rhythms. I called his name when he asked me to, but it was only to please him. Nothing made sense to me as he came inside of me.

"A baby?"

My head crushed the pillows beneath me. Alex slipped his tongue in my mouth, moaning in delight.

"I don't want a baby. What about school?"

"Don't ever leave me girl," he uttered, settling his rush.

I pulled my lips away from his. "I won't, I promise."

Quiet Reflection

After making love to Alex and one full hour of sleep, I was in no condition to go out. Since the villa included a full service kitchen, I made some tea and went to the back patio. It was already 5:00 pm and the sun was settling over the Caribbean waters. A small white table and chair was my resting place as I kicked my sandals off and got settled. There was a full ocean view in front of me to reflect on my life in its entirety. Something stirred inside of me to check on him. After a brief peek through the curtains, it was clear that he was in no condition to go out either. I kissed his forehead and covered his shoulders with the sheet. He looked so content and safe in our little world. The trauma he experienced was far worse than mine and I imagined that our quiet existence was all he wanted. I stroked my collar bone and wondered what we would have to go through to cope despite the secrets we shared. I wanted to put the past of Crescent Avenue behind, but I knew that Alex's dilemma would have lifelong consequences. Now that I knew, I wondered if I had the stuff to keep him settled and happy.

I returned to the patio and leaned against the doorway. The beauty of the ocean and its accompanied breeze was so relaxing I was convinced that we should never leave the island. I held my face up to let the sun bask against my cheeks. I sat down and observed my rising stomach.

"With classes starting in September, could I really be pregnant?"

We only used a condom on July 4th, but after he slipped the ring on my finger, we made love again without using one. I guess in Alex's mind I was his and that was that. My mind shifted focus as I looked at the crashing waves coming on shore in a thunderous applause. The water was as daunting as my life; small waves rifling towards shore, suddenly being sucked back into a more powerful force. Powerless to the elements, baby bubbles surfaced and quickly dissipated as the large swell took over. The house on Crescent Avenue claimed me mentally, *had Alex done the same?* I wanted a donut, smudged over with peanut butter.

"Damn Shanelle, why did you make those promises?" I loved him too much not to, but did I have a choice? I took a deep breath and watched the swell of my midsection rise and fall. Suddenly, a warm hand gripped my shoulder. A soft kiss molded my cheek. Alex knelt down next to me.

"Can't sleep?"

I stroked his face. "No babe, just thinking."

Alex convinced me to make a mad dash for the bathroom to get dressed for dinner. I pulled my hair back in a ponytail and grabbed a sundress. It was tight but bearable as he rushed me with a blaring tone.

"Hurry up Shanelle, I told them dinner at six o'clock."

"I'm coming!" I shouted, "I need to get my sandals on." Embarrassing as it was, Alex had to fasten them for me as I rested on his hips. He slid his hands up my legs and grabbed his treasure. I pushed him away angry and curt.

"Stop. Is that all you can think about?"

Alex backed up, letting my ankle slip away.

"Let's go."

Candy's face was a breath of fresh air once we got outside. She hugged me and said, "You look cute."

"You're gorgeous as ever Candy," I sang back with charm.

Clinton rolled his eyes in Alex's direction.

"C'mon man, let's sit up front so they can compliment each other all night."

We boarded the minivan and took an evening tour before dinner. The bumps and gaps in the road knocked our shoulders together.

"What's wrong?" Candy asked, "You don't look like you're going to be married in two days."

"Not now Candy," I whispered. There was nowhere for me to go and I was in no position to say no to the idea. As we exited the vehicle, Alex extended his hands.

"Still mad?"

"No, just a little confused."

Alex put his arms around my shoulders. Reservation tackled his thoughts as he cracked his neck. "I've got cold feet too, but we're going to work this out. No secrets right?" A long pause filled the space between us. He pulled me towards the beach and glared into my eyes.

"Tell me you don't love me Shanelle. Tell me that I didn't wait a whole year to make love to you for the first time. Tell me that I haven't been there for you through school, your bills, your brother, the weight thing and now the food issue. Tell me now and I'll leave you alone."

My face anchored to the sand. The island breeze, along with Alex's cinnamon complexion did nothing but enhance his love for me. I grabbed him around his waist and blurted, "I'm sorry."

A sigh of relief rushed from his full lips.

"No need to apologize baby. Let's eat and you are going to eat."

The four of us sat down to a splendid dinner complete with lobster, grouper fish, conch fritter, cabbage and rice and peas. I was in seventh heaven as I sampled Candy and Alex's plate after heartily eating my own. Alex smiled at me in sheer delight while Candy watched me in dietary horror.

"Shanelle," Candy jerked forward, "When are you going to come up for air?"

Alex quickly rescued me, chomping in between his sentence. His pinky finger pointed in her direction coupled with a reassuring wink.

"Leave her alone, she's hungry."

Candy besmirched my high pitched giggles.

"Let's go to the bathroom girlfriend," she ordered. As light as she was, Candy flung me into the bathroom with an attitude.

"So, what's up girlfriend, you lost your mind or something? Alex is damn near finishing your sentences. Even Clinton said that you're not the person I described. Who's calling the shots?" Candy was ruthless. My formidable past crept into my neck as I swept my sleeves.

"Girl, do you know what you're doing?" asked Candy.

"Yeah."

"Shanelle I don't know whether to smack you or buy you a pregnancy test."

"I'm still going to school in September," I pleaded, wrenching my hands, "I didn't forget my plans."

One tear spilled from my face as she wiped it away.

"Loving Alex is a good thing, but don't let him dictate everything Shanelle."

"You're right Candy," I said. "Let's go back to the table."

When we returned, Alex and Clinton were joking about sports. They stood up to assist us back to our seats.

"Anyone care for dessert?" Alex asked.

We all responded in unison, "No!" The spontaneous comment brought brevity to the room as Alex stood up and asked me to dance. I took his hands as he led me to the floor.

"In one day lady," he courted with a smile, "you and me, man and wife, how does that sound?"

"Sounds wonderful."

"Are you sure you don't mind waking up to this face every morning?"

Blushing in between my gaze and bat of an eye I replied, "Nope, I don't mind at all."

I rested my head on his chest as the Caribbean rhythms swayed our bodies to and fro. Clinton and Candy held their glasses up as Alex held me close. The music, food and warmth of his embrace were all the comfort I needed.

Wedding Day

The sun rose on our wedding day with deliberate impatience, bursting through our sheer curtains and warming our tangled frames. I woke up to the sound of the phone ringing. It was Candy whispering in the earpiece. "Shanelle, come to my villa, Clinton went for a jog and I need to see you."

Alex was fast asleep as I untangled myself from his heavy grip. In lightening speed, I threw on one of his tee shirts and ran to villa number two. When I opened the door, Candy flashed a box in her hand. She turned it over in the palm of my hand.

"Pee on it now."

"EPT?" I asked.

"Yeah, an early pregnancy test. Take it," she demanded.

We rushed into the bathroom. Candy opened the package and said, "Don't fuck this one up, this damn thing cost forty bucks out here."

I put the stick into the stream. Candy placed toilet tissue on the counter top. "Put it down."

As the toilet began to flush, we watched the liquid spread across the lines. Two purple lines popped up. Candy's eyebrows rose to the occasion.

"What?" I asked.

"You're pregnant."

I grabbed the stick. "Let me see that box." Just as I began to read the instructions, a knock jolted the door.

"Shit," Candy jumped, "its Alex."

I quickly wiped myself and pulled my tee shirt down as the sound of Alex's flip flops headed through the front door.

"Is Shanelle here?" he asked.

"Yeah, she's in the bathroom."

Alex emerged and surveyed the coral décor.

"What's up, everything ok?" he questioned.

"Yeah, everything's fine."

"What's that?" He asked, pointing at the box in my hand.

Candy stood in the doorway folding her arms.

"It's a pregnancy test."

"Oh," Alex replied, scratching his head. He leaned against the tile wall with the palm of his hand.

"Well?"

"Well what?" I replied.

"Did you pass the test?" He turned around and looked at Candy. She shrugged her shoulders and backed off.

Alex closed the door and quickly pursued me as I backed into the sink. He looked down and grabbed my face.

"Tell me Shanelle, you're killing me."

"I'm pregnant."

Alex dropped to his knees and kissed my stomach in fifteen places. "Look at you! I knew it, I knew it, but I didn't want to say anything until I was sure. You just made me the happiest man in the world!"

Alex picked me up and carried me out of Candy's villa as she watched us in slow motion. Clinton was coming in from his jog as Alex exclaimed, "Man this is my lucky day!"

Clinton gave us the peace sign as he closed the door after our exit. When we got back to our villa, Alex laid me on the bed and squeezed the life out of me. "Girl, do you know how happy I am right now?"

I stroked his face and answered, "Happy indeed."

Alex rubbed his hands along my stomach as he sang a lullaby to his little seedling. He looked ridiculous, but I didn't say a word. I was amazed how such news gave him so much fulfillment, yet made me feel hollow and empty. When he finished, I got up, laid my white sundress out like nothing happened. Alex was in the shower singing and humming away all of his past sins and aggression. As he sang, my little island friends popped up to greet me. The Little One said, *"Barefoot, fat and pregnant."* The Big One replied, *"She's going to pack it on too, at least fifty pounds."*

I hoisted my dress in the air so it could fall flat on the bed for ironing.

"That test was wrong, my period is coming, I can feel it."

"Did you say something Shanelle?" Alex asked of my flighty conversation.

"No, I didn't say anything."

He grabbed me from behind and pressed his hands into my stomach.

"Today is our big day mommy."

"It sure is." I replied.

By 11:00 am we were standing before Reverend Timothy Simons. With his bible in tow, we took our vows before God, Candy, Clinton and the reverend's three children. His youngest daughter was five months old and cute as a button. I was attuned to the ceremony, but I couldn't help looking at her little hands and feet in the hot sun. She started to get fussy, so her older sister carried her into the house for a nap. The distraction gave me enough time to tune in to our nuptials.

"Do you Shanelle Brown take Alex Foster to be your lawful husband, to have and to hold from this day forward till death do you part?"

"I do," I replied. The cool wind forced some of the petals free from my gardenias sending them to the ground. Candy and I simultaneously watch them slip away and land onto the grass.

"You may now kiss the bride."

Alex obliged with a bear hungry tongue kiss, quickly surfing my ample ass with a subtle squeeze. It was as simple as that. Candy kissed me, Clinton hugged me and Alex smiled the whole time. There were no fireworks, orchestra or proud parents. The whole thing felt so surreal. I wondered if I was dreaming.

I had to say goodbye to Candy three hours after the ceremony. Clinton and Candy had to get back to Pittsburg. They didn't have the luxury of time that Alex and I had. She squeezed my hand in the back seat of the taxi and joked about our unexpected news.

"I'm not changing diapers unless it's a girl." Candy fussed.

Alex turned around as I gazed out the window. My engagement ring and delicate gold wedding band did little to ease my stigma. I remained quiet all the way to the airport as Alex occasionally looked back and winked. At the terminal, Alex and Clinton shook hands and exchanged business cards. Candy pulled me out of my trance and forced a smile on my face.

"I know you're going to miss me, but you'll be fine. School will be over in October and we'll be on the move in no time."

Her words did little to comfort me.

"How can I with a big ole belly?" I asked.

Candy pinched my cheek and hugged me. "Girl, you're going to be ok. Alex is a good man and he'll take care of you, just don't forget what I said. You have a voice too you know."

My eyes rested on the ground. "I know, I know. But listen, don't forget Alex is leaving Monday and I'll be by myself for a whole month. Call me."

Candy waved me off with the airline tickets flapping in the breeze. "Okay, I won't forget."

When we got back to the villa, Alex had the back deck decorated with white candles. Pink and white flower petals adorned the pool. A lobster dinner was waiting for our consumption.

"This is beautiful Alex, thank you."

"Anything for you Shanelle, let's eat."

We sat by the poolside as Alex made my plate. I poured wine for him and spring water for myself. I decided to exercise some self-assertiveness and said, "Hopefully my course schedule will be there when we get home. I signed up for International Politics and a creative writing workshop, I hope I got in."

"That's good," Alex replied.

"There's also a peer leadership class with a young professor from Rutgers, they say she's really good too."

"Oh yeah?" Alex asked.

I took a bite of some bread and said, "Eighteen credits is a heavy load, but I'm sure I'll manage."

Alex looked down at my feet and said, "You should put your feet up, they look swollen."

"They are, but I'm fine."

Alex took a deep breath. "We need to find a good doctor in the area, you need an appointment."

I looked down at my plate of food and swallowed.

"I've been cramping a lot lately; I think my period is late."

He took a sip of his wine. "Sounds like implantation to me."

"Implantation?" I asked. "What's that?"

"Oh, just our little one settling in, Mary had the same thing with my nephew."

"Oh."

Alex took another sip. "If it gets too much for you, you may want to drop a class or…"

"Oh no," I interrupted with a raised palm, "I'm going full steam ahead, I want to graduate in four years Alex, not five, or even six."

"Ok, ok," Alex replied. "I was only looking out for you and the baby's best interest."

I pushed my plate of food away. "I'm not hungry anymore."

Silence accompanied Alex's slow sip of wine. He put his glass down and wiped his moist lips as he continued to stare at me. He removed his tie and started unbuttoning his shirt. "Get in the pool with me Shanelle."

I looked at the water. It was warm and inviting as the moon shined against the rippling element. Alex stood up and dove into the deep end. He went underwater for a minute and came up for air.

"Get in mommy," Alex reiterated.

A steel drum band was playing in the distance as he extended his hand. "Don't make me wait baby, come here."

I started to take off my clothes, but he held up his hand. "No, I'll take them off."

Beads of water rolled off his handsome face as I stepped into the water. My dress bellowed up to the surface as Alex lifted it over my head. He bit into my breast as I grabbed his head. There was an intense tingling sensation that I never felt before. I enjoyed it, but it felt different. Alex began to kiss me as I held him tight. He hoisted my leg up and placed it around his waist. When our eyes met, I muffled, "I'm scared Alex. I don't know how to do all of this stuff, especially baby stuff. We were supposed to put this on the back burner remember?"

He pressed his forehead against mine. "I remember," he sympathetically toned, "but it happened already and there's no turning back right?"

"Right." I hushed.

Alex breathed a sigh of relief wiping water residue off my lips.

"Well then let's enjoy our time together. We have two days left on the island and we're going to enjoy it."

I started to yawn. "Sounds like a great idea." I stepped out of the pool and wrapped a towel around my body. Alex went to the kitchen area and placed a call back to the states. My eyes began to close the minute my head hit the pillow. I could hear Alex's conversation as he cleared his throat. The elation in his voice bellowed like a stadium microphone.

"Hey mom. Yeah, everything's fine, it's official. Shanelle? She's resting right now and for a good reason. No, I'm not kidding, she took a pregnancy test today. No kidding, I swear ma. Yeah, that is good news. What? No, we'll be back on Monday morning. No, we have a few things to straighten out, but she'll be fine. I know, I know ma, I'll tell her tomorrow. Right… Well she can drink orange juice until she sees the doctor. Ma? Before you hang up, I want you to know that I told Shanelle…, Ma, I had to tell her. She won't judge you ma, trust me, we'll be fine. Listen, I got to go, it's my honeymoon you know. I love you too… bye."

Alex quietly returned the phone to the base and shuffled around the kitchen. He sat on the bed and gently smoothed my satin gown along the side of my hip. He ran his hand down and around my stomach with the tips of his fingers. He kissed my cheek and said, "I love you Shanelle Foster." I balled up into a tight fetal position.

"He really does love me."

Sure, maybe I was too worn out for romance, but I knew he would understand. There was simply too much information in my brain sending me into mental overload. Besides, if I was pregnant, it only supported my need to sleep.

The sound of chatty birds woke me up at 8:00 am. Alex was already up and about, sitting on the deck reading the newspaper.

After a quick shower and ponytail prep, we headed out to Johnnie Canoe's for breakfast. Conch fritters, scrambled eggs and cantaloupe decorated my plate as I ate with smooth precision. I was surprised at how hungry I was as Alex beamed with pride. I didn't dare resist when he poured orange juice in my glass.

"Folic acid is the best thing for you right now mommy."

"Are you going to call me mommy from now on?" I asked.

"Yeah, it suits you perfectly; besides, you're too cute."

Slow sips preceded his comment.

"I'm glad to see you eating Shanelle."

I picked up a piece of his biscuit.

"Me too." A brief pause followed as I searched for the bathroom.

"I need to use the restroom," I said. My demise was cool and calculated as I headed for the door.

"Quick, wash your hands."

The first stall looked spotless as I went inside. Kneeling down, I held onto the toilet bowl handle, put my face over the bowl and with one swift action, I shoved my pointer finger down the back of my throat forcing up the goopy substance.

"Good one Shanelle," the Little One said, *"You can blame this on morning sickness too."* I closed my eyes and rested the palm of my hand on my forehead. My face felt hot and flushed. A woman skidded inside as I exited the stall. The rush of the cold water out of the basin relieved my dizziness and brought me back to focus. I felt much better as I patted water on my face. Pulps of orange juice sat on my gums as I rinsed my mouth three times.

"Are you okay miss?" The kind woman asked.

"Yes, I'm fine, thank you."

When I staggered out, the Big One griped, *"Wish you could spit that little bastard up inside you too, huh missy?"*

I shook my head, quickly returning to the table.

"What's got your face all turned up?" Alex asked.

"Nothing, my stomach is just a little upset," I replied.

"Oh." He remained fixed on my flushed face.

"Upset my ass," the Little One said.

"Are you ready Alex?" I asked, patting the corners of my mouth. His napkin fell on the table.

"Sure, let's go."

We caught a taxi to the Artasda Zoo to see the famous flamingo run. It was cute, but the warm swell of the Bahamian sun beating down on us sent me into a dizzy spell. Purging was a bad move. Alex carried me by piggyback and hailed a taxi. Once we settled in, my husband ordered some crackers to settle my stomach and put a cool compress on my head.

"We're staying in for the rest of the trip," Alex said. "I don't need you getting sick away from home."

I didn't want to be sick, pregnant or pampered. A good nap was all I needed. Alex ordered two turkey sandwiches and fresh fruit. It was a good choice because I was starving and didn't want to admit it to him.

Alex sat down next to me and gently put his hand on my thigh. "Is that okay?" He asked.

"What?" I replied.

"Touching you like that?"

I put my hand on his face.

"Don't be silly, of course you can."

"Funny," Alex remarked, "I did that the other night and you damn near took my head off."

"You're right."

"Well how will I know, because the other night didn't sit right with me."

I took a sip of water and looked at him. "Just ask."

Alex stood up and planted a kiss on my forehead. "I'm getting in the pool. Oh, I'm also asking."

"Okay, give me a minute, I'm coming." I thought to myself, *"Mr. Foster is smooth, very smooth."*

Alex left the sliding glass door open and began to do laps. I wanted to finish eating and sit for a minute while he waited. A small notepad and pen was sitting on the table. I turned it around to see what he wrote.

"Dr. Robinson, obstetrics. Well isn't he the eager beaver."

I tore away his notes and put it aside for safe keeping. Another small piece of paper glared at me with serious repercussions well beyond my control. I needed to write something for myself. A poem or even a song would have settled my strange reality. So much had happened in the last few weeks; I wondered how I would remain sane for myself and the little piece of life inside of me. The title came quickly as I watched Alex methodically cut the waters surface with his lean arms.

The Dance

I left a cold place a brief time ago,
an abyss of cruel intentions.
A beautiful place became me
in the warmth of cinnamon arms.
perhaps my naïveté suppressed
a tale of unspeakable wrath,
hidden among the maple trees,
down a horrendous path.
Innocence is a place I found,
wherever sorrow appears.
Tucked away in mental anguish,
Buried in a million tears.
A delicate hand rests inside his
sweet and protective touch.
Security forces surrender.
Your love means so much.
You lead, I follow,
A dance among stars.
A tiny seed grows within.
Determination my love,
how lucky you are.
Is this a paradox?
A rare treasure?
Only two should know.
Appearing so confident,
hidden emotions ebb to and fro.
The path beside me so complex,
a delicate life strengthens and grows.
The maiden sighs today,
it settles beneath her brow.
He who ponders deadly sacrifices,

hand in hand we take a bow.
She awaits...
Time...
Perpetuity...
He waits...
Seasoned...
Perhaps too secure,
Alex my husband, now and forever more.

I signed it Shanelle Foster, the first time I ever accepted my new married identity. I left it on the table for Alex to read and joined him in the pool. He was at the opposite end when I stepped inside. The forced temperature upon my skin made my nipples hard as goose bumps rose up my arms and legs. He said nothing, but stared. I backed up against the edge and rested my arms on the pool's edge. He looked at me with a devilish grin and went under as I watched his body swan out to my side. The sound of the water rippling between us was the perfect orchestra. Alex took my bra and panties off, placing it on the edge of the pool as he bit my breasts. A sharp pain ripped through me as I grabbed his head. He picked me up and carried me out of the pool and onto the bed soaking wet. Alex buried his face in Kitty and rocked her into a sweet melody. He turned me over and kissed the small of my back and ran his hands up and down my legs as I called his name. He bit my back as he entered me and ran his hand up the nape of my neck and hair. The feeling was so intense, unlike anything I had ever felt before. His words were unforgettable.

"Shanelle, you feel so good, I'll die for you girl."

My body began to shiver as I released my own pleasure onto him. Alex flipped me over and continued to grind me. Soon after, he collapsed on top of me. The weight of his body was too heavy, especially on my stomach.

Alex quickly rolled off. He placed his hand on my stomach with shaken worry.

"I forgot did I hurt you?"

My lower lip poked out as I grabbed his face.

"No, we're fine."

He smiled, sitting up to face me.

"I like the sound of that. Do you think you're coming to terms with this?"

I wiped my forehead with the palm of my hand. "I don't have much of a choice do I?"

Alex immediately got off the bed. His heavy feet pounded towards the shower.

"Shanelle!" Alex ordered.

"Yes," I replied.

"Get in here."

"Excuse me?" I asked.

Silence followed. I didn't like the tone in his voice, or the way he called me. Anything that sounded like the path I used to follow needed immediate rejection. The only thing I couldn't reject was his baby. I looked at the swell of my stomach. After the orgasm I had, it seemed to double in size. I went to the bathroom hoping to see Aunt Flo, but she was nowhere to be found even after the pounding Alex gave me. He peeked through the shower curtain.

"Shanelle, it kills me when you say things like that. Do you know how happy I am? Damn, it's like everything is going my way."

"That's just it Alex, everything is going your way. But how about my way? Or better yet, how about our way? I'm starting my sophomore year in college and you're leaving for a month, why does it seem like I'm carrying the brunt of all of this, babies, books and missing you."

"Whoa, whoa, Shanelle," Alex shouted, vigorously scrubbing his head as he yelled over the stream of water, "The last time I checked, I was heading out the door everyday to put you through school. I'm not asking you to give that up, we need that."

"Yeah, but you're trying to break me down to nine credits and sleep exhaustion. I would have preferred to go full steam ahead without,"

Alex stepped out. The eyes of a grizzly bear faced me.

"Without what Shanelle? Are you trying to tell me some-thing?"

I sat down on the toilet defeated. "There's nothing left to say Alex."

"Damn," he lamented, grabbing my upper arms. "Look at us having our first argument on our honeymoon. I don't want to do this."

"Me either." I saddened.

"You punk," The Little One teased.

"Let's order some ice cream from room service, I need something sweet," Alex mumbled.

The order came in five minutes. We ate my favorite chocolate chip mint with hot fudge. The last remnants of a honeymoon left us that night as the real world rolled in. Alex crossed his ankles and leaned against the headboard with the remote skillfully locked in his hands. I placed my bowl of ice cream on my swollen tummy and wolfed down cold spoonfuls. We left sentences unresolved. Emotional entanglement rested between us in the form of two pillows. I got up to brush my teeth while Alex hurled his first post wedding verbal assault.

"Leave me some toothpaste Shanelle."

I cut him a look like a woman possessed.

"He's on top of his game tonight," The Big One jabbed, as I stared down at a full tube of Crest. Alex came into the bathroom, pretending to look for something. He brushed against me just to make his presence known.

"Looking for something?" I asked.

He stood behind me and placed his hands on my hips. After he kissed my neck he said, "Yeah, my dental floss."

I picked it up and handed it to him. I took his other hand off my hip and flitted out. The heavy comforter was a quiet surrender for the night. I didn't want him near me anymore. Parts of me felt hurt on the inside. The other parts looked for repressed places to hide. Alex climbed into bed and snuggled next to me. He tugged and pulled until we fit like a perfect puzzle piece. I was still angry at him, but his hands softened the places that hurt. His antidote for the evening was forgiveness. He palmed my swollen stomach with his right hand.

"I love you Shanelle."

Back to Reality

It felt good to reach home. It was late when we arrived and Alex had to leave the following morning. He went through the mail and sorted mine into a small pile. I shuffled through the letters looking for my fall class schedule from St. James University.

"Hey Alex, I got all of my classes."

"That's good," he replied. A phone call for Alex interrupted my moment. "What's up mom? Yeah, we just got in."

His tone softened. "I missed you too." His next response was my demise.

"A crib? It's a little early to be talking about that ma, besides we just got back from our honeymoon."

I shifted through the letters like an oversized deck of cards with no Joker in sight.

"That's right dammit, stop sweatin' a crib, ask me how I'm doing or something. Shit, talk about the weather if you must." I laughed on the inside. I found it difficult to act like a new wife or a lady in waiting. Grandma was on the other line, setting up shop like I was starring in Rosemary's ugly ass baby.

"I'll look at it later." Alex hung up the phone and chuckled.

"Can you believe my mother?" He asked. "She's already passing down antique baby furniture."

"I hate antique anything."

Alex cut me a stern glare.

"Our baby is going to have brand new everything anyway." He stood behind me and wrapped his arms around my waist. "And you're going to need maternity clothes right?"

I pushed his hands away and snapped, "No!"

"Shanelle, you complained your clothes were too tight…"

I didn't let him finish. "Well, I'll just buy some bigger clothes." I pulled and tugged at my shirt in two different directions and then looked at the bathroom for sanctuary. "I need to pee."

Alex rolled his eyes.

"Thanks for sharing."

The full-length mirror behind the bathroom door was calling my name. I closed the wooden frame and immediately removed my clothes. After my eating fest in the Bahamas, I looked like a swollen cow. There was no curvature in my waist. My breasts were swollen two times their original size and my thighs were stuck together. My shoulders sagged to enhance the disfigured image I saw in the mirror. In two short weeks, the tiny being inside of me and my uncontrollable eating habits held my body hostage. Looking away for a minute offered no resolve as the voices began to giggle. I turned to the side. My ass ballooned out so big, I was sure Alex's nephews would ask for a ride sidesaddle.

"Step right up ladies and gentleman. Get your three dollar ticket to see Shanelle's big ass."

I closed my eyes to think it away, but the ugly image was still there. *"Damn,"* I thought, *"How am I going to cover this shit up?"* I got so angry, I contemplated breaking the mirror, but a small tap at the door quickly resolved that thought.

"Shanelle, are you okay in there?"

In a defeated voice I replied, "I'm fine."

Alex's next question could have ignited world war three.

"That was a long trip, are you hungry?"

I mimicked his question with my lips, swaying my head to and fro, "Are you hungry are you hungry?" My hands rested on my hips.

"Well?" He asked.

"No, I'm fat enough as it is."

Alex sucked his teeth. "Look, stop acting like a baby and come out of the bathroom."

"I'm not acting like a baby, I'm having one, remember?"

"Well, I'll tell you one thing, you're not going to get any smaller in there. Besides, I'm leaving in the morning and we need to go over some things."

I don't know why I did it, but I opened the door so Alex could see me in all of my fat naked glory. Alex raised his arms in the air and reached out to me.

"You look good to me juicy girl, so don't think you're going to get any sympathy."

He fell to his knees and kissed my stomach in ten places. "What's up Pumpy? It's me, Daddy."

I put my hand on his head.

"Pumpy? Where did that come from?"

"That's my son's nick name. I know he's going to be a big one."

The ceiling became my focus.

"This is unreal."

A smack on my ass followed.

"Like I said, you'll be ok, mommy." He picked me up just to prove his manhood.

"Damn girl, you're still a lightweight." We plopped on the couch. Alex took off his tee shirt and put it over my head. He knew I loved his scent, especially at the end of the day. Even after a smelly plane ride, I was still enticed by the smell of his clothes. The last thing I wanted him to do was leave. I cupped his face and kissed his lips as he spoke to me.

"Listen; don't forget to pay the cable and public service. Whatever expenses you need for school has to be paid by check. I left five hundred dollars for you in my dresser. Use the JC Penny credit card if you want to pick up bigger clothes." He winked at me as a comforting gesture.

"That's right," I replied, "Bigger clothes, not maternity clothes."

Alex cleared his throat.

"Shanelle, I don't want you looking sloppy, like I don't take care of you. Make sure you buy some clothes. I'll call you in the morning on the road. Jack is going to drive so you can have the car while I'm gone."

Alex paused for a minute and adjusted my ring.

"I want you to make a doctor's appointment tomorrow. If you have an emergency, call Captain Fisco, that's the only way you can reach me."

I tugged at his ear. "Promise me you'll be safe Alex. I've heard about friendly fire."

Alex put his finger to my lips.

"I'll be fine; it's you I worry about. Will you go to my mother's if you get lonely? You can sleep in my old room. I've got tee shirts there too."

I nestled my head in his neck and whimpered, "I'll be fine."

"Baby girl, a month will fly by so fast. Just keep yourself busy, you'll see."

I didn't say a word. I wanted him to stay, but I knew how much his job meant to him. His need to help others was part of his redemption.

We took quick showers and climbed into bed. I remembered falling asleep worrying about him leaving me and the emptiness I would feel. Nestled in his embrace, I began to escape into a world of fretful dream sleep.

"One more game," Steven said, as he slammed down the game piece. "No, I don't want to play Sorry anymore; I beat you fair and square."

His voice dipped to anger.

"Sit down."

I looked at him and laughed.

"Why don't you sit down sore loser."

He jumped up and put me in a choke hold as I screamed for mercy. "Ok, ok, you won!" My plea didn't satisfy him as he gripped my neck.

"Who's the number one soul brother on the planet?" Steven yelled. His grip tightened around my neck. I gasped for small amounts of air.

"You Steven, you're the number one soul brother."

He mashed my head into the floor.

"You better not tell mommy either or I'll kick your ass real good the next time." My eyes rolled back into focus as Steven dragged me by my ankles into the living room and threw my feet to the floor. He slammed the door to the family room and said, "Don't come back either, Good Times is on and I want to see Jay Jay kick Thelma's ass too."

I rubbed my throat as I minced into the kitchen to make a pot of rice before Mrs. Viv got home. As soon as I stepped onto the black and white tile floor, I fell into a dark and scary abyss. I started to scream in mid air. I reached out my hands and called for salvation.

"Help me God please."

Suddenly, I stopped. I was in the embrace of Alex's strong arms.

"Shanelle, its ok."

Alex placed his hand on my heart to reduce the tempo.

"You're drenched too Shanelle."

Even in my dazed state of confusion, Alex's presence calmed my fears. The clock suddenly became my enemy. Alex shifted his body weight and looked me in the eyes. "I've got to leave in two hours Shanelle. I didn't want to leave like this."

"It was just a bad dream."

"Steven?" he guessed.

I scratched my head.

"Yeah, I always knew something was wrong with him because his temper just got worse over time."

Alex sighed and slid his fingertips onto my scalp.

"Did he ever hit you?"

His massage induced a slow and steady answer. "No, I'm mean, yeah, but not punches, more like choking and pushing. I guess he knew that if he left a mark my parents would finally take my side."

Alex's fingers slowed down. "I made a few phone calls to a buddy of mine on the North Orange squad. I didn't get all of my info yet, but I want you to stay clear of your parents' house and the Garvey Projects. Especially Garvey, he made some serious enemies over there. I know you have to pass that way to go to St. James. "

Alex picked up my chin to hear my answer. "Ok?"

I grabbed his wrists to keep his hands in my hair.

"Ok, I will."

Alex looked at the time.

"Damn."

I squeezed him tight to confirm his sentiment.

"I wish you didn't have to go Alex. Who's going to hold me at night?"

Alex tucked the sheet into me and held me tighter.

"The maiden sighs today?" Alex softly asked.

"You did read it after all." I smiled.

"Yeah, it was nice. I packed it in my bag with my favorite picture."

"In my bikini?" I wiggled with delight.

"No, the one of you writing poetry."

Alex cleared his throat. "Not to change the subject Shanelle, but I feel terrible leaving you. Just hold on to me right now and remember this place. When I come home, we'll start where we left off."

Early morning bad breath didn't stop our love. Alex put his hand under my back and enticed my hands onto his dick. A natural moan churned inside of me as my breasts began to ache. Alex put me on top of him as I took center stage. His face strained as my thighs worked a smooth and easy rhythm. He clutched my ass and sped up my pace.

Alex quickly teased me.

"Look at my baby getting her skills up."

My thighs began to tremble into a full collapse as Alex took over. He rolled over on top of me and held my legs up. Twenty minutes passed until he came. He looked at the clock and said, "Take a bath with me before I go."

The sunlight had yet to rise. We lit three candles and placed them inside the edges of the shower stall. We lit one for our love and one for our marriage. Alex lit the last candle.

"This one's for Pumpy."

We slipped into the tub together. The hot water melted us into one soapy being. Alex slid his massive hands down my thighs and massaged them with long hard strokes. He claimed me by marking my back with a big ass hickey. Every now and then he held my hand up and stared at my wedding ring. I got out of the tub first and quietly donned some satin pajamas. I sat on the bed and watched him pack a few clothes. He put his favorite baseball cap on my head while he continued packing. He also wrapped his favorite pictures of me in tissue paper and put it in the side pocket of his travel bag. Watching him was unbearable. I crawled under our covers. I pulled his baseball cap down so he wouldn't see me crying. Before the sun rose, Alex slipped off to training with a kiss to my forehead. He carefully removed his hat from my head. His fingers tucked the curly strands behind my ears.

"I love you Shanelle. Remember what I told you." Alex picked up my favorite teddy bear.

"Hold him until I get back." He kissed my stomach in two soft pecks.

"Be good to mommy Pumpy."

I closed my eyes. I didn't want to see him leave. He wasn't coming back at noon or tomorrow. Thirty days was too long for my heart or nerves to endure. It wasn't until I heard him close the door that the realization of my emptiness kicked in. I squeezed my teddy bear tight and quietly cried myself to sleep.

Surprisingly, after five hours of sleep, waking up at eleven a.m. felt pretty good. The phone rang twice before I anxiously picked up.

"Hello."

"Hey baby," he said.

"Hey, where are you?"

"Just outside of Philly." Alex replied. "We just left a diner."

"Oh," I pouted, "Say hi to Jack for me."

"What are you doing today?" he inquired.

"I don't know, but I'll stay busy like you said."

"Don't forget, Tammy's home for a few more days, maybe you can go to the beach with her."

I wasn't interested.

"I'll call you later," Alex droned, fumbling papers. "We're about to get back on the road. I love you, take some vitamins Shanelle and make a doctor's appointment."

"I love you too and I will."

I looked around the room. I packed a small bag with shorts, a tee shirt, Nike sneakers, a brush and some Nunile. I put some mascara on and pulled my hair back in a tight ponytail. The mirror smiled back at me today. Amazingly my skin was clear as a shiny button with no acne. A plot began to form.

"Let me see what's up on my side of town." I grabbed three hundred dollars, the check book and my class schedule. The slam of the front door should have been a warning as I headed for the car. Alex left a full tank of gas and Parkway tokens. I put on my sunglasses and turned on Kiss FM. Eric B. and Rakim came on as I put the car in first gear and headed out of Lakewood for some action.

First stop, St James University. I paid the 145 exit toll and decided to cruise through North Orange before I headed to the campus. I donned my sunglasses and headed down Oakwood Avenue. Kids with white tanks and shorts were running with basketballs to Garvey. I looked past the swell of the crowd headed toward Garvey Street. It was a clue that the summer league pick up games were in full swing. Without hesitation, I hung a right and headed there. The same 'ole crew was out and about. I saw Big Booty Brenda, the local skank who knew everybody's business. I called from the window.

"Brenda, who's playing?"

She swerved up to the car to get a better look.

"Hey Shanelle."

Brenda did a full inventory search of the car as her fingers played a melody on the door.

"Mookie's over there entertaining with his ugly ass."

She pointed at me and said, "When you see Steven, tell him he better pay me my fuckin' money." I shook my head.

"We don't talk anymore."

Brenda jerked her neck out.

"Talk my ass, family is family; you'll see his tired ass at a fuckin' barbecue or something."

An heir of royalty rested in her tipped hand as she stalled her words.

"Just-tell-him-what-I-said-please."

Brenda rolled her eyes and turned her lip up as she pulled back. My face molded in disgust as her funky smell lit up the entire car. It almost made me pass out as I looked for a parking space. She was probably pissed off with some Steven bullshit but I didn't care, he wasn't my problem anymore. I got out the car and put my shades on the top of my head. I brought an Italian ice from Rockies and headed up the block for the game. The quad was packed to watch Mookie play on the hot asphalt. On the mini courts, little kids were practicing their skills in between the, "Oohs,' and "Aahs," of Mookie's game. In the heart of the projects, the swell of the crowd was black, Puerto Rican and some wannabees. The weird thing was watching old men in khaki pants with press pads in their hands hungrily waiting to recruit Mookie. They took notes and stood in separate huddles calculating the lure it would take to get him to Villanova, Duke, Marquette, you name it, they were there. They were going to have to work hard too. His mother, "Mama Barb," as we called her, made sure her baby stayed out of trouble and ate a good meal. She fed the whole damn neighborhood too. The good heart she had did little for Mookie's education, but she made sure that nobody went hungry. She sold five dollar chicken dinners from her apartment five days a week and gave the Peppermint Lounge a run for their money. Mama Barb always said that chicken and rice came cheap. People trusted her food too because she kept a clean apartment and a white dishrag continuously soaking in bleach. Amazingly, she managed to keep every roach in the project out of her place with monthly boric acid treatments. My stomach started growling just thinking about her perfect white rice and brown gravy. On a hot ass day like today, you would think that all I wanted was coconut Italian ice, but I moved through the crowd and rolled right up on Mama Barb to buy an early dinner.

"Hey Shanelle, go help yourself," she said, as I handed her some money. The rest of the cash I flashed was a mistake, because sticky finger Tamika walked up to me to get a piece. She grabbed my ring finger as I shoved my wad into my pocket.

"Damn, you doing 'aight girl with that ring on your finger."

A good compliment came first, then a pitiful story to get some money.

"Look here," she sniffed, wiping her crusty nose, "I need to get some bread and milk for my babies, can you loan me twenty?"

Never look a feign in the eye, my brother used to say. If you did, they'll spot your weakness and be your friend for life. I focused on the court and picked up my plate. One scoop of rice and gravy went in my mouth.

"I calculate three dollars and forty-five cents, what are you gonna do with the change?"

Tamika quickly sucked her teeth. My question, the food in my mouth and the hot swell of the sun pissed her off as she bounced away.

"Forget you Shanelle. Anyway your brother owes me some money. You better tell him to come see my ass."

"Yeah whatever," I shot back, scooping up rice. Shifting my interest, I fixed my attention on Mookie and his legendary slam-dunks. There were others with different intentions. Among the crowd were bookies, gun-runners, pimps in training and hookers in heels. Little did I know federal agents were staked out in apartment

7H shooting rapid fire photographs of the underground economy. Vehicles parked along the side were also subject to evidence and inventory. Lucky me, they even took a photograph of my energetic bite into a chicken leg as one of the most ruthless crime suspects strayed up to me in the crowd.

"Yo, Shanelle, what's up?"

"Hey Rico, nothing much."

"You kinda far from Seven Oaks."

"I don't live there anymore and it's not Seven Oaks."

Mama Barb's delicious product melted down my throat as my heart began to thump in my shirt. I knew what was coming next.

"Look, you know I always had a crush on you and I'm always gonna look out. You need to step up outta' here because Steven made some crazy enemies." He moved in closer, "Everybody's lookin' for him."

A hard gulp choked me as I cleared my throat.

"How's Nikki?" I inquired of his younger sister.

"Good," Rico replied. "She made it out. Nikki's a varsity point guard at Pitt."

Nikki and Rico's parents had enough sense to keep their daughter in St. Amelia's for as long as their five jobs could carry them. We weren't that cool in high school, but I was happy for her because she was a good ball player. My empty plate piled into the garbage as I licked my lips.

"Let me get up outta here."

Rico shot spit to the ground and remarked, "Yeah, you do that and tell mama boy Steven to come see me."

I marched to the car with keys in hand.

"Damn," I thought, *"Steven really fucked up."*

I rolled up the windows and headed towards Shoprite, nixing the thought of stopping at the university due to the intense heat outside.

As soon as I arrived, Gina the sales clerk spotted me.

"Shanelle, long time no see! I hear you're married now!"

The other cashier Maria chimed in too. "Yeah, she even put on honeymoon weight, look how chubby and happy she looks."

"Hi, Gina," I replied. "Yes, I'm a fat old married woman."

Maria added her two cents as she tallied the produce. "Your mother is here somewhere sweet heart. I think down aisle two."

I was in no condition to run away. A quick glance down the aisle was all I needed to spot Mrs. Viv. She was scrutinizing a can of Alpo holding a small basket in her hand. My body hardened for a moment as I gathered courage in my balled fist. She was humming her all time favorite.

"I'm coming up, on the rough side..., I finished the verse for her just like old times. *"Of the mountain. I'm doing my best to make it in."*

My timid voice chimed in tune, "Hi mama."

"Shanelle," she gasped with wide mouth surprise.

"My baby, how are you?"

She engulfed me in a back breaking squeeze. I embraced her as far as my arms could reach as my body melted in her arms.

"I'm fine mama, really..., I'm fine."

She continued to hug me, smoothing my back in a nurturing exchange. Suspicion set in as she softly pushed me back.

"Look at you, all grown up and married now."

I flashed my ring. The sparkling gem barely held her attention as her eyes dropped to my growing mid section.

"Hmm," she said, "I see, I see. How are you feeling?"

"Fine mama," I replied, grabbing her basket and placing it on the floor. The contents surprised me. Ramen noodles, one onion, two bananas and a loaf of bread. Mrs. Viv always shopped by the cartful.

"You don't usually buy this stuff," I pitched with concern.

Mrs. Viv's face turned into a frown.

"Shanelle, I lost my job eight months ago and things have been rough. I'm still looking though..., even sending out resumes, but it's been hard. Your father got laid off too and he's doing free lance work right now."

I didn't dare ask about Steven or our visit to the house. I reached in my pocket and pulled the currency from the remainder.

"Here mama."

She took the one hundred dollar bill and folded it in half. It disappeared into her weary bra the old school way.

"Thank you baby."

Her pause was the first step in our healing. "I'm sorry Shanelle."

I stroked her cheek with my hand to suspend her apology. It was all I could do to fight back tears.

"I know mama, you did the best you could do. Don't worry about it I'll be fine."

"Can I call you?" Mrs. Viv's face was filled with regret. "You know…, at your place. I don't know if you're getting my messages at Candy's house and I found out from a complete stranger that you got married."

"I'm sorry mama," I sympathized, "we came by to tell you the good news, but you weren't home." As I pulled out a pen, Mrs. Viv reached into her bosom for the money.

"Write it on here, I want to show your father when I get home." She paused for a second.

"He'll be so happy when I tell him I saw you." She snapped her fingers and asked, "Can you stop at the house, he would love to see you."

A stinging sensation prickled my body. Alex's stern reminder flashed in front of me.

I promise Alex…,

My fingers jerked and curled.

"I'm sorry mama; I gotta get back to Lakewood now."

Mrs. Viv's face washed over with grief. I scribbled my name and number on the bill and placed it in her aging palm. She reached into her shirt and buried the money. She tugged on my shirt, toiling on her words.

"You're pregnant Shanelle."

My mouth dropped to the ground supported by a weighted anchor. I stood back and stuttered, "How, how did you…,"

She stepped towards me and smoothed my cheek.

"Looking at you is like looking at me when I was pregnant with Steven. You must be having a boy." A hollow wind carried me away with her revelation.

"Steven made me fat the minute I got pregnant with him. I was wearing maternity clothes at four weeks. My stomach swelled up so bad, your grandmother had to add elastic in the waist of my pants just so I could go out. Oooh girl," she breathed with relief, "I ate like a pig too, anything I could get my hands on." Her hand landed on my chin.

"Shanelle, are you all right?"

My voice became deep and demonic as I took ownership of the life growing inside of me.

"Does everything have to be about Steven? This baby isn't going to be anything like him, so don't go putting Steven into my pregnancy."

My fingers trailed my small pouch. Before this day came, I was wishing the entire reality away. Mentioning Steven spoiled my time. I was more than determined to win this war no matter what. A drum majorette played a tune in my head as I stood up straight and fixed my clothes. Loose strands of hair were quickly swept to the side as I glared at her in defiance.

Mrs. Viv didn't raise a white flag, but she did offer a sign of peace.

"I'm sorry baby; I wasn't trying to do that. Did you see a doctor yet? I can make an appointment for you."

I quick hug ended our exchange.

"I have to go mama; the parkway traffic gets busy at this time. I'll call you later."

I scurried out the door and jumped in the car. As soon as I sat down in Alex's bucket seats, the sensation to go to the bathroom overwhelmed me. I immediately looked around and decided to go to the Exxon station. Once inside, I released what felt like a gallon of fluid. The relief was so overwhelming that I had to stand outside to catch my breath. I put my hands on my hips and looked at the blinking light on top of the VA Hospital. I also stared at the phone booth that use to be my haven when I ran away. Memories rushed to the surface like a crashing tidal wave.

"Steven, whose wallets are these? Where did you get these watches from?"

"Stay 'outta my shit fat ass."

"Well, you left them on the table, I didn't know."

"You don't know shit, that's your problem. You need to grow up. Smoke a joint or somethin'."

"Steven, the doctor said you shouldn't smoke that stuff…"

I shut my eyes as I visualized him. One hard push sent me flying into the mirrored wall as my head broke a precut glass diamond that lodged into my head.

"Oww, look what you did. I'm bleeding!"

"So what! At least your head is not all fucked up inside, so quit your fucking whining Shanelle before I show ma those love letters for Derrick you horny bitch!"

The squawk of a black crow snapped me out of my trance. The need to eat again ravaged my taste buds as I rolled out of the gas station, anxious to reach home.

It took me two hours to get back to Lakewood. Once inside, I immediately noticed two phone messages.

"Let the games begin."

Mrs. Foster's grandma tirade began.

"And I saw the cutest little outfit today Shanelle, I was tempted to buy it. Anyway, I thought you would be home resting, but it's such a nice day. I brought you some vitamins from the store and some orange juice. Folic acid is good for the baby you know. Well, call me. I want you to look at this darling crib."

Tammy followed after the delete button tolled. She wanted me to join her chub club.

"Hey girl, I was going to pick you up for lunch and then swing to Belmar. I'm going to Lane Bryant's tomorrow if you want to go. Let me know, bye."

Thoughts of my mother quickly rose as I looked down.

"This baby won't be anything like Steven."

I grabbed the phone book. The first thing I needed to do was make sure my baby was okay. I sat on the couch and scrawled my finger down the list.

"Hmm, Dr. Cathy Swenson, she sounds nice."

Dr. Swenson's office, may I help you?"

"Yes, uh, hi, this is…"

"Can you hold on please, thanks."

Waiting, waiting, waiting, elevator music, waiting…

"Hi, can I help you?"

"This is Shanelle Brown, uh, I mean, Mrs. Shanelle Foster, I need to make an appointment."

"What insurance do you have?"

"Oh, I just got married and I don't think my husband added me on…"

"Well the office visit is two hundred and fifteen dollars and that doesn't include blood work."

I didn't know what to say. Alex didn't say to spend the money at the doctor's office.

"Hello, are you there miss?"

"Yes, I'm here, I'll call back, thank you."

"Well," I thought to myself, *"I tried."*

I quickly jumped off the couch and took a shower. As I stepped out, the scale was the first thing that came into eyesight. I avoided it in the worst way, but the swell of my stomach and baby talk by the world around me forced me to check.

"Step right up ladies and gentleman and look at the fat freak show."

Even if I wanted to get up and eat something, the heated afternoon at Garvey and the family reunion lulled me to sleep. By nightfall, emotional wreckage followed.

Ring, ring, ring, ring, ring, ring, ring…

"Hello,"

"Shanelle, it's me."

"Alex?"

"Yes, are you sleeping?" he suspiciously asked.

I grabbed the phone cord.

"I was, but I'm up now."

In a hostile and angry tone, he cleared his throat.

"Where did you go today?"

I cleared my throat, clueless to his line of questioning.

"Oh, uh… I went to North Orange. I was going to check on my courses but…oh, I got something to eat." I dazed out and recovered, "Oh yeah, I saw…,"

"I didn't ask you who you saw Shanelle, I asked where did you go?"

An official police interrogation set in as my eyes shifted back and forth in our dark bedroom. Quickly trying to recall, my eyebrow arched.

"Let me think, I went to Sandwiches Unlimited, no, not there, I mean Shoprite. Uh, I watched some basketball…"

"Yeah, that's it," Alex said, "Tell me about basketball."

My heart began to sink to the ground as I contemplated my error. "Mookie was playing…"

"Mookie?" Alex impatiently toned. Each word pulled with anger.

"What-the-fuck-is-a-Mookie? No, better yet, tell me, where did you see this basketball game?"

I stuttered briefly. "Ga-Garvey."

Alex yelled like a drill sergeant. "Garvey what?"

"Uh, Garvey Street Projects," I cringed, tucking my pillow under my arms.

Alex began to scream.

"Yeah, that's the answer I was looking for Shanelle, Garvey Street Projects, the very place I told you not to go!"

As Alex's wrath fell upon me in decorated black silk, all I could hear was the sound of tapping. I didn't know if he was in a phone booth or in a hotel room, but déjà vu came into being. Alex's response swept me into a dark wind tunnel as he continued his rant.

"Before I left, I specifically said not to go to your parents' house or the Garvey Street Projects! Why did my captain call me in the middle of training and say that my license plate showed up on a federal evidence stake out list? For your information Shanelle, the feds are over there taking pictures of every car, bookie, gun runner, drug dealer and wanna be gangsta. Never in a million years would I expect my wife to show up in those pictures eating a fucking two piece chicken dinner and…, and…," he bellowed, "Talking to the number one suspect in this damn investigation!"

The wind tunnel swept me up as chicken bones, marrow and unearthly debris rested on my lifeless body.

"Garvey, fried chicken, Mookie, Rico, who knew?"

Alex's rage continued as I listened to his alter ego blare into the phone.

"Did you forget I'm a cop? Did you forget you're my wife, more importantly, did you forget you're pregnant and you had the damn audacity to show up at that crime infested neighborhood!"

Jack stood in the back ground trying to calm him down.

"No man, get off of me, she needs to hear this!" He shifted the phone for clarity.

"Shanelle, do you know that I'm a laughing stock around here because my wife thinks she's a homey? Do you know you damn near made me lose my job?"

Icicles formed around my ears and feet as I nervously shook.

"This is our entire life! If I lose this job, we lose. What the hell were you thinking?"

I couldn't speak. I clamped my teeth into the bed linen.

"You better be glad Captain Fisco likes me and called in a favor. Now I'm fucked trying to figure out how I'm going to pay it back. But for now, I want you to do me a favor Mrs. Foster."

His demand bellowed through my hollow body.

"Get up off the bed and look out the window."

I couldn't move.

"Did you hear what I said girl?"

"Yes," I whimpered.

"Get up and go to the living room window now!"

I jumped up and rushed to the window in my bare feet.

"I'm here," I said, in a timid voice.

"Good, now lift up the blind, Shanelle."

Darkness settled outside as I stared into the parking lot.

"Are you looking?" he asked.

"Yes," I searched.

"See anything missing?" Alex asked.

I was clueless. His anger forced a response.

"Look at our parking space, number thirty-five!"

My heart crashed to the ground.

"The car, it's…"

"Gone!" Alex yelled, "Gone!" That's the deal I made with Captain Fisco and the Feds to keep you out of North Orange until this part of the investigation is over! Now you can stay at home and act like my wife instead of trying to front like some project chick!"

Alex's tirade shifted to his prodigy.

"Did you make an appointment today?"

"I tried but I didn't have…"

"Not good enough Shanelle. You've got time to watch somebody name Mookie, but no time for our baby. Be ready by nine o'clock tomorrow. My mother's picking you up for an appointment with Dr. Robinson."

Thoughts of his unborn child seemed to calm his voice. He cleared his throat. "How are you feeling?"

My response was weak and filled with hurt.

"Fine."

His next question was a test of my will on any given day.

"Are you eating?"

Tucked away in the deepest shame, my tearful voice jerked, "Yes, I'm eating."

"Oh I forgot," he wised off, "You had fried chicken today. Anyway, be ready in the morning."

What followed was the blaring sound of the dial tone. I shuddered silently as the voices gathered around me with sticks and torches, ready to burn Frankenstein at the stake.

"No he didn't," The Big One said.

"Yes he did," The Meek One retorted.

"He got some nerve talkin' to you like that."

"Who does he think he is, Steven or something?"

My body rocked back and forth as I held my ears tight. The sheets on the bed became a handkerchief as I buried my head deep inside the soft cloth and bellowed out in shame and humiliation. Suddenly, the phone rang again. Eternal hope rested for a quick minute as I heard the third ring.

"Please tell me you forgive me Alex."

I wiped my wet hands on my thighs and slowly picked up the phone. The sound coming from the receiver offered little hope as the voice of Steven came on loud and clear singing his rendition of Maurice White from Earth, Wind and Fire.

"Ohhh, ohh, oh, after the love is gone, what use to be right is wrong. Ha haaaa, what's up little sis, and better yet, how's my little big ass head nephew in that fat ass belly of yours?"

My body tensed up in fear.

"How did you get my number Steven?"

"The hooker that you are wrote it on that hundred spot you gave ma. Thanks for the get high money dummy."

Laughter rang out through the ear piece as I quickly hung up the phone. Steven wasn't finished, he was on a roll. In five minutes, the phone rang again. I knew it was Steven, but I couldn't take the chance if it was Alex. I needed to tell him that I was sorry.

"Hello."

"Hey Nell," Steven said, "Can you imagine my big head nephew runnin' around the house? I'm so excited I can't wait to pop that kangaroo in the back of his big ass head."

I rubbed my stomach like a she-wolf protecting her young. Mrs. Viv did even more damage to my psyche by telling him that I was pregnant. I hung up the phone and quickly called back. Mrs. Viv and Steven picked up the phone as I began to yell.

"Stop calling here Steven and leave me alone!"

The buffer between us was one hundred and thirty miles. It was the first time in a long time that Mrs. Viv took my side.

"Steven, leave your sister alone!"

Desperation filled the phone.

"Shanelle, Shanelle, are you there?"

I hung up and quickly ran to the bathroom for sanctuary. The voices were right behind me.

"No, no, no, I don't want you to be like him, please God, don't do this to me."

Tears began to fall. I forced myself off the floor and went into the kitchen. Among the cabinets and the refrigerator were the things I craved in times of stress. My mind shifted into hyper overdrive as I grabbed peanut butter and three bananas. I held them tightly under my right arm as I opened the door to the refrigerator. Cream cheese, goat cheese and left over fat free pudding were snatched from the first shelf. I topped it off with a half-gallon container of milk. With all of the contents tightly wrapped in my arms, I headed for the bathroom and closed the door. Under the evening twilight, on the cold ceramic floor, my sneaky eating device gripped my soul. Peanut butter and cream cheese went down first as

I forced hard swallows to calm my stress. The bananas followed in perfect unison as I took one bite and swallowed it whole. Sweat tremors kicked in and a small dizzy spell followed as my existence filled the entire bathroom with voices of shame.

"You're stupid, fat and worthless".

"Will you ever listen?"

"Hide in the closet where you can't be seen or heard. He's going to kill you anyway."

"Who?"

"Alex?"

"No."

"Steven. Well, maybe Alex. He's killed before."

"Steven would if you gave him a chance. Maybe Alex could kill Steven and then you can be rid of your brother. But then Alex may kill you just so he can have the baby all to himself. That's all he wants."

"This baby won't be sick like Steven."

"Yes he will as soon as Steven pops the little one in the back of his head."

I swallowed hard as I cursed them. Goat cheese and milk dripped from my mouth like a slow moving volcanic eruption. My heartbeat began to slow down. As the frenzy settled, my right hand slumped to the floor. My head dropped in exhaustion. The only support was the toilet bowl beside me as my shoulder rested against the cold tile. The voices dipped to a whisper.

"There, there, Shanelle, you're gonna be fine. Alex won't kill you, he loves you, maybe too much, but he loves you. Listen to him. He knows what's best for you. You're still a little girl, lost in Alex's world."

My body heaved up and down with two breaths of air as my eyes began to close. I was hung over like a scene from Lady Sings the Blues. The still of the night silenced my vice and accompanied me to another dream.

"Shanelle, open the door, it's me!"

"Steven, what is it now?"

"Open the door, they're after me!"

"Quick, hide with me Shanelle!"

"Not in the closet again Steven!"

"Shh!"

"Steven, let go of me, there's nobody out there."

"They're trying to kill me sis!"

"Steven, don't cry, nobody is going to kill you."

"They chase me all the time Shanelle."

"Who?"

"The voices in my head."

"Why don't you tell ma?"

"No, they'll put me away, I'm not crazy!"

"That's why you need to take your medicine. They'll go away if you do. I know, you're not crazy, shh, shh, there, there, Steven, you're going to be alright."

"Don't leave me sis, don't let them get me."

"I won't. They won't get you, I promise."

A soft shoulder rub awakened me. I blinked at pairs of shoes in various shapes on the bathroom floor. My clothes were stuck to my body like hard sticky paste. Finally in focus, Mrs. Foster took control.

"Tammy, wait outside. Mary, you clean this mess up and Debbie, help me get this child off the floor. Shanelle, can you hear me?"

I sat up and looked around at the Fosters.

"What time is it?"

"It's nine fifteen, you didn't answer the doorbell so we got worried and let ourselves in. Alex gave me a key before he left."

Mary picked up the empty wrappers avoiding the obvious.

"Wow, Shanelle, you're really eating for two. My niece or nephew will be as strong as a bull."

Mrs. Foster held me by the shoulders.

"Did you forget your appointment?"

"No," I replied.

Mary chimed in and said, "Ma you know that's the best sleep ever, especially the first trimester. Shanelle, do you want me to iron something for you?"

"Sure, my jeans are in the dresser."

I ran my fingers through my hair and watched the Foster women clean up my demise. I was too tired to care and I knew Mrs. Foster was going to tell Alex the sordid details. I exited the bathroom and saw Tammy sitting on the couch. Her face was as shameful as mine. She quickly said hello and put her head down.

I took a quick shower stretching my ear to listen to the ringing phone.

"Sure son, I'll take care of it. Yes, we're leaving for the doctor's office the minute she gets dressed."

"That was Alex. He was worried and took a break from training. He'll call you tonight at ten," she pitched from the room.

My hand fell to the side like a weighted stone. Mary handed me my jeans and a shirt.

"Here you go Shanelle, this looks cute together."

I grabbed the clothes and headed to the bathroom. The door closed behind me as they sat quietly in the living room. I didn't know what to think or to say, but I knew I needed to get to Dr. Robinson's office. I didn't want to disappoint Alex and I was determined to get this baby off to a good start. Steven's psychotic intentions forced me to worry about the innocent life inside of me as I brushed my teeth. I tapped my toothbrush and immediately thought of Alex. He was tapping something last night and it bothered me just like Steven's deadly blades. I slipped into my clothes and brushed my hair back into a ponytail. As I stepped out of the bathroom, the Foster women stood up to receive me with glowing compliments. It all sounded staged and rehearsed.

"You look great Shanelle," Tammy said, "You don't look fat at all." Mrs. Foster nudged Tammy with her elbow.

"Not fat at all," Mrs. Foster replied, "My grandbaby is going to take of all of your weight anyway." She grabbed my hand and squeezed it tight. "I made you some toast and wrapped it foil so you can have something on your stomach ok?"

"Ok." I replied.

"Good," Mrs. Foster said, "Let's go."

Dr. Robinson was a kind and caring woman. She made them wait in the reception area and spoke to me regarding my results.

"Shanelle, you're in good health. From the looks of things you are definitely pregnant, five weeks to be exact. Your due date is April twenty-seventh. In the meantime, I would like to see you in two weeks so we can listen to the heartbeat." She handed me a prescription and said, "This is for prenatal vitamins. You should take them everyday with food. Do you have any questions?"

I looked down at my stomach and wished Steven away.

"No, I don't. Thank you doctor."

"Help yourself to some magazines in the reception area Shanelle. Prenatal care is very important and that information is helpful. Please call me if you experience any bleeding or cramping."

I stood up, shook her hand and replied, "I'll see you in two weeks."

They greeted me with smiles when I returned. Mary, Mrs. Foster and Tammy stood up to get all the details as I scoured the magazine rack.

"Is everything ok?" Tammy asked.

"How many weeks are you?" Mary inquired. As Debbie leaned in for a response, Mrs. Foster quickly got them off my back and grabbed two magazines. She kept one for herself and handed one to me.

"It's been a while since I had a grandbaby around so I'd better read myself, right Shanelle?"

I took the magazine from her and smiled. "Yeah, you're right Mrs. Foster."

She put her hand on my shoulder.

"If you don't mind, call me mom, I would enjoy that."

"Sure, I would love to call you mom."

Mrs. Foster drove back to her house. Tammy showed me all the new clothes she purchased for school and we went over her class schedule. When she sat next to me on the bed, the mattress gave way as our shoulders pressed in a sisterly bond.

"At least you can blame your pregnancy Shanelle."

"Blame my pregnancy? On what?"

"You know the eating thing."

I turned away. "I don't do it too much, but when I get…,"

Tammy finished my sentence, "Upset? Me too and I don't know how to stop."

I looked her in the eyes. "That was so embarrassing this morning."

Tammy's eyes widened. "It doesn't matter in this house, they've been through it with me too Shanelle. You just have to learn how to control it when things get out of control."

"What do you do to stop?"

"I play basketball or take a long hike. I mean, you can look at me and tell it doesn't work that much, but I've been heavier than this. If it weren't for Alex's motivation, I would be worse."

"How did Alex help you?"

Tammy cleared her throat and sat with her legs crossed on her bed.

"Alex is driven in everything he does. He's an over achiever if you didn't already know. I'm the same way except for one big problem."

"What's that?" I asked.

"I let other people influence me."

"Oh." I replied.

"I'm getting ready to go to Pitt and I know I'm weak. The minute somebody acts like they're my friend, I'm bending over backwards getting my feelings hurt. After that, I start binging the minute I feel anxious or stressed."

I didn't want to chime in and say, "me too," but I knew how she felt.

"Alex talks to me all the time Shanelle. Before he met you, we used to run a mile on the beach or he would take me with him to the gym, just to keep busy. I only have one good friend and she moved to California last year. Hopefully I'll meet some cool people at Pitt."

I smiled at her and said, "I'm sure you will," I sympathized with a pat to her leg. "Hey, there's a girl I went to school with name Nikki who plays on the basketball team, you should hook up. I'm sure you'll find a nice guy too, you're cute as a button Tammy."

Tammy hugged me. "I was so jealous of you at first Shanelle, but I'm glad you're my sister now."

"Me too," I gushed. We trotted downstairs side by side as Tammy pushed me with her big hips at the last step. Mrs. Foster carried a steaming bowl of string beans to the table.

"Shanelle and Tammy set the table for me please while I get this salad together."

In unison we chimed, "Ok mom."

I felt so good being there I forgot all the problems that followed me the day before. Once the night began to fall, I asked the same question over and over again.

"What time is it?"

Mrs. Foster lamented, "Lord somebody take this child home so she doesn't miss Alex's call."

I chuckled, but I was nervous just the same. Not talking to him was driving me crazy.

Mary dropped me off. I rushed to the door after saying goodnight. I quickly noticed a soft illuminating light from the bedroom. Alex was sitting on the couch with a small duffel bag next to him. He peered straight ahead with little emotion. Reaching him, Alex lifted his hand and pulled me between his legs. His head rested on my stomach.

"I'm sorry Shanelle," he moaned against my belly.

His words melted me.

"They suspended my training and want us to come in for questioning."

I pulled his head up.

"Why?"

Alex exhaled.

"They want to know what you know about the people you were talking to in the photographs. Once their satisfied, I can go back to the training. They think you might be helpful."

Alex cursed under his breath.

"I wish you didn't have to Shanelle, but my job is on the line now."

Fumbling for excuses, I babbled, "I only know them from the neighborhood and school, I don't associate with them."

Alex quieted me with his fingertips. "I know baby, I told them that, but this is a big case and they don't want to make the wrong move. I just need you to be honest with them and we'll be fine, it's just a formality."

Alex cleared his throat and grabbed my hips to straddle his lap. I wrapped my legs around him as he looked me in the eyes and asked, "How's Pumpy?"

I looked down at my stomach.

"He or she is fine. I'm five weeks pregnant."

The smile on his handsome face stretched from ear to ear as all of his worries dissipated.

"You look cute mommy."

"Thank you," I blushed.

"What did Dr. Robinson say?"

"She said everything was fine. I have to go back in two weeks to hear the heart beat."

Alex stroked my stomach with his thumbs. "Make sure you remind me. I'm going to drive all the way back from Philly just to hear it."

"So you're not going to lose your job?" I asked.

Alex faced etched with strain as he squeezed my hand.

"I don't want to talk about it anymore. It's just a formality." He raked his lower lip with his teeth. "I don't need any attention on my life. You know why Shanelle. I told you my whole story and I'm trying to make good on the things I did wrong in the past."

I couldn't do anything but apologize but he wouldn't let me. He laid me down on the couch. His hands were so powerful; he could have easily popped my neck and ended my life right there. I squeezed my eyes tight as I tried to wrestle the thoughts away. Alex began to unbutton my shirt as he stroked the places I craved. He rubbed my stomach carefully sweeping his thumb under the seam of my panties, watching my back arch.

"Let's take a shower baby," I cooed.

He refused and lifted me up, quickly thumbing my panties to the floor. His hand gripped my ass as a deep moaned filled the room.

"I told you before I left that we were going to finish where we left off. We can take a shower later." He pulled me in closer and whispered, "I want you right now."

I unbuckled his pants as he watched them fall down to his ankles. There was nothing left to do but slide my tongue in his mouth. Alex sat down and hoisted me on his stiff dick. I cried out in pain as it pierced my insides and filled my existence. Our bodies molded as his hot breath crushed against my cheek.

"Ahh, damn I missed you, Shanelle."

Alex grabbed my hips and pumped me up and down as his powerful arms absorbed the shock of my weight on top of him. His head rested back for a minute. His mouth gaped open as he closed his eyes and bit down into his lower lip. He wrapped four fingers around my outer thighs and worked Kitty with his thumbs until my legs began to buckle beneath him.

"Baby," I cried out, gripping my nails into his shoulders, losing rhyme and reason. Alex lifted me off of him and stepped out of his pants, draping my legs around his waist as Kitty's juices coated his stomach.

Grunting to hold me up, Alex carried me to the bed as I carelessly fell back, bouncing once, finding a spot that would satisfy his time. Dripping with sweat, Alex hungrily buried his face between my legs, lapping up my clitoris with fat, long ice cream licks.

"Alex!" I trembled, "right there baby," as soft tremors rolled up and burst inside of me. He shoved his middle finger in my tunnel and pillow kissed my clitoris with his smooth thick lips. My head thrashed back and forth as he finger fucked me, slipping away to quickly grab his thick, long dick. Alex entered me again and cursed his own pleasure.

"Damn, I love you so much."

"I'm coming baby, don't stop."

A careless laugh escaped his hot mouth.

"I know baby, rain on me, I feel you."

He got on his knees and rested my ankles on his shoulders. Thrusting hard, watching me strain, his eyebrows rose and fell.

"Yes baby, it's your dick, enjoy it Shanelle."

Caught off guard, he leaned forward grabbing my rock hard tits. His other hand smacked the wall as he began to come, growling, groaning this time as he opened his mouth with wide eyes.

"Shit!" he cursed, focusing on my bouncing breasts, fucking me in a hurried frenzy. My rag doll legs fell on the bed as all the energy left my body. A few shivers ran up my arm and on to my shoulders as Alex rolled over taking me with him. Sweaty kisses piled against my neck. Relief and a bull's breath blew into my ear.

"Just like I said, I was coming back just where we left off."

My breathing calmed, cooled by his damp chest. I wrapped my arms around him. "I'm so sorry for everything."

Alex stroked my hair.

"Go to sleep Shanelle, we're going to be okay."

The fullness of the day and night took over as my dreams carried me through the early morning.

"Have a seat Mrs. Foster. I'm Special Agent Williams, Auto and Truck Hijacking Squad. To your left, Special Agent Daniels, Fugitive Warrant Squad. Next to Agent Daniels is Special Agent Phillips, Narcotics Task Force. Seated on your right, Special Agent Duncan, Evidence Agent and photographer, who by the way took those lovely pictures of you eating a five dollar two piece dinner at the Garvey Projects. So, Mrs. Foster, tell me about Steven."

"I don't want to talk about him?"

"Are you saying you are not going to cooperate with a federal investigation?"

"Alex, help me, I don't know what to tell them."

"I'm sorry babe, I was out back."

"Huh?"

"Come with us, Mrs. Foster."

I followed the agent to a secret back door. When it opened, they pushed me. Alex waved, "Shanelle, tell Willie James I said hi!"

My body quickly sprang from the bed. Alex damn near jumped out of his skin. I pulled the sheet off and escaped into the bathroom. Alex stood in the doorway wiping his eyes.

"Is something wrong with the baby?"

"No," I shrugged, "I had a bad dream and I'm hungry."

A jolt of bright lights strained my vision.

"My mother told me what happened in the bathroom."

"Oh," I replied.

"They sure do stick together."

We headed into the kitchen. Alex began to cut up watermelon and yogurt. He prepared one cup and put it on the table with a spoon and napkin.

"Are you worried about tomorrow?" he asked.

"A little, why?"

"You're eating." he professed, crossing his arms.

"Well, I am pregnant."

"I know, but that shouldn't be an excuse to eat this late at night."

I picked up my spoon and put the creamy substance in my mouth. Alex stood up and kissed my forehead.

"I'm going to bed. Don't stay up too late, we have a busy day tomorrow."

I watched him swagger back into the bedroom and slowly close the door. The spoon in my hand clanged against the table. The yogurt and fruit mixed together didn't have the appeal I needed. I watered a few plants and dried the sink with a paper towel. A few magazines left over from the previous month needed to be thrown away. I dusted off the TV and adjusted a hanging photograph. I returned to the bedroom and curled up under Alex. A good night sleep came at last.

Interrogation

I was expecting Alex to take me to a large white building with tinted black glass. Instead, he drove straight to Newark and parked in an abandoned factory on Frelinghuysen Avenue.

"Why are we stopping here?" I asked.

"This is it Shanelle, they have a facility here."

I grabbed his hand as we got out the car. Alex knocked on a rustic metal door three times as a man opened the door to let us in. Alex flashed his badge as the agent in black held the door for us. A freight elevator took us up three flights to a fully modern office. I knew I was in serious trouble just by the technology in the room. Agents in navy single-breasted suits shuffled down the narrow hallway with paperbound books and files in their hands. Women in short skirts with guns on their hips strutted past me like they meant business. Alex greeted a few people along the way, but he never smiled. A large conference room faced us at the end of the passageway. When we entered, twelve agents stood up to greet us. A buffed agent greeted us first. He shook Alex's hand and barely looked at me as he directed us to two chairs.

"Have a seat Alex, thanks for coming on time with your wife."

Alex cleared his throat and adjusted his tie. "No problem," he said. "We just want to get this over with."

His answer prompted all the agents to sit up and pay attention as they began to pick up their pens. The agent turned to me and said, "Shanelle, I'm Special Agent Russo from the Narcotics Warrant Squad. With me today are various agents from the bureau and its surrounding agencies. We called you in today because your husband's vehicle showed up on our photograph evidence list, including pictures of you talking to our lead suspect."

I looked at Alex for support. He patted the top of my hand as I surveyed the room of agents.

Agent Russo continued. "Shanelle, we only have a few questions for you, but we do know that your husband cannot be included in our undercover sting because of your association with the Garvey Projects and your brother Steven."

Agent Russo's message caused Alex to slip his hand away and fold them in his lap. I turned to apologize, but he looked the other way. Other agents held their heads down as they paid homage to the emotionally injured officer.

"Your husband has a great career in front of him, but our main concern is everyone's safety and protection during this sensitive operation."

My lips grimaced slightly as I stared at Agent Russo. He handed me a large envelope.

"Take a look at the photographs and tell me what you know about the individuals you were seen with."

Alex sat up straight and cleared his throat as I tried to concentrate. The first photo was Mookie's mother. I smiled slightly and said, "That's Mama Barb, she takes care of everybody, especially the kids."

One of the older agents to the far left of me threw his head back and joked, "Yeah, that's a good one."

The other agents started laughing as if they were all in on the secret. Alex began to tap his finger on the table. I held my lips together as I slid another photograph from underneath the pile. It was a photo of me and Rico. I spoke over the fading laughter and replied, "That's Rico, his sister and I went to high school together."

Agent Russo leaned into me and said, "Is that all you know?" Alex went on the defensive and said, "Yeah, that's all she knows, she doesn't live there, didn't grow up there and she had no business being there."

He stood up and adjusted his suit jacket as he grabbed my elbow to leave. Agent Russo motioned his hand in the air for Alex to wait.

"Just one more thing Mrs. Foster," Agent Russo said. "We have strong reason to believe that an urban bounty is on your brother's head for some expensive weapons he allegedly stole. Your husband was smart enough to warn you once. Take his advice and stay away from the Garvey Projects."

187

Alex turned his back on me and headed towards the double door. Most of the agents flashed a condescending smile as I held my head down low and followed. Agent Russo held the door open and said, "Alex, Captain Fisco said to report to work at your regular time tomorrow."

As the large door closed behind us, there was distant laughter from the conference room. Once outside, Alex loosened his tie and snatched it off. He trekked past the car and threw his tie in the air, clenching down on his jaw. I waddled a few paces behind him not realizing that he wanted to vent as my shoe slipped in a small pot hole filled with rocks. I began to brush off the side of my shoe as Alex turned in anger.

"So that's what's important right now, you're pretty shoes Shanelle?"

"No, I slipped..."

"Damn, I told you not to go there! Shit just keeps following you everywhere and you don't listen! You don't think either."

The voices heckled him. The Big One said, *"Last time I checked, didn't he kill somebody?"* The Little One replied, *"Lay low Shanelle, that tie is starting to look like a noose."*

Alex started the car. It never required so much effort, but I swear when he put his hands back on the steering wheel, he looked like he wanted to smack me in my face. I was immobile and two inches short of a beating. Alex sped down Frelinghuysen and then to Broad Street in five minutes flat. We passed Zanzibar and headed for the New Jersey Turnpike. He snatched the Turnpike ticket and shifted the gears in one swift motion. Another rant began.

"I asked you to do one thing Shanelle, one thing and you didn't listen to me. I ask my mother to do something and she does it. Any of my sisters, they do it. Here it is my wife, just short of one week married, baby on the way eating a two piece in the projects with the lead suspect in an undercover operation that I was lucky enough to get assigned to! Now, because of you, I'm back on the beat in a boring ticket assignment just because you felt like acting like a project girl!"

I reclined my seat back and processed the rest of Alex's rage. His Mazda felt like the closet Steven and I shared. I turned to the side silently numb and faced the passenger window as Alex weaved in and out of traffic.

"They're nice people Alex," I yawned, throwing his precious seedling in his face. "Besides, all this yelling is not good for the baby."

My good guess was right. He turned the radio on and shifted his gear down a notch. The engine raced and settled while Alex adjusted the station to CD 101.9. Defeated and exhausted, I slept the rest of the way home under the cloak of Alex's second rage.

Silent Treatment

Back at the apartment, the silence between us was deafening. Alex quickly made phone calls to his family. He spoke to his father first; slumped in the couch like he lost his best friend. I took a quick bath and climbed into bed for a nap. I could barely hear what Alex was saying but at least he wasn't venting on me. It was enough embarrassment and shame for one day and I didn't want to hear anymore. Neither one of us had dinner that night. Even though he was home, he chose to sleep on the couch. I wanted him to wrap me up in his arms, but he wouldn't come near me. The next morning, Alex quietly slipped in the bedroom and took his uniform and underwear out of the closet. I pretended to sleep as I focused on my aching heart. It felt like it was burning on the inside as my head began to tingle. Alex tiptoed around the room until it was time to leave. I could hear a few dishes clanging in the sink and smelled toast and bacon. I was too ashamed to get up and join him for breakfast, so I continued to lay there. Keys began to jingle in the distance. The bedroom door opened. Alex crushed the mattress and softly stroked my hair.

"Good morning," he said, sweeping my hairline with his thumb. "I'm leaving. I left your breakfast in the oven and cut up some oranges for you."

I grabbed his wrist.

"I'm so sorry Alex."

He kissed my forehead. "I know baby. I love you and I'll see you later."

I held on as he pulled away and headed to the door.

The pain of Alex leaving me was too much to endure. The sheets fell to the floor as I headed for the kitchen. In addition to the breakfast in the oven, I finished off the cream cheese and a cupful of peanut butter. The sound of the phone ringing instantly interrupted my frenzy. I forced the rest of the food down my throat and answered.

"Hello."

"Shanelle, hi baby, it's me, mama."

The tone in here voice took me back to childhood as I sat down on the kitchen chair. I wiped the residue from my mouth.

"Hi mama, how are you?"

"Fine Shanelle, I called to see how you were feeling?"

The soft compassion in her voice forced tears to my eyes as the eggs and bacon swelled in my throat.

"I did a stupid thing mama."

There was compassion in her voice.

"What happened?"

I wanted to tell her, but the bouts of isolation between the two of us could not compel my answer. I loved her, but I wasn't willing to risk more negative judgments. Besides, the news would only hurt her more. Most of it was about Steven's thievery sprees at Garvey.

"How's daddy?" I struggled, "I miss him so much."

She breathed a sigh of relief.

"We both miss you sweetheart; he was so excited when I told him I saw you at Shoprite. He wants you to visit."

My leg bounced, rattling the hardwood floor.

"I'm sorry mama, I can't, maybe we could meet somewhere."

There was a long pause between us.

"Why can't you come home Shanelle? We love you."

My fingers locked into a wad of hair.

"Then why did you do that to me mama? Why did I always have to pack my bags and go, I didn't do anything wrong."

"Shanelle, we didn't know what to do. We were so afraid of losing Steven in the streets. We did everything we could to keep him home and medicated."

Air filled my lungs and head. I felt dizzy. In retrospect, that kind of love led me into the streets for sanctuary. In fact, it led me straight into Alex's arms, good, bad or indifferent.

"Mama, the doorbell is ringing, I have to go. I'll call you later."

I didn't wait for her to respond. There was no one at the door, but at least there was silence. I immediately thought of Tammy. With nowhere to go, all I could do was stay busy. I took out a pen and paper, jotting down things to accomplish. Clean up, take a shower and write a note to my parents. The letter came first.

Dear mom and dad,

After all that's happened, I can still honestly say that I love you both. I want to hate you, but I can't. It's a strange paradox feeling this way, but I struggle with it every day. You missed an important time in my life so it's hard for me to tell you what's new. Everything is not so peachy keen because of the emptiness that comes from not having you in my life. We've got some wounds to heal and that's going to take time. Meanwhile, we're expecting our first baby on April 27th. The Fosters are my in-laws and have been very good to me. I'm trying to be a good wife and continue school. I haven't forgotten my dreams and maybe one day they'll come true. It's hard for me to say when I'll see you again. I resume classes at St. James in September. I have a full course schedule. Maybe we can meet in the fall when I'm on that side of town. Other than that, life is going in any direction the wind takes me.

Love Always,

Shanelle

I sealed the letter and quietly put it in an envelope. I looked around and decided that instead of binging, I was going to clean the apartment. Working on each room at a time, I dusted, swept and polished each room to a bright and shiny finish. I marinated chicken and took out string beans for steaming. A few citrus candles enhanced the aroma in the apartment. The TV remote needed to be where Alex left it last. For his own comfort and convenience, I needed to stay out of his way.

While dinner slowly simmered, I quickly changed the sheets and fluffed up the pillows. The voices giggled behind my back.

"She sure is making a fuss for him tonight."

The sound of Alex's key in the door and a quick look at the clock was my cue to greet him at the foyer. He strode through the door and immediately looked around. He smiled briefly and passed me by as my arms slumped from his immediate rejection.

"Smells good Shanelle, what did you cook?"

"Grilled chicken and steamed vegetables," I gazed at him, hoping to catch his glance.

Before he shut himself off from the world, Alex threw his hat and bullet proof vest on the coffee table. The bedroom door quickly slammed.

"Humph," the Little One griped, *"All that cleaning for nothing. You're so stupid Shanelle."*

My fingernail slowly tapped against the kitchen table as I contemplated my next move. There was nothing left for me to do. Five minutes passed. I sat at the table and put my head in my hand as my elbow rested on the table. Suddenly, Alex emerged, wearing black cotton boxers. His skin was smooth and his muscles were tightly etched in Olympic position. He grabbed the remote and plopped on the couch. Silence rested between us until the phone rang. When Alex answered, he stared at the earpiece and hung up.

"Wrong number?" I asked.

"Whoever it was hung up."

"Oh." I replied, wondering if it was Steven. Now wasn't the time.

Three steps forward, my toes gripped the floor. My hands gingerly rested at my sides.

"Are you hungry Alex?"

"Yeah, give me a minute Shanelle, I'm tired."

I quickly made his dinner and sat it on the table. His fork and knife were perfectly lined up next to his favorite plate. Three cubes of ices clanging in his favorite glass brought back a faint memory of the day I saw him at the wedding. He was so graceful and handsome that day. I would have given anything to turn back the clock and do it right this time. I peered at my stomach and then at Alex. His head was resting back in the fold of his arm. I traipsed into the bedroom and crawled under the sheets, hurt and defeated. Alex answered the phone again. In five minutes, it rang again.

"Hey Jack, what's up?"

"Nah. I'm cool; Captain Fisco said he was going to make a few calls to see if I can get another assignment. In a way I'm glad because I need to be closer to my wife."

I slid my body across the bed towards the edge and continued to listen.

"Nah man, you know I can't be mad at her too long, I'm crazy about her."

He laughed a little.

"Watch your mouth, that's my wife when you get finished. We'll work it out, but listen; I just saw point man on the news. They just bumped him up to maximum security. They said a few leaks got back to the runners and blew their cover down on Runyon Ave in Newark. Yeah man, no kidding. Even if they put me on, we won't be together anyway."

I didn't have any idea what Alex was talking about, but whatever information he shared with Jack seemed important.

"Listen, come by this weekend and bring your new girlfriend. We can grill on the patio. What was your score at the range?" Alex's feet hit the floor.

"Not bad, not bad. Ok, I'll see you Saturday."

I placed the sheet over my hips. My eyes began to close as I listened to Alex's fork hit his plate. He never asked me to join him so I stayed in the room. I don't know how long I slept, but when I rolled over he was stroking my hips with his fingertips. His face was an inch within mine darting a glance at my stomach. Finally making eye contact, Alex began to stroke my face and lips with his thumb. I searched for questions, doubts or simple rhetoric, but I couldn't read him. He buried his head in my neck and took a deep breath. I held him back as my body began to shiver in his arms. Alex ran his hand up and down my back until I began to moan. He slid down and rested his head against my stomach and began to kiss my belly button.

"Hey Pumpy, I bet it's nice and warm in there."

Giggling this time, my stomach heaved up and down. He palmed the space protecting our unborn child and warmed me over with his words.

"You look so sexy pregnant."

I didn't care what I looked like. I was happy to have him next to me in our sheet woven cocoon. Even if he needed space, at least he was craving me. I draped my leg on his back as an invitation to love me in anyway imaginable. In Alex's world, the only thing that seemed to calm him was caressing my stomach. He placed his head closer to my womb and quietly drifted off.

Alex slumbered into a deep sleep. He didn't feel me slip away. I contemplated eating, but made some decaffeinated tea and rolled up on the couch with a comforter. The remote became my friend into the early morning as I watched the Dukes of Hazzard thinking, *"Damn that Daisy, she's so skinny."*

Accepting Change

By the time November rolled around, there was enough family and holiday excitement to keep me busy. Candy finally came home after staying an extra month in Pittsburg. She hooked up with Tammy and Nicole one time as a courtesy to me, but I knew she wasn't feeling my sister-in-law. Candy got a job as a flight attendant for Continental Airlines. Missy traveled domestic and international flights four times a week and had the weekends off. She brought me souvenirs from all around the world including cute flowing tops to compliment my shape. We barely had time to spend together, so we made a point of hooking up on Fridays before I headed back to Lakewood. Every time she saw me she kissed my big belly like a happy fool. She was excited about being a Godmother, but she was hell bent on not changing pampers. Pumpy was growing by leaps and bounds. An ultrasound confirmed two months ago that Alex and I were having a boy. My face and stomach was as round as Florence from Good Times. The entire Foster family agreed that being pregnant with a baby boy made a woman beautiful. My skin was flawless and my hair grew past my shoulders. There was nothing but dreamy looks every time Alex stared at me. Change came with the comfort of knowing people loved me without ridicule and judgment. I decided that my world needed to stay that way, especially for my baby. The slightest negativity from anyone sent me into avoidance, so I simply wrapped myself up in the warmth of people who truly cared about me.

My classes were intellectually stimulating. I learned so much about myself and my ability to voice opinions about the world around me. I usually spent an extra ten minutes chatting with my professors about international politics and children's rights. Several professors encouraged me to seek an internship in Washington next year to see congress in action. I considered the thought by writing in my journal: *"Washington; a dream deferred for now."* In the meantime, the health and safety of my unborn child consumed my thoughts as I put my future career on hold.

I had small bouts of sadness at St. James because there weren't too many people interested in hanging out with the "prego girl" Ring or not, I didn't look fashionable next to any girl trying to make a name for herself. On sadder days, I watched girls my age hustle by in cute jeans and tops, holding hands with their college beaus. There was intellectual and social divide for me on a daily basis. It wasn't like I could hang out at the pubs with beer and cigarettes in my hand; it wasn't healthy for me or Pumpy. I met a few older women in my classes who rallied around my progress. I encouraged their youthful exuberance and they encouraged me to accept the things I could not change for now. Overall, I was glad to have Candy in my life because she was down with me no matter what.

As for Alex, he seemed to slowly forgive me after the Garvey thing. He settled back into his routine simply because I did the things that made him happy. That was his definition in our relationship. After several sleepless nights, I figured out that Alex loved me, but there was another side to him that didn't sit right with me. I only saw it twice, but I never wanted to see it again. My resolve was that acceptance to change made him a happy man. As long as he believed that I was conducting myself like a lady and being a good mother to his son, there was no need for him to act like a raging beast. Like some unwritten code of conduct, I was a loyal wife and he was a good husband. We respected each other's boundaries, but Alex defined my limits without any input from me. Alex defined his own code of conduct in our marriage. To the outside world, he looked absolutely perfect. It was a strange dynamic, but it beat the cruel abyss I left so long ago.

In preparation for finals, I stayed at Candy's house Tuesday through Friday and came home after hooking up with Candy. Alex brought me a used four door Toyota Camry to get back and forth. He had full confidence in me again in my decision not to return home or to Garvey. I called him from Candy's house every night before I went to bed. It was hard not being with him, but he knew how much an education at St. James University meant to me. One week shy of Thanksgiving, I stayed late at the library to study. The campus was fluttering with activity as students and faculty prepared for homecoming festivities. At five months, Pumpy was an active baby inside my womb, but usually settled in after seven p.m. My hands were glued to my belly all the time. There was nothing left to do but fixate on my growing stomach. It was a miracle of our love and I was growing fond of motherhood as the days went by.

Bonnie was at Morgan State University raising hell and selling jewelry to get by. She was still kickin' it with her grammar school sweetheart and she called every now and then to say hi. Memories of all my friends filled my face with a soft smile as I sat at the table. I picked up my pen to jot down a few notes, when suddenly; an old friend walked up to the table and placed a biology book next to me. I looked up in complete astonishment.

"Shanelle?" he asked, smoothing his face over with wide eyes.

"Derrick?"

I followed his handsome face as he walked around the table next to me. I immediately stood up, reaching on my tippy toes to hug him. Derrick leaned in like I was a delicate swan. He rubbed my back in small circles.

"Wow, it's so good to see you. Look at you."

Derrick grabbed my left hand and studied my ring finger.

"Married too. My how time flies, who's the lucky guy?"

Charming as ever, he placed his hands behind his back and tapped his foot while he waited for an answer. I folded my hands across my stomach and blushed, "Alex Foster, he's a police officer."

Derrick shook his head up and down and placed his hand under his chin in heavy thought.

"Ah yes," he replied, "Honor, serve and protect."

I began to rub my belly and chuckled.

"Yes, you can say that."

I wanted to know more about him so I tapped his arm and said, "So, what's been up with you after all this time Dr. Johnson?"

Beams of bright light bounced off his wide eyes.

"First year medical student, Gross Anatomy, merit scholar, little bit of this and that."

I egged him on, tapping his arm.

"And, how's your love life?"

He rocked back and forth.

"No one special. I was holding out hope for you."

His almond shaped eyes and warm smile melted my frame. I didn't feel anything for him, but he made me feel special.

"Enough about me Shanelle, how are you feeling? Look at you. Pregnancy suits you, you're beautiful."

I held my head down, but he picked it back up.

"Keep your head up lady, there's nothing down there except feet and shoes."

He leaned in and whispered, "I'm sorry, maybe you can't see your shoes."

Like old times, I smacked his arm, peering up at his mature, charismatic smile. "Shut up Derrick!"

He grabbed my hand, gently sweeping it with his thumb.

"You know I'm just playing Shanelle."

Derrick looked around at the patrons staring at us and softly whispered, "Do you want to go to the sub shop for coffee, uh, well maybe milk and cookies?"

The child trapped inside of me giggled.

"Sure."

Like the days gone by, in an innocent gesture, Derrick picked up my books and escorted me out of the library. There was a chill in the air so he stopped and waited for me to button up my swing coat.

"Nice and warm now?" He asked.

"Yes, I'm fine," I said, as my face blushed over like the good ole days. Crisp leaves in red, yellow and brown swept by us as we casually strolled across the campus. Derrick carefully slowed down his pace. He looked down at me.

"You look so cute waddling like a little mama duck."

I put my hand through his arm and said, "You know you're the only person who can get away with a comment like that."

He patted my hand. "I know Shanelle, I know."

The black iron gates of the university faced us as I referenced my vehicle. "Let's put my books in the car so you don't have to carry them."

Derrick looked down at me and said, "It's no bother Shanelle, I'll carry your books anytime."

I felt like a teenager all over again as I continued to hold his arm, glancing up with a smile.

"Still the gentleman Derrick."

"Always Shanelle."

Derrick escorted me to a booth in the back of the Campus Sub Shop. He helped me out of my coat and held my arm as I sat in the booth. I smoothed out my clothes and crossed my ankles as Derrick went to the counter and ordered two caffeine free hot chocolates with whipped cream. His side profile was so handsome. I was sure he found some new hair care products to tame his wild wooly hair. Derrick's new mustache made him look more mature as he waited to pay the cashier. A few guys came in the store and gave him his proffers.

"Yo D, what's up, how's life at Cornell Med?"

Derrick shook hands and pounded chests with them as they looked up to the mighty alumni.

"Can't complain," he said, walking away with a smile. He slid into the booth and passed the steaming cup towards me.

"Be careful, it's hot."

I couldn't resist asking, "Like I used to be?"

Derrick leaned into the table and said, "You're still hot, Alex is a lucky guy."

I looked down at my bulging belly.

"Yeah he is lucky."

Derrick viewed the scenery around us.

"Are you happy Shanelle?"

I sighed, swiping the tip of the frothy cream.

"Sometimes I'm happy and sometimes I'm relieved that all of that stuff is behind me." My metal spoon clanked the mug.

"What about you Derrick, are you happy?"

Derrick leaned back into his booth and took a deep breath.

"Academically yes, my life is on the fast track. I just haven't found my soul mate. You know how much I want that Shanelle."

He cleared his throat.

"Remember all the plans we used to have?"

"Yes," I blinked, watching his smooth full lips.

"It takes a lot to juggle your time and attention between medical school and a relationship. I barely have time for myself."

He paused, placing his mug down.

"Some of the women out here are not hearing it Shanelle. They're not willing to put their lives on hold while I waste away in a library."

I sipped my hot chocolate and sat back.

"Hmm, sounds like someone I know."

"I think if I stayed local I could have convinced you Shanelle."

My watch flashed in front of me.

"We'll never know Derrick."

He nodded. "You're right."

"Hey," I questioned, "whatever happened to Portia?"

Derrick leaned forward.

"Bad news, Ricky called me and said that she left Spelman. He said she went to a frat party and things got out of hand. Portia cried rape and her father went storming down there with a pocket full of money and expensive attorneys. I'm not going to mention the school, but two leading scorers were expelled after the indictment. You know Dr. Davidson had to get her out of there. She was getting death threats from across the country for messing up the point spread the night she was attacked. Basketball is big business down there. I heard she's lying low taking classes right here at St. James."

"Really, I haven't seen her at all."

"She probably doesn't want to be seen," he guessed.

"How's your mom?" I asked.

"Good," Derrick replied. "She asks about you all the time."

"Oh, that's nice, tell her I said hello," wiping my lips dry.

"Listen, I better run, it's getting late."

"Where do you live Shanelle?" Derrick asked.

"Lakewood, but I stay at Candy's house during the week."

"Oh," Derrick replied.

I slid out of the booth and reached for my coat.

"It was really good seeing you again. Thanks for the hot chocolate."

Derrick grabbed my hand, stalling for time.

"It was really good seeing you again too Shanelle."

He helped me put my coat on and waved to the guys behind him.

Even though we said our goodbyes at the sub shop, Derrick escorted me to my car and watched me pull off. I peeked at the rear view mirror thinking, "It was really good seeing him again."

By the time I got home, Candy's father Leonard retired for the evening. He left a note on the table that read, *"Page Candy through the airline dispatch. She has a layover in D.C. and call Alex now, he called three times."*

I glanced at my watch. It was nine-thirty and I knew he was worried. Alex picked up on the first ring.

"Shanelle?"

"Hi baby," I softly toned.

"Why are you getting in so late? I was worried."

"I stayed at the library to cram for finals, but I'm okay."

"How's my son?"

"He's just fine. I love you."

"I love you too baby," he moaned, "I wish you were home lying next to me."

I stroked my collarbone longing for his big bear hug.

"Alex, I have finals and I need to study."

He rolled over and switched the phone to his other ear.

"I know I'll see you tomorrow after work baby."

Long distance love filled my throat.

"Okay."

"Goodnight mommy."

"Goodnight Alex."

As I ascended the stairs, a tight cord squeezed my heart. The need in his voice led me straight down the stairs back to the phone. I dialed the number and exhaled.

"Hello."

"It's me."

"I know, what's up?"

Pausing first, looking at someone else's walls, I drifted off with my refrain.

"I think I'm going to transfer to Monmouth University. Don't get me wrong, I love St. James, but I want to be closer to you."

Alex swallowed and paused.

"Sounds good. I'll call tomorrow and get an application."

I went to the blue room and climbed into bed. I was craving Alex, but I knew it wouldn't be long before I saw him.

The next day I met Candy for an early dinner. She looked exhausted, but wanted to see me just the same. She handed me a gift bag with two outfits for her Godson.

"Candy, stop buying everything and wait until he gets here."

She pushed my hand away.

"Girl, stop telling me what I can and cannot buy. You know I'm going to spoil him and when I have my own, you better spoil mine rotten too."

She pinched my healthy cheeks.

"You look happy, what's new?"

I ordered a Greek salad and handed the waitress the menu.

"No big surprises, I'm just trying to make sense of everything. You know, the baby, classes and Alex."

"Alex is your toughest challenge I bet," Candy replied.

"Yeah he is, but we'll work it out as long as he gives me space. He is trying Candy." I smoothed the white linen table cloth and focused on a passerby.

"Oh yeah, I'm going to take two classes in the spring just to get ready for the baby and transfer to Monmouth University."

"Well, that's good, but you know we won't see each other as much. I'm getting ready to do Newark to L.A. three times a week to cut down on my fatigue. The money is nice, but I'm tired. Clinton and I are getting more and more serious and it's hard keeping up with his sexy ass."

"Do you love him Candy?" I asked.

Her eyes danced a bit as she sipped her diet ice tea.

"Oh Shanelle," Candy exhaled, "You are such a sucker for romance. But yes, since you asked, we're in love."

I grabbed her hand expecting the best.

"Please have a big wedding but wait till Pumpy's born so he can be in it with us."

"Oh, now you're planning my wedding?"

"Well you were trying to plan mine! Just give me the date and I'm there girl."

We toasted our glasses and ate over chatty small talk. Candy looked so pretty being in love and I was genuinely happy for her. Parts of me wanted to hop on the next flight and hang out, but I could sense she wanted to slow up her pace too. Candy gave my belly a good rub before she hugged me goodbye. To her surprise, Pumpy gave her a swift kick.

"Shanelle, did you feel that? He kicked me?"

Catching my breath, I laughed out loud.

"Of course I did silly. Let me get on the parkway. I'll call you later."

Candy hopped in her two seater and waved, "Ok, I love you."

By the time I got home Alex greeted me at the door and took my overnight bag.

"Dinner's ready if you're hungry."

Alex carried my bag to the laundry room area and said, "I'm proud of you baby."

"Why?"

"Well, I used to worry, but not as much now."

"I know," I proudly stated, "I'm trying to stay focused. Besides, as long as there's no pressure in my life to do and be all these things, I think I can manage."

I went into the bedroom and picked out a white sheer gown that fell just pass my booming ass. It was his favorite piece because it gave him easy access. Alex nuzzled in my neck and blew air into my ear. His firm hand led me to the edge of the bed. Alex knelt down and talked to my stomach. My eyes rolled back in my head as Alex laid me down and put his face between my legs. He bit Kitty right through my panties as I rubbed the top of his head. The sheer fabric and his thick tongue filled his mouth. He slid my panties off and finished me off while he massaged my thighs. My legs slumped to the floor in pure fatigue.

"Not yet, I'm not finished and you need to eat."

He slid behind me and kissed the small of my back. "C'mon Shanelle," Alex said, "Get up." I rolled over and rested my head under his chin. I pleaded with him to let me sleep, but he wouldn't let me. "You're too sexy to sleep right now and besides, I want to make love to you."

Alex picked up my robe and helped me put it on. We sat on the patio and ate dinner under the stars. He picked my feet up and rested it on his legs while we ate steam vegetables and shrimp. He caressed my chin with his hand.

"I'm a lucky man Shanelle."

I put my plate on my lap.

"So what makes you so lucky?"

It didn't take much for him to answer.

"Remember the night we met again at the wedding?" He asked.

"Yes," I replied, "I remember."

Alex held my hand against his chest.

"You looked like the sweetest angel in pink when I realized it was you."

I giggled in the dark as my big belly pressed into his flat stomach. "Actually, I was wearing fuscia," I gloated, placing my plate down.

"I remember when you walked out. I followed you to make sure you didn't leave me again."

"Oh?"

"My palms were so sweaty; I had to wipe it on my tux."

"Yes, that beautiful Armani tux, you were so handsome."

He chuckled, bobbing his head.

"I still got it going on girl."

I slid my hands down the back of his boxers and said, "You can say that."

The clock alarm kicked in as Vaughn Harper's silky voice emitted through the speakers. *Very Special* by Debra Laws serenaded us as we danced in our bare feet.

"We better enjoy this now," Alex said. "When Pumpy gets here, we'll be too tired."

My voice was light and sweet.

"We'll put him between us that's all."

Alex sang the entire song to me as he stroked my back and breasts. He was so smooth he danced me back to the bedroom and on to the bed. He couldn't pick me up like the old days. I was finally too heavy for him to sweep me off my feet. Making love at five months became a chore too, but Alex was good at taking his time. In fact, creative foreplay was his specialty. I bit my lip as he laid me on my side and entered me. It was the easy way to make love without Pumpy getting in the way. Alex bit my neck and stroked my nipples into hard rocks. My stomach tensed up as Kitty grooved to the swell of Alex's entry. He grabbed my hand as we locked our fingers down to compliment his release into me. The pleasure he felt kept him engorged as he continued to rock his manhood into me for another five minutes. Suddenly, the phone began to ring. Both of us were too exhausted to pick it up, but we managed to strain our ears as the answering machine went off in the living room.

"Hi son, uh, hi Shanelle, it's me Pops. Look here, call me when you get a minute, I have some news for you."

Alex jumped up and returned the call. His conversation sent chills through my body.

"Hey pops what's up?"

Erie silence followed.

"When?" Alex asked.

"Just you? You don't think that'll look suspicious?"

"What time is your flight?"

"Ok, uh, no, I'm off tomorrow so I'll take you to the airport, no problem."

"Shanelle? She's fine; we were in bed when you called. Ok Pops, I'll see you tomorrow at six."

"What happened?" I asked.

Alex slid under the covers, rubbing my arms to ward off the shivers.

"Grandma Mae, she passed away this morning."

He shook his head as I offered my sympathy.

"She lived a good life Shanelle and gave me a new one.

Pops said that Grandma Mae had cement poured in the pet cemetery last month. She had a playground installed for all of her grandkids and great-grands. She must have known she was leaving. I'm just sorry I didn't say goodbye."

I pressed my forehead against his cheek.

"Alex, there's so many ways to say goodbye, just think of something and we'll do it. I don't want this to eat you up inside."

He got off the bed and put his sweat pants on.

"Where are you going?" I asked.

"The beach, do you want to come?"

I was worn out and exhausted, but I didn't want him to go alone. I threw on a heavy Gap sweat suit and a baseball cap as we headed out the door. I leaned my head on his arm as he quietly dealt with his grief. I didn't know what to say to him as we trudged through the damp sand. The cold air awakened my senses as I inhaled. Pumpy moved for a minute as I rubbed my stomach to connect with him. Alex held my hand and looked up at the sky. Tears continued to stream down his face as he stepped from side to side.

"I looked for you in the stars Shanelle and asked God to send you to me. I also asked Him to forgive me for the awful thing I did that night to protect my mother's honor. I'd do it all over again if I had to and keep atoning for my sins until I die."

The wind pierced through our skin so hard that Alex had to wrap me up in our blanket as he held me. Alex continued to look at the dark waters and said, "Thank you Grandma Mae for what you did for me. I love you and I'm sorry I never had a chance to say that to you."

It was too cold to sit and reflect. Alex could feel me shivering through the blanket as he wiped his final tear away.

"C'mon, let me get you home where it's warm."

I think if there was no forgiveness in the world, the cold sand would have opened up a large vacuous hole and sucked us straight to hell. I traipsed lightly across the sand unsure that it was going to happen like a bad nightmare from the past. I looked up at my warrior and squeezed his hand. All the things I needed were within my reach as Alex ceremoniously accepted his faults and asked for forgiveness. I squinted as the sharp wind cut into my face. A kind voice spoke to me.

"Stay by his side, forget the past, trust him and no harm will come to me in the dark of night or light of day."

In some strange ceremony, when we arrived home, Alex and I washed away our past with a hot shower. We cried in each other's arms and forgave each other for the squabbles and doubts that came between us. Pumpy was our greatest joy as Alex kissed my stomach under the covers. He set the alarm for five o'clock and within an instant we were sleep.

Flash Back

The sound of the phone ringing woke me up as I rolled over on Alex's side of the bed. I looked at the clock. I stretched my arm across the bed and answered.

"Hello."

"How's my little nephew Shanelle?"

"Steven, I told you not to call here."

Another voice chimed in from the living room to emphasize my message.

"Yeah Steven, you heard my wife, she told you not to call here, do I need to come over there and remind you?"

A dial tone followed Alex's threat as I hunched down under the covers. I didn't realize he was home and I was scared that the past we buried last night came right back. Alex reached the bedroom door and stared at me. I immediately confessed.

"I'm sorry Alex, he only called here once. He stole the money I gave my mother. It had our phone number written on it. You were so mad at me after Garvey I never got a chance…"

Alex put his fingers to my lips.

"Shanelle, relax, its ok."

My stomach was heaving up and down so fast Alex laid his hand on my belly to settle me down.

"Don't do this, I'm not mad, I just want you to be safe, that's why I flipped out about Garvey."

I searched his eyes for the truth and leaned back on the bed while Alex went to the fridge for some water.

He opened it up, handed it to me.

"Shanelle, your brother is in the red with a lot of people. I can't say much, but he's basically a wanted crack head. I'm surprised he had the balls to call you, but whatever is going on, he must be desperate."

Alex kissed me on the forehead and grabbed his car keys.

"Where are you going?" I asked.

"I have a few errands to run, I'll be back by noon."

As Alex rolled out of the parking lot I nestled back under the covers. Intuition was the last thing on my mind as my eyes shut. Just as my world became a safer place, a blue wall of silence fell over North Orange for operation Sitting Bull. In the year that it took Alex and I to fall in love and conceive a child, I accepted everything he did without question. I was so blind; it didn't make sense to ask. Ultimately, everything happens at great sacrifice and that day, redemption fell on Garvey Street. The point man Alex referred to by phone was the infamous criminal I saw on the news months ago. He was Rico's first cousin from Garvey. Rico was second in command for Garvey, even though point man lived in the Fordham section of the Bronx. Six caseloads of glocks, five kilo's of coke and five hundred vials of crack were stored in Mama Barb's apartment moving in and out under the guise of five dollar chicken dinners. Steven fucked up because he decided to take advantage of Mama Barb's drunken Friday night stupor and shoved a handful of crack vials in his pocket along with three glocks. His addiction forced him to brag about what he stole and how "stupid," Mama Barb was for letting him into her apartment. Steven even had the nerve to smoke with the hood snitches. Word got back to Rico in thirty minutes. That "hot" gossip blazed a trail throughout North Orange and that's how Steven became a wanted man. No matter how small the loot, disrespecting a king pin was a guaranteed death wish.

Rico's house phone was wiretapped for the last six months and the feds knew that Steven would prove to be the fall guy in the operation. Alex had his own "fall" in mind. He was cool with Dominick, aka, Nick, a sneaky cop who smacked the knuckle heads around at Wayne Valley basketball games. Since Steven bit into Nick's profits by stealing the weapons and drugs, Nick was ready to pay Rico a personal favor. Nick gave Alex the heads up since Steven was related to me. Alex acquiesced with silence and hence the job was given the green light. Alex's only request was that Nick kept Steven out of a body bag.

As the sun began to settle on Garvey, Nick went on to the roof and dragged Steven's cranked out frame to the eleventh floor. Nick ravaged Steven's knees with a Billy club and flipped him over for one good crack against his scull. After that, he hoisted his body head first into the garbage shoot for an eleven foot fall into the needle and roach ridden garbage heap. Luckily, the remnants of an old mattress broke his fall as an elderly woman lifted the wall shoot and screamed in horror. The paramedics took their time. By the time Steven's mangled body made it on a stretcher to North Orange Memorial Hospital, Steven was paralyzed from the neck down and lost his ability to speak.

Nick received a handsome reward, including a promotion to detective and an antique World War II starter pistol. The feds criminal wrap sheet on Steven's crime sprees in New York City and the surrounding areas of Essex were enough for the feds to close the investigation on Steven without question. After a fully executed warrant, no weapons could be found at Mrs. Viv's home. She cursed the federal officers, but fed the local officers who had been kind to her over the years. As for Steven and Mrs. Viv, well she was happy just tending to her dear boy without the worry of his drug addictive ways. She lobbied hard to get him on permanent disability and Medicare without question or inquiry. After a month long stay in Kessler, the prodigal son returned home again to Mrs. Viv's loving arms as she fed him mash potatoes and his favorite cherry Kool-Aid.

My life would never be the same again. Rumors of the shake down in North Orange ran rampant in three towns and followed me everywhere I went. My final resolve was to empty out my locker at St. James and remove all the left over clothes I left at Candy's house. Candy's advice was simple.

"Fuck em,' you know people only care about themselves at the end of the day. Besides, even if Alex had anything to do with it, you're his wife and you need to stay by his side even when things get rough."

As crazy as it sounded, for now, all I needed to do was to stay calm for the baby and keep Alex happy. That felt a lot better than my regrettable past.

That's Life

Mrs. Viv expected sympathy when she called to tell me about Steven's "terrible accident." I was more worried about what was taking Alex so long to get home because it was already nine-thirty p.m.

"Mama, I'll call you later, it's Alex."

When I reached the door, he staggered in with beer on his breath. I pushed him off me and said, "Where were you I was worried to death!"

He laughed and said, "Just celebrating with Jack, I'm sorry I forgot to call you baby."

I tightened my robe around my stomach. He grabbed my arm and said, "C'mon now, Shanelle, don't be mad, you know this is not like me."

"You're damn right this is not you and I don't like it one bit Alex."

Alex started laughing as he began to take off his soiled clothes. He took off each piece and stated his intentions, "Feisty one huh? Didn't you forget I'm your husband, your lover, your savior, provider and daddy to our son, don't you forget that sweetie."

I didn't like his tone, folding my arms against my swollen breasts.

"Sweetie my ass, sleep on the couch, you stink."

Alex dropped his hands to the sides.

"I'm going to take a shower and get into bed right next to my beautiful wife."

I took my robe off and laid it across the foot of the bed. Alex took a shower and started singing a Larry Graham song. I turned over twice as my stomach hardened and settled down. Alex stood at the sink and brushed his teeth. He came to the entrance of the doorway with a mouth full of frothy toothpaste.

"You still love me right?"

I wanted to vomit, but he was too charming. I put the covers over my head.

"I know you can't resist me girl." He went back into the bathroom and began to gargle. When he walked back into the room, Alex began to tease me by reciting the poem I wrote for him on our honeymoon. He pulled the sheet off and threw it to the floor.

"The maiden sighs today, it burrows beneath her brow, he who ponders deadly sacrifices, take a final bow."

"Alex, you're drunk," I warned, "go to bed."

He slid next to me and put his arms around my stomach.

"Pumpy, mommy's mad at me, but she'll forgive me, joy comes just before dawn."

After a few tosses and turns I finally went to sleep. There was so much confusion in the things he said, I could hardly make sense of it all. I simply decided to let it go for another day.

Special Delivery

I closed out the fall semester with a B plus average. I signed up for two independent study classes for the spring which cut my commute down to one day per week. By the time March rolled around I was ready to pop. Alex was promoted to detective and received a healthy raise. He was so diligent at saving his money; we were able to put a down payment on a three bedroom house in Brick, New Jersey. I spent most of my time shopping for the baby. The sky was the limit for Pumpy's nursery. Alex's mother damn near cashed in her pension to make sure Pumpy was set with every need and want. Alex and I went to my last doctor's appointment together. He hung on every word Dr. Robinson said regarding labor and delivery.

"You don't have to rush to the hospital the minute you feel contractions Shanelle. I would like you to bear with the pain as much as you can and call me when the contractions are at least fifteen minutes apart. The baby is in position. He's going to come when he's good and ready so be patient with him and be patient with each other."

By the time April 1st arrived, I completed my classes and bunkered down for Pumpy's arrival. I spent most of my time nesting in various ways. I tested the rocking chair, double checked the harness points on the car seat and dusted the blinds. Mrs. Viv called intermittently to check on me. She was so busy taking care of Steven's acute care status; she barely had time to talk. When she did call, she bragged about his accomplishments like he was a new born.

"Today Steven said, 'Ahhh, ahhh', for the first time Shanelle. I was so tickled pink I had to write it in my diary."

"That's nice Mama," I replied. Deep in the crevice of my brain, I remembered when Steven used to heckle at mentally handicap people. I smirked to myself thinking, *"Karma is a bitch."*

"Girl, Steven made a big stink on himself today. It was so bad; I had to call the aid to help me."

"Wow," I thought. *"Instead of him smearing it on the walls, it can finally reach the toilet bowls."*

"Listen mama, I've gotta' go, I'm going to the Fosters. Its family night and I don't want to be late."

There was a long pause in the phone. Mrs. Viv began to cry. "Look at me carrying on about Steven and here you are getting ready to have my first grandson. How selfish of me. Are you ready for all of this Shanelle?"

"Sure mama, we're ready, I have a wonderful husband and we're going to be great parents."

Avoidance on her part came quickly.

"Well would you look at the time. I have to feed Steven now. Take care Shanelle."

I didn't say goodbye. I hung up the phone and rubbed my stomach.

"Oh Pumpy, your granny is a piece of work. We won't try to change her. She has to do that on her own."

As time marched on, it became more and more difficult to get around. Alex wanted to make us more comfortable so he traded in his Mazda for a red Jeep Cherokee. I was thrilled because it was just enough room to stretch out for the three of us. Alex took me for a ride after we left the dealership and headed for the beach. It was a chilly day, but the warm sun felt so good against my face, I begged Alex to walk with me along the shore line. I waddled around for a little while, but the false contractions got so intense we had to sit down. Alex sat behind me as we practiced breathing together. He rubbed my legs down as we reminisced about all the days we spent on the beach together. Dusk began to settle on the sky as Alex held me in his arms. The water was so enchanting, with the exception of the cold wind, I didn't want to leave. Alex got up and extended his hand to help me up. When he did, there was a sudden pop between my legs. It felt like someone popped a champagne cork inside of me. Suddenly, a huge splash of water crashed between my legs like a busted water balloon.

"Alex, something's wrong."

He looked down at my legs.

"Shanelle, your water just broke."

The sweet and pungent odor whipped through the wind and into my nostrils. My nose scrunched up but I remembered thinking how good it felt just to release the fluid. Alex turned towards the vehicle.

"Damn, the jeep."

"Don't you start Alex."

He started smiling.

"Take off your pants."

I looked around. The coast was clear. I held onto Alex's back as he peeled them off. He turned them inside out and wiped the excess off my legs. Suddenly, a numbing pain shot through my back. A lightening strike spiraled up into a tight ball and landed in my stomach with sharp agonizing tugs and pulls. I bent over thinking the pain would quickly subside.

"Owwww, Alex! It hurts, it hurts, help me."

Alex put his arm around my waist.

"I know baby, it's a contraction, remember?"

I looked back at the crashing waters and contemplated running into the ocean. Maybe a large whale would swallow me whole and put me out of my misery. Alex had other plans.

"C'mon Shanelle, you can do it mommy, let's get to the car."

The pain started to diminish as we hastened back to the Jeep. Alex made me wait on the side walk while he covered his precious passenger seat with anything he could find.

"Alex!" I shouted, "They're leather seats, let me get in!"

My husband grimaced at the amniotic fluid trickling down my leg.

"You're right, I'm sorry."

It didn't matter what I said, he didn't want it on his darling seats. He grabbed the paper mats off the floor and hoisted me on top of the crumbled paper like a senior citizen sitting in three layers of cheap diapers. I rolled my eyes as he scrambled to the driver's side.

"Ok, let's get you home."

"Home?" I demanded, "Take me to the hospital now!"

"Shanelle, the doctor said…"

My balled up fist ended his lecture.

"Doctor this, doctor that, it's not what she says, this shit hurts!"

A sharp pain shot into my pelvic area.

"Help, oohh, help me, I can't take this!"

Alex took off down the street like an angry kidnapper.

"Shanelle," he calmed, "Your contractions are twenty minutes apart, we have to go home first."

I held the bottom of my stomach and growled like a demonic pit bull.

"Take me to the hospital now."

"Okay, I'll take you now."

After a quick check by Dr. Robinson, she sent me home to ride out the storm.

"Shanelle, listen to me, you can do it. You're not even dilated yet. Go home and rest. Call me when the contractions are ten minutes apart."

I cried all the way home. There was nothing that Alex could say or do to console me. His nerves got the best of him as he drove to his mother's house. I stayed in the car and damned them to a life of misery.

"I'm not going to make love to Alex again. He better not come near me or I swear I'll cut him!"

Another sharp pain shot through me as Mrs. Foster scurried out of the house, happy and calm.

"Are you having a contraction Shanelle?"

"Yes!" I whimpered.

"Look at me and focus on your breathing."

Her voice was so soothing and calm that I was able to settle down. Alex breathed a sigh of relief as he helped his mother get in the back seat.

Three hard contractions came in the time it took to get home. Mrs. Foster was consistent in getting me through each one as Alex nervously patted my hand.

Once we reached home, Mrs. Foster escorted me to the shower for a quick wash up. Alex packed the car with my bags and Pumpy's new car seat. The contractions became more and more intense as I cried to the heavens.

"Please help me, I can't do this God."

"Ok Shanelle," Mrs. Foster softly replied. "You can do this. Look at me and focus baby."

Alex laid my clothes out while Mrs. Foster helped me towel off. My compassion for others kicked in when the contractions stopped. I hugged Alex and apologized for yelling at him. Another contraction came and I damned his existence again.

"This was all your idea; you should have this baby, not me!"

Alex ignored me, flicking his wrist up to reference his watch.

"Mom, it's time to go, they're fifteen minutes apart."

"Who am I chop liver?" I asked. "I'm the one having this baby!"

The two of them coaxed me through my tirade. "You're right Shanelle, you are certainly right, are you ready?" Alex asked, rubbing my lower back.

"Yes, I'm ready."

They put me in the back of the car like I was a criminal. I guess it looked too embarrassing riding in the front seat thrashing my head around like a crazy person. The pain was so intense; I put my foot against the rear window of the driver's side and called on all of my biblical heroes.

"Moses, Matthew, Luke, John, Joseph, please deliver me."

Mrs. Foster looked at Alex hiding a smile.

"She's rolling some serious holy dice for this delivery."

I didn't find a damn thing funny and neither did Alex when he saw my filthy sneaker resting on his precious window.

"Shanelle, take your foot down."

"Shut up!" I screamed, as I bore down on my teeth.

Alex cocked his neck to the left and turned on the radio. As we rolled into the emergency entrance, I grabbed Mrs. Foster's sweat jacket and covered my face. The emergency room nurse met us at the car and tapped on my window. Alex jumped out and held the door open.

"Well, well, well," she doted, "who's hiding, a celebrity? Why are you covering your face?"

I took the sweatshirt off my face and cried like an I Love Lucy, episode.

"I'm having a baby and I don't want to do this."

She was sympathetic to my cause, but a smart ass in the same breath.

"Oh dear, I'm sorry sweetie, you made your bed, now you have to…"

"Don't even go there Nurse Ratchet!" I replied. "You don't even know me!"

The seemingly kind nurse looked at Alex and said, "Feisty one, good thing there's a shift change in fifteen minutes."

They escorted me down the longest hallway of my life. The nurse parked me next to a small window while a frail woman asked for our insurance cards.

"Excuse me," I said. "I really need something for the pain."

"I know sweetheart, your doctor will help you."

Alex put his hand on my shoulder and said, "Hang in there babe, we'll be upstairs soon."

I looked at her with puppy eyes. "Can I leave my socks on? My feet are cold."

The nurse went to a small cabinet and pulled out a pair of socks with grips on the bottom.

"Here," she said. "Put these on, the doctor's going to let you move around freely to get through some of your contractions."

Mrs. Foster and Alex sat upright and attentive as they watched my every move. Alex was more than happy to get a break.

I went into the small bathroom and changed into my gown. All I could do was hold onto the bottom of my belly and pray to God for forgiveness. My back was throbbing and the cramping intensified with each shot of pain.

"Alex!" I screamed. "Here comes another one!"

He came into the bathroom and wrapped his arms around me as I hugged him back. As the contraction deepened into a painful swell, Alex rubbed the lower portion of my back with hard strokes.

"Breathe Shanelle, that's it breathe."

"It hurts."

"I'm sorry it hurts baby, but you can do it Shanelle, just breathe."

I wanted to collapse to the ground, but Alex was strong enough to hold me up. After the pain subsided, we returned to the waiting area. The nurse took me by wheelchair to my private room. The minute Alex opened the door, I began to relax. Another nurse returned with medical machinery, including an intravenous drip. They poked, prodded and taped me up like an old shirt hanging on a clothes line. The next contraction came with so much intensity; the nurses had to wait for me to ride it out. I begged for mercy and forgiveness.

In two seconds, Dr. Robinson arrived

"Doc, you gotta help me!"

"Ok Shanelle, settle down. Is your contraction over?"

"Yes," I cringed.

"Ok, let me check you and we'll see what we can do about the pain."

She examined my cervix and said, "Sorry Shanelle, you're only dilated two centimeters, let's hold off on pain medication for an hour."

I immediately started crying. Alex rubbed my back. She looked at me with concern in her eyes and said, "I'm going to take a nap because I just finished a cesarean section, then you can have all of my attention, ok?"

She held my trembling hand and wiped my face. "You'll be fine, your little one likes it in there, but we'll see him in due time."

Alex ran his fingers through my hair as the tears ran down my cheek. His hand got tangled in a ferocious knot as my head jerked back.

"Ow, that hurts Alex!"

Mom Foster immediately jumped in.

"Alex, why don't you take a break while I sit with Shanelle. Go get some coffee son, she'll be fine."

I rubbed my scalp so he could remember the pain he inflicted on me. Alex winked at me with his cocky ass and left. He didn't even ask me if I wanted anything. It only made me take out another, *"Pay back is a bitch,"* card and add it to my deck.

As for Mrs. Foster, she decided to do a little soul searching. Turning once, she leaned forward.

"Shanelle, I never got a chance to talk to you about what happened between me and Alex so long ago."

She grabbed my hand as I grimaced in pain. The swell in my stomach didn't stir up any empathy.

"That was a terrible thing that happened that night. As a mother, there's nothing you won't do for your son."

We locked eyes for a moment.

"The love between a mother and a son can be the most magical feeling on earth. At times I think there's nothing that I wouldn't do for him. I ask God to forgive me every night for what I put him through. I don't know if I'll be forgiven, but in the meantime, I'll be there for him until my dying day."

Mrs. Foster wrapped her arms around me and stroked my back in downward motions as I gritted my teeth. The contractions were becoming more and more intense as time went by. If the pain of labor had anything to do with my past sins and regression, I surely needed God to forgive me. Once the contraction subsided, I leaned back onto the pillows while Mom Foster fed me ice chips. Alex returned to the room with Dr. Robinson. She checked me again and to my surprise, I dilated to four centimeters.

"Good girl Shanelle, you're making progress! Just get to five centimeters and I'll authorize an epidural to relieve some of the pain."

Without further hesitation, four interns passed me onto another bed and shipped me off to delivery. Alex donned a surgical suit while they administered my epidural. He hugged his mother as they said a quick prayer for me and Pumpy.

I began to strain and push but the nurses stopped me.

"No, no honey, don't push yet!"

I tried to resist the urge as they wheeled me into an extremely cold operating room. It was so medicinal I felt like I was the bride of Frankenstein. I was in good company too. Alex stood next to me wearing throw up green. His arms were planted across his chest in bouncer mode while he waited for his precious Pumpy to be born.

"Ok Shanelle, take one deep breath and push for me."

I did what she said and came to a sudden halt as the sound of chicken necks in a grinding machine grated my eardrums.

"I can't, he's breaking me!"

Alex went into football mode.

"Ok babe, let's make this quick, you can do it. Listen to the doctor. Take a deep breath and push, I'm right here."

I took a deep breath and pushed. My response was deafening as the pressure from Pumpy's head ripped me from front to back.

"I see the head, good girl Shanelle! Take a deep breath and do it again."

Alex pushed my legs back as I complied.

"Quick, quick Shanelle, here comes the shoulders, you can do it."

One last push came as Alex's eyes widened. My head slumped onto the pillow with relief as Pumpy finally came out weighing eight pounds and nine ounces of joy!

Alex dropped to his knees and lifted his hands to heaven as Dr. Robinson announced, "It's a boy! It's a boy!"

She held Pumpy up for me to see. He quivered his lower lip and whimpered before a shrieking cry spouted. Alex sprang to his feet and turned away from us quickly wiping away his tears.

"Don't cry Pumpy, mommy's here," I pitched, as the nurses attended to him. I was amazed at his sheer size. He had a big Charlie Brown head, massive hands and broad shoulders like his father. In fact, everything seemed to emulate the Foster family tree. Alex planted fourteen Reese's Peanut Butter kisses on my puffy cheeks. He approached the attending pediatrician and asked, "Ten fingers, ten toes?"

The pediatrician laughed.

"Yes, Mr. Foster."

Alex continued his inventory over his brand new race car.

"Penis?"

"Check."

"Hearing?" he asked.

"Looks good, he's following your voice right now."

Alex bent down in sheer wonderment.

"Hey man, it's me, your dad."

Pumpy released a Billy goat snort. The bond began right there as the pediatrician passed our little bundle to his father.

Like a delicate egg in the fold of his arm, Alex cried tears of joy.

"Hey, I would take you fishing but someone wants to meet you."

I held out my hands as Alex placed him in my arms. Pumpy was alert as he looked at his daddy towering over me.

Dr. Robinson and the attending pediatrician encouraged me to put Pumpy on my breast to nurse for a few minutes. My breasts looked too big for his mouth, but as Alex and Dr. Robinson exposed my breast to him, Pumpy immediately started thrashing his face back and forth to find my areola like a little pup. He opened his mouth and immediately latched on. Dr. Robinson stroked the side of his cheek as he began to suckle.

"Mrs. Foster was right, it is magical."

An instant attachment for him formed as I talked to him. The two minute ordeal put Pumpy to sleep as they tucked him into his bassinet and put an i.d. bracelet on him to match mine. Alex turned to the pediatrician.

"So doc, when does he go for the big snip?"

He tugged at his stethoscope and said, "Probably tomorrow, around ten."

Alex shook hands with him and said, "Do the right thing doc, just do the right thing."

He smiled and said, "Don't worry, it'll be perfect."

Our new life with Pumpy had just begun.

Happily Ever After?

On day three of my hospital stay, we left in a balloon and flower trail of glory. Pumpy was officially named Troy Alexander Foster, but we still called him Pumpy. Mrs. Foster followed behind us as Alex cursed every driver on the road.

"Slow down you idiot, we have a baby."

I looked at Alex like he was crazy. Suddenly everyone was a nut just because of his son. I sat in the back with Pumpy at Alex's request. I was calmer then he was. Alex was determined to keep me home with him and I didn't mind because I wanted Pumpy to have a healthy start.

Boxes of pampers, flower arrangements and money in festive envelopes were waiting for us. I held Pumpy in my arms and went straight upstairs to his Noah's Ark nursery. Alex peeked in on us as I immediately went to the rocking chair and nursed him. He was always hungry. Pumpy sucked hard for five good minutes and then passed out like I slipped him a Mickey. While he was sleeping, I carefully changed the dressing from his circumcision and changed his pamper. Mrs. Foster peeked in but kept her distance. They were giving me just the right space to be with my son.

The smell of chicken soup drifted into the room as I turned on his nursery monitor. Afterwards, I joined them downstairs for something to eat.

Mrs. Foster put a hot bowl of chicken soup on the table for me as I sat down.

"It smells wonderful," I said.

Alex kissed my cheek.

"You're doing a great job mommy."

I grabbed his wrist to make the feeling last a little longer. "Thank you, I needed to hear that."

I stayed with Alex and Mrs. Foster for a few minutes. Even though the nursery monitor was on, I wanted to check on him. I quietly slipped upstairs under the watchful eye of Alex. When I reached upstairs, my breasts began to leak the closer I got to his nursery. I stuck my head in the bassinet to listen to him breathing. He looked so peaceful tucked away in his quiet existence. Weariness began to set in as I sat in my rocking chair thinking about the world around me. Having Pumpy was Alex's greatest joy. Giving birth to him aroused feelings of motherhood, but not blissful happiness. My eyes began to soften as I searched for answers in my thoughts. The window facing me stirred up feelings of loneliness and sorrow as soft rain began to fall. Tears falling down my cheek accompanied the orchestra outside as I quickly jotted a poem in Pumpy's baby book.

Rainy Days

The search outside my window
Offers no purpose to my refrain.
A spring breeze gracefully pirouettes
as I watch the pouring rain.
I hope the rain cleanses me
while falling softly to the left.
An innocent redemption,
placed inside a delicate nest.
Upon the highest mountain,
welcome to the lair.
delicate thoughts of your touch,
Breathlessly awaiting innocent air.
Focus on reflection,
will it ever be explained?
Let it happen naturally,
Find solace in my refrain.

Alex stood in the doorway as I closed our son's baby book. He knelt down in front of me and placed his head in my lap. Alex looked so humble as if he was a peasant before my throne. Reality offered a different conclusion. In my weakest hour, he swept me off my feet and defined the person I had become. There was no way I could abandon the notion of being a good mother to his son. I wanted the same things, but it was much too soon. Our little miracle was Alex's sweetest redemption. My mind, heart and womb were the place that cultivated Alex's grand scheme. Deep inside, I knew I had a greater destiny. The temper festering inside of him needed to stay there while I figured a way out. I began to close my eyes as I stroked Alex's head. He nestled his cinnamon face in my lap and squeezed me tight as Pumpy began to stir. The sound of a faint whimper prompted Alex to fetch his son. He lips met Troy's warm cheek as he spoke to his little miracle.

"Hey little man, you hungry?" Alex laid him on the changing table and carefully changed his diaper. Pumpy's chubby legs jerked back as the cold air hit his bare skin. Pumpy began to pee but Alex was ready for him.

"C'mon son, that old trick, I was ready for you." Alex wiped him down and carried him to me as I lifted my shirt to nurse him. He grabbed his camera and began to take pictures of his son's first day home. Pumpy nursed for six straight minutes and went right back to sleep. Alex turned on a lullaby and tucked Pumpy back into his bassinet as I wearily climbed into bed. Life stood still for me as his massive hands tucked the corners of the sheets around my body like a cocoon. His lips pecked my moist mouth.

"Sleep tight baby."

I stared out the window for signs of life. Clean air whipped under the sill and soared through my nostrils. The serenity of the moment claimed me as I settled into Alex's and Pumpy's world.

Joy at Dawn

The smell of eggs and bacon engulfed the bedroom. I rolled over and stretched, blinking twice to focus. Pumpy's bassinet was right beside me. Luckily he started off on the right foot. I had to wake up twice for a feeding. He slept the night away like a good baby should. Alex huddled next to me, clearing his throat, "I'm off today, ma's downstairs cooking breakfast if you're hungry."

I sauntered to the bathroom, unwittingly glancing at my body. No voices stirred as I slowly brushed my teeth. I stepped into the shower and carefully washed my raw and achy frame. Parts of me felt alive and other parts of me felt like jello. After I got dressed, I joined Mrs. Foster in the kitchen.

"Good morning Shanelle, how did you sleep?"

"Great, Troy only woke up twice and went right back down after Alex changed his pamper."

"Good!" she replied. "Magical isn't it?"

Our orange juices glasses clanged in an instant toast.

"Very magical," I gushed with pride.

Just then the doorbell rang. Mrs. Foster got up to answer as my fork scraped my teeth. The excitement in her voice was a sure fire sign that Tammy was home from college and strapped down with company.

"Nikki, it's so nice to meet you. Shanelle's in the kitchen, come on in."

I clutched my robe shocked at the sight. It was Tammy and Nikki, Rico's sister from Garvey. My chair scraped the floor, pushing back to create distance between us. Nikki and Tammy hugged me with reservation. I backed up, searching the entrance for Alex.

"What brings you here?"

They locked eyes and laughed at their inside joke. The quick glance between them wasn't a girlfriend glance; it appeared a bit more intimate.

"Oh, Tammy and I are hanging out during the break," Nikki chuckled, "Besides I'm kinda' in between housing right now."

No doubt she was. The feds hauled Rico and the rest of her drug smuggling family out of Garvey so fast there was no way she had time to recover her things. The New York Times did a full expose on the reputed family and standing in my kitchen was the good black sheep of the family. Alex's heavy feet charged into the kitchen sending me out of my skin like the coat of a freshly sheered lamb. He ordered my life with a firm finger as his neck cocked to the side.

"Shanelle don't you hear my son? He's hungry."

I tightened my belt and grabbed two slices of cantaloupe. Alex pushed past me so fast he almost knocked me down. I gripped the banister, shoving the sweet fruit into my mouth as I listened to his tirade. A verbal war ensued the minute I reached the top landing.

"Who do you think you are Alex, I came to see my nephew and Nikki has known Shanelle since high school!"

I picked Pumpy up and settled his cries as he latched onto my areola. His tiny hand smoothed over my robe and gripped the soft edge.

"Tammy," Alex blared, "you've got a lot to learn. I'm sorry Nikki, being here is a conflict and you're smart enough to know why. Now that you know who I am, you have to leave."

Mrs. Foster jumped in as I rocked Troy back and forth. His quiet suckles calmed me like a sweet melody.

"No ma, that's not an option either. Not my house or your house!" Alex shouted.

The front door slammed. I strolled to the window burping our miracle. Small circular rubs produced a small burp. Pumpy held his head up wide eyed and attuned.

Tammy stormed down the walkway holding Nikki's hand as they marched to the car. Before she got inside, her eyes trailed the house as she spotted me. I smiled as a quiet tear trickled down my chin and into the burping cloth. I raised my hand and gave her the peace sign as she quickly reciprocated with a smile.

"At least you're free Tammy."

I would have given anything to jump in the car and ride off into the sunset. Like anything else in my life, it was a dream deferred as Pumpy cooed and smacked in my ear. I sat down again to take the pressure off my stomach. I sang a snippet of *Sweet Thang* by Chaka Khan as his gazing eyes fixated on my face.

"I will love you anyway, even if you cannot stay.

Alex appeared in the doorway massaging his neck.

"Tammy's upset, but I can't jeopardize our safety," he said, taking Troy from my arms.

"Hey man," he grunted, lifting Troy up and parachuting him back down again. Alex pulled his baby bundle into his chest and pitched, "I love you Shanelle even if I don't say it enough."

I turned my attention to the window. The smallest strand of hair brushed my eyelash. Pulling it back behind my ear, air rushed my nostrils as I exhaled, "I love you too Alex."

Fly Away

Four months passed as Troy grew by leaps and bounds. Alex and I competed against each other by capturing the most precious pictures on film of our pride and joy. Troy was the chunkiest baby in South Jersey and every beach comber and well wisher stopped us to admire him. In fact, nursing him throughout those early months brought my shape right back to regular size. The appeal of my premarital weight enticed Alex every night, but we only averaged three times a week. One good thing about our little Troy was his need to get in between us. Alex adored him, but called him a cock blocker. I immediately began taking birth control pills and worked out feverishly to combat any extra weight gain. Candy came to visit us three times since his birth. She was the only friend that Alex accepted in our quiet life. It was a great relief having her around as we talked about her fashion layout for the upcoming nuptials planned for the spring.

On a bright day just before dawn, we drove to the beach to take a morning stroll. The view was spectacular as an orange sun began to rise above the ocean. Alex wrapped us tight in his arms as Troy pulled at my shirt happily nursing at my breast. His fat chunky foot sat in Alex's mouth as Troy laughed in between sucking. "It can't get any better than this Shanelle," Alex said, as he kissed my neck.

I took Troy off my breast, kissed his cheek and handed him to his father.

"I guess you could say that." I replied, pushing my son's food supply back into my sports bra. I inched closer to the shore and watched the sunrise against the backdrop of my family. Alex loved this time of day including the glorious view the ocean provided every morning. The majestic waters pulled and tugged on my emotions as I thought about the day we were reintroduced. He broke my virginity, put a ring on my finger, and claimed me as his wife and mother to his precious son.

"But what about me?"

"Get organized Shanelle," I whispered out loud.

"Did you say something?" Alex asked from a distance.

My head rattled to and fro.

"Funny."

I learned that bit of advice from the great Alex, himself. I turned back one last time watching him poke and prod at Pumpy's fat belly and chunky toes. A few birds flew over the vast ocean as the winds carried my thoughts in the salty breeze.

"This butterfly needs to spread her wings and fly."

Welcome to Love's Twilight, the Conclusion

The under cover federal sting operation called "Sitting Bull," shut down too soon. Now that I look back on all the things that happened to me, instead of closing up shop, the feds should have obtained a warrant to wiretap Rico's phone calls in prison. If they did, maybe Alex would be alive today.

Wiretapping, photographing and surveillance ended on the day of the bust. Federal agents from the joint narcotics and weapons units closed up shop with a firm handshake as black Chevy Caprices drove out of the Garvey Projects. Confident in their drugs and weapons seizure, they made their presence known by driving down the pothole riddled street in a slow, parade like procession.

Scorned residents followed closely behind and flashed their middle fingers. They were happy to have less crime in their neighborhood, but furious that two staples in the community were headed to federal prison.

Life at Garvey was a double edge sword. Mama Barb, the fearless cook for the entire apartment complex and the second lead suspect, was hauled out of her apartment with tight plastic cuffs cutting her chubby wrists. Back inside, federal agents made a mockery of her two-bedroom flat as they kicked, flipped and showed off items that had nothing to do with their investigation.

"What the hell is this?" one agent asked, as he held up a cold jar of fresh hog mogs soaking in cloudy vinegar. The sight of pig skin and flesh caused his face to scour in disgust.

"Damn," he replied, "We may have to call in the Haz Mat unit for this shit."

A senior narcotic agent laughed.

"Quit playing Dobson, we're looking for controlled substances. Make sure you check the ice cube trays too, if they're empty, let them sit out so we can swab the interior for residue."

Shattered glass stuck to the senior agent's feet as he dragged the soles of his shoes across Mama Barb's bedroom floor for one last photograph. Evidence of her morning routine caught the agent's attention as his eyes shifted to a small light flickering on her Rowenta iron. Mama Barb usually took a shower after her chicken dinners were packed. She never had a chance to dress herself. The agents squashed what little dignity she had by forcing her out of the apartment in a soiled housecoat riddled with grease stains. Mama Barb's auburn highlights stood straight up like a rooster under the still of morning twilight. Her moist slippers did little to compliment her style or gait as she hobbled down the walkway to a government vehicle.

Anxious members of the press stood by with their feet planted firmly to the ground. They had a field day at her expense, as flashing light bulbs forced her eyes into a startled reaction.

News of arresting agents entering the building spread through the complex like wild fire. The weak, weary and the nosey jumped out of bed, hobbled to window sills or ran downstairs in tee shirts and doo rags to see the commotion. The child that stood out the most along the horizontal fence was little Corinthia. Mama Barb rocked that girl in the comfort of her bosom and on her hip for the first two years of her life, while her mother hit the streets looking for a hustle and a hit. The sassiness in her two-year old voice won Mama Barb over every time she came to her door with a bag of chips and a quarter juice in her hands. Corinthia had butter brown skin, thick eyebrows and piercing green eyes. Silver caps gripped every tooth in her mouth, so Mama Barb did everything in her power to keep her away from sugar.

Corinthia gripped her petite two-year old fingers through the iron fence and wailed in shivering agony as if it were her own mother. In her short time on earth, this was Corinthia's second psychological abandonment. The older kids held on to Corinthia's shoulders just to keep her from jumping over the fence and into Mama Barb's arm.

Mama Barb turned her head around to give one last instruction before she got in the car. She jerked her head back up and shouted, "Kia! Take Corinthia to Ms. Jenkin's house until her mother gets home and don't give her any candy!"

Because of Mama Barb, many children escaped the wrath of Child Protective Services just by living near and dear to her heart.

No matter how kind, the motherly love she provided ended on the day of the bust.

As for Rico, he went out in grand style with shackles on his wrists and legs escorted by four buffed federal agents. He looked good no matter the time or trouble. Rico pimped out of the quad with a cocky ass grin on his flawless face. He even flexed his muscles to enhance his "Enter the Dragon" tattoo on his bicep. Residents shouted from their apartment windows in various temperaments and languages.

"Keep yo' head up Rico!" One of his boys said, as he pulled his handkerchief down past his mouth, quickly pulling it back up again.

"We love you," said one of his many adoring girlfriends. Tamika looked up to see what window it came from. She was pissed off when she saw him leave. He tipped heavy even if it was a five-minute blowjob. Seeing Rico leave was a financial hardship for her because she didn't have to go far to turn a trick.

That night, the feds celebrated at Krug's Pub on Ferry Street. It was the same night Alex came home drunk when I was pregnant with Troy. He participated on the evidence inventory team when the bust was completed. Captain Fisco waited for things to cool down before he convinced the feds to let Alex take part in the clean up operation. In retrospect, that was the reason why Alex was so pissed off about Nikki coming to the house when Troy was born. If the feds or Captain Fisco heard about Nikki's visit, Alex would have been in big trouble.

Jack was also at Krug's Pub for the grand cigar and cigarette filled celebration. They sat around in black boots and fatigues to toast their success, while I lay in bed wondering where my husband was. It took a while for me to put the pieces together. The New York Times was the only paper that provided a succinct timeline of events. I should have been trying to figure this stuff out before Alex was gunned down, but I didn't have a reason to be suspicious.

My life and life at the Garvey Street Projects would never be the same. Nobody reaped any immediate benefits from the bust except for the local cops and feds. They dipped, sampled and split up their cut without blinking twice. They had a solid case against Rico and Mama Barb. That was all they needed to shut their operation down for good.

Payback

Rico sat in jail cool and collected despite his sixteen count federal indictment. After a momentary pause, he spit in the corner of the hallway, slicked his curly damp hair back with his hands and picked up the pay phone.

"Yo Flaco, call my sister and tell her she owes me one. I need info on Foster. I could fuck with Nick, but I'm gonna need him for now; I know he still wants in. We need to send him a warning that he's still our bitch. In the mean time, I'll fuck up another good 'ole boy on the take."

Rico was pissed off that an eleven month operation got by him without any word from Nick. A payback was the only way Rico could put Nick on notice that his turn was next if he didn't cooperate in the future. He could have easily killed him, but he always had valuable information for Rico, including new spots in other parts of North Orange that was open and accessible to drug trafficking. Rico definitely wanted revenge, but chose Alex instead.

Rico's cousin and underground flunky hung up the phone and called Nikki.

"No," Nikki said, "I don't see Shanelle too much, she just had a baby."

Nikki cleared her throat while she stroked Tammy's perky nipples. "Nah," she answered with little suspicion, "He threw me out of his house a few weeks ago because of the investigation."

Tammy rolled over and whispered, "Who's that?"

Nikki covered the phone and said, "Shh, it's my cousin."

The conversation ended just like that. Nikki quietly hung up the phone, rolled over on top of Tammy and slowly kissed her to silence any lingering curiosity. Flaco dropped the phone on the receiver and smiled with criminal intent. A promotion was long overdue and he knew this job would do the trick.

Flaco was Rico's first cousin. He grew up in East Orange with his mother and younger sister. After one rape trial ended in a hung jury at the ripe old age of eighteen, Flaco fled to the Bronx until things settled down. He tried to make a name for himself out there, but he failed. When he went back home to his mother's house, she changed the locks and forbade him to return. His little sister revealed a dirty secret to their mother, which confirmed her suspicions about her son's seedy appetite. Desperate and nowhere else to go, Flaco sought refuge with Rico and he quickly put Flaco to work. His main job was quick stick ups and getting information passed on to Rico from the outside. On the day I went to Garvey to watch Mookie play basketball, an undercover street agent, wearing a wire, picked up Rico and Flaco's conversation right after Rico told me to leave. No wonder the feds and Alex were so adamant about my safety. The conversation went down like this:

"Damn, who was that sweet piece of ass that just left; I swear I know her from somewhere?"

"That's Shanelle, Steven's little sister?"

"Word?"

A photograph from the seventh floor captured Rico pulling a drag from his cigarette before he dropped it to the ground.

"Yeah, but she's off limits, she's married to five-o, one of Nick's boys."

"Word?"

"Yeah, Magilla Gorilla, you've seen him before."

"Right, right, but I remember a nice piece of ass when I see one."

A second photograph captured Flaco snapping his fingers as he recalled our association. "We can snatch her up to get to Steven."

Rico could be heard saying, "Don't fuck with her man, she's got enough problems!"

It was enough dialogue to force the feds to take a closer look at me and figure out why Rico was so invested in a cop's wife. Strange as it sounds, Rico looked out for me in a small way by telling me to leave.

When we were younger, Rico walked me home from Metcalf Park in the Valley. When we reached Scotland Road, he asked me if I wanted an Italian Ice from Cocquelle's Bakery. He was too cute to resist on that quiet summer day. He nervously pulled four crumpled bills out of his pocket. He told me he was going to be rich. I believed him as I licked my dessert and thanked him for my Italian Ice.

Once outside, he planted a cold kiss on my cheek. It was an innocent slice of fifth grade affection that meant more to him than to me. We rarely saw each other as years went by, but every time I ran into him, we shared an innocent smile of the childhood we left behind.

I think his boyhood crush stayed with him even in his darkest days of deviancy, but it wasn't enough to keep Alex alive. Garvey was his family's lifeline and keeping it under his control while he remained in jail was his number one priority.

Alex was as vigilant as Rico was about controlling the world around him. He blamed the whole thing on Tammy after she left our house with Nikki. Alex told her on too many occasions, that when the real shit goes down, families stick together no matter the reason. Unfortunately, love and lust had Tammy so mixed up she was blind.

Rico went back to his cellblock confident. He knew four visits with his sister would get him the right information. Like clockwork, Nikki visited her brother over an eleven-month period. On every occasion, she had diarrhea of the mouth, especially when it came to me and Alex.

Two weeks before Candy's wedding, Rico put in a bid for a female shooter.

"Listen Flaco, let Gigi do the job, that bitch is good yo, she never misses. Make sure you saw off the handle and barrel."

One Week of Happiness

"Happy birthday dear Troy…happy birthday to you!"
The noise in our kitchen was enough to make the meekest child cry out in fear as friends and family sang happy birthday to our son. Troy balled up his fat fingers into two fists and blew out the candles like a champ. He clapped in unison as everyone cheered for him. At one year old, I wasn't surprised. I practiced with him for an entire week simply because I had so much time on my hands. Gone were the days of juggling classes and exams. Alex's constant need for me and tending to Troy's every whim took me away from my dreams. College took a back seat on the highest bookshelf in our house. Just talking about school stirred Alex in the worst way. He was so worried about the trial and the intrusive press coverage surrounding the Garvey Street bust, he found little time to relax. A fretful thirty pound weight loss had everyone buzzing about him. Some speculated that he was hitting a crack pipe, while I begged him to eat because he looked so thin. So much was going on in our lives; I decided to wait until after the trial to resume classes. He loved the idea and became a calmer man. His greatest joy was coming home to us every night. After a good meal and thirty minutes of his own time, he was truly the king of our modest castle. The domestic hustle and bustle did little to enhance my self worth. I felt like an old maid all the time and my girl Candy made a point of reminding me every time she saw me. Troy's first birthday was no exception.

"Shanelle," she said, after handing me the cake knife, "Go upstairs and take that raggedy ass sweatshirt off, you look like a bum."

Even though Candy whispered her message, it landed right in Alex's ears. He cut Candy a look as he passed out two slices of cake and then grabbed me by the arm.

"She looks good to me no matter what she wears."

Alex kissed my forehead and winked at me with love in his eyes. When he let go, I looked down at my clothes and said, "You're right Candy, I should change."

Alex, of course, had other plans.

"Shanelle, make my father a plate and wrap it up, he's ready to go."

I looked at Alex and then Candy before I responded.

"Uh, ok, I will."

Troy grabbed my leg as I bounced into the kitchen.

"Ma-mee, Ma-mee, up!" he said, as he stretched his arms in the air. I scooped him up and kissed his chunky chin as he playfully smacked my cheeks. I quickly switched him to my other hip as the phone rang. Alex and I picked it up simultaneously as the intruder started his inquiry.

"Mrs. Foster, do you have any comments regarding your brother Steven's mysterious accident at Garvey?"

Alex's response was swift.

"Hang up the phone Shanelle."

Alex dealt with the call. With less than two weeks to go before the trial and Candy's wedding, He was damn near going crazy with anger and suspicion. Candy was getting on his last nerves too, because she was a gossip pipeline from North Orange to Brick, New Jersey. Candy quickly came to my rescue and fixed a plate of food for Alex's father. While the Fosters bid us goodbye with hugs and kisses, Candy slapped some foil over his plate and threw it in a Shoprite bag. Once they were out the door, she followed me upstairs to Troy's room.

"Shanelle," Candy said, "Why don't you spend the night at my house so we can go to Mueller's in the morning?"

"What's at Mueller's?" I asked.

"I want to make some baskets for the bridal party."

"Why?" I asked, "It's just me and Bonnie anyway."

"Don't worry about it Shanelle," she impatiently toned, "Can you come?"

Candy started taking Troy's birthday outfit off while I ran some water in the tub. He was sleepy, but he needed a good bath to get him through the night. After pouring some baby bath in the water, I picked up Troy and put him in the tub. He laughed and splashed the water so hard that Candy stood back to avoid getting wet.

"I don't think that's a good idea," I doubted. "Alex really likes me to be home and we just finished Troy's party." I handed him a yellow duck and said, "Hey, we'll get up at five o'clock and meet you in the morning, that way we'll have the whole day."

Troy let us know his father was coming just by the sound of his heavy footsteps.

"Daaa-dee! Daaa-dee!"

Alex's entrance into the bathroom immediately crowded our space. He threw a towel over his shoulder as we stepped out. Candy followed me out and sucked her teeth at the sound of the bathroom door closing. What followed was an orchestra of a grunting father bear and baby bear. Candy glanced at me and whispered, "That shit sounds ridiculous and so does your plan, but at least we can go to breakfast first."

Candy helped me straighten up Troy's room. A quick peck on the cheek followed as the toy box closed.

"Let me get out of here, Clinton has a flight in the morning. I'll get everyone out. You get a good night sleep. By the way, great party."

Candy playfully bid me farewell with a Miss America wave. Peering over the balcony, I could hear laughter from a distance as she teased the lingering guests.

"Black folks, y'all sure don't know when to go home." She side glanced Jack and blurted, "Oh, I'm sorry Jack, you don't look it, but I swear you got some black in you too."

Warm steam escaped from the bathroom. Alex cracked the door and looked in my direction. I smiled as I listened to him try to make sense out of his baby babble.

"You did?" Alex asked, "And then what happened?"

Troy continued his raucous and held his head back. Alex stood up and lifted him out of the tub. Our son had so many shiny rolls on his skin, Alex had to separate the creases and wipe out the moisture so he wouldn't get a rash. After a puff of baby powder escaped from his pamper, Troy's eyes opened and closed. Alex turned on his night-light and put our baby giant in the crib. Then he put his arm around me as we watched Troy snuggle into his warm surroundings. Alex rubbed my shoulders. Even though we were in tune to our sleeping son, it didn't take long for him to start asking questions.

"What time are you coming home tomorrow?"

I took a deep breath.

"One o'clock, Troy will probably sleep the whole ride home."

Alex followed me into the bedroom and put on a dry tee shirt. He didn't care that guests were shuffling out the door as he pulled me on top of him. He exhaled in my neck while I kissed the stress lines on his forehead. We stared into each other's eyes like any couple searching for serenity during times of happiness mixed with stress. Alex closed his eyes and began to think out loud.

"I love you Shanelle."

"I love you too," I replied.

My eyes met his.

"Let me help you Alex, talk to me, tell me."

He immediately shook his head to negate my concern.

"There's nothing to tell Shanelle, don't worry, everything's fine."

My lips quivered slightly with doubt. "You're getting so thin Alex; you don't feel like a teddy bear anymore."

He seemed surprised at first and then remembered his brawn and strength by looking at a picture of us on the beach last year. He stretched out his fingers and slowly pressed them into my back.

"You're right." Alex pinched my earlobe. "If anymore calls come in Shanelle, just let the machine answer." After that, he immediately lifted me up off of him and quietly went downstairs. It was definitely my cue to get off his back about the ordeal we were going through. There were so many phone calls I couldn't keep up with the endless questions and requests for interviews. The press was frustrated with the case because nobody wanted to talk, especially the good citizens of Garvey. Steven's mysterious accident put everyone on notice to mind your damn business. The local cops made sure it stayed quiet by posting extra police officers in the day and evening. Candy kept clippings from the Essex Chronicle to keep me informed, but none of it seemed to matter because I was so far away. Meeting the girls the next day brought me right back into the action.

Bonnie met us at the Harris Diner for breakfast with all the dirt.

"Look at fat boy Troy," she exclaimed, quickly grabbing him as she tried to put him in a wooden high chair. His fat legs quickly resisted as he kicked the chair with his white Stride Rite shoes.

"He doesn't like high chairs," Candy said.

Bonnie winced as she handed him back to me.

"Girl, what are you feeding him?"

Candy laughed. "Girl she just took him off the titty last week!"

Bonnie's eyes stretched in disbelief.

"Damn Shanelle, were you enjoying that too?"

The waitress passed out the menus as Troy bounced up and down on my lap.

"I'll pretend I didn't hear that you freak." I replied.

Bonnie smirked.

"Speaking of freakin' at the Freaknik, what's up with Tammy and Nikki, I hear they're closer than close."

Candy busted out laughing, but I didn't find it funny.

"You don't even know them," I said, "So you need to mind your business."

Bonnie sipped some of her water as her eyes shifted between two conversations, "I love you too Shanelle. Don't get me wrong, I think Tammy is cool, but does Nikki know how to mind her own business?"

I put some bread in Troy's mouth to calm him down and asked, "What do you mean by that?"

Bonnie's constant pursuit of hot news kept her connected to the underground gossip.

"Me and Andre saw Rico's cousin Flaco last week outside the Shelter. You know they lit up a spliff and started talkin' about this and that. Anyway, Flaco said that Nikki kicks it with your sister-in-law for free food and a bed at Pitt."

I didn't know who Flaco was at the time, so I asked out of sheer curiosity.

"Who's Flaco?" I asked.

"Oh," Bonnie said, "That's his punk ass cousin from East Orange." She paused a minute and said, "Yeah, I think he used to live on Fourth Avenue." Bonnie smirked. "He beat the rap on a rape charge, but Andre doesn't care because he said his weed is too, too nice."

"Yeah well, I'll talk to Tammy, but I can't pick and chose my sister-in-law's partners."

Candy picked up her fork and said, "Yeah, whatever, I choose, capital DIC...," I quickly covered her mouth and fired back, "Candy chill!"

Bonnie shoved some pancakes in Troy's mouth. Candy pushed my hand away and rolled her eyes. "Anyway, like I said, I prefer the pipe."

Bonnie chuckled.

"Hold up, hold up, girl are you free basing now?"

Candy flashed us a condescending smile while brushing her hands clean.

"Girl don't play with me, you know what I mean." She pat her lips with pink gloss and ordered the day.

"Anyway, we're all set, right?"

Bonnie and I chimed in together.

"Yes Candy."

"Good," she replied, "Dinner at Forno's Wednesday night."

"Forno's?" I replied, "You know I can't make that."

Candy slammed her compact mirror down and lifted her hands to the sky as Troy quickly mimicked his Godmother.

"Don't tell me, Alex right?"

Troy banged on the table as I bounced him on my knee to settle my own frustration. Before I could entertain her comment, Candy continued.

"Do me a favor Shanelle and take Alex to the next level."

Bonnie and I leaned in for a piece of advice.

"Alex is stressed the fuck out with all of this trial shit. He was riding your ass when I got to the party, during the party and after the party if my memory serves me correct. So do your marriage a favor, dim the lights, pour some wine, take a few sips and get on your knees girl."

Candy sat back in confidence. Bonnie chuckled offering a quick high five.

"If you do that three times a week, Alex won't give a damn what you do. You see how fast Clinton brings his ass home to me after a long flight. They don't call it a cock pit for nothing girl."

Troy raised his hand in jubilee, full from his meal.

"Yeee, dee dee, mamee!" he clapped, bearing a toothy grin.

Candy pinched his cheek and teased him in whiny tone, "Even fat boy Troy knows what's up."

I got off the subject by concentrating on Bonnie. "So what are you doing for the rest of the week?"

"Nothing," Bonnie replied, "Just hanging out with Andre and getting cute for Candy's big day."

She grabbed Troy's hand shaking it gently and said, "How is this Budda gonna make it down the aisle with his fat self? Are you going to bribe him with cookies?"

Candy sighed, "He'll be okay, Alex is going to carry him if he gets cranky and his Auntie Tammy is coming for back up."

I came up with the idea just so Alex and I could enjoy ourselves at the wedding. Tammy only saw Troy at Mrs. Foster's house after the argument she and Alex had when he was born. Honestly, I didn't think he was going to hold out that long, but he was determined to keep us safe from Nikki's crime family. Alex's good intentions meant little to the reality unraveling behind our backs.

Rico's grand scheme fit right into my idea. He wanted "Gigi," to saunter into the wedding disguised as Nikki and blow Alex away. In retrospect, Tammy fed her brother on a platter to Rico with her big fat mouth.

Bonnie looked at the two of us and smiled as she rubbed Troy's hand. Candy picked up her glass of water and smiled at me as we shared a momentary lapse in conversation. If we only knew what was ahead of us, we would have called off the whole wedding and went into witness protection.

Candy threw her napkin down and signaled the waitress.

"Let's go ladies, there's plenty of stuff to get done. I need your help picking out dry flowers and that's it, so let's drive separate cars."

Bonnie motioned to Candy. "This is the part where I get to say that you're starting to work my nerves Miss Bride-to-be."

Candy got to Mueller's first and parked in the lot. As usual, Bonnie had to make a stop so we waited on the sidewalk for her at Central Avenue and Martin Luther King Boulevard. Troy stood between my legs as Candy looked for her car.

"Where's that girl?" she asked.

"You know she likes to get lost, but she'll be here."

Cars were driving so fast I had to pay close attention to Troy as he tried to wander off. I barely had time to notice Candy's astute attention to a car slowing down in our direction. She tapped me on my shoulder and asked, "Who's that waving at us?"

I picked up Troy as a white Toyota Camry pulled over. A light skinned woman with an attitude peered over her sun glasses as Derrick suddenly stepped out. He seemed relieved to get out the car because of his height. His big feet and green scrubs immediately gave him away as I looked up at him with Troy in my arms. Derrick was so fine he just took my breath away. He looked older and more mature than ever. He cut his hair shorter and faded it on the sides. I smiled when I looked at him in his scrubs because I was proud that he stuck to his goals. I don't think he would have settled for anything less.

"What's up Doctor Derrick?" Candy said.

A small smile caressed my face as I stared at Mr. Handsome.

Derrick gave Candy a quick hug and immediately focused on me.

"Shanelle, it's good to see you." He kissed me on my cheeks and left his trademark cologne lingering on my neck to enjoy a quick memory from the past.

Troy grabbed my sunglasses, put them in his mouth and began to gnaw on the edges. I glanced at the woman in the car first and then looked at Derrick. He immediately stretched his hands out to hold my son and said, "What's up little man?" Troy extended his left hand out first as Derrick took him from my arms. He smiled at Troy and said, "So, this was the big miracle holding your stomach hostage?"

I smiled from ear to ear and quickly smoothed out my clothes. "Yes, that's him."

It was strange looking at the two of them. Derrick looked completely comfortable holding my son as the woman in the Toyota beeped her horn and defiantly yelled, "Rick, are you coming?"

Derrick hesitated before turning, "No, I'll get a ride, call me later."

The window rolled up and she immediately sped off towards downtown Newark. Her actions didn't faze Derrick in the least as he tickled Troy's fat tummy and immediately paid me a compliment.

"Wow Shanelle, he's healthy as a bull, what's his name?" Troy patted his shoulders while Derrick smiled at him.

In between my answer, smart ass Candy shrugged her shoulders and motioned silently with her mouth.

"Rick?"

She covered up her silly grin and laughed to herself. I put my hands on my hips and boasted, "Ask him, he'll tell you."

Derrick immediately looked at Troy and said, "What's your name?"

A mouthful of spit accompanied my son's answer as he belted out, "Toy!"

I quickly corrected his pronunciation.

"His name is Troy."

My attention turned to the Toyota as I watched it turn down University Avenue. "So," I joked, "Who the heck is Rick?"

Derrick laughed out loud exposing his pearly white teeth as he hoisted Troy in the air and said, "Can you say Derrick?"

Troy mimicked him like a baby parrot.

"Deh dick!" he babbled.

"Wow," Derrick replied, "He's smart too."

"Thanks Rick," I replied.

Curiosity stirred inside of me.

"What happened to Cornell Med?"

"Nothing," Derrick replied, "I volunteer at University whenever I come home. I'll be there this summer too."

I took a deep breath and continued to gaze at him. I was thrilled to see him and curious at the same time. In between his playtime with Troy, he continued to glance at me and then quickly look away. Candy broke up the reunion.

"Here comes Miss Bonnie."

When she exited the vehicle, Bonnie quickly apologized and sized up the scene.

"What's up Doctor Derrick?"

He gave her a quick peck on the cheek.

"What's up with you? I see the three of you are still friends."

Bonnie replied, "We wouldn't have it any other way."

Derrick checked his watch and pitched, "Ok, my ride left me, which one of you can take me to University?"

Candy took Troy from Derrick arms and sassily answered, "Shanelle of course."

Candy winked at me and snatched the diaper bag from my hand. "Make it quick cupcake."

I knew Troy was in good hands. He always went with Candy and this time was no different. I pointed to the Jeep Cherokee as Derrick put his arms around me.

"It's so good to see you again Shanelle."

"Thanks Derrick," I gushed.

As we got in the car, I could feel his eyes all over me. I turned the ignition key as his fragrance began to light up the car.

"What?" I asked, forcing back a smile.

"Nothing, you look great. The last time we saw each other you were waddling like a duck remember?"

I turned at High Street nodding with a fond memory etched in my head. "Yes, I remember."

"I do have a confession," he admitted.

"What's that?" I asked.

"I wanted that to last forever."

I fixed my attention straight ahead as cars pulled over at the New Jersey Institute of Technology. I slowed down a bit surprised to hear his admission.

"As fat as I was…"

Derrick gazed at the commuting students.

"You looked absolutely sexy pregnant, did anyone ever tell you that?"

"Yeah, my husband."

Derrick turned his head.

"Right…, your husband."

I wasn't trying to rub it in his face. My lips parted, but I couldn't speak. Derrick leaned back in his seat and asked, "Are you happy Shanelle?"

In order to avoid the question, I pulled an Alex move and turned on the radio.

"So," I asked, "How many years left of school do you have?"

"This is it," Derrick replied. "I graduate next year and then my residency starts at University Hospital in July."

"So you're coming home?"

Derrick rubbed his face. "I have to Shanelle; you know I need to be with my community. There's a lot going on in pediatric AIDS research."

Derrick stroked his chin and rephrased his concern

"I've been following the stories in the press Shanelle, I hope everything's okay."

I stopped at the traffic strumming my fingers on the wheel.

"Are you going to practice pediatrics?"

His answer was filled with confidence.

"Of course, I can't wait. I hope my patients are as healthy as Troy, you're doing a great job with him." He locked eyes with me and boasted, "Did you hear the way he said my name?"

I chuckled along with him. "Yeah, he's something else."

Our laughter faded into silence.

"We do a good job with him, especially his father."

Derrick's lips pressed together as a tweak of sadness gloomed over him.

"Pull over here."

Derrick turned the radio down. He took my right hand off the steering wheel and held it in between his hands. A soft flutter in my stomach stirred as he silenced me with a soft friendly kiss, quickly pulling away.

"Don't say anything Shanelle, I'm leaving," he whispered.

His thumb stroked my hand.

"Derrick, I…,"

He placed his lips to my ear.

"Every time I see you, I swear I never want to let you go."

Our eyes locked for a second.

"Don't get me wrong, I'm happy for you, but I regret letting you go even after all these years. With the trial coming up, I hope you'll be safe."

I didn't utter a word.

"If you ever need me Shanelle, just look me up, my phone number is listed."

I cupped his face.

"Thanks Derrick, I'll be fine."

He grabbed my wrists and wrapped his fingers around the back of my hands. His thumbs pressed into my palms and forced my fingers to close. I slowly pulled away. The freedom in his eyes begged me to follow, but I couldn't. He took a deep breath and immediately got out of the car. I flashed half a smile, watching him casually walk away to fulfill his dreams. If it wasn't for Troy, I would have stayed with him just because.

When I got back to Muellers, Candy quickly handed the cart to me filled with dry flowers and my babbling son.

"Maa-mee! Maa-mee," he rejoiced as I cuddled into his fat neck.

"Took you long enough," Candy teased, "I hope you got everything off your titties, oops," she winked with a tribute to Betty Boop, "I mean chest with Rick."

Bonnie's lip poked out.

"Damn, I'm mad I missed the trophy girl, what's with the Rick thing?" Her finger pointed towards the sky. "I'll tell you one thing, Rick sure gets better looking with age."

"Yeah, he does," I replied. "He's still a sweetheart too."

My girls knew not to beat me up over our reunion. We all quietly wished it away as Candy showed me her floral arrangements.

When we got outside, Candy took Troy out of the cart while we loaded her trunk. The two of them looked so cute together walking up and down the driveway. She shook her head in shame and said, "C'mon Troy boy, you need to get your practice in, Lord knows your mama picks you up too much."

Candy was right, I did cart him on my hip a lot, but it was everything Alex wanted. By the time I got home it was three o'clock. Troy talked himself to sleep halfway down the parkway and then slept the rest of the way. The minute we got in the door, he unleashed his toddler hood on me and started tearing up the place. I confined him to one room and let him play with his dinosaurs and jumbo blocks. The constant routine of cleaning up and getting ready for Alex seeped into my blood stream as tension slowly crept up into my head. Bonnie, Derrick and Candy had it made in their "free to go where they damn well please," lives. The routine of chores and taking orders was no different than the shit I used to put up with when I was home. I looked at the front door briefly and then looked at Troy. He was the anchor that kept me from temporarily leaving. I sat down to catch my breath as I thought about my life. *Get up, take a shower, cook breakfast, lay out Alex's uniform, feed Troy, feed Alex, kiss Alex goodbye, walk Alex to the door with Troy on my hip, "Wave bye bye to daddy." Clean up, play with Troy, watch Sesame Street and play with Troy. Take him to the park, put him down for a quick nap, take out dinner, clean the bathroom and adjust the blinds for sanity. Chat with Alex and take his lunch order. Wake up Troy, prepare their lunch, feed Troy, put him down for an afternoon nap, feed Alex, sex him up in thirty minutes and tell him you love him. Fuck, I'm only twenty-one years old, give me a break!*

At my age and youthful tenacity, I began to feel like a wind up doll. Seeing Derrick and the girls made spit well up in my throat as I lamented over the thought of freedom. A slight reprieve to my routine came to me in the form of left over food from Troy's birthday party. By the time Alex came in the door, Troy was in his highchair pulled up to the table dropping green peas on the floor. Alex came home in a good mood and full of small talk. He took a quick shower and changed into some sweat pants and a tank top. After he wolfed down his food like a human vacuum, he pinched his son on his cheeks and kissed his irresistible face. Alex playfully forced his head into Troy's chest while he banged on his father's big head. When Alex grew tired of the joust, Troy threw a handful of green peas on the floor. I immediately grabbed his hand.

"No Troy, that's not nice."

My adoring son had payback in his heart as he looked at me with two fists and spouted, "Deh-dick!"

The guilty look on my face gave it away as Alex looked my way.

"What did he say?"

I grabbed a cookie to silence Troy.

"I don't know."

Alex sat down and quickly pulled me on his lap. The instant I sat down, I could tell the natives were restless. I kissed his lips and said, "Somebody missed me today?"

Alex stroked my back with his heavy hand and whispered in my ear, "We missed you real bad Shanelle."

Troy threw more green peas at the both of us to get our attention. My shoulders slumped in defeat. The two of them vying for my affection was a bit out of hand, but I knew I needed to tend to Troy first to take care of Alex's appetite. Troy stretched his hands out and recited, "Up ma-mee, up!"

Alex quickly cleared his throat. He hoisted me off his lap and abandoned us for the TV room. His feet crushed the vegetables on the floor, which instantly spoiled my stomach. Parts of me wanted Alex, the other half of me wanted to kill him for putting me in this complacent routine.

"C'mon Troy," I said, "Give mommy and daddy some adult time." Troy giggled his way to the floor while I fetched a paper towel. Of course his curiosity led him straight to the mashed up peas. He held his fingers up and blurted, "Nasdy!"

I amused him and said, "Yes, that's nasty Troy," as I wiped him down with a paper towel. Alex turned up the volume on the TV. I carried his son upstairs while Troy waved goodbye to his father. He was such a good boy, I was sure he was going to give us twenty minutes. I ran to the bathroom to brush my teeth as Troy babbled in the background, "Dadee, dadee!"

At least Alex had enough sense to quietly come upstairs. I put my fingers to my lips. Alex tiptoed into the bedroom and slid under the sheets. An emotional pendulum rocked back and forth between loved and unloved. My heart of hearts told me that he really loved me, but at times it felt like lonely love. I stood in the door way and took off my clothes while he watched. He sat up and reached out his hand. The part of me that felt unloved began to click like the sound of a musical mobile. A tear welled up in my eye, but nothing enticed him to ask me what was wrong or if I had a nice day. He wanted me and nothing else mattered.

Alex pulled me into his body and moaned as our skin came into contact. He used his right hand to stroke me into a natural arousal. Off in the distance, Troy spanked his dinosaur in the background exclaiming, "Nass-dee dee-no!"

Alex pressed his forehead against mine. He caressed my face and whispered, "He's getting dino back for those nasty green peas."

Soft pillows and crisp sheets crushed beneath his body while he raised our level of intimacy.

"You're a good mother Shanelle. I know that if anything ever happened to me, my son will be okay."

My heart began to flutter up and down like a moth stuck in a net.

"Alex don't talk like that, nothing is going to happen to you."

Alex stroked my arm. "I know, I just wanted you to know that you're a good mother."

I pulled my face away and immediately straddled his hips. Alex placed his arms behind his head and smiled at me.

"What's wrong?" he quietly asked.

The pendulum rocked to loved again as I thought about life without him. Desperation became my focus.

"I'm worried about you Alex. I don't know what's going on and you're losing so much weight. Should I be worried?"

I searched for an answer. Alex took a deep breath and began to kiss me as I pleaded with him.

"Don't ever say that again, okay?"

The pressure of his fingertips rested into my scalp with a gentle massage. He slid them down to my shoulders and lower back with more intensity while I began to moan. Slowly but surely, Alex eased my stress away with an intimate whisper.

When I looked into his eyes, an instant vision of Derrick flashed in front of me. Butterflies danced in my empty stomach. Alex apologized for upsetting me and cuddled my weak heart. Exhaustion from the entire day sink in as he kissed me all over and worked out his own stress. I closed my eyes and let him do all the things that pleased him. My body was filled with pleasure and tension as I turned my face towards the window and contemplated tearing freedom mixed with love into four equal pieces myself, Alex, Troy and independence. Alex grabbed my load and squeezed it tight as he released his love deep inside of me. Listening to him claim me did little for the small glimmers of hope I hid.

"Don't leave me Shanelle," he strained.

"I won't."

"I need you Shanelle."

"I know baby," I replied.

"I can't live without you girl."

Off in the distance, Troy was tugging and pulling on his sheets. He eventually settled into a quiet nap which gave us more time together. In retrospect, we were lucky to have such a good baby. His sweet disposition allowed us to make love three more times up until Saturday, a day I shall never forget.

Bloody Wedding Day

Saturday came with full sun and seventy degree temperatures. Troy woke up early that morning so Alex took him for a long stroll on the beach to settle him down for the day. I took full advantage of my time by shaving my legs and packing Troy's diaper bag. When they got back Alex gave him a bath and put him down for a nap. We discussed our last minute plans for the wedding while Alex took a shower. He told me he was going to shower again at Clinton's house because he knew he was going to get sweaty during the drive. He packed his own bag and flirted with me the whole time. When he finished, he had his hands all over me and I knew I would have to oblige before we left for the wedding. I don't know what revelations came to him at the beach, but while we were in the kitchen, he sat me on his lap and told me that he wanted me to go back to school in the evening while he watched Troy. He picked up the sports section with one hand and looked at me for a response as I kissed his neck in a million places. Alex rubbed my lower back and said, "I want you to go back to school Shanelle, I just wanted my son to have a good start. We were having so much fun at the beach this morning; I started to wonder if you were still having fun."

I didn't need him to go into the particulars, the fact that he brought it up meant that he cared about my needs and wants. Alex picked me up and threw me over his shoulders. His large hands spanked me which complimented the mood, because I was suddenly feeling like a very naughty school girl. Just like the good old days, we began to play football for lovers. Alex made me play the quarterback and immediately tackled me to the ground. The pillows we threw on the living room floor supported my fall as Alex fell on top of me. I laughed to the top of my lungs as he tickled my stomach and yanked my panties down. He had to cover my mouth twice so Troy wouldn't wake up from his nap. Alex took cool whip and cherries out the fridge and made a sundae out of me as I covered my mouth and squealed. We could hear Troy stirring over the nursery monitor and changed our playful tone to sweet love making so he wouldn't hear us again.

Alex's last words to me were simple.

"This tasty girl of mine."

"That's me."

"Says who?" Alex whispered.

"You baby," I winked in a coy tone.

"I like the sound of that."

We kissed for an eternity. His tongue whipped and weaved in my mouth as he sucked my tongue and grinded against me. It was the last kiss we would ever share. If I had known, I would have never left his side on that pillow filled living room floor.

Preparation for Alex's murder took place in an abandoned building on Freeway Drive East. Gigi, Rico's hired shooter, stared at the ground and contemplated two techniques for firing the weapon inside the church.

"I think I'm gonna pump it inside the church," she said, as she held it up in the air. "Yeah," she continued, "That's more my style."

Her accomplice took the weapon from Gigi and surveyed it twice, making sure to smooth out the splinters on the handle. Gigi looked into a cracked mirror hanging in the abandoned room. She scooped her hair up into a ponytail and compared it to Nikki's picture in her back pocket.

"Yeah, we do kinda' look alike."

Her accomplice gaged their similarities and nodded. She placed the sawed off shotgun in Gigi's long duffel bag and said, "Good luck, this one's for us."

Her accomplice couldn't wait for Gigi to get the job done. Flaco promised with a handshake that five thousand dollars would cover the hit. Two one way tickets to Miami were in her possession as she held her fist out to Gigi.

Gigi gave her a pound and left. Mangled debris crushed under her feet as glass and broken needles wedged into the soles of her sneakers. She closed a steel door at the bottom of the landing and began to focus while her partner stood up to leave. Gigi's friend and their tickets to Miami didn't have a chance. A silencer was placed to the back of her head before she could react to the cold steel piece. In one instant, she fell to the floor in a bloody heap.

Gigi awkwardly stepped into a stolen BMW driven by Flaco. He was wearing black leather gloves. Flaco was smart enough to wear them for the get away, but didn't think to wear one when he gave Gigi a picture of Nikki. Gigi noticed the gloves, but quickly assumed he didn't want to leave fingerprints in a stolen car. He turned to her and said, "Let's eat first; we still got time before we go to Shiloh."

Candy's wedding arrangements defied perfection. Even though she did most of the planning, Clinton added a special touch of class by ordering four late-modeled Rolls Royces in white. He also requested that the photographer shoot pictures in black and white. As I pulled up to Clinton's house, he was pacing out front like a normal groom on his last day of freedom. Just the sight of Alex calmed him down as I dropped him off. Alex waved with a wink as I drove off with Troy.

Candy and I could barely speak to each other when I reached the church. She knew not to panic even though I was supposed to meet her there an hour earlier. She looked absolutely beautiful and I didn't want to ruin her makeup with my silly tears.

We sat around for an hour as I laughed about the good 'ole days. As I touched up Candy's lips, I told her how handsome Clinton looked in his tux. Bonnie poured three glasses of champagne while Candy's mother rolled her eyes at us in disbelief. In friendly unison, two gulps were all we needed as the glasses were snatched from our dainty grips.

Bonnie graced the aisle like an elegant swan as a saxophone player serenaded us from the balcony. When it was my turn, Alex eyes widened as I strolled down in my gown. A soft wink from him was our last flirtatious gesture. Troy came down the aisle to the sound of adoring laughter. He looked like an overstuffed penguin wobbling back and forth in his stubby tuxedo. He occasionally stopped and stared at the people admiring his performance. By the time he reached the front three rows he was pulling on his bow tie with one hand and dangling the pillow with the other. Tammy stood up and coaxed him to stand next to Clinton as the wedding guests quietly clapped for his toddler performance.

The saxophone and clarinet player didn't play the regular wedding march. Instead they played an instrumental version of Luther Vandross' *A House is Not a Home*. The entire church was reduced to tears when Candy came down the aisle. Enchantment filled the air as Candy and Clinton exchanged their vows before God. We were so caught up in their romantic kiss; no one except me caught the eye of someone who appeared to be Nikki quickly stalking along the pane glass walls of the church. Oddly enough, as she reached halfway down the aisle, God lead my son to toddle to his aunt. I quickly looked at Alex and wondered whether he spotted the mysterious stranger. Unfortunately, his guard was down and while he clapped for Candy and Clinton's intimate kiss, the shooter made her move. She quickly pumped her gun back one time as I opened my mouth to scream. The sound of the shotgun exploded in the quiet church like a bomb. Alex's massive frame split wide open in multiple directions as blood splattered against Candy's gown in bright red polka dots. A ten second pause silenced the entire crowd as the shooter hauled ass out of the church. When she jumped in the vehicle her adrenaline was pumping so hard she didn't realize that Flaco had a gun pointed at her head. He fired two shots at point blank range and jumped into a black sedan driven by one of Rico's soldiers.

Back inside, family and friends hid underneath the pews for cover. Andre jumped up and ran down the aisle out of the church, followed by Clinton. They stopped dead in their tracks at the sound of a car peeling around the corner. Sunlight pierced directly in his eyes as Clinton bent down to witness Gigi's lifeless body slumped over the passenger seat. Andre held up his hand like a sun visor to get a visual of the assailants in the getaway car. His mind raced with confusion as he tried to figure out who they were.

Surrounded by an array of white candles flickering at her side, Candy's senses kicked in as the tips of her fingers trembled violently to communicate with her husband.

"Clinton no!"

Bonnie's innate thrill for danger and excitement caused her to take off running down the aisle. She caught up with Andre and grabbed him as they surveyed the damage. Andre quickly whispered in Bonnie's ear under the swell of their heavy breathing, "That was Flaco in the car."

Bonnie cupped her mouth and gasped in disbelief. As for me, I was too stunned to move. The crowd around me whimpered and cried under the pews. I immediately looked at my screaming son as he gripped his ears. Tammy began to scream.

"Alex! Alex! Oh God my brother!"

I turned towards my fallen husband. He was slumped on the ground with his massive hands slightly curved above his head. I tripped over my gown quickly rushing to his bloody frame.

"Alex," I whimpered, briefly pausing as the tips of my fingers pressed into his damp bloody tuxedo. My gentle prod had little effect. I changed the tone in my voice to a quiet plea.

"Alex, wake up baby…Alex please."

I pressed my lips to Alex's mouth and tried to breathe life into him with a delicate whisper.

"Please Alex, I'm sorry. Don't do this to me and Troy, wake up baby."

A tear fell off my chin and splashed on his face. Nothing moved him as my knees sat in a pool of his blood. I began to rock slowly back and forth. I picked up his limp arm hoping he would rise as a distraught guest began to pray in the distance.

"Oh Lord, please don't test us on this beautiful day."

Her words began to gain momentum as she bellowed out, "Jesus! Jesus! Why?"

More guests began to gain composure as I lay across Alex's chest to protect him. The blood oozing from his open wound quickly absorbed into my satin dress. While I continued to lay there, an aging gentleman tried to assist me.

"Get away from me! Don't you touch me!" Drool escaped my mouth as I quickly wiped it away causing Alex's blood to smear across my cheek and chin. I buried my face in Alex's neck as the sound of sirens blared from a distance. Bonnie had enough sense and composure to call the police from the pay phone out front.

Clinton and his father quickly ushered all of the guests out of the church as the sound of rolling wheels and keys jetted down the aisle. Clinton's father came back and struggled to pull me off.

"Help him," I begged, slumped in the knees.

Paramedic number one checked for a pulse, paramedic number two placed his lips to his receiver.

"University, we have a DOA in transit…massive gun shot wound to the chest, black male…"

A loud crackling sound forced us into silence.

"Stand by for Newark P.D."

I reached out to the paramedic, stamping my feet.

"No! You have to take him now. Do something please."

Clinton interrupted the paramedic's response.

"He's a police officer."

The paramedic paused. His fingers press the button again as he quickly changed his tone.

"Be advised, we have an officer down."

"Do you have identification? Over."

The paramedic faced me for an answer.

"Alex, Detective Alex Foster!" I yelled.

A stern voice followed.

"Okay, prepare him for transport to University, over."

The paramedic responded, "On our way. Over."

Small tremors tormented me. Weak and helpless, my knees knocked together like two bowling balls while they lifted my sweet Alex on the gurney.

The sound of a fussy baby quickly jolted me out of my trance. My poor son was reaching out for me opening and closing his hands. Tammy trembled towards me while Troy forced himself out of her collapsed arms. Her anguished tone was reality for all of us. Alex wasn't going to wake up. In fact, he was dead on what was supposed to be a celebrated day. Troy gripped his hands around my neck while Tammy and I followed the stretcher with bellowing sobs. Bonnie met us halfway down the aisle. I looked back as Candy stood weeping in her husband's arms. On the most beautiful day in her life, she gained a cherished husband and my husband was gone in an instant.

Tammy rushed to the telephone to call Mrs. Foster. I climbed into the ambulance with Troy in my arms as the world began to move in slow motion. Bonnie snatched the phone from her hand and told my mother-in-law the regretful news. Tammy gained focus and ran up to the ambulance to get in with me and Troy. The minute she did, the doors slammed shut and rushed from the stunned crowd. At least six squad cars flew by us to the chaotic scene. Tammy grabbed me and Troy as we huddled together shivering in shock. The paramedic covered Alex's face with a sheet and then began to tend to us.

"Are you injured?"

Our heads shook in unison.

"Are you his wife?"

Troy began to reach for Alex to no avail.

"Dadee?" He called.

Tammy buckled over, leaning into my neck as she unleashed a pitiful moan. There was no comfort in listening to Troy beg for his father.

My voice trembled at first, but I remained calm.

"Daddy..., daddy went night, night Troy." I said.

"Ni, night?" Troy asked, as he tugged Alex's bloody sheet.

"Yes baby, Daddy went night night."

Newark police officers were waiting for our arrival as they stood guard to usher Alex's lifeless body through the double doors. Hospital personnel began to split us up as Alex went one way and we went another. I ripped myself from the nurses with Troy in my arms screaming for Alex to come back to me.

"Please save him, I'll do anything, please save him!"

Troy began to cry again as an officer restrained me in a tight squeeze. My denial grew faint and weak as hospital personnel gathered around me.

"Is there someone we can call?"

"Would you like to speak to the chaplain?"

"Your son looks dehydrated; can we get him some juice?"

There was no direction or purpose in their questions. I wanted Alex and everything that came with his love. Suddenly, out of nowhere, a familiar voice peeled back the crowd with his hands. I quickly looked up and found relief in Derrick's eyes.

"Derrick," I rambled on, "Please, Alex was shot…"

"I know Shanelle, I heard about it in the trauma unit, I'm so sorry…"

I begged for his kindness, "Please take me to him."

"Okay, Shanelle," Derrick said, "Just relax, we'll get you there. We need to get Troy admitted first to make sure he's okay, is that all right?"

He didn't wait for an answer. He took Troy out of my drenched arms and handed him to a nurse.

"This is Nurse Sheila Hendricks, she's going to check him from head to toe, he's in good hands."

The confusion and commotion was too much for Troy but I had to let him go. He started kicking violently as the nurse gently stroked his back and soothed him with a soft voice. My eyes shot back and forth for Tammy. She quickly shook her head and followed the pediatric nurse down the hall. The warm disposition in Derrick's voice slowed my heart rhythm down and caused my shoulders to relax. Derrick grabbed my blood soaked hand and led me down the hallway.

"You'll be able to observe everything Shanelle, but you won't be able to go inside until they're finished. Even though Alex is…" Derrick paused first and then continued, "Well you have to get cleaned up first to keep the room as sterile as possible."

Derrick handed me some tissues and escorted me to a small changing room equipped with a shower.

"Shower off and put these scrubs on when you're finished. After that, I can take you to see him, okay?"

Shock began to settle into my feet and hands. Derrick put his hands on my shoulders and pleaded with me.

"Shanelle, listen to me, you need to see him. Go inside and clean up. After that I'll take you to him."

Derrick wiped a tear away and reassured me with a nudge.

"Go ahead Shanelle, I'll be right outside this door."

My eyes followed a trail of absorbed blood running down my dress and shoes. I looked at my bloody hands and immediately felt a need to wipe them off.

My warm shower was quick and vigilant as I talked my way through my misery.

"He's going to be fine, I know it. He's so strong and brave; God will take care of him. It's not his time yet."

Soap mixed with blood foamed up and slid down my frame. I followed the trail as a dark swirl of rich red blood effortlessly flowed into the drain. There was so much wasted, I began to wonder how he could survive. Doubt and troublesome voices crept into my psyche.

"It's God's way Shanelle, Alex is dead."

I turned away from the shower stream in denial.

"He's not dead! God wouldn't do such a thing!"

I immediately turned the shower off and stepped outside to a pure white towel. Left over makeup mixed with blood along my hairline smeared on the fabric. Two strokes at my hairline wiped it away as I quietly continued to sob. I quickly got dressed and drifted outside. Derrick stopped pacing and ushered me and the police officer to an observatory room. Once inside, one look at him confirmed the voices' declaration. Alex was dead.

Derrick and the officer stood back as I snailed up to the window. A round bullet was being removed from a gaping wound in his chest. A nurse stood near with a tray containing four bloody bullets similar in size and shape. There were no monitors, tubes or IVs hooked to him. The doctor said a few words to another nurse who quickly jotted some notes. He pulled back his gloves, looked up and motioned Derrick to meet him.

Derrick exited while I peered through the window at my lifeless husband. One tear quickly fell and splashed to the ground. My mouth pressed up against the mirror as vapors quickly formed and disappeared with my breathing rhythms. Derrick returned with his head held low.

"Shanelle, I'm so sorry…"

I couldn't bear to hear it from him.

"He's dead right?"

"Yes, he is."

"There was nothing they could do to save him right?"

Derrick wiped my tears away.

"No Shanelle, the impact was immediate," he paused, "I'm sorry."

Wishing upon a star I mumbled, "Can I see him?"

Empathy coated his deep voice.

"Sure."

Derrick held the door open for me. A numbing sensation rushed through my body and rested in the soles of my feet. Alex felt cold, so I tucked the sheet around him like the comforts of home. I forced his hand into mine and squeezed it tight.

"Alex, it wasn't supposed to be like this."

My fingers traced the outline of his eyebrows and hairline. I searched his face for an answer, but nothing came. A sweet memory of the first time he smiled at me flashed before my eyes. Nervous laughter escaped my lips along with pitiful tears. Even thoughts of his sweet redemption couldn't bring him back.

"You wanted a son and I gave you one. Troy needs you so much, especially now. How am I going to manage without you?"

The walls around me began to shrink.

"Please Alex, tell me what to do. I'm scared without you in my life."

My hands trembled in unison. I quietly kissed his cheeks, nose and eyelids.

"I love you Alex. Troy loves you too. Stay with me in my thoughts baby, we need you."

A soft creak in the door announced the Fosters. I wondered how much time had passed because they lived so far away. This was the first time we gathered together with such heart felt sorrow. Mrs. Foster walked in and fell to her knees as Mr. Foster held her limp in his arms struggling to brace himself. Derrick smoothed my shoulder, parting his lips with information.

"Troy's fine. He's sleeping in the pediatric unit when you're ready."

A mournful and deep wail swelled in my stomach. Derrick quietly walked away and closed the door behind him as my legs and knees buckled beneath me. The sound of Mrs. Foster's screams was the last thing I heard. She lifted her hands up to God and begged for mercy. Passing out on the cold sterile floor was the perfect escape.

Saying Goodbye

People huddled around my hospital bed with messages of encouragement and hope. Despite the stoic expression on my face, there was nothing they could do except weep for me.

Bonnie stood at my bed crying and wiping snots away while the side of my face rested against a crushed white pillow. Sunlight from the window was the only cue to keep my eyes open as she spoke to me.

"Shanelle, just say something, please. Everything is crazy now. Cops are everywhere, people are calling me about funeral arrangements and I don't know what to tell them. You can't just lay there, you have to do something."

She was my girl, but she couldn't bring Alex back or breathe life into me. Bonnie left with Andre hurt and defeated, turning at the doorway with a message of hope.

"I love you Shanelle and I'm sorry."

My sister-in-law Mary came after Bonnie left. She brought my son into the room dressed in a white polo shirt, jeans and new sneakers. Fisting balloons in his hands, he searched the ceiling, squealing at the colorful display. Troy banged on the balloons while Mary offered words of encouragement.

"We've been making arrangements for Alex. Troy is fine, well you can see that."

She placed Troy on my lap hoping to stir my maternal instinct. A juicy open mouth merged with my cheek for his own enjoyment as he weighted the balloons down with a quick jerk and pull. Troy crashed his head against mine and serenaded me with baby babble.

"Mamee? Mamee!" He gave up when I didn't respond. Mary picked him up and straddled him on her hip again.

"We all need you Shanelle. Mom and Dad will be here later to pick you up for the funeral tomorrow."

She smiled briefly, tracing her nephew's chin as he smiled.

"Don't worry about Troy, he'll be fine."

Troy's chunky wrist sailed in the air, persuaded by Mary's adult hand.

"Say bye bye Troy."

I fixed my eyes on the linen. Troy's face resembled Alex's more than ever.

"Mama, night, night?" Troy asked, in a high-pitched tone.

I didn't flinch, but my heart hurt deep inside. Mary turned on her heels and quietly walked out so I wouldn't see her crying.

I continued to lay there without the will to get up. As the sun lent itself to the other side of the world, Candy and Clinton came for their first visit. My best friend piled onto my bed hoping to illicit a response.

"C'mon girl, at least squeeze my hand, you're stronger than that."

Clinton stood at the foot of the railing.

"We don't want you to be alone. If you want to stay with us for a while it's okay. You and Troy are welcome in our home."

Candy squeezed my hand harder and began to cry. Her lips trembled as she spoke.

"If you want to be alone, we understand too, but you may want an extra hand with Troy."

I shifted my head to the other side and let go of her hand. I didn't want Candy or Clinton. I wanted Alex. Since he wasn't coming back, there was no need to answer. Candy slid off the bed and into Clinton's arms for consoling. Clinton began to coax her out the door but she resisted.

"Alex's obituary was in yesterday's and today's paper. The funeral is tomorrow so you better snap out of it. Anyway, your son needs you."

Clinton's urgings were futile as she slid around his side, hanging onto his wrist.

"Okay Shanelle, I feel you, but you know in your heart you have got to get up from that bed."

The sound of an ambulance echoed in the distance as the door closed. A food cart parked just outside as nurses hurriedly talked about their patients. My left hand stretched into the air and forced the sheet off my body. I sat up straight and stroked my hair into place. My hospital scrubs were worn to wrinkles and riding up past my knees. A sudden knock on the door dulled my senses. Derrick poked his head through the opening.

"Hey, just thought I'd check on you, today is my last day."

A sliding chair vibrated against the floor as he pulled up to the side of my bed and referenced my dangling feet.

"That's a good start."

I sipped some water, breaking up the dust lodged in my throat.

"What?" I groggily asked.

"At least you've decided to put your feet near the ground; it's a good place to…,"

Slightly weak and loosing equilibrium, Derrick grabbed my shoulders as I stumbled to stand. Remorse filled his eyes.

"Derrick," I blurted, "Can you take me home?"

His hand pressed against my lower back. He braced me against him and grabbed one of my hands.

"Sure, I guess I owe you one right? That day at Muellers, you gave me a ride."

I pressed on, mindful of the traffic commitment.

"It's a two hour drive."

Derrick picked up the phone and started to dial. He tucked my hair behind my ears and said, "Sure, I'll take you home Shanelle."

His head rose as he focused on the phone call.

"Hi Mrs. Henderson, this is Derrick Johnson, I'm going to say goodbye from here, I have to help out a friend. Please tell Dr. Davidson that I'll call next week about the research grant."

He continued to nod and accept her lingering compliments about his time spent at the hospital. Derrick ended the call and snapped his fingers.

"Oh, wait here, you need your bag, it's in the locker."

Restless and empty headed, I shuffled to the window and stared at the hustle and bustle of life outside. A young mother pushing a stroller on Bergen Street was my cue to get home. Derrick quickly returned, shuffling my personal effects in his hands along with floral sentiments from visitors. I grabbed his wrist, pushing the flowers away.

"I don't want them, give them to the nurses."

Derrick quietly shook his head and held the door open. Nurses gathered at the desk and wished me well while I signed my release form in a wheelchair.

"Take care Shanelle," a kind nurse said, propping a teddy bear for Troy on my lap. "We'll be praying for you and your family."

I turned and quietly waved without looking back. An orderly tried to assist Derrick with the transport to the lobby, but he refused.

"No chief, she's with me. Thanks anyway."

The orderly tucked his hands in his pocket and stepped back with a smile.

"Doc, you didn't even start your residency and I like you already. I hope all the first year residents are like you man."

Derrick skillfully wheeled me onto the elevator and nervously patted my shoulder.

"Comfortable?" he asked, searching his pocket for car keys.

The back of my nodding head reassured his friendly task.

"Okay Shanelle, let's get you home."

The two hour ride home was entertained by the sound of racing engines and occasional motorcycle brigades. I motioned a few turns to him once we got off the exit. When he pulled up, a squad car idled with an astute officer sitting inside. He exited his vehicle and quickly donned his hat, offering heartfelt condolences.

"I'm so sorry for your loss; Alex was a great officer."

While he exchanged courtesies with Derrick, I thanked the officer and headed up the quaint pathway in slow motion. White and yellow tulips in full bloom settled my heartbeat as I looked at the front door. Derrick escorted me up the steps and placed my bag on the top landing. He stepped back two spaces and brought me up to date.

"I'm going back to Cornell on Monday, but I'll be at the services tomorrow. If you need anything, my number is in the bag."

When I opened the door, Derrick handed me an envelope.

"When things settle down, I hope you get a chance to read this."

His lips parted and closed. My fingers tapped his wrist.

"Thank you for taking me home Derrick."

The closing front door separated us as his goodbye trailed off in the breeze. In a robotic trance, I walked inside. My hands settled at my hips as the envelope Derrick gave me quickly fell to the floor. Alex was everywhere. I stroked his utility belt hanging from the doorknob. Slow steps lead me to the kitchen where his lingering fragrance rifled my nostrils. I quickly changed my course of direction and held on to the banister. The love we made on Candy's wedding day was evident from the pillows resting carelessly on the floor. My fingertips dappled my collarbone to calm the pain growing inside my heart. I turned around again and looked up. I would have paid anything to see him standing at the top of the stairs waiting for me. His fragrance was the only thing calling me. A zombie's march led me to the front entrance of our bedroom. I quietly walked by and took off my disheveled clothes. Alex loved to be clean all the time and I wanted to feel him after my shower. Droplets of water splashed against my face. A sturdy washcloth drenched in lather trailed across my frame as his hopes and dreams caressed me.

"Shanelle run away with me. Let's take that day back at the beach and make it ours this time. My heart and soul is telling me that tonight is our chance and I'm never going to let you go."

"I want a son Shanelle."

"All I want is for you to be safe and happy."

"Be good to mommy Pumpy."

"Shanelle, promise me you'll never leave me."

His words were so vivid, I had to respond.

"I promise Alex, I'll never leave you."

I patted my neck and slowly buried my face in his thick terry-cloth bathrobe while his scent engulfed my senses. He was everywhere I turned, especially in the bedroom. I took his favorite baseball cap off the dresser and put it on my head. My hands softened his side of the bed with gentle sweeping motions. His body was so massive, I could feel the impression in the mattress while I molded into his frame. Passing the time with tears, I turned on the radio. Al Green sent his condolences in one of Alex's favorite songs. I turned over to listen as he soothed me through my agony.

"You make me feel so brand new…"

I shook my head recalling the day I saw him at the wedding. A baby picture of Troy came into view. His smiling eyes were as charming as his father's. I laughed at first and then wiped my nose, relieved that I had a precious gift to love. My body began to ache for both of them as I looked at the clock on the wall. It was just after nine o'clock. I needed to see my son.

Mr. Foster's arms and legs stiffened like an army cadet before she spoke. Alex's baseball cap concealed my puffy eyes as I stepped inside surprised to hear Troy scampering in the background.

"Shanelle, when did you get out of the hospital, we were leaving in an hour to pick you up."

His question went unanswered. I walked up to Tammy and snatched Troy from her arms. Anger welled in my throat as I fixed my suspicion on my big mouth sister-in-law.

"Why couldn't you just listen to him Tammy?"

Mrs. Foster barreled down the stairs by twos, quickly adjusting her robe.

"What are you talking about Shanelle?" Tammy glared.

"Don't play stupid," I yelled, "He warned you about Nikki's family. You fed Alex on a fucking plate messing around with Nikki!"

Tammy hurled the next insult.

"Me? You got some nerve girl. Who's the one hanging out in the projects with Rico? Don't think I don't know either because Nikki told me all about it!"

Casting a vicious glance, I fired back.

"Tammy please, I was watching a damn basketball game. Besides, I bet Rico told Nikki the whole thing. Did you ever think about that? I bet they're on the phone every damn day catching up with my life."

Troy bounded to the floor as I quickly jammed my finger in Tammy's face.

"Haven't you heard, payback's a bitch and we all got it with your big ass mouth!"

Tammy's hand sailed through the air crashing against my face with the intensity of a tennis serve. Her next comment sent me over the edge.

"You crazy bitch, if Alex never met your demented ass this would have never happened!"

My swollen fingers wrapped around her throat.

"Get off of me!" she yelled, jerking back and forth. Mrs. Foster scooped Troy off the floor and covered his eyes to no avail. Troy fought her off with a slide of his chubby hand wide eyed as his grandfather intervened.

"Break it up!" he ordered, pushing and prying at us until the veins in his neck surfaced. Tammy gained dominion and control by kicking me in the pelvis. I fell back with my hands between my legs screeching in pain. She jumped up, finger combing her hair, ready to finish the fight.

"You're as crazy as your fuckin' brother!"

Troy lashed out, pointing his tiny finger.

"Ti, Ti, not nice!" he chastised.

Stinging in pain, I rolled over to soften the blow, cringing in a fetal position. Tammy bolted up the stairs as I regained my stance, running to the bottom landing.

"Go ahead and run you blabber mouth, I hate you!"

"Shanelle!" Mrs. Foster roared, "We're all upset, but don't think you're going to walk in my house and carry on like this. We've all been through hell with Alex gone. You don't think Tammy is broken up over this?"

Her head rattled to and fro as Troy's lips began to quiver. Spit flew from her mouth as she fought back her well earned tears.

"The papers are making a mockery of our entire family, so it's best we stick together before they rip us apart!"

Weary from the exchange, my shoulders slumped in defeat.

"I'm sorry, but Alex would be here if…,"

Mr. Foster placed his hands in the sky as I rehashed the loss of his son. He planted his hands on my stiff joints and squeezed life back into my weary soul.

"We don't know where Alex would be Shanelle. All of this is God's plan."

I snatched Troy from Mrs. Foster's arms and headed for the door, blinking in rapid successions. Mr. Foster lunged forward, quickly shielding my exit with his long arms.

"Why don't you stay here? You don't have to go Shanelle; we can help you with Troy."

My answer became apparent the minute I scooped up his diaper bag.

"No! I can take care of him myself. I want to go home and be with Alex!"

Troy enhanced my sentiment by pointing towards the door. "Adex! Adex!"

Meeting him in the eyes, I smiled and held him close as he clutched my collar for comfort.

Mr. Foster's pleaded one last time.

"Shanelle, you're in no condition to drive, at least let me take the two of you home."

"No, we'll be fine, you have to stop fixing things all the time, Lord knows I only need to show up for the funeral. You did everything without me; I'm his wife for God's sake!"

"I'm sorry," Mrs. Foster urged, wringing her restless hands, "We had to do something. We couldn't get you to talk for the last two days. The nurses said you were in shock."

Troy felt like an anchor in my weary arms. I switched him to my other hip as he quickly snatched my keys and gnawed on the leather strap. I wiggled it from his grip and rocked him as his damp face settled into my neck. Succumbing to their sorrowful control I heaved, "What time is the funeral tomorrow?"

Mrs. Foster nervously rubbed her upper arms.

"Eleven-thirty." She paused for a minute, turning towards the closet, rubbing her hands to ward off the cold.

"I hope you don't mind, but we bought a suit for Troy to wear." She handed me a small dry cleaning bag with a tailor ready white suit enclosed. A new pair of Stride Rites and white socks accompanied the package. Troy's hand wearily wrestled with his ear as he began to whimper. Mrs. Foster stroked Troy's chubby cheeks.

"Night night baby, Grandma loves you."

A truce settled in her heart as her hand slip around my waist.

"I'm sorry Shanelle. We'll consult with you from now on. A limo will pick you up at ten-thirty to take you to the church." She paused briefly, looking at the clock. "Did you eat? I have some left over stewed chicken."

A wrapped plate landed in my hand. Mr. Foster quietly picked up his keys and followed me out the door. *Your Love is King*, by Sade followed me home as tears streamed down my face. I would have done anything to have Alex driving the car and telling me what to do next, but it wasn't going to happen.

Mr. Foster carried Troy inside. We exchanged a glance before he quietly left, slipping through the door like a thin ghost. I looked around his room for a minute and turned off the lights. I walked into the bedroom after checking on Troy and changed into one of Alex's tee shirts. He had enough to last a lifetime. I adjusted his baseball cap on my head and turned on the TV as the world around me continued to evolve. News reporter Carmen Rivera quickly appeared. She was poised outside a familiar haunt pitching the latest drug bust update.

"I'm currently at the Garvey Street Projects as North Orange police detectives question various people about the female assailant who shot Detective Alex Foster at Shiloh Haven Baptist Church on Saturday. Sources tell us that the shooter was fatally shot after she got into a stolen black BMW. The shooter of the female assailant jumped into another getaway car. Newark Police are currently combing the car for possible fingerprints. A source close to Detective Foster's wife said the female assailant was able to enter the church without suspicion because she looked strikingly familiar to Nikki Rivera."

Switching hands, Carmen raised her hand to sweeten the sordid tale.

"Interestingly enough, Nikki Rivera, is the sister of federal inmate Rico Rivera, who is currently under indictment for various drugs and weapons offenses stemming from the Garvey Projects. The twist in this story Bill is that Nikki Rivera and Tammy Foster, the sister of the murdered detective have been intimately linked. Nikki Rivera is a lead scorer at Pitt University and Tammy Foster; we are told is her dormitory roommate. Most people are speculating that this was some form of retribution for the drug and gun bust that took place right here at Garvey."

I squeezed my eyes tight as pieces of Alex bodies flashed before me eyes. The reporter paused for a minute and motioned her hand to a disheveled man standing in the background. "We have one brave resident of Garvey who may have some information."

"Yeah, uh, uh, uh, uh, um, looka here, uh, I don't mean no harm. We's good folk, you know, just trying to make a livin'."

He paused to wipe the white pasty residue from his mouth.

"Yeah, like I was trying to say… uh, we love da police."

Carmen snatched the microphone from his hand.

"Thank you sir. As you can see, there is sentiment here in Garvey, but this investigation is certainly not over. Back to you Bill."

The TV blackened with a quick hit from the remote. I rolled over and squeezed my eyes tight.

"Be strong Shanelle, you can do this."

I picked up the phone and called Candy.

"Who took you home?" She inquired.

"Derrick."

"Derrick?" she pitched, startled by the answer.

"Where's Troy?" She asked.

"Sleeping," I yawned, sitting up with regret.

"I'm sorry this happened on your…,"

Candy cut me off.

"No, I'm sorry for you Shanelle," she sniffled, "I'd give anything to see you with Alex."

"The funeral," I recited, "It's tomorrow."

"I know," Candy sympathized, "I'll be there, don't worry."

With what little strength I had, I rolled over on Alex's side of the bed and set the alarm. One hour later, Troy woke up crying for his father.

"Daadee," he whimpered, reaching for the bedroom's empty space. I picked him up and trekked the hardwood floor to settle his nerves to no avail. Desperate for sleep, we piled into bed, both settling onto Alex's side. Troy buried his head against my breast and found solace against the crumpled sheet, rubbing it between his fingers. I didn't want him to start picking up bad sleeping habits so I put him back in his crib after twenty minutes. My feet scraped the floor as I slumped back into bed. I turned to my husband's empty side, dry mouthed and exhausted.

"Goodnight Alex."

They Come and Go

Without fail, a limousine escorted us to Metropolitan Baptist Church in Lakewood for Alex's funeral. News reporters and well-wishers from near and far lined up in front of the church, somberly looking through the car windows at any glimpse of the family.

When I stepped out, flashing cameras immediately lit up to take a picture of the fallen officer's wife. Mr. Foster escorted us behind Alex's maple and gold encased coffin. Flowers filled the church in every direction as the weeping audience stood up to receive us. Quiet whimpers and sniffles passed us by while we walked down the aisle. I held Troy tight in my arms and patted his back sensing his confusion and hoping he would quickly fall asleep once everyone was seated.

A young man from the balcony sang *His Eye is on the Sparrow*, while we slowly positioned ourselves to our seats. Mrs. Foster began to wail for her precious son lifting her hands to the heavens.

"Lord Jesus! You should have taken me! Not my son, not my son heavenly Father!"

An usher quickly rushed to her side and fanned her flushed face as the reverend began to speak above the organ's melody.

"Trust in Him and He will not lead you astray. Let the church say amen." The audience rang out his request, *"Amen!"*

"Today is a day that I stand before you to provide funeral services for the Foster family. Now, it is not too often that I have to provide services for parents who have lost a child. So I ask you today to trust in Him and He will not lead you astray. Now, y'all ought to know that I watched Alex Foster grow up in this very church. He comes from a good God fearing home with parents that have worked their entire lives to watch their children become wonderful adults. In my time here, I watched this child of God grow from an infant to a young boy and then a man. And if it were not for his family's faith and Alex's love of the Lord, I don't think Alex would be in peace right now. But you're going to have to trust me when I say that Alex is in a better place. No matter how hard that sounds, no matter how many nights you weep, if you trust in God, he will not lead you astray. I'm also asking that you pray for this family, especially his young wife

and son. Alex may have left us a little too soon, but faith will be with us every day of our lives. His son, his wife and his family need our prayers during this difficult time. Not even the devil's bullet can stop our faith in the almighty Father..."

Troy's head fell heavy upon my shoulder. I placed him across my lap while the reverend continued. I looked at Mr. Foster and offered him a soft smile while Mrs. Foster cried on his shoulder. I turned around to look at the audience. Oddly enough, just behind Candy sat my father in a black single-breasted suit. He was sitting by himself and I wondered whether Mrs. Viv was with him or home tending to Steven.

Before the final procession took place, an officer handed me the American flag and Alex's police photograph. I kept my eyes focused on the ground until the limousine doors swung open. My body felt hollow and empty at the gravesite. A massive crowd gathered to wish Alex farewell casually turning to witness the spectacle at curbside.

"Can someone help me with my son?'" Mrs. Viv inquired, struggling to hoist Steven down from his handicap ramp while he mumbled in his wheelchair. A few good men gathered around to help them as my father quietly took over. To my surprise, Mrs. Viv politely pushed him.

"Thank you," she smiled, adjusting Steven's plastic eight-inch lobster bib. I closed my eyes and tried to wish them away.

"Why did she have to bring him?"

It was considerably cool that day and I was relieved the crowd dispersed quickly. A few well-wishers walked up to me to express their condolences, including Derrick. Mrs. Viv watched me from a cautious distance while he softly pressed my body into his chest for a final hug goodbye.

"I'm so sorry Shanelle; I hope you find the strength to keep moving."

When Derrick walked away, my father appeared with open arms.

"Wow, look how big Troy is getting." He quickly changed the subject to avoid his own guilt.

"I couldn't leave without saying goodbye Shanelle. I'm sorry about your loss."

The past didn't matter anymore. My head swiftly turned.

"Leaving for where?"

"North Carolina," he replied, "Viv and I decided to split for a while…, it's for the best."

I put Troy down as he immediately clutched my leg.

"Well, don't go just yet, we need to talk."

My attention focused back to Troy as he toddled off.

"Why don't you stay at my place, just for the night so we can talk."

He searched my eyes and followed his grandson.

"Ok, but I'll get on the road in the morning."

Mrs. Viv's hurried steps almost knocked Troy over.

"Ma, be careful!"

I abruptly shielded Troy from Steven. Even though he was no longer a threat, there was no remorse in my heart. Mrs. Viv tried in earnest to appear concerned.

"Oh, I'm so sorry, I almost hit my grandson. Look at him with his handsome self."

Mrs. Viv tugged and pulled on her worn dress.

"Shanelle," she bantered, "I'm so sorry about your loss, I hope Alex left you well so you don't have to struggle anymore."

Her flying dagger flew over my head as the Fosters huddled together and stared at my freakish family.

"Listen," I ordered, "The repast is back at the church mom. Dad, you can follow me to the house if you want."

Mrs. Viv grabbed my wrist, gripping her nails into my skin.

"Whatever he tells you," she bewitched, "I'll always be your mother."

My father put his head down and shamefully stepped in tow towards his car. Mrs. Foster broke up the commotion.

"Shanelle, are you coming? The limos are leaving,"

I peered above the crowd, searching for my father's car.

"No, go ahead, I'll get the car seat out and ride back with my dad."

"Okay sweetheart. We'll catch up with you later."

Candy, Clinton and Bonnie approached me from behind with a group hug. Candy stroked my face and smoothed away strands of hair.

"We're going to get back on the parkway. Clinton has a flight going out at four. If you need anything Shanelle, just give me a call."

Bonnie squeezed me tight and forced back her tears.

"Andre sends his love Shanelle. If you need anything, just call me."

A slow march led us back to the vehicles as my dad struggled to strap Troy into the car seat. Cursing under his breath, a final click relieved him.

"There you go sport, all set."

We exchanged a timid smile. I only wondered what would come next.

Revelations

I was glad my father accepted the invitation to go back to the house. It kept my mind off the real issues even though I wasn't ready for new ones. I showed him the guest room and offered him a wash-cloth and towel. His over zealous compliments made me nervous as Troy ate a few bites of his sandwich. Rocking him, he fell asleep and accepted the warm surroundings of his crib. I changed into sweats, made a sandwich for my father and poured juice in ice filled glasses. A fragile face and restless hands possessed his thin frame. His eyes shifted to the floor while he caressed his drink.

"Dad," I asked, "Tell me, what is it?"

"Shanelle, I want you to know that I am sorry for everything that happened to you. I feel like such a failure for not looking out for you the way a father should. I've been carrying this guilt with me for so long, I guess there's never going to be a good time to tell you."

He paused to pick up a napkin and wiped his brow. "Today is probably not the best day to tell any of this to you, but Vivian was determined to come here and ruin whatever peace you have left."

My heart began to pound under a sharp sewing machine, ready to burst on the final stitch. I stared out the window as a puffy white cloud drifted against the backdrop of the bluest sky. The strain in my heart became heavier and heavier, but the slow moving cloud was my cue to keep moving forward.

"Dad, just tell me. Start from the beginning."

Even though I gave my father the green light, I began to float away.

"I guess a resurrection is impossible, huh Alex?"

"You're right baby it's impossible."

"Can you believe my father is here?"

"I can believe it, he's got something heavy on his heart, listen to him and find your way, I'm right here."

I put my hand on top of my father's wrist as he began to tell his story.

"When Vivian and I got married, we were anxious to have children right away. It was her dream to have a house full of kids. After Steven was born, we waited a year to have another child. Unfortunately, Vivian had three miscarriages, one after the other. She was so driven to have another baby it became an obsession Shanelle."

He took a deep breath and turned his glass in slow circles.

"She blamed me for everything and it put a strain on our marriage. I buried myself in work and started coming home late just to avoid her. She made such a fuss over Steven because he was the only thing that could keep her mind off of getting pregnant again."

My father sighed. I connected with Alex again.

"I don't think I'm ready for whatever it is he's going to tell me."

"You'll be fine, I'm here."

"Vivian put on so much weight; the doctor told her that she would be better off losing fifty pounds before she tried again."

"So what happened? She got pregnant with me?"

His face coiled with strain.

"I had an affair with another woman," he stalled, "Vivian's not your mother."

My fingers lay flat against the table. What little light shining through the window began to fade as the room darkened around me. My voice cracked underneath the swell of my own question. Small beads of sweat formed around my hairline.

"What do you mean she's not my mother?"

My father put his hands up and folded them in front of his mouth.

"Please let me finish Shanelle, or I'll never get this off my chest. I had an office affair with a woman named Clara. It only lasted a year, but before I knew it she was pregnant with you Shanelle."

"What!" I screamed.

Shaking his head, racked with emotions, the words continued to spill from his mouth.

"Vivian accepted you because…"

Standing, gaped face and shocked, my voice blared in denial. "Stop this daddy."

My father jumped up pressing my shoulder with a firm hand.

"Vivian's not your mother, but she raised you like you were her daughter."

I stormed out of the kitchen, but he stopped me mid way.

"I'm sorry Shanelle, your mother died in a car accident when you were two weeks old. I had to tell your mother, uh, I mean Vivian, well she is your mother, she raised you... well, the truth is, there was no one else to take care of you but me and Vivian."

"Why are you doing this to me?" I yelled. "I just buried my husband for God's sake!"

"If I didn't tell you, Lord knows Vivian was prepared to do it today. I'm sorry Shanelle, she never forgave me for the affair and I couldn't take it anymore. She blames you for Steven's paralysis and I couldn't let her do that."

"Me!" I jerked forward, facing the cruel reality. "I didn't do anything to him, he brought this on himself daddy!"

"You're right Shanelle, but there's no convincing her because of what I did so long ago. She accepted you because of her faith, but she couldn't forgive me."

My arms folded as he looked at my hands. My wedding ring was the only ornament on my fingers.

"Your ring," he paused, "Where's the ring I gave you?"

Years of sweltering one-sided memories exploded.

"The ring? You're worried about that damn ring?"

I wiped my tears away ready for the storm.

"I did exactly what you said daddy. I kept myself pure until the man of my dreams swept me off my feet! But trust me, I ran to him out of desperation. Thank God he was a good man in his heart. You did nothing to protect me. For years you went to work while she whipped my ass and stroked Steven's ego. I cooked and cleaned up Steven's filthy habits while you looked the other way, busy on a train to New York, hoping that dear Mrs. Viv wouldn't throw you out. Look where it got me, locked up in closets, walking the streets, beat up and trying to survive. No wonder none of you came around when Troy was born! I'm real easy to forget. What was I to you, some fucking sacrifice for your adultery? I hate you!"

Troy cries bellowed through the nursery monitor. I ran up-stairs to settle him down to no avail. The last thing he needed to hear was instability in my voice. My voice trembled as I sang to him, *"Yes, Jesus loves me, yes Jesus loves me, because the bible tells me so."*

He gripped my shirt and refused the floor with a few kicks at my side. By the time I came downstairs with Troy in my arms, the front door was ajar. I held onto Troy for comfort and used my foot to slam the door shut. Silence overwhelmed the room until Troy gave me new energy.

"Dadee? dadee go bye bye?"

His damp fingers fished inside his mouth for relief.

"No baby, that wasn't daddy, daddy went to heaven."

Troy stared at the window pouting his lips to practice his mastery of the English language.

"Headen?" He squeaked, tugging my hair.

"Yes, baby daddy went to heaven, but he's with us."

Coaxing him to the floor with a silly song, I fought back tears and cleared my throat. Troy picked up an envelope off the floor and handed it to me. I knew it was Derrick's letter, but I wasn't ready for condolences. I placed it carefully in our letterbox for another day. Suddenly, the doorbell rang.

"Good afternoon, are you Shanelle Foster?"

"Yes," I replied.

"My name is Neil Harrison from Prudential. I'm your late husband's insurance agent."

His suit and business card looked official so I let him in the house. A squad car passing by eased my worry. I directed him to the kitchen and offered him some coffee.

"I'm sorry, I can't stay very long, I have a few stops along the way."

I sat down next to him while he took an envelope out of his briefcase. Troy clamored alongside me and plopped himself on the floor with one of his favorite toys. The insurance agent smiled.

"Mrs. Foster, I know this is a difficult time for you, but your husband left specific instructions with his father to make sure you received the proceeds of his life insurance policy immediately upon death."

Mr. Harrison placed the envelope on the table along with an application.

"You also have insurance on the house. Once this form is filled out and processed, your mortgage will be free and clear."

He stood up and exclaimed in a rushed tone, "Alex left you well off Mrs. Foster. I know the money won't replace him, but at least you'll be able to provide for yourself and your son."

He passed Troy, playfully scrunching his soft hair.

"Call me if you have any questions."

The visit was so abrupt I didn't know what to say except, "Thank you, Mr. Harrison." When I walked back into the kitchen, Troy was pulling on the refrigerator. I washed his hands and placed him in his high chair. Juice in a toddler cup complimented his snack. I sat at the table and slowly opened the envelope. The check from Prudential looked like a practical joke, but it had my name on it bearing Four Hundred and Fifty Thousand Dollars written in the box.

"I can't believe it."

A phone call to the Fosters confirmed my doubt. Mr. Foster took his time and talked to me despite his aching heart.

"I didn't think they would come today Shanelle, but that's what my son wanted." He sniffled a bit and tucked his sad tone into a loud cough.

"I have another check for Troy from his father too. We spent our lives saving money in case we ever had to go to court for that thing in Virginia, but it's over now."

"Well why don't you keep it?" I replied. Mr. Foster quickly responded. "No Shanelle, I gotta follow Alex's wishes to the letter. He loved you so much and you have to make sure that Troy is taken care of, that's all he wanted for the two of you."

I held on to the phone cord like it was a lifeline to Alex.

A wilted napkin absorbed my tears.

"I know and I will," I replied.

Mr. Foster cleared his throat.

"What's my grandson doing?"

"Eating as usual," I chuckled.

"Well," Mr. Foster said, "We have plenty of company here. You and Troy are welcome to come by tonight if you get lonely."

"Thanks Dad, I love you."

"We all love you Shanelle, come by later on okay?"

"I will."

I hung up the phone and walked to Alex's make shift office. The check went into a mail slot for deposit. I decided to put Troy in his playpen while I rested on the floor. He sat up and grabbed his toys.

"Be a good boy for mommy while I take a nap."

It wasn't long before I drifted off to sleep. A stage of grief took place in the form of a dream. It must have rested there until today. Never had I been faced with such despair, happiness and hopelessness.

A soft shade of light began to shine in a six by six foot padded room as the voices from my past and present appeared. My dear friend Nemesis was wearing a tight, full-length red dress. Her hair was slicked back in a ponytail with a fully bloomed white flower tucked behind her ear like Billy Holiday. She took a seat at the head of the table and quietly lit a cigar with her head cocked to the side to enhance her sophisticated demeanor. In a sultry voice she sang, "Bring her in boys."

The Big One and the Meek One pulled the curtain back with their grubby hands and pushed my chair out from behind a black velvet curtain. My mouth was covered with duct tape. I was confined to a crisp white cotton straight jacket. Desperate pleas of help were muffled behind the thick sticky tape as my head thrashed back and forth.

"Okay," Nemesis said, "Let's bring this meeting to order."

Nemesis put the cigar in her mouth and spoke while it bobbed up and down. "Let's face it Shanelle, I did a good job at keeping Derrick out of your panties, so we can't blame him, he certainly loves you."

She looked at her cohorts and asked, "Did you see the way he handled himself at the hospital? Shanelle couldn't ask for a better man. He's so caring, confident and more importantly, she'll be safe. I don't think anyone would have a need to hunt him down like a wild animal. Alex must have really done some dirt behind that badge to get popped like that."

Nemesis removed the cigar and pressed her lips together to contain her worry. She sighed briefly.

"I guess we'll never know."

She smiled and looked me in the eye.

"*Shanelle, open the letter. You're working my nerves already; dropping it here and there. Troy is going to need a father. As for you..., well an empty bed is no place to be on a cold winter night. You know winters are rough on you with the whole Steven thing.*"

The Meek One covered his mouth and giggled as he held my face still.

"*Steven did a good job of running you out of that house and right into Alex's loving arms. Don't get me wrong, he was a good man, but a little too controlling. We won't blame him, but he sure had a way of stressing you out.*"

The Big One hurled an attack.

"*Yeah, she can throw down can't she, peanut butter, toothpaste, all kinds of shit.*"

Nemesis resumed her puff.

"*Now, now, Steven, Mrs. Viv and dear daddy sure did a number on her, nobody can deny that. But the real question is, can she forgive and just let that shit go?*"

The Little One started growing fangs.

"*Hell no! Let's light a fire, torch the damn house and throw rocks at it, better yet,*" The Little One turned my face into his demonic eyes and growled, "*Go ahead and kill yourself, then you'll never have to worry again!*"

I rocked my head out of his hands and looked at Nemesis with a quiet plea of strength.

"*No, not Shanelle, she's too strong, she's a fighter, just wait and see.*"

She extinguished the cigar and crossed her hands.

"*You're not going to leave that precious boy behind without his mother. Your own mother did that to you in a tragic accident. Troy deserves to know you and love you. He also needs a father and Derrick is right there waiting for him.*"

Troy managed to hit me with one of his toys, jolting me out of my dream. His eyes were as handsome as his father's as a message from Alex popped up.

"*Get organized Shanelle.*"

Rico was so impressed with Flaco; he had to call him to give him his props.

"Yo man, your shit was smooth like that, I gotta give you credit."

Flaco bobbed his head in agreement.

"Yeah, yeah, right, right."

Rico took a drag from his cigarette and threw it to the ground. He used his brand new white Nike sneaker to crush the lit embers in front of him.

"Call Nikki and tell her not to go back to Pitt. She needs to be by my side with Mommy and Papi for the trial. Oh yeah, tell her to drop Tomboy Tammy and start hanging out with the fellas, she needs to be around family now. Last but not least, send Gigi's mother some money for the funeral and a nice arrangement, we owe them that much."

"Okay, I'll take care of it," Flaco replied.

Three days later, Nikki called Tammy to let her know she was picking up her stuff from the dorm room.

"But why? Just finish this semester," Tammy pleaded.

"No, I gotta be with my family right now baby, they need me."

"But I need you," Tammy said.

Nikki sighed.

"Things are crazy right now, so I think we should lay low for a while."

Tammy went to the refrigerator for some deli meat.

"How long?"

Before Nikki ended the call she gruffed, "I'll let you know."

Tammy hung up and buried her sorrow in three sandwiches, Doritos and two Sunkist sodas. She took two bites at a time before she swallowed, hastily wiping her tears away. Mrs. Foster stood in the doorway and watched her daughter's quiet torment.

"Do you feel better now?"

Tammy stood up, threw the can in the garbage and yelled, "Leave me alone mom, suddenly Shanelle's a damn angel, just because Alex is gone. What about me? I miss him too and it wasn't my fault!"

Mrs. Foster rubbed Tammy's back while she wept for her lost brother and girlfriend.

"Tammy, it's going to take time to heal. If you want to take a semester off that's fine, but its best that you go back to school and continue your regular routine."

Before Tammy went back to school, Mrs. Foster gathered everyone for dinner. Despite the tension in the room, we all agreed to resume our lives without any comments to the press. Mr. Foster hired an attorney to be our spokesperson during the trial. Luckily the police had a good tip on Alex's murder. Unknown to any of us, Andre the entrepreneur had a keen sense of eyesight and a strong scent for the smell of reward money. Without a word to anyone, he was secretly working with the police to nail Flaco for Alex's murder. Fifty thousand dollars from crime stoppers had Andre's mouth watering for legitimate money to start his own business. It wouldn't be long before Andre collected his reward.

Even if Rico thought things were going his way, it didn't work out in his favor. The trial lasted five months and he was sentenced to thirty years under the toughest federal sentences. Racketeering, money laundering, extortion and witness tampering followed his demise, while Mama Barb picked up a fifteen-year bid. Poor Mookie wept like a damn fool in front of the news cameras. His so-called basketball career was over in the blink of an eye. The stress of the trial sent him into a weed and drinking binge just like Steven. Without the academic smarts and his mama to back him up, life was too unbearable, so he moved to Maryland with his aunt.

Amazingly, Garvey began to flourish with green grass and a small community garden. A few residents banded together to form a community watch group. Under the watchful eye of the North Orange police, peace came again in the form of happy children laughing under the early twilight with fewer junkies around. Alex may have thought differently, but they were really decent people just trying to survive.

My Turn

Seventeen months passed by and I was still in the thickest stage of denial. Jack kept me posted on the murder investigation, but parts of me felt like he was keeping information from me. To keep busy, Mrs. Foster convinced me to drop Troy off for the day to sort my mile high mail. Candy and Jack agreed to come over and go through Alex's clothes for the homeless. I considered it a good start. Everything Alex owned was neatly in its place. The pillows we threw on the floor from our last interlude were still on the floor. Troy made a few adjustments, but I forbade him from going in the living room.

Jack said very little when he came. He and Alex were so close; it was difficult for him to organize his belongings. Alex's badge, hat and smaller incidentals were placed in a keepsake box for Troy. All of his other belongings were eventually boxed up and hauled away. Jack met me at the bottom of the stairs for a hug goodbye.

I grabbed his wrist when he reached the bottom of the stairs. I wanted him to tell me more about Alex since there was so much controversy during the trial and investigation. He seemed insulted that I asked and pulled me into the kitchen while Candy went to the bathroom.

"Look around Shanelle; he was a good police officer and a good husband. There's no sense in you trying to figure out anything else, just hold on to your memories okay?"

Jack pressed his fingertips into my shoulders. A quick glance suggested there was something more, but if there was, Jack wasn't going to tell. He promised he would call, but I knew he was lying. I held on to him for a little while and stared into his eyes again for closure. Jack grabbed me by the hand.

"Remember what I said, he was a good man. Troy ought to grow up and learn the same thing. Listen, I better run, you take care okay?"

He could barely fight back the tears as he left with Candy standing by my side. When the door shut behind him, we went back upstairs to survey the damage. Empty hangers were swinging back and forth. A cool breeze whistled underneath the opening from the window and forced clean air into my lungs. The hangers began to clang together like church bells on Sunday morning.

"C'mon," I said, "We can let the bedroom air out while we open the mail."

Candy and I went into the kitchen. She quietly picked up the phone to see what Clinton wanted for dinner. Her voice sounded calm and relaxed as they exchanged messages of love to each other. I think the tragedy they experienced solidified a perfect bond of matrimony. I looked out the window and wished I had Alex around to talk to me. When I did talk to him, the words never came back. They followed me in nature's smallest gifts, an ocean breeze, morning birds or leaves cascading to the ground. Candy sensed my longing the instant she sat down.

"So what about you? Don't you think it's time?"

I picked up a stack of mail and passed it to her.

"Separate them first and then we'll open it."

Candy picked up one that stood out among the rest.

"This one doesn't have anything on it except your name."

I looked at Candy and quickly put my head down.

"I know Derrick gave it to me the day before Alex's funeral."

"How come you didn't open it?"

I scanned my checkbook and recorded the balance from my cable bill. Candy tapped the table for a response. Cringing at the thought, I took a deep breath.

"I don't want to read it."

"Shanelle," she whined, "It's been…"

I finished her sentence. "Yeah, seventeen months to be exact since Alex died."

"Shanelle, just see what he has to say. If you didn't care, you would have thrown the letter away. But you didn't, so read it girl."

Candy picked up a letter opener and handed it to me.

"You open it," I asked, pushing the instrument away.

Candy cut away at the envelope's thick seam. She cleared her throat and read Derrick's heart-warming words.

Dear Shanelle,

Words cannot express how sorry I was to see you at the hospital. All I can say is that I am sorry you lost your husband. I had to write something just to let you know how I feel. It's something you taught me a long time ago. Anyway, I can only pray that you will open this letter and read it one day. Knowing you the way I do, avoiding me may be the best thing for now.

Candy handed me the first page. I gazed at the paper keying in on his meticulous handwriting. Candy's voice softened.

Shanelle, you've gone through so much in your life, I can't imagine any person other than you who has to once again overcome such a crazy reality. Seeing you with your son downtown that day convinced me that despite it all, you would weather the storm. If some time has passed before reading this letter, I hope this makes sense to you because I'm going to take a risk and just say it. Do you remember our hopes and dreams for the future? My dream of becoming a doctor tested our relationship and I had to leave you behind. I realize now that there was little I could do to help you escape the past, but something deep inside of me often wonders if it's ever too late? I believe in destiny Shanelle and I know you do too. I put the poem you wrote to me in this envelope so you could remember the words you wrote to me. It hasn't been ten years, but I'm ready to see if we can finally have a meeting of the minds. Shanelle, call me.

(212) 333-1212

Candy pulled the poem out of the envelope. I snatched the thin piece of wispy paper as a small grin cascaded across my face.

"Well?" Candy asked.

"Well what?" I giggled, recalling our high school antics.

"Call him. If you don't, I will. Damn Shanelle, you're not a mummy. See what he has to say. I'm not trying to shove him down your throat, but he still has hope, call him."

"Hope in what? I have a son, he doesn't want me Candy."

"Duh…," she quickly fired back, slapping her thighs, "He picked Troy up, asked his name, took you home. Don't be silly."

I cleared my throat trying to find calm.

"Besides, you know I promised the Fosters that I would lay low."

Loose change rattled in her head. Candy pressed her fingers into her temples.

"The last time I checked, the trial was over, the police aren't parked outside the door and Barbara Walters isn't trying to call your ass for an interview. It's time to take a small step forward Shanelle. Just call him."

Having her fill, Candy finished me off.

"Look, you're doing a great job with Troy, just like Alex would have wanted. But you need some adult stimulation in your life."

Honestly, there was no way I considered myself unavailable. All of my time with Troy replaced my need to binge on food. I was sure that once I pulled my sweatshirt off, I wouldn't mind what was underneath. Derrick just kept popping up but he was there for me when the chips were really down. Despite my problems, he was the only person that really connected with my future dreams. Alex constantly boxed them up and peeled back the tape at his leisure. I had to admit, if it wasn't for Alex, I wouldn't be able to afford any dreams.

Clean air drifted downstairs from the open windows. New perspectives became my friend as I inhaled the crisp scent around me. I watched my fingers uncurl and plant down on the table.

Candy jumped up and danced a jig.

"Whoop! Whoop! That's my girl."

Blushing, I picked up the phone. Candy called out the numbers.

"212 333-1212."

Three rings blared into my ears. A well spoken woman chimed in.

"Hello."

My eyes grew wide. I contemplated hanging up. She inquired again. "Hello?"

Candy snapped her fingers in three rapid successions.

"Oh, hi, hello, may I speak to Derrick please?"

She paused. I'm sure her hand landed on her hip.

"May I ask who is calling?"

I looked at the letter for strength.

"This is Shanelle…, returning his call."

Candy gave me the thumbs up sign, mimicking a silent circus seal clap. I covered the mouthpiece. A few muddled voices carried on in the distance. When Derrick answered, I exhaled.

"Hello?"

"Derrick. Hi. It's me, Shanelle."

A brief pause suspended our time. He cleared his throat. I wondered what he was thinking, but it didn't take long to find out.

"Hey, I was beginning to give up on you."

There was relief in his voice.

"Did I catch you at a bad time?" I asked.

"No, I have a study group over, but we're just wrapping up."

"Oh."

"So, I guess you finally read my old letter?" Derrick wittingly inquired.

I clutched the phone cord.

"It was nice, really nice."

Derrick rode the tail end of my feelings.

"It would be nice to see you Shanelle. It's been a long time."

I caught Candy's eye and quickly looked away.

"I wouldn't mind seeing you again, where do you want to meet Derrick?"

"My money's kind of tight these days, so I couldn't take you to a fancy restaurant. Can you meet me in the city on Saturday night?"

Relaxed by his casualness, I said, "You know I'm not a fancy restaurant kind of girl. Let's keep it simple. How 'bout Ray's Pizza in the Village?"

Candy nodded with approval.

"Sounds great, six o'clock?"

"Six o'clock is fine," I replied. When I hung up the phone, Candy ushered me along with a push.

"Pack a bag for you and Troy and stay at my house for the weekend, I could use the company."

I looked at her puzzled.

"Why, aren't you doing Newark to D.C.?"

Candy's head fell on my shoulder.

"Clinton and I are trying to get pregnant and he is wearing my ass out girl."

"What!" I jumped, "Am I going to be a Godmother?"

"Not yet, but one day God mother."

Bouts of maturity strengthened our bond as we shared a quick hug. Candy wouldn't let me out the door unless I had a cute outfit on and a full face of makeup. She stayed with me while I packed our bags. She also went for the ride to pick Troy up from the Foster's house. When Mr. Foster opened the door, he blinked twice.

"Shanelle, hey, you're all dressed up, what's the occasion?"

I quickly replied, "Nothing, where's Troy?"

Candy greeted Mr. Foster and walked in behind me.

"Troy's outside with his grandmother. You're early; I thought you weren't coming until eight."

I walked towards the back door.

"I know, I'm going to spend the weekend at Candy's and we need to get a jump on traffic."

Mr. Foster smiled.

"That's good. You know you can leave Troy here if you like."

I shook my head in the middle of his sentence.

"No, he's coming with me."

I knew the Fosters would take care of my little man, but I wasn't ready to leave my lifeline on any given day of the week. Having him close kept me sane. Mrs. Foster was in the back planting when Troy spotted me.

"Mommy mommy!"

I picked him up and nuzzled in his neck. He was getting so tall and thin; it felt like I hadn't seen him in weeks.

"Wow," I exclaimed, "I think you grew some more."

Mrs. Foster got off her knees and flicked away loose particles on her pants. She looked at my attire and immediately began an inquiry.

"Hi Shanelle. Hello Candy. You girls going out for a change?"

"Yeah, I'm going to Candy's house for the weekend."

Mrs. Foster's sentiment was the same as her husband's. "Oh, Troy has extra clothes, so he'll be fine Shanelle."

"I'm taking him with me."

Her curiosity continued. "Well if you go out, who's going to watch him?"

I was annoyed at first, but it was time to take a stand in a modest way.

"I'm going out mom. Candy's going to watch him."

Mrs. Foster's trembling fingers yanked at her gardening gloves finger by finger. Her stance planted firmly into the ground as if Alex was buried directly beneath her feet.

"I see," she mumbled.

Candy checked her watch, nudging me along.

"We better get going Shanelle."

I returned to the house to collect Troy's favorite toys. Mr. Foster took the initiative to change his pull up and put his jacket on as he got on his knees to hug his grandson.

"Troy, be good for mommy, I'll see you when you get back."

Tickled by his antics, Troy's pointer finger shot into the air leading a horse drawn chariot race. "I'll be back Pop Pop!"

Tears cascaded down Mrs. Foster's face. I grabbed her wrist and reassured her of our safe return.

"I'll stop by and see you on Monday, ok?"

She quickly swept her emotions away into her soiled shirt sleeve.

"Okay Shanelle, see you Monday."

Derrick

It felt good going to Candy's house. They purchased a four-bedroom home in Livingston, which added some much needed color to the block. Troy stayed awake for the entire drive so I was more than happy to put him down for the night. We quickly nominated Clinton as the babysitter and went to the Short Hills Mall for a mini shopping trip. Two bags landed at my sides as we departed from Bloomingdales. Candy tugged my ponytail.

"You need to do something with that curly mop of yours before you meet Derrick."

"I know Candy, don't start."

She leaned with an unintended secret.

"When he looks at you after all this time, I want him to be blown away."

My eyes slammed shut to avoid a flashback of Alex's bloody demise on the church floor. Candy grabbed my wrist.

"Oh Shanelle, I'm so sorry."

"I know, you didn't mean it, I'm fine Candy, really."

The next day I kissed Troy goodbye and went to Bloomfield Center for a manicure and pedicure. A doobie came next including a long over due clipping. I couldn't believe how long my hair was, so I made her cut it to my shoulders to shape my face. Candy finished me off with some light makeup to last me through the day.

It felt good to get dressed up. I couldn't remember the last time I put on an outfit. Candy loaned me her silver hoops and a small leather bag. I decided to drive into New York to meet Derrick so I wouldn't have to walk in new leather boots.

By the time I got to the city, I realized that Derrick and I didn't speak to each other since Candy came over. I wondered if he was going to stand me up. I stood outside Ray's Pizza looking like a nervous idiot for fifteen minutes. Tight lipped and antsy, I turned to leave, quickly changing my expression to a bright smile as he stood in front of me grinning from ear to ear. Derrick looked like he could afford more than a slice of pizza. A fresh shave left his skin taut and smooth. His cologne rifled my nostrils. He was distinctive as any New Yorker in signature black attire, including a turtleneck, casual slacks and a black leather jacket. One hand was comfortably tucked in his pants pocket. His other hand hid behind his back. His almond shaped eyes lit up when our eyes connected for a star dust gaze. Derrick took the flowers he was hiding behind his back and put them on top of a mailbox. I looked down for a second as he quickly picked my head up like the glory days of our past.

"There's nothing down there Shanelle except feet. Besides, I need a hug."

My leather jacket was open when I embraced him. Derrick didn't reach around the outside of my jacket. Instead, he slid his hands underneath and wrapped his warm hands around my back in a sweet caress. I didn't realize it at first, but he lifted me right off the ground and nuzzled his face in my hair. He inhaled and held his breath with a subtle moan. Our combined energy seemed to satisfy his soul.

"Ahh, it's so good to finally see you again Shanelle."

Having him hold me felt wonderful. When our eyes met again, all he could do was smile. He held my hand up and spun me around.

"Gorgeous as ever," he bragged. The flowers, still within reach landed in my hands as I held them up to my nose. Derrick tapped me with the tip of his finger to remove small strands of hair from my face.

"Thank you Derrick."

"You're welcome."

Scrutinizing his ensemble I said, "It doesn't look like you want pizza."

Derrick looked both ways as yellow cabs drove down the Avenue of the Americas.

"You're right, I'm not in the mood for pizza. I just want to be with you."

We crossed the street when the coast was clear and headed towards Washington Square Park. There was a slight chill in the air, but Derrick's fast pace and warm hand kept me comfortable. I waited for him to speak first as we dodged the oncoming traffic.

"What are you wearing Shanelle, you always smell so good."
My heels clicked along the sidewalk.

"Tresor, by Lancôme."

"I like it, it's soft and sexy."

I laughed.

"I bet you say that to all the ladies."

Derrick quickly shook his head.

"The only girl in my life is called T-cell."

"A medical term?" I asked.

"Yep, I live and breathe her." He stopped in the front of the Hagen Das Ice Cream store.

"Want some?" He asked.

"No thank you." His eyes quickly darted to my hips.

"You look great. I hope you're not worried about the weight thing."

I shook my head.

"Trust me; Troy put an end to all of that."

Derrick turned to the cashier and grabbed his chocolate cone.

"How are the two of you doing?" His face was filled with concern.

"It's day by day for me Derrick. Troy was only one when it happened so he doesn't remember much."

If it was a hot day outside, Derrick's ice cream would have melted because he was riveted by my story. I grabbed a napkin and handed it to him. I remembered how kind he was to me on the day of the shooting.

"I never got a chance to say thank you for everything you did for me that day."

Derrick pulled me away from the counter as a courtesy to the incoming patrons. He grabbed my hand.

"Shanelle, you did thank me, but you were a million miles away. Rightfully so, you lost your husband."

Derrick watched the wind blow my hair.

"Let's sit in the park."

"Sure," I replied.

Washington Square Park was lit up with colorful people huddled in groups or strolling by with loaded shopping bags. Derrick turned towards me and pinched my earlobe. He was making a small fuss, but it felt nice.

"I'm glad you called Shanelle."

"Me too," I blushed.

Derrick surveyed the crowd.

"Even though all of these people are sitting in the park, it feels like it's just you and me here," he remarked, rubbing the back of my hand. He leaned back studying my face with concern.

"Are you okay Shanelle, you've been through so much."

My pointer finger met his thick lips.

"You look great Derrick; I hope all is well in your life."

Derrick tossed his tattered napkin in the trash.

"Hmm," he said, "I feel like I missed a lot of down time, but I'll catch up. I'm happy I stuck to my goals."

Derrick was so convincing when he spoke. As people strolled by, they struck a glance at his handsome appeal. I stroked his smooth face with my hand.

"I'm so proud of you."

He held onto to the moment, thumbing my palm before a kiss landed on my knuckles. Keeping my hands warm, he rested them on his lap. A pause followed before nervous laughter erupted between us.

"Do you think we really had a chance back then Shanelle?"

I immediately answered, "No, we didn't."

"How about now?" he asked, squeezing my hand.

Finding focus into the night, I firmly questioned, "Why me?"

"I don't know, Shanelle, it just feels like I need to take a chance." Derrick pulled me off the bench and wrapped his arms around my waist. I laid my head on his chest and closed my eyes. His heart was beating fast as he continued to rub my back.

"It feels good to hold you again Shanelle."

Trust me, I enjoyed the hug, but I wasn't sure if Derrick was saying the same thing to other women. I wasn't looking for any drama after all this time. Pulling away, my head leaned to the side.

"Derrick, do you have a girlfriend?" I asked, planting my hands at my waist. He sat down on the park bench and pulled me into his sturdy frame.

"Shanelle, I had a girlfriend, but it didn't work out. It's hard trying to find someone as sweet and sincere as you. I think they're all lined up waiting for that MD to get behind my name."

"You're right," I said, "You worked hard for that. You need a real woman by your side to support you."

"Like you?" he queried, raising his eyebrow.

His question caught me off guard. Derrick's shoulders rose and settled as he continued. "Real woman like you," he paused, pointing his finger. "Tough and not afraid to follow a dream."

My lips spread across my face and retreated to a pout.

"Derrick, you know what's been going on in my life. I didn't follow my dreams. I followed someone else's."

"You mean Alex?"

I blinked once, grinding my teeth as my fingers curled into tight balls.

"Yes, Alex. In my crazy mixed up world, I ran to him and gave him everything he wanted, even Troy."

Derrick placed his hands on my waist.

"You're a good mother," Derrick pitched, leaning forward with a smile. "Is it too late? Your only twenty-one…, well make that twenty-two, next week right?"

I blushed.

"Yes, "I'll be twenty-two."

A pair of weightless hands shot into the air.

"Well, what's the problem? Go back to school; you have your whole life ahead of you Shanelle."

Searching his rich hazel eyes under a bright lamp post, a subtle smile escaped. Blinking twice, my teeth raked my lower lip as his thumb lifted my chin.

"You're right."

A soft pinch followed. A giggle escaped with a yawn.

His warm arm weighted my body as I leaned into him.

"You look tired Shanelle, are you ready to go?"

I perked up, not wanting to leave him.

"I can hang for another hour or two."

"Good!" Derrick replied. "I don't want you to go, but I know Troy probably misses you."

"Candy's watching him for me. He's in good hands."

Derrick patted my leg.

"Let's go to the Blue Note."

My throbbing feet wanted to head home. I perused the ground hoping to find pavements made of goose down pillows. Reading me like an old preschool acquaintance, Derrick teased, "You had to be cute and buy those new boots?"

His knees came within an inch of the cold cement. Flashing a set of pampered teeth, he laughed, "Take them off, I'll give you a piggy back ride."

I grabbed his wrist tickled by his high school antics.

"You're crazy!"

"No, I'm a medical student and anything goes. Besides, this is New York. It wouldn't matter if I was naked."

Blinking once, my stomach fluttered at the feel of Derrick's hand pressed against my hip. An instant flashback from our lust filled days passed by as Derrick's naked splendor appeared in front of me.

"I think he could stop traffic."

Flowers in hand, I boarded his back coupled with a giddy girl daze. Derrick carried my boots and walked four blocks to the jazz spot as passerbys teased our intimate moment.

"Can I get a ride too?" an old lady chortled, gripping her wrinkled shopping bags.

"What a gentleman," an elderly Latino man boasted, "She'll give you the world if you keep that up."

My chin settled in his neck as the fragrant flowers passed through my nostrils.

"Happy?" Derrick asked, striding along with ease, my weight presenting an effortless task under his solid forearms.

"Yes, I'm very happy right now."

Upon arrival, we settled in a seat near the back of the club for privacy. Derrick propped my feet up and pressed his knuckles into the sore spots of my foot for instant relief. A local artist played his saxophone as we quietly locked eyes. His hand reached my face tenderly sweeping my lips with his thumb. I grabbed his wrist and clasped his hand watching it fall into my lap. Derrick turned away and ordered a drink while I sipped on spring water. He leaned over and whispered, "Are you sure you're doing okay?"

A weighted velvet curtain shut my eyes as the melody swept me into Alex's warm embrace. My lips trembled at the thought.

"I still miss him."

Derrick continued to treat my ailing toes and arch.

"It takes time Shanelle; just take it day by day."

He pulled me closer to him coaxing my head on his shoulder. We ordered dinner and enjoyed the rhapsody. Nothing else needed to be said. Even if Derrick wanted me back, that was going to take a season or two. We were still the same in many ways, but time had changed us. Thirty minutes passed before the waiter presented our dinner. We shared small talk and samples of food. I was glad we were catching up, but there was little about my life that I wanted to divulge with the exception of Troy.

The clock forced our priorities to the surface. He paid the bill and picked up our jackets from the coat check. Once outside, Derrick shielded me from the street. Satisfied that I was slightly away from the hustle and bustle, he tugged my earlobe again.

"This can't be our last time seeing each other Shanelle."

A tattered piece of paper appeared. I wrote my number down including Candy's. He folded it in two and slipped it inside his tailored jacket pocket.

"Right next to my heart."

My eyes settled and rose.

"That's sweet," I flirted. "Look at us all grown up now."

"How about that." He winked.

I searched the busy street as the wind tossed my hair into a careless heap. Derrick swept it behind my ears as I struggled to find the right words.

"Derrick there's so much time between us I guess I'm afraid of getting hurt."

He planted his feet, crossing his arms across his chest.

"It was just dinner in the city Shanelle. Besides, I couldn't do that to you."

Gnawing on an imaginary piece of gum, I pleaded my case.

"Derrick, you can have anyone you want, and I do mean any woman. Why me?"

He bent forward smoothing my shoulders with his hands.

"How about this, let's not try to figure out all this stuff right now. Let me prove how much I care for you first. I think everything else will fall into place. Besides, it's your turn to figure out what you want." He stepped in closer, pulling the lapels of my coat. "I know what I want and need already."

Derrick cleared his throat.

"Think about it Shanelle, if you go back to school while I start my residency, we're going to be busy. In order for me to be a competent doctor, I need to be three steps ahead of myself. I don't have time to be out there chasing skirts."

He paused to strengthen the intensity in his answer. "Trust me; I'm not interested in chasing skirts. But you might get a little frustrated if I'm not able to spend enough time with you. If there are breaks in between, I'd like to reacquaint myself with you again."

My maternal instincts rested in my curling fingers.

"What about Troy?"

Derrick laughed. "How could I resist him? It'll be a good excuse to act like a kid again."

A bright bulb went off in his head. "Listen, if you're going to be around, meet me for dinner at my mom's house tomorrow." Bring Troy," he gloated, "I would love to see him and so would my mother."

A brisk walk led us back to Ninth Street as our eyes connected more times then the passing traffic. When we reached the car, I flashed my keys and offered him a ride back to his apartment.

"Next time Shanelle. It's late and I want you to get back to Troy in one piece."

My pocketbook dangled on my arm as I leaned against the Jeep. Derrick stepped forward. His head bent to the side. A pair of almond shaped eyes and smooth lips softened. A kiss was eminent.

My lips puckered and relaxed as I stretched my chin forward, quickly releasing a loud giggle.

"Shanelle, before I let you go."

"What?" I gushed.

Derrick put his lips next to my ear.

"Can I squeeze your nose, it's so irresistible."

Any attempt to curtail him failed as I tried to smack his hand away.

Derrick grabbed my waist.

"Sike!" he teased, pulling my hips forward before bunkering into a deep, longing whisper, "I really want to do this.'

His thick warm tongue slipped into my mouth. Sweet and sour delicacies riddled my taste buds and instantly turned my nipples to rocks as I moaned against him. I pulled away quickly staring at the ground.

"What's wrong Shanelle?"

I grabbed his face, smoothing his warm skin.

"Nothing, kiss me again."

Derrick obliged and held my face in his hands while he slowly explored my mouth. His hand traced the small of my back with three fingers just below the waist of my jeans. It was a new and wonderful feeling. I didn't want him to stop, but he did, resting his forehead against mine.

"Okay," he heaved, rattling new cobwebs out of his head, "We need to leave New York City. Don't forget about tomorrow."

"What time?" I asked, yawning into my hand.

"Around five, come casual so we can wrestle."

"And what about your mother and Troy?"

Derrick laughed. "My mom has some old Sesame Street footage on video. We'll send them upstairs after dinner. She won't mind."

I didn't have a chance to answer. Derrick's moist mouth met mine for another kiss. The car keys dangling from my finger were wrestled loose as his hand pressed me against him. Derrick pulled away and kissed my cheek as the key slipped into the lock. When he stopped, the car door opened as I slipped inside. The engine turned over into a quiet hum while I rolled down the window. Derrick tapped my nose.

"Remember Shanelle, it's your turn. I'll see you tomorrow."

Besides the pleasurable feeling between my legs, deep down inside, it was the first time in a long time that I felt good. The rearview mirror showcased Derrick hail a taxi with a firm gait and raised hand. I smoothed the remaining lipstick across my lips and turned on the radio for the ride home.

By the time I got back to Candy's house, Troy was occupying Candy's living space with blocks and board books. Candy was smart enough to give him a bath and put his pajamas on while they sat on the couch and listened to mommy's puzzled life. Troy climbed in my lap.

"I think I'm going to attend late registration at St. James. What do you think?"

Candy hugged me.

"Sounds like a plan, you can stay here if you want, there's enough room."

"Oh no," I shuddered, mindful of my life with Troy. "I'm getting an apartment, but you can help me out and watch Troy while I go to class."

Candy playfully poked Troy in the stomach.

"Girl, the Fosters are gonna have a fit if you come back here."

I nodded my head in agreement. "Candy, I can't let anyone decide for me anymore, it's my turn, you know what I mean?"

Candy gave me a high five. "Girl, do your thang! Alex left you straight and you'd be crazy not to go back to school."

"Oh yeah," I pitched, "Derrick asked me to come to his mother's house for dinner. He wants me to bring Troy."

Before Candy could answer, Troy stood up on the couch and rubbed his eyes. His tiny hand rested in mine as we climbed the stairs with Candy in tow.

"Are you going to bring him?" Candy asked.

"Of course, wherever I go, he goes."

The three of us crawled into a feather downed bed. Troy' quickly fell asleep underneath me while Candy and I knocked knees in girl talk.

"So tell me about Dr. Derrick."

I put my hands under my head and sighed. "He's the same in some ways, but different in other ways. One nice thing about Derrick is that he likes to be out. With Alex, we were always huddled in the house like Alex wanted to escape from the world. Derrick seems like he wants to enjoy the world around him. I guess being cooped up in a library all day makes him stir crazy."

The drone of heavy breathing took over. Candy was fast asleep supported by the weight of her forearm. I put a blanket across the two of them and quickly took out my journal. Nothing meant more to me than three simple words.

Take your time

Abundance on earth,
Wrought with guilt and pleasure,
Time can only measure
My intensity
Intertwined with my passion for life.
So much of what rests within me
Cultivates our child.
Each grain of sand
Sweeps in various directions
Some of which I cannot control
While some embeds in my conscious and
Rests with my soul.
Strong conviction,
Stand tall,
Loving thyself first
Sharing with others
I finally behold,
An innate constitution to survive
This crazy test of time
Please stand back
As I claim what is rightfully mine…
Self love.

I put my pen and paper down and walked into the guest bathroom. There in the mirror, a reflection of Alex came to me in my thoughts. I closed my eyes to feel him as a warm sensation flowed through my body. A cool breeze from the window caressed my face and whispered to me that everything was going to be ok. I opened my eyes and looked at the reflection of myself. There was clarity and calm. No voices entered my head and taunted me. I began to sing an old song and thought about seeing Derrick and his mother again. I also thought about staying an extra night at Candy's house so I could go to St. James for late registration. If Candy couldn't watch Troy, at least I had his stroller to get him around the campus. I took a deep breath and sighed. For once in my life, the things I decided to do on my own felt free and easy. Derrick was right; it was "my turn."

I kept Troy on a tight schedule Sunday afternoon so he wouldn't be a crank pot at dinner. He was teething a-lot so I decided to give him some Motrin before we left. Candy wasn't happy with my fashion choice or Troy's comfortable Gap sweats. I wanted to have fun for a change and I knew Troy was up for the challenge. By the time we arrived at Derrick's mother's house, I could smell dinner from the walkway. The September foliage and her comfy house brought back memories of the refuge Derrick provided for me in the past. I made a checklist in my mind to stay an extra day to give Mrs. Viv a visit and speak my peace.

Derrick opened the door before we announced our arrival. Troy walked in with mayoral status and the interest of a local plumber. He was dying to fix anything and pointed to an old sailboat positioned on the fireplace. The lady of the house soiled her clean apron and wrapped her arms around me.

"It's so good to see you again Shanelle, make yourself at home."

By the looks of things, it was easy to do. Derrick took Troy on a tour of the house, banging on anything that looked broken. Ms. Johnson laughed. "Derrick was the same way at that age; I think boys are programmed for tools."

Derrick stretched across the living room floor when they returned and let Troy bang on his "broken heart." Troy laughed hysterically while Derrick jerked his body up at every strike. I was glad he was spending time with Troy because I didn't do those things with him at home. We were always reading or coloring our time away. I got up to offer my assistance to Ms. Johnson, but Derrick pulled me down to the ground in a juvenile tussle.

"Derrick, stop!" I urged. Ms. Johnson peeked in and smiled at our giggle filled romp. When Troy slipped away, He slipped me a quick kiss.

"I missed you," he reflected, "Did you miss me?"

My eyes locked onto his soft lips.

"A lil' bit." A smile escaped before Ms. Johnson ushered Troy to the bathroom. Derrick took the opportunity to snuggle next to me as my fingers trailed his forearm with a few thoughts.

"So," I paused, clacking my tongue against the roof of my mouth, "Do you have a girlfriend?"

"No," he replied, "Do you have a boyfriend?"

My hand fell heavy upon his leg. "You know I don't have a boyfriend. Stop playing. The only boy in my life is Troy."

I sprang off the floor and turned towards my ravenous son. Ms. Johnson and Troy were anxiously waiting to eat. Before we dined, a simple grace resounded through the dimly lit dining room. Derrick squeezed my hands and kicked me under the table. It felt good having someone I could be silly with instead of being so serious all the time. Troy sang while he ate his food to Ms. Johnson's delight. Derrick's kept a Christmas morning grin until the doorbell rang. Ms. Johnson's eyes orbited once as she got up to answer the door. A high pitched voice in the background greeted her as Derrick dropped his table napkin on his seat.

"Give me a minute Shanelle."

Before his exit, a trench coat draped woman stepped into the room with a box tucked under her arm. She glanced at me, darted a phony smile towards Troy and locked onto her target. The box bounced into Derrick's grip reminiscent of hot potato.

"Playing house?" she quipped, whipping her hair to the side.

The weighted box fell to the floor to Troy's admonishment.

"Dat's not nice."

Ms. Johnson returned, grimaced in the face with her table napkin wrenched between her aging hands. Derrick offered cordial introductions.

"Bridgette, this is…"

"You must be Shanelle," she interrupted, paying particular attention to my carefree ease. Derrick jumped in with certainty resting in his voice.

"Yeah, this is Shanelle, if you let me finish. This is her son Troy."

A mouthful of food garbled his greeting as his chunky hand raised.

"Hi lady."

Ms. Johnson's shoulder bounced up and down as she covered her wide mouth. Bridgett made her final announcement before turning on her high heels.

"Take care Rick."

She air kissed his mother with little emotion.

"Bye Bridgette, take care."

Derrick escorted her to the car. We could see them through the window as Ms. Johnson patted the corners of her lips.

"Lord forgive me but I can't stand that girl," she toiled, turning her plate. "Now that she saw you, I guess that's the last I'll see of her."

The window became my immediate focus. I thought of the sunglass girl peeling away from Mueller's just before the wedding. I glanced at my watch and focused on cleaning. Like a failing game of Three Card Monty, stupidity and impatience etched my nerves the more he remained outside.

Ms. Johnson grabbed my wrist.

"Shanelle, she's an old friend trying to hang on. Derrick dumped her a long time ago."

Refusing to let go, she squeezed tighter, honing in on her sentiment.

"Don't runaway because of little Ms. Pris."

Troy grabbed the serving spoon from the macaroni and cheese dish. Ms. Johnson took the utensil and delighted in his hearty appetite.

"This boy reminds me of Derrick. God bless him, he can sure put away some food."

My eyes shifted back to the window. The car was long gone. Blinking once, Derrick appeared in the entrance, motioning for me. My defenses kicked in the moment I stepped outside. A cool breeze rifled through me as my foot swept away small pebbles. Derrick tugged my sleeve.

"C'mon Shanelle, you know I've been straight up with you."

His words served little purpose as I continued to clean the ground beneath me.

"I'm not trying to be your rebound girl you know. I've been through too much Derrick."

His weighted hands landed on my shoulders commanding my attention.

"Shanelle, we broke up a long time ago. I know what I want and that's you."

I turned away shifting my thoughts to Troy.

"Derrick, I've got a lot going on, including my son. So it's not just me to think about. He's on my mind every waking moment of the day. So if you want to be with me, Troy has to fit right in too."

Derrick took my hand and walked down the front path to the sidewalk.

"Look Shanelle," he reflected with sincerity, "My life is straight as this sidewalk, graduate from Cornell, four year residency at University and right into pediatric medicine." He cleared his throat with a final appeal, leaning over to face me. "Has anything stopped me yet?"

"No." I replied, curt and distant.

His hand met my waist.

"Do you think I have time for nonsense with the life I mapped out for myself?" Looking up, sincerity rested in his eyes against a star lit sky. Despite his tone and honesty, doubt rested in my gut.

"No, but what do you want from me?"

Derrick relaxed his shoulders.

"Shanelle, just be you, I don't want a machine, a toy or somebody to lie to me to make me feel good."

Derrick grabbed my hand with a gentle shake and whisper. "Tell me Shanelle, is it too much for you right now?"

I knew he was referring to Alex and I was grateful for his concern. I took a deep breath and squeezed back.

"No, I like your plan. That's cool."

"Good," Derrick calmed, clearing his throat, "Let's go back in the house and finish dinner."

By the time we reached the living room, Troy was finished for the night, fast asleep in Ms. Johnson's warm arms, snuggled against the couch. With a playful pinch to my love handle, we went into the kitchen and cleaned everything in sight. A cup of ice cream occupied our time as I chatted about school.

"I'm going to register at St. James tomorrow."

Derrick eyebrows stretched and softened.

"That's good, how many credits?"

"You know me," I boasted, "Eighteen of course."

"Who's going to watch Troy?" he asked, swallowing the creamy remnants and licking his thick lips.

"First I have to see what classes are available. Then I'll work something out with Candy."

Derrick put his spoon down. "Can I make a suggestion?"

"Sure," I replied.

"My mother retired six months ago and she could really use the company during the day. You can drop him off here and walk to St. James."

The offer was tempting, but I wanted to run it by Candy first. I searched Derrick's eyes for a possible conclusion.

"Let me talk to Candy about it first."

Sensing doubt, he sat back with a smile.

"Okay Shanelle."

He stood up and put the empty dish in the sink. I walked up behind him and placed my hands around his waist. He turned around and hugged me back.

"What was that for?" he asked.

"Thanks for listening; I'm excited about going back to school."

"I'm happy for you Shanelle," Derrick answered.

I peered at the clock and sighed as we concluded the evening with a soft kiss. Derrick trailed behind me into the living room and picked Troy up from his mother's sleeping arms. He wrestled Troy's thick arms into his jacket. Derrick looked awkward, but I didn't mind his initiative. Ms. Johnson rubbed my arm as I thanked her for dinner.

"Shanelle," she recalled, "I remember when I met you at Livingston Mall. You were so sweet and still are. In fact, you remind me of myself when I was your age."

Ms. Johnson followed us to the foyer as our voices rattled Troy from his nap.

"Goodnight. Take care of that sweet boy."

She bent down as my son planted a wet kiss on her cheek.

"Shanelle, it was nice having the two of you over. I hope we can do this again."

Derrick carried Troy to the car and put him in his car seat. My little man was so spent; sleep was his immediate need as he gripped the seatbelt. Derrick pressed my hand against his heart.

"I'll call you when I get back to the city."

I kissed him on the cheek and blushed, "Okay, you do that." My return to the car was short lived as his schoolboy charm returned with a gentle tugged.

"Dance with me Shanelle."

A girlish giggle escaped as he swirled me around and pulled me into his sturdy frame. Derrick serenaded me on the street as we stared at Troy. A few honking horns complimented our time. There was no way I could go wrong in his arms. Derrick was an emotional anchor, but I still felt free to do whatever I wanted. I reached up and grabbed him around the neck as he picked me up and spun me around. We were catching up on old times, but moving forward in the right direction. After a long kiss goodnight, Derrick closed the door and tugged my earlobe. Delaying the time, I held my puckered lips up for one more as he obliged.

"Get home safe."

"I will Derrick, goodnight."

"Goodnight baby," he whispered, as I pulled off in the distance.

Back to School

The next day, with Candy and Troy on my heels, we went to St. James for late registration. My transcript placed me in my junior year with thirty credits to graduate. After looking at the course schedule, we agreed to a three day schedule while Candy cared for Troy.

Going to the Bursar' office to pay my bill was the highlight of my day. Because of Alex, I could afford school and provide an even better life for our son. In my heart of hearts, I knew he would be proud of me.

When we exited the building, early fall foliage fell from the trees in bright yellow and red leaves. It was Alex's favorite time of year as hints of nature's pleasure feathered down in front of my face and landed on the ground. I smiled as I looked into the sky happily holding Troy's hand. Candy sensed my sentiment and smiled.

"I'm proud of you Shanelle," she said as Troy handed her a chunky leaf to admire.

By the time we reached Candy's house, they headed upstairs for a nap. I went to Joyce Leslie's to pick up outfits for school. On the way home, stopping at Mrs. Viv's house was a must. I needed to bury some old issues.

Mrs. Viv was out front, tending to her wilted garden. A "House for Sale" sign was staked on the front while she dug into the dry dirt. There was no sign of Steven. She turned with haste at the sound of my concrete grinding footsteps.

"Shanelle," she said, in a surprised tone.

"Hello Vivian."

She quickly smoothed her clothes and began to chuckle.

"So, I'm no longer mom, momma or mommy, just Vivian huh?"

She scoured me over from head to toe and quipped, "I take it your father told you what happened?"

The sight of falling shingles from the roof offered a humble distraction to our dilemma.

"Yeah, he told me."

A symbol of my half blood landed as a black crow positioned on the gutter.

"Where's Steven?" I asked, searching the smeared windows for a grimacing stare.

"It was too much for me without your father. I had to put him in long term care."

Compassion for my son slowly rose to the surface as her gardening tools fell limp in her hand.

"How's Troy? Let's see, he's two right?"

"Yes, he's two years old," I droned.

Envious of my outward stability, she went into classic attack mode.

"That boy is going to need a father Shanelle."

I mumbled under my breath, "Yeah, you're one to know."

"What did you say?"

I ignored her and focused on the ailing symbol in front of her.

"What's the asking price for the house?"

"I'm not going to get much for it because it needs so much work."

"A house of horrors, I bet it does."

"Do you know where you're going to move to?" I asked.

"South," she flatly replied.

Realizing that this was possibly our final farewell, my hands fell at my sides.

"Well, let me get out of here, take care Vivian."

Her aging hand shot up in the air. Vivian plopped back into the dirt fixated on the burial ground beneath her. The helpless mums she stuck in the ground didn't have a fighting chance as she beat a circular dust cloud into the earth. I started up the car, thrilled at the fact that someone else gave birth to me.

The front door to Candy's home opened to the smell of baked chocolate chip cookies. Clinton shared a relaxed seat by his wife's side while Troy lay sprawled across the floor playing with new blocks. They were spoiling him rotten, but for the moment, it didn't matter because it gave us a sense of family without the Fosters around. Troy jumped up and scrambled into my arms. His wet lips met my face as he bellowed out, "Mommy! Mommy! Mommy!"

A hard tickle to his chunky belly filled the room with baby filled scream.

"Mommy missed you too sweetie."

I packed a small bag and chatted with Clinton before my long ride home to Brick. A pit stop at the Fosters was a must. I needed to tell them about school. I knew they were going to be devastated, but I had every intention of letting them see Troy, especially during the weekend. Just before I walked out the door, Derrick called, anxious to hear about my academic adventures.

"Hey, how did it go? I didn't hear from you all day."

"It went great, I'm registered. Classes start tomorrow."

"You sound happy Shanelle," he pitched.

"I do?"

"Yeah, I can hear it in your voice."

My fingers curled around the phone cord.

"When can I see you again?"

Derrick remained poised. "Here in New York?"

"No silly, come to South Jersey this weekend. We can take Troy to the beach and then have dinner."

A long pause followed.

"What?" I asked, "Did I say something wrong?"

"No," he uttered, "I just thought that."

His voice drifted away as my limp hand fell at my side.

"I'd like to see you, is there any harm in that?"

"No, that's fine," he sighed.

The conversation ended with little fanfare. By the time I reached the Fosters with my news, a tidal wave of emotions spilled onto the floor. Mr. Foster buried his head as he sat on the couch.

"Sell the house," he griped, "Why do you want to do that?"

I stood up and planted my position.

"I'm going to buy my parent's house in North Orange, gut the whole thing out and put an addition on it. There'll be plenty of room when you visit."

Mr. Foster lips abruptly parted but nothing followed. I pressed on with confidence.

"I'll use the proceeds from me and Alex's…," I paused for a minute. Saying his name was strange, but I continued my quest for freedom. "I'll use the proceeds from the sale of the house for Troy's education. Maybe he can go to St. James Prep one day."

My pride for North Orange did not sit well with them. Mrs. Foster scratched her forearm with a stern warning.

"Shanelle, Alex used to tell me that North Orange isn't a safe neighborhood."

My hands planted into my waist.

"Well, that's where my heart is telling me to go and I want to complete two degree programs at St. James. It's five minutes away and that's that."

A tear trickled down Mrs. Foster's face as she gazed at Troy. I met her needs first.

"Troy can come for long weekends. I'm not going to keep him away, you're his family."

Mrs. Foster's desperate eyes searched the hardwood floor.

"What about Thanksgiving and Christmas?" she asked.

My hands shot up in a peaceful surrender. "Especially Thanksgiving and Christmas, you think this boy wants to miss your fried turkey?"

Troy scrambled across the floor yanking his grandmother's wrist rejoicing, "Nana, I'm hungry!"

Her weighted shoulders slumped into her chest. Smiling eyes exchanged as the two departed playfully swinging arms into the kitchen.

Mr. Foster entered my space and placed his hand on my shoulder.

"Shanelle, let's sit down and talk" he pitched while I shifted my body against the couch.

"Now I know you're ready to handle everything and that's fine. But I just want you to rethink the house thing. Why don't you hold on to the house? It's close to the shore and you can use it as a second home in the summer. Trust me; you'll want to get to the beach when the weather gets warm."

His hand landed on my knee with a sigh.

"You know how much Alex loved the beach. Don't you want Troy to have that love too?"

A warm sensation flowed through my body and settled in my fingertips. The corner of my mouth lifted and fell.

"You're right," I laughed turning towards a rustic cabinet in the corner, "besides, you have to take Troy fishing too."

The door gave way to a mini commotion with Troy leading the way. Mr. Foster leaned in to me as my voice rose in the room, "I'll keep the house as long as you look after it for me while I'm gone."

The Fosters responded in humbled unison, "Sure Shanelle, we will."

A quick hug ended our visit. Mr. Foster busied himself with a set of keys and an old newspaper curled in his grip. Their last minute antics delayed our departure as Troy fought off his grandfather's musing, shielding his head from a tap and poke. The turning door handle swept a cool breeze inside as Mrs. Foster struggled to her knees to kiss Troy.

"I'm having company Saturday," I announced, placing one foot out the door, "Can you watch Troy for me in the evening?"

Mrs. Foster's knees buckled, quickly using her fist to brace her dramatic fall. Mr. Foster rushed to her side, nervously winking at me.

"No problem Shanelle, Troy can come anytime, day or night."

Saturday fell on me in one heap. I completed three days of classes, unlimited playtime with Troy and a long ride back home to Brick on Friday night. I was so busy; Derrick and I didn't catch up until Friday evening to confirm our date.

"I'll be there in the morning," he yawned.

I placed the phone down on the receiver. Troy was off in the distance singing to himself, happy to be home. Thoughts of Derrick began to consume me. I was longing for his affection and company. Before I could blink, he was ringing my bell with a snorkel sticking out of his mouth. When we greeted him at the door, Troy screamed with gaping eyes. He raised his chunky hand and shouted, "Hi, Mr. Dee!"

Derrick's fingers curled into a pair of claws as he pretended to be a sea creature. He chased Troy into the kitchen while I ran upstairs to grab some bags. I returned to find the two of them rough housing on the floor. Troy pounded his chest compliments of his father's personality.

"Are we ready?" he asked, hoisting Troy into the air.

"Weeeee," Troy gleefully pitched with his arms stretched out in mid air flight. Once a safe landed was secured, Troy grabbed his Sesame Street towel and whipped it around his neck. Derrick leaned into me and planted a kiss on my cheek.

"Hey beautiful," he smiled, strumming my neck with his thumb. I watched his hand fall at his side quickly slipping into mine with a slight shake.

"It's good to see you Derrick," I blushed.

"Let's go mommy." Troy ordered, breaking up our mini interlude.

"That's right," Derrick confirmed, nudging Troy's shoulders out the door, marching like toy soldiers to the delight of a nosey neighbor. A traffic free drive and a few love songs complimented our scenic drive to Point Pleasant. Troy and Derrick quickly posted camp with the blanket and kicked sand on each other's feet. After a full forty minutes of horseplay, Troy ate a snack and drifted off to sleep. Derrick took the opportunity to snuggle next to me.

"Can I share that beach chair with you?" he referenced with a point of his finger. It was a breezy September day, but cool enough to oblige. I stood up and let him sit first before I plopped between his legs, wiggling first to find warmth between his thick thighs. I turned and locked eyes with him, exclaiming, "Hey handsome."

Derrick strummed my lips with his finger before he grabbed my face. His thick tongue slid into my mouth as my body began to melt. He paused and trailed his tongue up my neck, ending at my earlobe. "Shanelle," he whispered, "I couldn't wait to kiss you again. You taste delicious."

Derrick massaged the side of my thigh as I turned around to face the ocean. He buried his neck into mine as my nipples became aroused. Kitty began to wake up after a long hiatus as the lion in his pants began to stir. We giggled under our breaths and shared slices of a sweet tangerine. Troy began to wrestle himself from his nap and immediately began to stretch.

"Can you take him to the bathroom to pee; he's just getting the hang of the potty."

Derrick hoisted Troy on his shoulders, looking up to assure him.

"No problem, we can handle it."

I watched them walk away as seagulls glided and dipped alongside of them while Derrick motioned their movements, encouraging Troy to do the same.

"See the birdie Mr. Dee," Troy pointed.

"That's a seagull man."

"A seagull?" Troy mimicked as their banter trailed away.

Temporarily blinded by the intense sunlight, I blinked and continued to watch my late husband's son being whisked away by my old love. The vast ocean quickly settled my feelings. It felt good being with Derrick and I was willing to take a chance with him. Needless to say, Troy adored him. The quick chase and plop on the towel resolved it when Troy returned.

"Mommy can we go to Mr. Dee's house to play?" he asked, tugging at his shorts until his underwear settled into place.

"Aww," I teased, "Are you having fun Troy?"

Derrick dropped to his knees anticipating the charge as they fell back for another tackle. Derrick lifted his chin, quickly avoiding a playful punch to the jaw.

"You think?" he laughed, poking his fingers in Troy's quivering stomach.

"Oh yeah, you've definitely one him over."

We quickly wrapped up our day at the beach and dropped Troy off at the Foster's house. I didn't want to hide our relationship anymore, so hand in hand, we walked up to the door with Troy in tow. Anxious to see his grandparents, a mighty toddler fist struck the door in three loud thuds.

"Nana! Pop Pop, open the door!" he belted out to our amusement. For a two year old, he was picking up speed in the language department. Derrick nervously adjusted Troy's overnight bag on his shoulder as the entrance way opened with disbelief, then surprise.

"Shanelle," Mrs. Foster uttered, sizing up Derrick with inquisitive eyes, "You're early."

"I know. I didn't want to keep him in the sun all day." Forcing my lips open again, I paused and announced, "Mom, this is Derrick..., Derrick Johnson."

Troy pulled Derrick by the fingers exclaiming, "C'mon Mr. Dee!"

Mr. Foster came into the living room wiping his hands off from his barbecue. Troy gripped his grandfather's thigh imitating a young lumber jack in training.

"Pop Pop, that's Mr. Dee!"

Derrick walked up and formally greeted him man to man.

"Nice to meet you," Mr. Foster teased, glancing at Troy, "Uh, Mr. Dee, care for a beer?"

Derrick's shoulders relaxed as he shook his head laughing, "Sure, just call me Derrick and thanks for the offer."

The threesome headed out back while Mrs. Foster came out of her trance.

"He looks familiar."

A soft smile erupted from my weary past.

"He's hard to forget." I replied, searching my jacket pockets for lint balls.

"Oh," she mumbled, dabbling at her neckline with two trembling fingers. "Like Alex?"

My eyes settled to the floor as the sound of Derrick's voice in the background rose them to the surface.

"I hope you're not upset that I brought Troy early?"

Mrs. Foster gazed at Alex's picture on the wall.

"No honey, I understand."

Laughter filled our ears as we searched the window. From the looks of things, Derrick was a shoe-in with Mr. Foster. He was pointing at the joints in his body while Derrick nodded with acute medical interest.

"Good Lord, what is he doing?" Mrs. Foster inquired.

My proud demeanor came to life with my rising chin.

"Derrick's graduating from medical school this year; he's probably getting some tips."

"Oh," resonated through the air and hollowed out down the hall. The Three Musketeers came back in the house and continued to chat about medical ailments. Mr. Foster pointed towards Derrick.

"Honey, Derrick's going to be a...,"

Candy coated caution layered her quick response.

"A doctor, yes, Shanelle told me. Good luck with that."

Flushed in the face, Derrick's eyes scrolled over Alex's photograph. Mrs. Foster's lip pulled inward resembling a tight anus weary of a hemorrhoid eruption.

"Thanks," he mouthed quietly, spotting another mounted picture of Alex on the wall. Dropping to my knees, I began to hum pulling Troy into my frame.

"Be good for mommy. I'll pick you up tomorrow."

"Troy be good mommy. I love you," he toned, pounding his fist on top of Derrick's hand.

"I love you too baby, don't forget to call me to say night night."

"Okay, mommy, Troy don't forget."

Mr. Foster walked us to the car and ordered our day with his own agenda.

"Listen Derrick, I'm grilling tomorrow after church, so stay a while. Tammy's in town too. She's been asking for you Shanelle."

"Thanks," Derrick obliged, squeezing my waist as a Miss America wave met complimented Mr. Foster's smiling eyes. Derrick slammed the door shut and calmly walked to the driver's side.

"I won't make any promises, but we'll try."

Nodding, Mr. Foster brushed gravel with the heel of his shoe.

"I understand y'all enjoy yourselves."

The empty street lined with bursting floral buds and a sharp blue sky became our escape route. Derrick's palm fell on top of mine as our anxious fingers locked into place. Turning my head slightly to the right, Mr. Foster appeared in the side view mirror wiping his hands clean turning to find his wife at his side while Troy remained on the side walk waving goodbye.

Derrick and I returned to a quiet house. I immediately showed him the guest's quarters and bathroom to unwind from the beach. I wasn't sure what Derrick wanted to do with our time, so I turned on Kiss FM to break up some of the tension while I steamed vegetables and placed some marinated meat in the skillet. I think we knew we were going to hit the sheets, but I wasn't sure how or when. Derrick appeared from the distance looking buffed, attentive and full of sexual adventure. A fresh shower enhanced his cocoa brown skin and smooth exterior. An old love song was playing on the radio. Derrick's hand smoothed my skirt over my ass as he whispered, "You used to be my girl, and I'm ready for you to be my special lady."

"I like the sound of that," I turned, facing him, pressing my cheek against his chest. Having him there with me enticed my energy and longing for him. Derrick pulled my hips against him and swayed back and forth. His voice dipped to a deep, longing whisper.

"I like the sound of that too."

My cooking utensils fell to the floor.

"This feels like déjà vu Derrick."

He buried his face in my neck and replied, "It does Shanelle, but I just don't know how to make it right. I don't even know if you really want me. This is your world not mine."

I grabbed his face as we began to breathe in unison.

"I want you to feel comfortable Derrick; you're more than welcome here."

Derrick's hands planted into my waist. My feet left the ground as he placed me on the counter top, filling the empty space between my legs. Longing for him to stay, I strummed his neck and whispered to him, hoping it would settle his nerves.

"We can go somewhere else if you want, but I want you here with me."

Derrick's baby stubble brushed my face, sliding down with multiple kisses to my chest and stomach. I leaned back and allowed him to fill the empty spaces of my lonely heart. The softest kiss complimented a warm embrace as my eyes began to close. The sensation made me crave him in greater intensity as I made love to his tongue. The phone began to ring, but we continued to kiss. Derrick massaged my back and called my name as I ignored the world around me.

"Are you going to get that?" He moaned.

I didn't want to, but hurriedly scooped up the receiver with a quick and steady voice.

"Hello."

"Hi mommy!"

Derrick backed away as my arms reached out for him. I jumped off the counter to temporarily talk to my son, who suddenly seemed annoying to me. I leaned back and wondered what the hell my wonderful two year old wanted.

"Yes sweetie, you having fun?"

Derrick laughed, quickly teasing my broken grammar.

"Are you having fun?" he quipped, flashing his pearly whites.

"Troy having fun mommy, I love you."

I playfully smacked Derrick's bicep and gushed, "I love you too, call mommy when it's time for night night."

"Okay."

Derrick planted his feet and pulled me into his frame. Mr. Foster cleared his throat and bellowed through the earpiece.

"Sorry to bother you Shanelle, he missed you."

Static filled the phone. We connected at the hip. I ran my hand up Derrick's shirt, while his teeth sunk into my neck.

"Shanelle, are you there?"

"Yes," I sighed, masking my moans into Derrick's chest, "I'm here, thanks for calling dad. I told Troy to call me when he's ready for bed, goodbye."

A click ended my lifeline to the Fosters. Derrick grabbed my hand and pressed his fingers into my palm. He held it up and merged it with his thick, warm lips.

"Come closer," he ordered, carefully embracing each finger with a gentle massage. He held my hand against his heart and rubbed my ass with his other hand. We resumed a comfortable position again as I connected with the countertop. Derrick paused for a moment and stared.

"What is it?" I blushed as our foreheads met. Derrick's eyes trailed down to my engorged titties, peeking at them with flared nostrils and a determined finger. I held my lips next to his, licking his moist skin and asked, "Will you take a chance with me?"

Derrick pressed his chest against me, pulling his tee shirt off and carelessly whipping it off his arm. He cupped my face with his hands, swallowing my chin, meeting my lips and licking them to and fro.

"You know that Shanelle. I've wanted it since beginning but it was difficult then. I know what I need to do now."

His fingers met my lower back as he piano keyed each verte-brate, his appreciation for the human body apparent in his touch. Our eyes closed and opened. Derrick lulled me to the edge of the counter.

"The stakes are higher this time. Are you sure Shanelle?"

I sealed his answer with a sloppy kiss.

"I'm sure Derrick. It's our time now. Just remember I need my space to finish school."

Heavy panting ensued. His lips met my ear.

"All the space in the world, no pressure."

Derrick pressed his nose against my skin and inhaled. The space and heat between us swelled my nipples into rocks as he pulled me to the floor, kissing the top of my head and plying his finger through my tousled hair. We walked upstairs to the guestroom. The master suite was off limits to the outside world. In my heart, I felt like the time was right, but not in a room that was filled with Alex's love.

We reached the queen size bed. Derrick headed for his bag and pulled out some condoms. A nervous smile etched his face as he grabbed my wrist.

"We won't call it safe sex, how about safe lovin'?"

Silence filled the room.

I remained silent.

"Are you ok?"

"I'm fine," I breathed, stroking his cheeks, "I'm going to take a shower."

Derrick curtailed my plans by pulling me between his legs as he sat down.

"Don't hide from me baby. Take your clothes off right here," he pleaded, tugging at my shirt. His finger slipped along my waistline. I stepped back and lifted my shirt over my head, listening to him moan as his thick lips merged with my belly button. He used his pointer finger to slide my bra strap off my shoulders. Derrick continued to seduce me with his eyes as he placed his hands behind my back and unhooked my bra. He watched it fall to the floor, slowly raising his eyes to meet mine.

Derrick spread his legs and whispered, "Come closer Shanelle, you're too far."

Derrick wrapped one arm around my waist, planting his teeth into my left nipple. Trembling now, my legs buckling at the knees, Derrick lulled me into silence by sucking on my breast.

"Look at you," he paused, gently biting down, "You were a constant dream in my head."

"And now it's real," I whispered, moaning against him.

Derrick skillfully slid my thong down with his right hand as it quickly fell to the floor. His hand settled into Kitty's den, his other hand toyed with my lips as two of his fingers slipped into my mouth.

"So sweet Shanelle," he sang, spreading my juice against my ass and tasting the remnants that rested on his fingers. My face warmed over and flushed away my color, changing my cheeks to red.

"Derrick wait," I pleaded as my head spun out of control, a spell falling over me.

"Shh," he quieted, licking my nipples and searching for more nectar. Gripping my thighs, he swirled my clit with his thumbs and spread the juice on my legs. He turned me around and bit my back with soft intensity as my head slumped to the side. Gently pulling me onto his lap, Derrick grinded me against the thick bulge tucked in his boxers and explored me, taking bites along my back and shoulders. I turned and straddled his lap feeling the power between his legs desperate to be released. We locked eyes and smiled. Derrick wrapped his arms around me. Tears welled up in my eyes as our skin pressed together. Derrick serenaded me with a whisper.

"Shanelle, you feel so incredible, I want this to last forever."

Goosebumps scrambled up my arms.

Arching my back, pursuing our long awaited needs, I tongue kissed him with a momentary break.

"I want you. Do it now."

Without hesitation, Derrick slipped a condom on and laid me down as his weight crushed me. He spread my legs with his hand and buried his face in my neck. I wrapped my hands around his neck and took a deep breath. His taut, cocoa brown skin felt tight and smooth. Derrick thrust his bulging dick inside, sliding along my tight walls, quickly filling me with his enormous size. I shifted my hips and ass to find comfort as my face contorted in pleasurable pain.

"Derrick," I moaned, letting the moment take me.

I cried out feeling his lips meet mine. He sucked my tongue with excitement, his nostrils releasing hot air against my face. My nails dug into his back as he fucked me like a well oiled machine set on maximum control, our sweat merging into beads and pooling into my belly button. Derrick flipped me over and spread my legs apart like easy scissors. He kissed me in places that stirred up new arousals as my face pressed against the cool, damp sheet. He slid his hand under my stomach and grunted as I moaned for him. Derrick cemented my feelings.

"I've wanted you forever Shanelle. I can't believe I'm inside of you."

His sweat trickled on the back of my neck as Derrick mixed words and exploration together. In just the right places, Derrick made love to me like I was a work of fine art. His love of the human body took me to heights of physical pleasure. Derrick flipped me on my back and massaged my pressure and pleasure points at the same time. He placed his hand under my ass and talked me through my first orgasm.

"Arch your back baby and inhale. Don't breathe until you feel it coming"

Trembling, watching me coo, he placed my fingers on my clit and begged me to stroke it as a small erotic ball welled up and burst inside of me.

"That's it baby, it's yours, enjoy it."

Derrick's dick grew thicker and harder. We used our own energy to create a symphony of erotic music by scratching the sheets and hitting the headboard. Derrick tripled in size. He braced himself in a firm push up and rammed his dick inside of me as he released himself. Goosebumps riddled his upper arms. He cried out like a warrior at battle as I dug my nails into his skin. Trembling, shaking, Derrick collapsed, covered in sweat as he pulled me into his arms. I smoothed his silky chest hairs as he stroked my ass with his fingertips.

"Shanelle," he groaned, licking his lips, catching his breath, "I don't know what to say. What did you do to me?"

"What did you do to me?" I asked.

His hand trailed my back. "I'm glad we waited."

"Why?"

"Even after all this time, you're everything I imagined. I like the way you respond to me and yourself."

He cleared his throat and sat up while I repositioned my body on top of his.

"You're just you. There's nothing fake or pretentious about you and I love that."

A gentle smile erupted as he continued.

"It's not just making love either Shanelle. We missed out on a lot of fun. We had to grow up fast. I'm not trying to get that back, but it feels good being with someone who understands me."

"Just don't forget Troy," I sighed, "There's no me without him."

Before Derrick could respond, the phone rang.

"Hi mommy!"

"Hi Troy," I replied with a wide grin on my face.

"Are you going night night now?"

Derrick stroked my face as I waited for an answer.

"Yes, mommy."

Derrick said, "Tell him I said goodnight."

I handed him the phone.

"Tell him yourself."

"Hey man, are you going to bed?"

"Hi Mr. Dee, I go to bed now."

"Goodnight,"

"Night, night," Troy yawned, slamming the phone down in true toddler fashion.

Derrick stretched relieving his wide mouth with laughter. He sat up and said, "He is too much. I'm starving, are you hungry?"

My head fell heavy upon his lap. "No, I'm happy. You go. I understand. We can cuddle later."

He playfully smacked me on the butt.

"Well, I'm going to make myself at home and fix something to eat. I also need to hit the books."

"That's fine, book worm."

I watched his hard gait head for the shower. Thinking of him enticed my feet to the floor. The minute he saw my naked frame his eyes rolled up to the ceiling.

"Here she comes, trouble!"

"What?" I coyly blushed, wriggling my dry toes into his soapy stream of water.

"Admit it Shanelle, you can't resist me in a shower. Matter of fact, I think it was the last time I saw you naked."

"Yeah, I was wild and on the run, but you took good care of me."

Derrick grabbed my face.

"Shanelle, with the things you were going through, that was the right thing to do. I'm just glad we're together again."

Water pellets struck my face. Derrick brushed them away with his thumb. He felt wonderful in my arms and I didn't want to let him go. Derrick pulled my body against him. His firm dick planted against my thigh.

"What kind of vitamins are you taking Derrick?"

He knelt down and bit my hip. Water splashed against his charming face.

"Roots and herbs in my tea 'gal." He laughed out loud and said, "Don't leave me hanging Shanelle."

I wrapped my arms around him and rocked him back and forth.

"This isn't a big shower Derrick."

The beating water drowned our moans. Derrick's free hand reached for a towel, quickly stepping out to wrap me warm in his arms. Falling damp onto the bed, Derrick's playful tongue scooped and licked Kitty to my girlish delight as my legs and head thrashed against the firm mattress. My orgasm forced his erection inside of me with screaming pleasure as he put my legs on his shoulders. He never took his eyes off of me as we rocked each other into the late evening. By the time we finished, Derrick was rejuvenated for three hours of studying well into the early morning.

I woke up to the smell of a cheese omelet. I took a long hot bath before I joined Derrick downstairs. Fatigue weighted his shoulders. His head rested in his heavy hands.

"Get any studying in?" I asked, kissing him on the forehead.

He pinched me on the arm. "I had no choice, now I need some sleep."

I was so spanked by Derrick's love making; I didn't care what he did. "Okay, I didn't make any plans today, so relax. Besides, you need to rest before the ride back."

"Are you going to the cookout?" Derrick asked.

"For a little while. You don't have to go if you don't want to."

"Good," Derrick replied, "I need some sleep."

"Well," I said, clearing soiled dishes from the sink, "I'm going to get this place cleaned up and pack for the week. I have a few chapters to read and then I'll go over there."

Derrick shook his head. "That'll work, are you staying at Candy's tonight?"

"Yes," I replied.

Derrick's hands slid across the table, using his forearms as a pillow.

"Well, we'll leave together then."

I turned, briefly smiling at his overwhelming life.

"Sounds like a plan."

I cleaned the house and quickly packed Troy's bag for the week. Without thought, I walked into the master bedroom and suddenly paused. There was brevity in the room as thoughts of Alex appeared in the photographs we shared with each other. I picked up his photo and stared. My fingers swiped a thin layer of dust. I placed it next to Troy's baby picture and continued to tidy up the room. A ringing phone jolted me from my task.

"Hello."

"Oh, hey Shanelle, it's me Tammy, I was getting ready to hang up."

"No, I'm here, what's up? Better yet, what's Troy doing?"

My question seemed to calm her agitation. "He just came back from church with mom and dad. What are you doing?" she asked.

"Not much," I replied, as I tip toed past Derrick.

"Well," Tammy gushed, rushing her words with baited breath, "I wanted to come by and talk before the cookout."

I stepped back from the guestroom.

"No," I paused, pulling on my tee shirt, "It's not a good time, we can talk later."

"Shanelle," Tammy pressed on, "I hope you're not holding a grudge."

I shook my head. "No Tammy, I have company right now."

A twenty-second pause followed.

"Oh," she stalled, "Well I'll talk to you when you get here."

"No problem, can you tell ma to put Troy down for a nap at two o'clock, I won't be staying long."

"Okay Shanelle."

I hung up the phone and checked on Derrick again. He was sound asleep and stretched out across the bed. A crumpled sheet beside him feathered down as he turned his face away from the blinds and sighed. I quietly closed the door thinking, *Things are getting better as each day goes by."*

Shanelle versus Tammy

Troy was the first person to greet me at the door when I arrived at the Fosters. There was relief in Mrs. Foster's eyes when she saw me coming through the door solo. She wasn't ready for Derrick and her greeting to me was an instant reminder.

"Girl, this child is just like his father. He wants and wants until he gets it." She threw her head back but cut her smile off as she headed for the kitchen. Tammy strolled downstairs while Troy sat on my lap waiting for his shoes to be tied. She must have gained forty pounds and her face was riddled with acne. To boot, her eyes were blood shot red. Tammy sat down next to me, tugging at Troy's collar.

"So," she said, "You're headed back to North Orange?"

"Why?" Troy's feet hit the floor.

"I dropped out of school. They don't want me here."

"Why?" I asked.

"Long story."

Troy ambled into the kitchen, entertaining himself with high pitched preschool banter. His chunky fingers soared through the air with a clap. Turning away from him, I focused on Tammy and blinked. "Nikki?"

Tammy's lips curled up and spit air out of frustration.

"Alex is gone," she pouted, "But you're starting to sound like him." Sniffling now, she wiped her nose clean with her forearm playing tribute to her flared nostrils like a violin.

"So what does all of this have to do with me?" I asked.

"I need a place to stay," Tammy said.

"Well you can stay at the house…"

Tammy cut me off, "No, I mean up there."

"North Orange?" My question was filled with surprise.

I remained poised. "Where's Nikki, in North Orange?"

Tammy stood up. "I'm not sweatin' her. Please Shanelle, get serious."

"Well where is she now?"

Tammy put her head down. "North Orange."

"Look at you, Nikki's got you all strung out. You don't know if you're coming or going on any given day."

Tammy sucked her teeth and rolled her eyes. I put my arm on her shoulder.

"Look Tammy, I'm staying with Candy until I get a place and it's going to be awhile. Why don't you get a job down here and get your head together."

"No," she ordered, curling her fingers in frustration, "Stop trying to tell me what to do Shanelle. Look at you; you got your life all figured out now, new man chillin' at your house, cute kid, money a nice car…"

"Tammy please, you don't know me, you may think you do, but you don't. Besides, you need to worry about yourself and figure out what you want instead of chasing Nikki."

Tammy retreated, smoothing her clothes as her feet stomped up the wooden staircase. I went to the backyard and ate a small salad. Trust me, the entire family was watching, but food wasn't an issue anymore. As long as there was no stress around, I was okay. This time Tammy was peered from the window desperately searching for freedom.

"I can't stay Ma," I said, "I've got to get back on the road."

Troy took my cue and slid off the bench while he waved goodbye. She grabbed Troy by the wrist and squeezed him tight. He patted her back and said, "Next time Nana, Troy be back."

Mrs. Foster struggled away from her grandson's embrace. Wiping her knees free from debris she asked, "Why don't you make a plate for Derrick?"

"Thanks, maybe I will."

Mr. Foster handed me a plastic bag and walked me to my car.

"I'm glad you're going to keep the house Shanelle, you'll be glad you did. Call me with the address to your mother's house. I'll be down tomorrow and take a look at it before we put in a bid."

Hearing him say "your mother," froze me into temporary shock. My thumbs smoothed the wrinkles in the bag.

"It's a long story," I saddened with wide eyes, but in my life, she's only Vivian to me."

Mr. Foster stepped back; his bottom lip falling without words. I searched the ground quickly finding his face calm and composed. He scooped Troy up and allowed him a free hop into the car. Troy climbed into his car seat as I wrapped my arms tightly around Mr. Foster's neck.

"We'll be home Saturday morning okay dad?"

"Okay Shanelle, see you Saturday." Mr. Foster stuck his hand through the window and tickled his grandson's stomach while Troy fought him off with wild feet and hands.

"I love you Pop Pop."

"Aww, that's my little man, I love you too Troy."

Mr. Foster stood on the sidewalk and watched us pull off quickly turning towards his cherished home.

Time Heals

Life pulled a fast forward on all of us in a matter of months. A quiet sale with a ten thousand dollar profit sent Mrs. Viv packing to Virginia. Needless to say, she took Steven with her. With what little money she had, Steven was transferred to a long term care facility just outside of Fredericksburg. Little remorse rested in my heart for him and Mrs. Viv. I quietly disconnected them and went along with my life like I was supposed to do. Alex would have wanted that for us. Besides, the Fosters were like surrogate parents to me even when the chips were down.

Speaking of parents, when Candy couldn't button her jeans anymore, she finally announced that she was pregnant. We didn't have the nerve to tell her we knew just by the sight of her nose. It spread across her face so fast; we were convinced she was having a girl. As a result, Derrick and Clinton had ample opportunities to exchange small talk about raising children. Candy was more than happy to stay home during her pregnancy because the sight of food and cooking oil made her sick all the time. She didn't have the courage to board an airplane and tend to needy people on tight flights.

Mr. Foster hired the best licensed contractors in town and gutted the house from top to bottom. By the time the house was completed, there were no haunting memories at the front door or in the attic. Butter cream paint with white trim coated the living room and dining room walls. Solid wooden doors graced the bedrooms that use to lock at night from Steven's perpetual thievery. The attic, by design was converted into a bright day room with bursting beams of sun from an oval skylight. The third floor became a colorful sanctuary graced with colorful paintings I purchased from a famous Bahamian artist.

Against my better judgment, on the first day of spring, I let Tammy move to the third floor while I continued my classes at St. James. Her college dreams at Pitt were long gone and she was looking for direction from anyone who understood her immediate cause. Nikki crept in and out her life behind our backs and the Fosters accepted my departure as long as I looked out for their daughter. I made a pact with Tammy to help her get on her feet while she lived with me for six months. Even though I didn't need the money, I made her pay rent to keep her disciplined. She got a job at a dental office on South Center Street and registered for classes at St. James.

Tammy was three semesters short of a degree and looked to me for determination. We kept our class schedules on the refrigerator to keep up with one another and every now and then I let her babysit her nephew. I had to remind her about leaving junk food in the house. It was disturbing to watch her put on weight so fast. I tried to get her to focus, but smoking weed got in her way. She learned her way around North Orange real quick and picked up weed in the Valley before she came home. I never saw or smelled it in the house, but Derrick and I could see it in her red eyes. Whenever Derrick came around, she turned into Medusa as evil snakes hissed and cajoled at his mere presence. Derrick liked Tammy, but he was suspicious of my codependency.

"Shanelle," he said one night over flirty phone banter, "Every time I come over there she's high. Now don't tell me you don't notice?"

"I do notice."

"Well, are you going to do something about it?"

"Derrick, I gave her six months to get her act together and that's it. She's got to get her own place, she knows that already."

"I'm not telling you what to do, but you've got Troy to worry about first."

I didn't want to worry Derrick with my simple life. He was studying around the clock and getting ready for graduation. I didn't think it was fair for him to take on my responsibilities.

"Well look at you getting all protective over my son."

"Please Shanelle, you know that's my little man and I'm going to look out for him and his stubborn mama."

"Oh now I'm a mama?" I asked.

"Yeah," he said, "My sexy mama."

I blew Derrick a kiss over the phone. There wasn't much else that needed to be said because we both needed to hit the books. He mentioned one more thing before he hung up the phone.

"I have to start looking for apartments in Jersey. My lease is up in two months."

"When does your residency start?" I asked.

"Late July," Derrick replied.

"What about your mother?"

"Shanelle," he droned.

"Okay, you'll figure it out Derrick. Get through your finals and graduation, something will come up."

The next day I headed for class. A notice caught my eyes from the political science bulletin board.

"Internships available in Washington D.C. See Professor Jeffries."

Without hesitation, I snatched the notice off the board and headed to his office.

"Hi Professor Jeffries."

He peered above his glasses. "Shanelle, what brings you here?"

I handed him the notice. "I want to go to Washington, what do I need to do?"

He smiled. "Great. Give me a writing sample and resume tomorrow morning?"

"I'll get it for you today."

He held up his hands. "I'm sure you'll have no problem, what's your GPA?"

"A three point forty-five."

"That's even better." Professor Jeffries scribbled my name on a post it note and stuck it to his computer.

"Bring it tomorrow. I'll give you the slip to register."

I felt lightheaded as I walked out of the building. A pay phone off in the distance connected me to Derrick.

"Washington? That was quick."

I held the particulars in my hand.

"The Children's Advocacy Center, 1500 M Street."

Derrick laughed. "Can you take Troy to work too?"

My heart immediately dropped to floor.

"Shanelle?" Derrick asked, "Are you there?"

"Oh, yeah I'm here. Damn, I forgot I had a son!"

Derrick's sarcasm got the best of him. "So what now Miss Shanelle?"

My fingers piano keyed my forehead. "Let's see, I can't rely on Tammy, I need her to watch the house." My eyes stretched with wonderment. "And Derrick has no apartment and doesn't start until late July," I squeaked. "Come with me!" I jumped, shaking my head to and fro with excitement.

"Me?"

"Yeah, well you're going to be homeless in two months and you need to take a break after your exams. C'mon, help a sista' out and don't make me beg!"

Derrick groaned filling the phone with worry and stress. "We can't afford to go Shanelle."

He didn't know what I was worth, so I kept him at bay just to see if he would be down for the struggle.

"I get by with Alex's Social Security checks, we can wing it, rice and beans are cheap."

Derrick hesitated. "Well, I know a few people in Silver Springs, Maryland. Let me make a few phone calls."

"So you're going with us?" I asked.

"Is that what you want?"

"Of course!" I shouted.

"Well, you only live once, let's go."

The heels of my feet served as a mini rocking chair. "Thanks Derrick."

A long sigh followed, "Anything for my girl."

"Washington!" Mrs. Foster shrieked, "Shanelle, can you just focus on one thing at a time?"

Mr. Foster wedged himself between us using his hands as a barrier.

"No!" I yelled back. "I can focus on as many things as I want. I'm twenty-three now and the last time I checked, I don't have to answer to anyone."

Mrs. Foster's facial expression was unforgiving.

"Well what about Troy, do you mean to tell me he's going with you?" she asked.

"Of course he is, he's my son and I'm not leaving him behind."

She was quickly losing control as she rubbed at an ulcer fermenting in her stomach.

"You need to understand that I'm trying to move on with my life. Maybe I looked settled when Alex was here, but I gave up so many things that I don't want to regret ever again. Derrick and I are going to work out Troy's needs and he'll be fine. But if I decide to do a million things all at once, I'm entitled." I caught my breath and pleaded with their emotions. "I said before you guys are the only family Troy has. What I meant to say is that you're all the family we have, so please don't turn your back on me now."

Mrs. Foster held her hands to her mouth and began to cry. Mr. Foster pulled us into a huddle. She immediately grabbed me. I whispered in her ear to reassure her self-doubt.

"I promise, we're coming back Mom."

When she released me, Mr. Foster handed her a wilted tissue from his pocket.

"We couldn't ask for a spunkier daughter-in-law Shanelle. We'll be fine, it's just taking this ole' girl more time to adjust. You have our blessings."

That evening, Troy stayed overnight with his grandparents while I packed. I kissed Alex's picture and quietly talked to him while

I straightened up my bedroom. An anxious ring from the door sent me flying out my skin.

"Somebody's really happy to see me!"

I pulled Derrick inside of the house and squeezed the life out of him.

"Hmm, you feel so good holding me Derrick."

Derrick smacked me on my butt. "Okay lady, let's rustle up some food, I'm starving."

Derrick and I sampled so much food during the preparation; we were full by the time it was finished. A thundershower began to fall and we quickly ran around the house shutting all the open windows. By the time we caught up with each other, we were at the top of the staircase heaving for clean air. Derrick grabbed me by the waist. I lifted his damp shirt and planted my lips against his chest.

"Let's go," I gushed, quickly running to the bedroom for a condom. I returned to the guestroom to find Derrick completely naked.

"Excuse me, did you read my mind?" I asked, cat crawling onto the bed.

"I think I know you by now Shanelle. I missed you too."

Derrick placed his hands behind his head and let me take over. I covered his mouth when I mounted him and watched his face relax. Derrick palmed my butt and pumped me up and down as sweat trickled down my face.

"Damn Shanelle, you feel so good."

"Shhh, let me finish," I whispered, losing a desperate battle. Derrick grabbed my hips and rolled over quickly stretching my legs up. My ankles wrapped around his neck. I reached back to grab the head board as he entered me deep and long. I tried to speak, but words failed me as one of his firm hands grabbed my erect breast, squeezing it tight as I screamed his name anxious for him to grip the other. Derrick pulled out and flipped me over, pulling my ass towards him as his thick dick slipped back in, his hands planted on my waist.

"Ahh," he moaned, happily ramming me from behind as my forehead hit the mattress, restless from his energy. He continued to pump, full of stamina, bending over to bite my back, his hand reaching under me to squeeze my titty. Time pressed on until he fell on top of me, a pool of wetness merging us into one, he bit my earlobe and announced his arrival.

"I'm comin' baby."

Derrick kissed my hips and inner thighs as I begged him to hold me. He wiped the sweat off my forehead and said, "Shanelle, you're a piece of work." He got up and opened the window to let a cool breeze quiet our frenzy. While I nestled into a deep sleep, Derrick took a shower and packed the jeep. By the time he climbed into bed, I was curled into a tight ball. Derrick rubbed my legs and back until I melted into his frame.

After a restful nap, we loaded the jeep with last minute items, including Troy, who was singing in the backseat for the drive down. A couple of good connections made our transition easy too. Clinton knew a pilot who was looking for someone to sublease his apartment in Georgetown for three months while he vacationed in Europe. Since we were considered good friends of Clinton, we were lucky enough to get by without a security deposit. I gave a check to Candy to cover three months rent and told Derrick that Mr. Foster was handling my expenses. Derrick still needed to feel like the man of the house so he picked up a research assignment at D.C. General.

By day I was researching child care legislation and preparing a database for the agency. It was arduous work, but I loved every minute of my time in the office. Every night, Derrick and Troy met me at the Metro station so Troy could enjoy his time on the train. He loved it so much; he cried every time we got off. Derrick was patient with Troy. Deep inside, I knew he was reliving the childhood he never had with his father. From the looks of things, Troy was a lucky little boy.

We went out to dinner at least two nights a week once Derrick started receiving a paycheck. Being in the heart of Georgetown forced Derrick and I into great political debates and wonderful lovemaking at night. We fell in love in D.C. and we knew it without saying it.

Back at home, paint fumes, or the voice of Steven began to possess Tammy's soul on the third floor. During the fifth week of my internship, she called Nikki for a Friday night pleasure party.

"Fuck it," Tammy said, "Bring whatever and whoever, let's do this."

Private parties in a college town spread quickly, even during summer session. Since Nikki went both ways, she made a few phone calls on both sides of the track. By eight o'clock, a medium sized eclectic crowd began to trickle into my newly decorated home with weed, Hennessey and Colt 45 in tow. Of course, Nikki called Flaco to bring in the good shit and he was more than delighted to crash my pad and smell my sheets for a turn on.

"Where's Shanelle?" Flaco asked.

"Just come on dummy, I wouldn't be asking you if she was here. She's in D.C."

"Aight, aight," Flaco replied. "I'll be right over."

When he got to my house, Flaco and Nikki went upstairs to roll a blunt. Nikki excused herself on the second floor to use the bathroom and told Flaco to wait. His innate scent of a woman lead him to my room with sinister eyes. He surveyed my bed and opened my dresser drawers. A pair of pink panties went into his jean pocket before he walked out to meet Nikki. He laughed to himself thinking, *"Weed and pussy, two of my favorite things."*

Before Nikki opened the door to the bathroom, a pair of keys caught his attention. He quickly shoved them into his pocket. My panties muffled the jingle as Nikki opened the door and looked into his mischievous eyes. Nikki and Flaco headed to the third floor while Tammy worked her way through the crowd downstairs. She went into the kitchen and found a pretty brown skinned sister searching for a snack.

"Looking for something to eat?" Tammy asked. She closed the refrigerator door and eyed Tammy's boyish charm up and down with a seductive smile.

"I was hoping someone could eat me." she replied.

Tammy extended her hand and led her upstairs. She called Nikki down from the attic and whispered their intentions. Nikki looked the temptress up and down and asked, "Don't I know you?"

She grabbed Nikki and Tammy's hand and replied, "Does it matter?"

"No, not at all," they sang in unison.

The three of them went into the bathroom and fired up a blunt while Nikki watched Tammy and the familiar girl freak each other out in my brand new bathroom equipped with a new shower head. Tammy took the shower head off the cradle and rocked herself off with fast pellets while the temptress bit at various body parts below her waist.

Meanwhile, Flaco made himself comfortable on Tammy's bed in the attic. His brain riddled with confusion and haze from his stimulant relaxed his eyes to two slits. His dry lips parted as he fixed his sight on the ceiling. A defect in the contractor's job after the installation of the skylight caused excess rainwater to puddle into a soft spot. In a matter of weeks, the moisture dried up and formed a brown shape reminiscent of a T-Rex dinosaur.

"What the fuck?"

Flaco rubbed his nose and stood up to study the damp shape. Using his fingers as a probe, he poked and peeled away at the sheet rock until a six inch piece gave way revealing a tin box. The bedroom door shut. He peered over the discovery and pried it open.

"Oh shit," he mumbled, blinking twice.

To his surprise, the three missing glocks and empty crack viles Steven stole out of Mama Barb's apartment were ready for the taking. Flaco positioned a gun in each hand and proudly boasted, "Word up."

His next move infuriated Rico.

"What the fuck do you mean you're at Shanelle's house? Look dumb ass, take the guns, hang up the damn phone and get the fuck out of there!"

Dazed by his high and gloating at his discovery, Flaco laughed as the phone disconnected. He carelessly turned as the gun fell to the floor. The loaded glock dislodged and fired into the ceiling.

Startled by the noise and his own stupidity, Flaco bolted down the stairs by threes, leaving the third gun and a set of finger-prints.

Back in the bathroom, the pretty stranger quickly jumped out of the shower, startled by the commotion.

"What was that noise?"

Nikki passed her a towel.

"That's my cousin goofing around."

Tammy quickly reacted, "Flaco's here?"

Nikki sucked her teeth. "Well you said whoever, whatever."

Sensing the tension, the temptress quickly slipped her arms through her shirt sleeves. Tammy grabbed her arm.

"Wait, don't go."

She smiled, licking her moist lips.

"It was cute, but that sounded like a gun shot, I have to go."

Nikki grabbed her by the waist. She traced her finger along her panty line and zipped up her jeans.

"You never told me your name," Nikki flirted back.

She opened the door as her hair sailed up and landed on her back.

"Portia."

The commotion from the third floor, including Flaco's quick haul ass exit from my house sent everyone running for the front door. Neighbors immediately called the police.

"Yes that's what I said; I heard a gunshot at the Brown's house, 122 Crescent Avenue."

The anonymous neighbor sighed in frustration.

"Oh, it's been a while, but they're at it again."

Countdown to Flaco

Two pictures hung on the evidence wall at Newark Police Department's homicide division. One was a mug shot of Flaco and the other photo was Rico's. Alex's murder investigation was left up to the local police, but a liaison from the feds was assigned just in case there were any left over issues from the sting operation.

Andre's tip was critical. Even though they had the case wrapped up in eight months, they needed to nail Rico as a co-conspirator. By the time a wire tap was granted, Rico said very little about the killing. As far as Rico was concerned, the job was done and there was nothing left to talk about. Although silence protected him for the moment, Flaco's flagrant stupidity opened up a new can of worms.

"So what do we have so far?" the chief of homicide asked. "I need to put this case on the table tomorrow and issue an arrest warrant for Flaco Santiago."

A slim veteran detective placed a file on the table.

"It's a solid case, we've got his fingerprints in both cars and the wood shrapnel found next to the corpse in Building One on Freeway Drive matches the shrapnel found in the shooter's duffel bag. The drive to Shiloh was three miles. We have video surveillance of both suspects leaving McDonald's on Broad Street twenty minutes before the wedding started. Tire treads from the...,"

The heavy set chief stood up and adjusted his belt. "Look, we need more, I don't need the word 'circumstantial' following this case. We have a dead detective to answer for, you got that?"

The liaison assigned to Alex's murder investigation stood up to receive a phone call.

"Shots fired? How many? Who's responding? Okay, I'm on my way."

A room full of homicide detectives stood up to hear the agent's lead. As he shoved his arm through his sleeves he stated, "We've got shots fired at 122 Crescent Avenue. They want the task force assigned. As soon as I have more information, I'll let you know."

Tammy was too afraid to call me in D.C. while the police and the feds scoured the third floor for fingerprints and ballistics information. A call came in an hour later with the information. Three sets of fingerprints matched Flaco's; one on the door, the abandoned gun and ceiling. The liaison quickly ran downstairs and began to interrogate Tammy.

"Look, we all know who you are, so tell me something. Why would you let him into your sister-in-law's house for a party?"

Snot drizzled down Tammy's red nose. "I didn't know he was here, Nikki invited him!"

"Nikki?" the officer pitched in a sharp tone.

Tammy wiped her nose. "Yeah, why?"

"C'mon now, your family kept a low profile for the entire trial, you don't think you're putting Shanelle and yourself in jeopardy by hanging out with them?"

Silence occupied the space between them. The officer pulled a card out of his pocket. Tammy's eyes stretched as he shoved it in her hand.

"Kid," he ordered with a military glare, "Pack up and go home. You live in Lakewood right?"

"Yes," Tammy quivered.

"We need to talk to Shanelle and I don't think she's going to be happy when she hears the news."

Tammy packed her bags and took the Forty-Four bus to Penn Station. At ten o'clock that night, she called Mr. Foster from a payphone and told him her half of the story. After that she boarded a train home to South Jersey.

My feet and hands were trembling so badly when I got the call, Derrick had to finish the conversation.

"What time did it happen?"

He shook his head and jotted down a few notes before hanging. My head fell into my hands as I mumbled, "Call the airline and book a flight for the three of us. We can leave the jeep at the airport parking lot."

Derrick's eyebrows shot up.

"Shanelle, we don't have that kind of money. Do you know how expensive that flight is going to be?"

I headed to the bedroom to pack a small bag for Troy.

"I'll explain everything later. We need to get back to the house."

An all points bulletin blared over the police wire for Flaco's arrest. Flaco hid out in a tree and shrub filled lot parallel to the house until things cooled off. He peered over the bushes as police searched my premises for evidence. A hurried flight from Washington National Airport to Newark interrupted Troy's sleep scheduled as I rocked him on my hip and allowed him to snack on crackers. During takeoff, Derrick and I discussed the speculations surrounding Alex's murder. He quietly watched me wolf down his meal and my meal without blinking twice. Derrick patted my hand.

"What?" I asked, wiping my mouth dry.

"Nothing," he replied, turning his attention towards the black sky. When our flight landed, I called Candy from the airport. Clinton picked us up and drove us back to their house to get Troy settled in the guest room. Clinton handed us his car keys at the end of the driveway.

"Don't worry about Troy, just take care and be safe."

Derrick extended his hand.

"Thanks man, we will."

When we pulled up in front of the house, an empty beer can decorated the walkway. Derrick picked it up and wrapped his arm around me as we headed inside. The stench of sweaty bodies and weed immediately engulfed my nostrils. Derrick checked the basement and shut the door leading into the kitchen.

"You don't want to go in there Shanelle. Maybe we can find a cleaning service to take care of the mess."

My stomach began to sour. Charging the stairs, I ran to the bathroom with Derrick in hot pursuit. His forearm blocked the slamming door as he watched me force my food to the surface. Rattled, he shook his head and balled a washcloth under a stream of water. He turned as I began to heave from the instant relief.

"Is this your comfort zone Shanelle?

"I'm trying my best not to Derrick."

He planted his feet and leaned against the countertop.

"I haven't done this in a long time."

His hands rested on my shoulders with a gentle pull.

"There's no way out unless you get rid of this baggage and heal. That's why I'm here. Let me help you."

My lips began to quiver.

"You can do Shanelle, I know you can."

Our eyes met in the confined space. Derrick kissed my forehead.

"Let me get something to settle your stomach. There's a twenty-four hour pharmacy on Broad Street. I'll be back in forty minutes."

By the time Derrick got in the car, I was laying on my bed resting with a cold compress on my head. Just outside, Flaco smiled as he watched Derrick pull off in Clinton's car. Under the cover of darkness, Flaco appeared from the brush and sprinted across the street. The first key slipped into the lock with a quick turn. Flaco placed one foot on the bottom of the stairs. My eyes opened. The exhaust of a delivery truck heading down South Center Street buried the sound of eight steps. My fingers nervously tapped my thigh.

"Derrick? Derrick is that you?" I called.

There was no answer.

"Tammy?"

My body began to freeze.

Flaco heckled at my desperation and fear. In a high pitch voice, he mimicked, "Derrick, Tammy, is that you?"

He kicked the door open and stepped inside. His stench engulfed the room as I backed up against the wall.

"What do you want?"

He threw his head back and scratched his stubbly face.

"You, sweet ass," he replied.

Three steps brought him closer to the bed. I quickly pulled the lamp cord and revealed his face.

He put one hand on the bed and used the other to pull the gun out from behind his back.

"You prefer the lights on?"

"No!" I yelled, "Leave me alone!"

I watched his eyes shift to the light cord. Three hurried steps brought him closer. I looked down at my night stand. A sharpened pencil sat in my reach as he smiled at me. Before he yanked on the cord, in one swift motion, I grabbed the sharpened number two pencil and rammed it right into his eardrum. The slanted strike forced the pencil halfway down his ear as he screamed in horrific pain. He managed to knock me to the ground with a swift backhand. I jumped up and bolted for the door while he dropped to the floor in pain.

Halfway to the convenience store, Derrick quickly remembered that he left his wallet. He patted his empty pocket and turned around. By the time he turned the corner of Crescent Avenue, I was barreling out the front door begging for help. He immediately threw the car into park. I ran into his arms and gripped my nails into his back.

"He's in the house, he's in the house!"

Derrick pulled away from me and began to run towards the front door. I managed to yell as my knees fell into the cold grass beneath me, "Derrick, please don't leave me!"

It was enough to make him stop in his tracks. All I could see was another man I loved dead in my arms from a bullet or a knife. As the commotion continued, the neighborhood watch took action.

"There's a woman in distress at 122 Crescent Avenue. No shots this time, just screaming."

A squad car responded in less than five minutes while Flaco hid in the attic.

Derrick held me tight as I shouted to the officer, "He's still inside, upstairs!"

Backup units responded with the K-9 Unit in tow. Flaco managed to pull the pencil out of his ear, but the excruciating pain of his damaged eardrum humbled his surrender. A flashlight in his face shamed him into a tight ball as his arms hovered over his head.

"Flaco Santiago," the officer stated.

"Yeah," Flaco replied, as he held his throbbing ear.

"You're under arrest for the murders of Alex Foster and Gigi Ramirez."

Flaco peered into to the light, grimaced with pain. Bending slightly at the knees, he braced himself as two officers pulled him off the floor as one recited the Miranda warnings.

The Truth

The next day, with Derrick by my side, we met with the local and federal task force to discuss Alex's murder. This time we met in Morristown with five new agents. We sat at an oval mahogany table. The view overlooked the downtown area. Derrick sat to my right and held my hand under the table. I wondered what was racing through his mind as he heard the inside story.

I was assured that Alex was not a crooked cop and that he was secretly working with law enforcement to eradicate corruption among local and federal officers. During Alex's training in Philadelphia, the feds conducted satellite conferences with certain officers who were part of the inside sting. When the feds told Alex that I was at Garvey, they showed him all the evidence including Flaco's statements to Rico when I left. Alex's reaction to Flaco and Rico's conversation brought out the worst in him. The feds said that Alex was so irate; they had to pull him from the job because they didn't think he could go undercover again without killing Flaco. Since I was the only person in the room that knew about Alex's unfortunate childhood, I pressed my lips together without reaction. They were right; Alex would have killed Flaco to protect my honor. Amazingly, he kept his composure and remained a loyal officer. While I continued to listen, the feds also said that Alex was sworn to secrecy. He was forbidden to tell me the entire truth no matter how difficult it was for him. *Poor Alex, the secrets he had to keep must have weighed so heavily on his heart, he had no choice but to keep me like a caged butterfly.*

I looked at the agent and asked, "How come Flaco wasn't arrested after the operation?"

The agent cleared his throat.

"Honestly, we didn't have anything on him. He was a messenger for Rico, but most of his information had nothing to do with the investigation."

The agent folded his hands.

"In fact, that's why we were so surprised to hear that he was bumped up to third in command when Rico was arrested. When we started looking more closely at Flaco's activities after the murder, we realized that Rico needed to do something that wasn't obvious to any of us."

"Killing my husband?" I asked.

The agent nodded his head in agreement.

"We also have strong reason to believe that Nick knew about the hit and didn't warn us because when we pulled Alex from the investigation after the Garvey incident, Nick couldn't reach him by phone and assumed Alex turned on him. In fact, your husband was working with us the entire time."

Still searching for answers, I asked, "What about Jack?"

The agent took a deep breath.

"Jack and Alex were loyal officers. Jack is doing some inside work for us right now but has to keep a low profile. He was instrumental in our case against Detective Nick Damiano."

While the agent continued to speak, my shaky hand rose in mid sentence. "Something doesn't sit right with me. If my husband was such a commendable officer, why was he such a wreck before the trial?"

The agent pressed his lips together and focused on his answer before he spoke.

"Mrs. Foster, we had a solid case against Rico including taped conversations and video surveillance." He paused and said, "Well, you know all this, but Alex knew with certainty that he was going to have to testify about the bounty on your brother Steven. There was little he could do without blowing the investigation. The defense team in this case was prepared to make a mockery of your dignity by sensationalizing this case with the photos of you at Garvey. Frankly Mrs. Foster, he didn't want that to happen."

I put my hand on top of Derrick's hand.

"I need to leave now."

"One more thing Mrs. Foster."

"What is it?" I blinked.

"Along with the murder charges, we're adding on attempted rape and some other charges. We may use that as leverage to get him to testify against Rico, but we in no way want to diminish your rights as a victim of assault."

Derrick put his arm around me. Events from my past boiled to the surface, but closure for Alex was more important.

I held out my hand.

"Do what you need to do, I'll cooperate."

By the time we got back to Candy's house it was already three o'clock. Clinton and Candy listened to us tell our harrowing story while Derrick bounced Troy on his lap. I quickly excused myself and went upstairs to place a phone call to the Fosters. They were relieved to hear from me and surprised that the police made so much headway in Alex's murder. Mr. Foster put the phone on speaker mode so Mrs. Foster could speak to me. She was glad to hear the news and wept while she tried to contain herself.

"How's Troy Shanelle, we miss him so much."

"He's fine; we're at Candy's house now."

"So what are your plans?" Mr. Foster asked.

"Well, our flight leaves back to D.C. tomorrow night. I'll bring him to the house next weekend if you like." I would have let him stay for a week, but thoughts of Tammy didn't sit well with me.

Mrs. Foster exhaled into the phone, "That would be wonderful Shanelle," she replied.

Before I hung up the phone, I asked Mr. Foster to put 122 Crescent Avenue up for sale.

"Okay Shanelle, I'll take care of everything."

Derrick came upstairs to check on me. I hung up the phone while he knelt down on the floor.

"I'm fine, really."

"Really?" he asked.

"I'm ok, trust me, Dr. Derrick."

"I don't want to be a doctor in your eyes, just Derrick, okay?"

"Sure," I replied.

He cleared his throat and continued.

"Even if I were a zookeeper, I would still want you to talk to someone; you've been through a lot."

I folded my hands.

"I doubted Alex and I feel horrible about that. All he wanted was for me to be safe and to be a good mother to our son."

"Shanelle, it's not like I'm trying to compete with Alex but I have to admit, after hearing what the feds had to say, he really loved you and did everything he could to protect his family. I'm sure he's looking down at you and thanking you for doing such a good job at raising Troy. Don't be so hard on yourself, just hold on to the things that matter."

He didn't need to say anything else, I knew he was right.

"I'll look up someone in D.C., I promise."

Derrick pulled me off the bed. "Good, that's what I wanted to hear."

We got back to D.C. without fail, but I remembered feeling extremely numb inside and out. I called in sick the next day and sat around with Derrick and Troy like a mummy. Derrick knew I was feeling the emotional brunt of my ordeal. He left a book on the kitchen table. The chapter heading read, "Post Traumatic Stress Disorders." Honestly, I didn't know where to start or end, but it was time to pick up the phone and talk to somebody. By that evening, we found a therapist in the area who was willing to meet me. By nightfall, my mind was made up, I didn't want to go.

"Derrick, just give me a chance. I'm not backing out; I just need to figure out that part of my life that seems so empty."

Derrick was concerned, but forgiving.

"Look, if it doesn't feel right after I try it my way, then I'll go."

Derrick voiced his own perception.

"You know Shanelle, just because Steven had a few things rolling around in his head, doesn't mean you're crazy. I just want you to feel like the decisions you make aren't based on stress or anxiety. I never told you this, but I felt like that was the reason you married Alex. But don't get me wrong, it's also the reason I told you it was your turn."

The revelation sent chills through my body, but he was right. The only thing I needed to do was put the pieces together without help from anyone. My father's revelation left a huge gap in my life and I was craving a biological connection with someone. With earnest, I began to think about the things my father told me after Alex's funeral.

"Her name was Clara," I said to Derrick. His face was full of compassion.

"I'm so sorry Shanelle," He said.

"When we get back to Jersey, I'm going to my father's old job to see if anyone remembers her."

Derrick ran his fingers through my hair.

"That sounds like a good idea."

"What about you Derrick?" I asked, "Do you ever wonder about your father?"

Derrick pressed his forehead up against mine.

"Yeah, but I buried it Shanelle. Besides, it would hurt my mother if I did and I couldn't do that to her."

"Do you feel connected?" I asked.

Derrick sighed. "Honestly I do. I know I won't make the same mistakes my father did." He paused as he looked for rationale in his answer.

"I look at Troy and even though he's not my son, I want to do the right thing and be there for him."

It was the first time I heard Derrick talk about a real commitment to my child. Derrick grabbed my face and said, "I want you by my side Shanelle. I told you before, once I start my residency, I'm going to be working around the clock, but I want to come home to you."

I pulled the sheet up to my neck. "Well, I'll have my degree by the end of the summer session. In September I'll start my masters program."

Derrick leaned on his elbow. "Well, we'll be busy getting in debt together I guess."

I laughed at first because debt wasn't an issue for me at all, but I still wasn't ready to share that information with Derrick until I had a better idea about where our relationship was going.

"Well, I told Mr. Foster to put the house up for sale. I don't want to go back there. Whatever money I make on the proceeds can help pay for my expenses."

Derrick pulled me into his frame.

"I'll camp out at my mother's house until I can find an apartment. I think we should do this the right way."

"What do you mean the right way?" I asked.

"Shanelle," he sighed, "Don't play with me. We're shackin' up now, but I did it because it was last minute. When we get home, I need to make a respectable woman out of you my sugar shack girl."

I chuckled.

"We'll see. In the meantime, I'm going to enroll Troy in pre-school three days a week."

Derrick stroked his eyebrows and said, "Good, he's more than ready, Lord knows he gets all of our attention."

"He's a lucky little boy," I gushed.

Derrick wrapped his arms around me. "I'm a lucky man Shanelle."

"I'm just as lucky as you are Derrick."

His finger poked my stomach. "I hope you can close some chapters in your life now."

"I will," I replied, "As soon as I find out some information about my real mother."

Loose Ends

My internship in Washington wrapped up in three weeks with a few contacts and a solid A plus on my research paper. In that short period of time, Mr. Foster arranged for a mover to pack up the house and placed everything in storage down in South Jersey. The house was sold in three months to an out of state couple. Needless to say, the neighbors were glad to see the last member of the Brown family leave the neighborhood.

Derrick and I scoured the newspapers for weeks to find two decent apartments that were reasonably close in location. After an exhaustive search, we ended up finding a real estate agent who found a two family house in Montclair with two vacant apartments. The arrangement was perfect for the two of us because it allowed us to have our space and be close to each other. Troy loved the arrangement too because a common access door allowed him to go up and down the stairs between the two of us without a fuss.

By mid September, we settled into our planned routines. Derrick was six weeks into his exhaustive residency at University Hospital, Troy started preschool and I started my Masters Program at St. James University. To keep the Fosters happy, we agreed that Troy would spend every other weekend with them, including Mondays. Mr. Foster drove him back on Monday afternoons and Derrick was usually there to greet him at the door. Each time Mr. Foster brought Troy home, they spent hours talking and grunting about sports, the trial, politics and life in general. It was Derrick's only day off, but I think he looked forward to the time he spent with Mr. Foster and Troy. I knew Mr. Foster cherished their talks because he was filling the void of his cherished son.

On a cool sunny day in November, I walked in the house and found the two of them standing in the lobby shaking hands and laughing.

"Hey Shanelle," Mr. Foster said, "I was just leaving."

"Well, look at the two of you, what are you so happy about?"

They both responded in unison, "Nothing!"

The look on their faces was suspicious, but Troy distracted me.

"Look mommy, I found two worms!"

I pretended to be happy to have his happy discovery on my living room floor.

"That's nice, but take it outside."

Mr. Foster patted Derrick on the back and gave me a hug.

"Listen, let me get on the road, I'll give you a call later." He suddenly remembered something with a snap to his fingers. "Oh yeah, mom wants all of you over for Thanksgiving, can you come?"

I looked at Derrick and immediately thought about how we were going to work it all out. Derrick immediately erased my doubt.

"Well, I have an early shift, but if my mother can come with us, we would love to."

Mr. Foster smiled and said, "Hey that sounds like a plan."

"Great!" I replied, "Maybe your mother can stay the weekend at my house. We can walk on the beach, Troy really misses that."

Derrick agreed with a nod. "Well, I won't be able to stay, but that could work."

We said our goodbyes at the end of the walkway while Derrick hid a secret from me. It was written all over his face, but he wouldn't tell me.

"What?" I asked. "You're keeping something from me."

"Nothing," he replied, grabbing a football from off the lawn. "Troy, long pass!"

Troy took off and caught the bomb. He fell backwards, and immediately threw the ball into the grass.

"Touch down!" he yelled as he clapped his hands. Derrick put his arm around me and said, "Like I said, nothing."

While Derrick opted to keep his secret to himself, I walked into the kitchen to unearth another one.

"Yes please, New York City, may I have the number to the Emory Roth Group?"

I scribbled the number down and sat at the table. Derrick washed his hands and handed Troy a paper towel to dry his hands.

"Hi, good afternoon, can you connect me to personnel; I'm trying to obtain information on an employee who used to work there."

Elevator music followed. I searched Derrick's eyes. He gave me a thumbs up and ushered Troy back outside with two apples in tow.

"Hi, is this human resources?"

"Yes it is how can I help you?"

"Um, well, my name is Shanelle Brown, my father William Brown…"

"Yes, Shanelle, how are you, this is Betty Roberts, I remember your father."

"Oh great," I replied. "Well, I was wondering if you could help me find out some information about my mother Clara…"

"Excuse me?" Betty asked, she seemed startled, but continued, "Clara died in a car accident years ago, if this is some kind of a joke…"

"I'm sorry," I replied. "But to be honest with you, my father told me that they had an affair and when she died, my father took custody of me…"

Betty began to muffle the phone. I couldn't hear the commotion.

"Shanelle, I have to ask, how old are you?"

"Twenty-three."

Betty immediately gasped. "I can't believe this. Can you come to the office today? We have a box of her belongings in the archive office, but no one claimed it. I think she has a sister in Virginia, but we couldn't reach her."

My heart started to beat in rapid succession.

"Can I have your address?" I asked. I quickly jotted the number down as Derrick walked back into the house with Troy.

"Is everything okay Shanelle?" Derrick asked.

"Everything is fine, there's information on my mother at the office."

Derrick's eyes widened when I told him.

"Do you want us to go with you?" He asked.

"No, keep Troy, I know you're tired. Can you manage?"

Derrick kissed me on my lips. A tap on my thigh followed. I looked down at my growing pride and joy.

"Yes?"

"Can I have a kiss too mommy?" Troy asked.

"How about three?" I replied.

Troy giggled and held his face out while I pecked him three times.

Derrick walked me to the door and wished me good luck as I headed into the city.

By the time I reached West 35th Street in Manhattan, I got so nervous I had to pull over and catch my breath. I placed my forehead on the steering wheel and talked myself into bringing closure to my life. I jumped back into traffic and searched for a parking space. A tiny elevator took me to the eleventh floor of the Emory Roth Group. When I reached the desk, she stood up with a dropped jaw. She kept her composure and said, "You must be Shanelle, Betty is expecting you."

"Thank you," I replied.

The woman walked around the desk and put her hand on my shoulder. "I've been with this firm for thirty years and I knew your mother. It's amazing how much you look like Clara."

An elevator door opened. A woman with slim hips stepped off and immediately gasped. Betty grabbed my hand and blurted, "I can't believe it, you look just like your mother."

Tears spilled and crashed to the ground.

"Please, can you tell me about her, do you have a picture?"

We stepped on the elevator together and immediately began to probe each other with questions.

"So what are you doing now Shanelle? How is your father?"

"I'm in school; he's fine I guess. What did my mother do here?"

"Oh," Betty replied. "She did a little bit of everything, public relations, marketing, she was phenomenal."

"Really, I can't wait to see a picture of her."

Betty led me to a small copy office and reached up to retrieve a dusty box off the top shelf. It was marked, "Clara R. Johnson."

"Johnson?" I asked. "That was her last name?"

Betty said, "Yes, that's right."

"Oh," I rolled my eyes in my head and thought, *"With my luck, Derrick is probably my long lost cousin."*

Betty eased my worry.

"There are so many people with that name though, it's common. I do know that Clara had a sister in Fairfax, Virginia, but they had a strained relationship while she was here."

"Oh," I replied. "You sure do know a lot about my mother, were you close?"

Betty cackled, "You might say that."

"Is there somewhere I can sit?"

"Take your time, the only thing I need you to do is fill out a claim form for the contents in the box."

"Sure," I replied.

Instead of sitting on a chair, I plopped down on the floor and took the lid off the box. I immediately inhaled at the sight of a three by five inch picture of her. She was standing up with her hands on her hips smiling wider than I ever smiled in my entire life. I stroked the picture with complete joy and bellowed out, "Hi mama, it's me Shanelle."

I quickly looked around to see if anyone heard me. My pointer finger stroked the entire frame of her body. She had thick thighs and a big forehead just like me and Troy. I began to laugh as Alex's references to Sade's head came to mind. More photographs followed along with happy tears. She had wild wooly hair like I did and I wondered if she ever used Nunile.

At the bottom of the box, there were little messages and love notes to my father.

On one she wrote:

To Mr. Brown,

How quaint are we.
The sweetest apricots.
Satin sheets and forget me nots.
Suddenly love makes three.

A love untold,
Beauty behold,
Our love child wrapped in white gold.

Sadly our gem cannot shine,
Your love will never be mine
We have yet to be defined.
Except for the garnet ring I wear...
So surreal and consciously sublime.

This life belongs to us.
Forever yours in the eyes of our love child...
Clara

I held the poem to my heart and began to cry. My whimsical need to write poetry came from mother. The precious ring my father gave to my mother was passed down to me to protect my virtuosity. I cried harder because I cursed my father out when he asked me about the whereabouts of my garnet gem. Knowing that it was my mother's ring brought more tears of joy to my eyes as I wiped my hands on my jeans just to gain composure. I couldn't wait to share the news with Derrick, so I placed everything back in the box and headed back to Betty's office. By the time I reached her, she could see the relief in my eyes.

I gave her a hug and filled out the forms. She gave her co-worker a pocket camera and took a picture.

"Good luck Shanelle, I'm glad we didn't get rid of the box."

"Thanks for everything, "I waved as I got on the elevator and waved goodbye. I felt like the luckiest girl in the world.

Derrick met me at the door with Troy and Candy's big ass belly. She was ready to pop, but she couldn't wait to see my treasure.

Derrick chatted with us for an hour and then retired for the night with a warm kiss to my forehead. He was as shocked as I was about my mother's resemblance. Troy gave him a high five and said, "Now go to bed Dr. Dee!"

Derrick laughed and asked, "Shanelle, when you get a chance, can you pull my car in the driveway so I won't get a ticket."

Candy and I were laughing, but I managed to respond, "Okay, I will, goodnight."

I fed Troy his dinner and sent him to bed without a major fuss. He was already worn out from the long trip up from South Jersey. Candy and I continued to scour over every ounce of my mother's life while I rejoiced in her beautiful spirit. Candy said of her, "She seemed like she was real down to earth and fun to be with, just like you girl." I kissed Candy on the cheek.

"Thank you little mama."

She rubbed her belly and pouted, "Girl one more week. I can't wait until the princess gets here." She stood up to leave while I picked up her pocket book.

"Did you figure out a name yet?"

"Bianca Noel," Candy replied.

"Cute," I said, "I like that."

She turned to leave. "Don't forget to move the good doctor's car."

I grabbed his jacket and put it on while we headed for the door. When I walked outside, the car was already parked. I waved goodbye to Candy and thought, *"Derrick must be going crazy, he already parked the car."* I reached into his jacket pocket to hang his car keys on the hook by the exit, but there were no keys. Instead, my hands felt a small velvet box. I took it out of his pocket and stared. I laughed at first because I knew Derrick was a pure clown and I didn't know what he was up to. I checked on Troy and quietly walked upstairs. I turned the door knob but it was locked. We never locked the inside doors because it was easier for Troy to get to us.

"Derrick?" I called.

He didn't answer. Three knocks followed.

"Who is it?" He asked in a burly voice.

"Stop playing Derrick, open the door," I said.

"What's the password?" he asked. I could tell by the brevity in his voice that he was smiling.

"We don't have passwords silly."

"Did you park my car?" he asked.

"You parked it, open the door."

"Shanelle," he whispered.

"Yes," I replied.

The door quickly opened.

"You finally said the password," Derrick said.

"I did?" I asked.

Derrick took the small velvet box out of my hand and said, "Did you open it?"

I shook my head no.

"You open it, it's probably a Hershey kiss, you practical joker."

As corny as he was, he got down on his knees.

"I may not have much to give you now, but I need to walk this earth with you by my side Shanelle. I want to be a father to Troy. I can't replace his father, but I think I'm doing a good job."

Derrick grabbed my waist and kissed my stomach with a soft peck. He looked up at me and said, "I'll support any dream or aspiration you have in this lifetime baby. You're the only one that did that for me. Just say yes Shanelle." Derrick took the ring out of the sleeve and slipped a petite emerald cut ring on my finger. "You can have anything in the world you want, just say yes. I told myself when you left that if you heard one more negative thing, Troy and I would be enough family for a lifetime."

That night we organized our lives for the future. A four year engagement, discreet nights of privacy and wild sex while Troy stayed with the Fosters during long weekends.

Truth be told, I needed to let Derrick know that I was financially stable. Before I did, I went to the bank and obtained a cashier's check for one hundred and forty-five thousand dollars. It was Derrick's loan balance from medical school. I remembered when Alex paid for my first year at Bloomberg College. He said he did it because it would only help us in the long run. He was right. Even though he was gone, my life with Derrick and Troy was a good thing and I knew Alex would be happy for me. The money wasn't an issue anyway. With him or without him, I knew I could make it on my own.

Family Affair

The feds and the prosecutors didn't let me down. An intense investigation brought Flaco to his knees in one double murder trial. He served Rico to them on a platter with his knees knocking together in pure fear. Redemption came to him in prison. There was little remorse from either of them as we sat in a packed courtroom to hear the sentence. Tammy cleaned up her act and sat quietly next to her father as she wept her guilt away. I sat next to Derrick and held his hand with pride and sadness. In my other hand was a trifold locket Candy gave me after Bianca was born. There were three delicate pictures resting inside each frame. One of me, Troy and the other was a refurbished picture of my mother. It was a sweet gesture from my best friend in the whole world. The locket was enhanced by my garnet ring. This time it was a source of maternal strength and emotional closure.

Four years couldn't come quick enough for us to get married. With the Fosters' blessings, Derrick adopted Troy six months before his fifth birthday. He told everyone he knew that his "police officer daddy," was in heaven and his other daddy was a doctor. With Derrick's help, we made a scrapbook for Troy so he could carry it around whenever he wanted. He was so proud of his two fathers, he took the book with him to school for his first day of kindergarten.

The following year, Derrick finished his residency and took his medical boards. Without fail, he passed with flying colors. He opened a flourishing pediatrics practice in Newark and worked day and night until he figured out a comfortable pace. As busy as he was, if Troy called he stopped everything to talk to his son. It didn't matter if it was a simple spelling word, Troy had his ear. I gave Derrick plenty of space when it came to the two of us. There was so much intensity in him to become a competent doctor; I made sure that his office ran smoothly by hiring two assistants and an office manager. At a minimum, the only rigors of his practice were the rise and fall of abused and neglected children.

Derrick's toughest case came to him when a distraught woman came in with her daughter. She was barely conscious when the woman brought the frail child in for treatment. Burns and three week old bruises covered her body from head to toe. Derrick was furious when he questioned her mother and signaled the nurse to contact Child Protective Services and an ambulance.

Derrick was startled when he opened the limp child's eyes to check her pupils. She had the most beautiful green eyes he had ever seen. He couldn't believe that anyone could be so cruel to a child. Derrick saw abuse before, but this case was different. Her mother, Cora Mae slipped out the back door and went back to her abandoned apartment. Fearing an immediate arrest for the harm she caused her daughter, she held her hands steady and slipped a noose around her neck. The strain of caring for a child born from rape was too much for her drug addicted soul. Her feet swayed back and forth as the police banged on the door. While her mother rocked under the force of the rope, Derrick finally convinced the little girl to recite her name.

"Corinthia," she softly whimpered.

When Derrick came home, he took a long shower. He piled under our thick comforter and smothered me with hugs and kisses. I took off my glasses and asked, "What's wrong?"

Derrick rubbed his eyes and placed his head in my lap.

"It gets crazy sometimes Shanelle. After four years of an intense residency, you think you've seen it all and then you get knocked for a loop again."

I stroked the fine lines in Derrick's brow. His skin was still smooth as satin as I kissed his forehead with caring confidence.

"Perspectives change when you look through the eyes of a child," Derrick said. "I can't imagine what that little girl must have gone through; she's only eight years old." I held his hand and kissed it with a soft peck. The stress in our lives stemmed from the social and medical needs of others, but Derrick knew when and how to turn it off. He turned his face into my neck and stroked my collarbone with the tips of his fingers.

"I'm taking Thursday and Friday off so we can have a long weekend. Let's go to the shore home, I need to get away."

"Sure," I replied.

That weekend we went to the beach. I rested on Derrick's chest as he read his New England Journal of Medicine. I was accustomed to his dual track mind while he stroked my hair and absorbed himself in medicine and science. Troy appeared as a silhouette just like his father did so long ago. He had Alex's broad shoulders supported by strong legs that were growing thick and firm as the days went by. Troy walked over to us. He picked up his football and said, "Dad do you wanna play?"

Derrick put his journal down.

"Sure, go out for a long pass."

I chuckled to myself as Derrick looked back and smiled.

"If he only knew."

Fun and frolic brought us home early that night. There was no need to don pretty panties or a cute bra for Derrick. As soon as Troy went to sleep, we made love without the song and dance of foreplay. Our skin intertwined under the sheets as Derrick locked his hands into mine under the brightest orange moon. I don't remember the last time seeing such a beautiful twilight and feeling so free.

Two years later, that same twilight graced an outside wedding on the beach as close friends and relatives held up their glasses in our honor. Bianca chased Troy in her lily white flower girl dress while he entertained his bratty little god sister by ducking and dodging her in the deep sand. Derrick's mother couldn't stop crying and neither could Mrs. Foster. The strangest family bonds formed and biology didn't matter.

I walked out to the shoreline with Derrick and stared at the moon. I quietly said hello to Alex with a whisper. His love kept me safe, Derrick's love made me whole. I bent down in my dress and drew a heart for the two of them as the water rushed in and quickly erased it away. Derrick slipped his hand around my waist and escorted me away from the seemingly quiet shoreline.

Three years of family life quickly passed as Troy grew before our eyes. The idea of motherhood swelled in my head day and night while Derrick passionately entertained my biological clock. On a warm September day, Derrick, with the help of a midwife, helped me bring into the world a seven pound one ounce baby girl. She was the little princess of the house and in Derrick and Troy's eyes, I was still the queen. We spent endless days at the beach house and put an extension on the back to accommodate our growing family. Raising a family and working part time as a freelance writer became my resolve. I also dusted off Alex's camera and took up his old hobby. It was all the therapy I needed with the life I left behind. Every time we spent time at the beach house, the ocean became my reflection in the warmth of Derrick's embrace. Life for me was empowering, simple, sexy and sweet.

Acknowledgements

Celebrating 16 years of marriage. I love you babe! Thanks for all of your hard work. JS and RS, I love you too!

My heartfelt thanks goes out to the staff at Nibiru's; Rafiyq, Ranisha, Darnell, Harry and Naomi. Thank you for your endless support and all of the wonderful memories.

Thanks again editors! D.S., T.S., T.R.

Thanks to ALL the book clubs across the country that have supported my work and continue to select my book for the monthly read. Special thanks to Sister Girl Book Club, Black Voices Book Club, One Mind Many Voices Book Club ----Hey Kae! Nubian Sisters out of Miami, Girl Talk Book Club and ARC Bookclub. LOCKSIE – What's good?

Good friends, Candy, Bonnie, Collette, Cindy, Delores, Maria, Lili, Rita, Daba and Sabrina.

Die Hard Moody fans, you know who you are. #1 from Brooklyn, "Hey Joy!" Dee from Texas, Yasmine Allen, Regan Payton, Patricia Strickland and Alese Jeter. Tony, Damon, Alex, Peaches, Michele (Thanks for the tickets). Erica, Linda, Simone, Tracey, Celeste, Nerajah, Wendy, Delicia, Ricky, Simone #2 and Tonya! Thanks for checking in during the wee hours of the morning!

Last but not least, "What's up Brooklyn?"

www.moodyholiday.com

Book Order Form

Pretty Paper Press
623 Eagle Rock Ave
Suite 267
West Orange, NJ 07052
Phone# 201-704-1105

QTY	DESCRIPTION	UNIT PRICE	LINE TOTAL
	Wild Innocence, A Novel	**$14.95**	
	Secrets, Portia's Story	**$15.95**	
	No Ordinary Love	**$15.95**	
	Three Days in Bed	**$15.95**	
	The Black Divorce	**$14.95**	
		Subtotal	
		SHIPPING	**$4.50**
		6% SALES TAX	
		TOTAL	

Certified check or money order payable to Pretty Paper Press.

25% Discount for Book Clubs orders of 10 books or more.

Questions? Call Moody at 201-704-1105